LARK RETURNING

LARK
RETURNING

Elisabeth McNeill

CENTURY

LONDON MELBOURNE AUCKLAND JOHANNESBURG

First published in Great Britain in 1988 by Century
Hutchinson Ltd
Brookmount House, 62–65 Chandos Place
London WC2N 4NW

Century Hutchinson South Africa (Pty) Ltd
PO Box 337, Bergvlei, 2012 South Africa

Century Hutchinson Australia Pty Ltd
PO Box 496, 16–22 Church Street, Hawthorn
Victoria 3122, Australia

Century Hutchinson New Zealand Ltd
PO Box 40–086, Glenfield, Auckland 10
New Zealand

ISBN 0 7126 1990 9

Phototypeset by Input Typesetting Ltd, London
Printed in Great Britain by Anchor Brendon

This book is dedicated to my beloved Borderland

THE FAMILY FROM THE ABBEY

Alice Armstrong, = Adam Cannon
1763–1813 | 1756–1815

John,   Jane, 1794–1849/Blaize Chardenel, 1782–1815
1794–1856 (in India)

Alouette, (Aylie) 1814–1901 = Hugh Kennedy,
1810–1885

Adam,   Hannah, 1858–1917/Gunther Von Egerlin
1853–1923 (in Canada)

Lark, born 1891 = (1) Sir Harry Lewis, 1896–1918
(2) Simeon Hepburn, born 1887

Blaize, Scotland, October 1812

'Where am I?' he wondered, and focused his eyes to look ahead. On the horizon he could see a line of softly rounded hills, their flanks covered with thick beech-woods. It was autumn and in the dying-year brilliance of the sun, the trees seemed to be on fire, glowing in brilliant red, gold, yellow and orange.

Perhaps it would have been better if he had died among the sun-baked lavender bushes on the plain outside Cuidad Rodrigo, for death in ambush would not be as shaming as the months he had spent as a prisoner, handed over by the Spanish to the British. Blaize Chardenel was a very proud Frenchman and the shame of being taken a prisoner by the boorish British bit hard into his soul. He had nothing but contempt for his new captors.

With two hundred other prisoners of war, he had arrived at the port of Leith and disembarked in front of the usual jeering crowd of loafers on a stone jetty lined along one side with stinking alehouses.

'Here's another Frog. Oh my, this is a bonny one, isn't it? Look at his fancy jacket! Hey, Froggie, where did our lads get you?' cried a group of ragged women as Blaize marched down the gangplank, deliberately straightening his shoulders as he went.

The march up a steep hill to Edinburgh was even more shaming because women and children lined the route, waving flags and chanting insults. He wanted to stop in the middle of the slimy, muck-covered cobbles and shout back at them, taunting them with their savagery and their filth, but he stared ahead, blank-eyed, trying not to hear their voices.

Yesterday they had stopped for the night at Valleyfield, about two hours' march out of Edinburgh. There, penned up like animals in stone sheds, were many Frenchmen – some of whom he knew and had fought alongside in Spain – but his own journey was not yet finished. With ninety other officers he was selected to march on for thirty miles more, into the southern hinterlands of Scotland, to a town called Melrose.

He knew the authorities always chose isolated places to station prisoners on parole because they were far from ports and escape was difficult. But that would be a challenge, thought Blaize, he would get away, he would foil them.

Now he walked alone, head high, one hand gripping the shoulder strap of his knapsack and the other holding a red-covered bundle bound round and round with rope. His scarlet Hussar's jacket was patched and stained, with the intricately looped gilt epaulettes unravelling in spite of the care he had taken to repair them, but nine months in captivity had levied a heavy toll on his once dandified appearance.

Behind him he heard the clatter of a horse's hooves on the loose stones of the road and one of the escort troop rode up on him. The man leaned down from the horse's back and pushed at Blaize with his long staff, yelling, 'Get a move on, keep up with the others.'

'Don't touch me, you peasant,' he spat out in French, using his bundle to thrust the stave aside. The man on the horse did not understand what the prisoner was saying and for a moment he contemplated bringing the stave down hard on the Frenchman's dark head, but there was something in the eyes staring back at him that intimidated the guard, something that warned him against violence or bullying. He drew back his arm and said gruffly before riding off, 'Just keep up, that's all, keep up with the others.'

It was dark as he stumbled up the slow rise of a twisting street lined with houses to a square and a market cross where a brazier was burning and a group of men awaited the new arrivals. French voices greeted him. 'Welcome brothers, welcome citizens, welcome to Melrose, you've come to the best place to be a prisoner!'

A ruddy-faced fellow of about his own age, eyes alight with friendship and goodwill, came up to Blaize and helped him off with his knapsack. From his accent, Blaize judged him to be from Normandy or Brittany but it was too dark in the square to make out which uniform he was wearing, if indeed his ragged jacket was a uniform at all. He was thickly bearded and the darting flames of the brazier sparkled on the golden earrings he wore.

'It's good to see some new faces. What's your name?' asked the friendly man.

'Chardenel, Blaize Chardenel, Captain in the Fourth Hussars, taken in Spain.'

'Like most of the men here. Where are you from?'

'My home's in Arles.'

The stranger smiled, showing fine teeth.

'Ah, the sun-filled south! I know Montpellier well, because I'm a surgeon and I studied there. My name's Jacques Lacoste and my home's in Rheims. I was surgeon on a privateer, captured a year ago, but this is a good place to sit out the war. You'll be very comfortable here, my friend.'

Blaize was surprised at this attitude from a Frenchman. He said gruffly, 'I don't want to sit out the war. I want to get back to fight for the Emperor. I don't care how comfortable you are here, you should be ashamed not to be fighting again.'

Lacoste just laughed.

'They all say that when they first arrive. Come on, you can billet with me. I've got some rooms in a house down the street with an old widow. She's well disposed to me because I'm treating her rheumatics and she thinks I'm some sort of wizard! Follow me.'

The autumn of 1812 was glorious and the sun which beamed down every day showed the little town of Melrose to its best advantage. Its centre was an ancient ruined abbey built of red sandstone round which the

9

town clung, tucked neatly into a bend of the river Tweed, surrounded by trees and orchards and with smooth green meadows stretching along the banks of the river. Apart from the old abbey, the most striking thing about the town was three tall hills called the Eildons that rose suddenly from the plain just behind the town, a triple crown of hills with their flanks dotted by flocks of sheep and streaked purple with banks of heather.

Every day Blaize climbed to the top of one of the guardian hills and stared over the spreading plains, trying to work out the best way to escape. Even in his misery he had to admit that the Border landscape was heartbreakingly beautiful – from the hilltop he could see silver rivers twisting lazily through tree-filled valleys; acres of untouched woodlands; viridian-green fields dotted with grazing animals and here and there a cluster of houses, the smoke from their chimneys drifting lazily up into the sky which was a soft shade of pigeon-egg blue, streaked with trails of soft white cloud that changed to a wash of pink and purple at evening. When spirals of grey smoke began to rise from the town's chimneys and a ghost-like mist drifted in from the river, it was time to go home. He turned back to his lodgings where his friend Lacoste would be waiting beside a well-laden tea table, chaffing the friendly, gap-toothed old landlady who hovered over him like a loving mother.

'Why do you go off on your own every day? What do you do with yourself? Have you found a girl so soon?' Jacques was always joking.

He never seemed low, never got depressed. His captivity sat lightly on him and he was one of a group of prisoners who had formed a theatre club that gave performances once a week to the people from the town. He also played the violin in the prisoners' orchestra and was a member of their recently formed Masonic Lodge, the creation of which had formed bonds with the men of Melrose, many of whom were also keen Masons. Jacques' open, friendly manner had made him many friends and local people consulted him on medical matters – consul-

10

tations which they paid for – and because Jacques was a good doctor, he was never short of money. He found Blaize's misery difficult to understand and as the weeks passed he grew worried in case his fellow lodger was about to succumb to the melancholy that sometimes seized men in captivity and which had already caused one suicide among the French prisoners.

Now Blaize sat down heavily at the tea table and said testily, 'No, I haven't found a girl. I'm not looking for a girl, I've a wife in Arles.'

'Humph, that's a long way away,' said Jacques, who was lavishly spreading bread with raspberry jam. He had an eye for the ladies and was already a favourite with the young women of the town who flocked to the theatre performances in which he appeared, booming out with his baritone voice and thrilling their susceptible hearts with his blond beard and glittering earrings.

'We're different, you and I,' said Blaize. 'This place bores me. I hate the stupid red-faced people. I hate their backward little town, their lack of sophistication. They are still living in the Middle Ages. They know nothing, these people . . .'

Jacques leaned back and stared at Blaize. 'And you wonder how they managed to beat you in Spain? You can't understand it, can you? Let me tell you, they're good people and they're good soldiers, my friend, as good as ours. If France is to win it will be a hard war, and now that we can do nothing to help, we can only hope. Believe me, I'm as good a Frenchman as you but I'm a realist. We're here, we're alive, we've given our word to stay here. All we can do is make the best of it.'

'I'm not staying. I'm going back to fight. I'm determined that I'm going to get away,' said Blaize, knocking over his chair as he marched out of the room without even tasting Widow Grant's teacakes.

When November came, winter set in and the winds began to blow from the north, biting through the thin clothing of the newly arrived prisoners till their very bones ached.

11

It seemed the weather was now determined to make up for the mildness of the autumn and show the Frenchmen what a Scottish winter could be like.

The three watching Eildon hills behind Melrose were crowned with snow from early in the month, and at night the pools in the fields round the town and on its streets froze to sheets of ice that reflected the moon and the stars in the clear frosty sky.

'You can't go walking about in this wind, you'll catch your death with only that jacket to cover you,' said Jacques to Blaize one bitter morning. 'Come down to the town hall with me and listen to our orchestra.'

To Jacques' surprise, Blaize agreed. It was 25 November and he did not tell Jacques that it was his thirtieth birthday. His gloom had been so cruel when he awoke that morning that he feared for his own sanity, and realized he must do something to help himself. So he accompanied his bear-like friend to the music room which the Frenchmen had set up in the first floor of a house on the corner of a narrow little road that led down to the abbey.

Jacques played the violin, sitting sawing away with his big red hands among a group of violinists, all more skilful than he.

Blaize listened, leaning against the music-room door, his eyes hooded and his head half down until the first piece was finished. Then he looked up and laughed. 'You're not much of a musician, my friend,' he told Jacques.

The big blond man was visibly nettled. 'No, perhaps not, but at least I try. I don't just wander about hating everything and everybody.'

Blaize flushed, the colour rising under his golden skin. Immediately he was apologetic.

'I'm sorry. I didn't mean to hurt you. I shouldn't have said that.'

'Are you a musician then?' asked another of the orchestra who disliked the sullen newcomer.

'I play the flute,' said Blaize.

'We need a flautist,' was the reply. 'Chaumier has a flute, he'll lend it to you.'

A man in the back row bent down, brought up a little wooden flute and handed it forward through the ranks of the players to Jacques' defender, who brought it over to Blaize.

'Let's hear you play that,' he challenged.

The flute was battered and felt light in his hands as he touched it lovingly, remembering many nights before all the fighting started, when he had been able to laugh, to make music and be happy. Something tightened painfully in his throat at the memory but he put the flute to his lips and blew a little trill . . . 'Yes, I can play this, it's a nice flute,' he said.

The orchestra played an old French country air which he knew and he joined in, making the notes soar, jump and dance beneath his fingers. The pleasure of making music won him over from his gloom and he closed his eyes in ecstasy, playing on alone for some moments before he realized that the rest of the orchestra had stopped and were listening to him.

Jacques was the first to speak. 'I bow before you, master,' he said with a good-tempered laugh. 'You're a real musician.'

Embarrassed, Blaize laughed too and, putting the flute to his mouth again, played some bars of music by Haydn which the orchestra took up after him in a ragged but enthusiastic fashion. They were playing away with gusto when the door opened and two men in dark blue bonnets and cloaks over black and white checked trousers came in and sat down in the row of chairs beneath the window. When the music ended they clapped and one of them limped over to Colonel Berton, who was the orchestra leader, and said, 'You are aiming at high things now, I hear, Berton. What was that you were playing?'

The colonel smiled and replied, 'It was a piece of music by Dr Haydn. I think it is one of the pieces he wrote in London.'

The newcomer looked at Blaize and said, 'The man

who plays the flute is very good. Is he one of the new arrivals?'

The colonel, who was senior officer among the prisoners and responsible for them, nodded. 'He was in the last intake. Like me, he was taken in Spain.'

The limping man now addressed himself to Blaize, who noticed that he had some sort of speech impediment which made him roll his Rs in a strange, guttural way.

He spoke first in English and then, thinking that he was not fully understood, switched to French – not good French it was true, but at least French after a fashion.

'Where did you learn to play the flute?' he asked.

'I was taught by a man in my grandfather's orchestra.' Blaize spoke English. He had been learning it ever since he was taken prisoner, in the hope that when the time came to escape, knowledge of the language would aid his getaway.

'In your grandfather's orchestra? He was a band leader?' The limping man was still using French.

But Blaize was determined to decide the language and replied again in heavily accented English.

'He had an orchestra in his home.'

Surprise made his adversary give in. His words this time were in English too.

'In his home? He had his own orchestra? Who was he?'

'My grandfather was the Comte de Florac. He was also very fond of music.'

Some of the men in the orchestra laughed but the limping man was too impressed to be aware of their amusement. He stepped over to Blaize and held out a hand.

'My dear man,' he said affably as if to an equal, 'you must come to dinner with me. Bring some friends – and your flute. We'll have a musical evening.'

And turning to the colonel, he said, 'Berton, I'll send my carriage tomorrow night for you and this accomplished young man. Bring another four friends as well and I'll give you all a fine dinner.'

*

14

'I don't want to go to dinner with him. I don't care if he is the local sheriff – whatever that means – I think he only asked us because he heard my grandfather was a count. If he had been a bandmaster or a woodcutter, there would have been no invitation for me.'

Jacques, who was tying a white cravat round his neck and patting his beard down over it with vast satisfaction, said, 'Don't be stupid. He wants to hear you make magic with that flute. We'll have a splendid dinner because Berton says he keeps a very good table and has a fine new house three miles up the river. We don't get much chance to go beyond the mile boundary, so come on, you'll get a chance to see the local countryside.'

Blaize spat derisively. 'Local countryside! It's a desert as far as I'm concerned – ruins, fields, hills and all those trees. It's like some place that's been stuck in time, at least three hundred years ago. There's no fine houses, no good buildings. Our fine houses in Arles have all been there since Roman times.'

Jacques laughed. 'Well, the Romans were here too, you know, so you should feel quite at home. The local people tell me that they had a fort and a temple up there on the nearest Eildon hill.'

Blaize followed his pointing finger and looked through the window at the slope of the hill where the sheep were huddled together for shelter among dead-looking bracken and gorse bushes. Not a building was to be seen.

'Oh, poor Romans, they must have hated it – almost as much as I do. Imagine sitting up there amongst all those sheep in this weather?'

Jacques laughed. 'Forget the Romans, put on your jacket with all its gold braid and let's go to eat the dinner of Mr Walter Scott, the good sheriff.'

The coachman was eager to talk as they drove along the tree-lined, snow-banked road that led out of the town.

'Oh aye, the Shirra's going to build a fine new house out there. He's changed its name already – Abbotsford sounds a deal better than Clarty Hole.'

Colonel Berton leaned forward in his seat. 'Clarty Hole? What does that mean?' He was interested in the local dialect and was making a collection of Scottish words and expressions.

'Clarty Hole?' The coachman laughed beerily into the thick collar of his coat. 'Clarty means dirty, filthy, full o'muck. You know what "hole" means, don't you? He likes words, does Maister Scott. He's a bit of a poet, you ken.'

The solidly built old farmhouse that was once Clarty Hole stood in a pleasant garden full of ancient trees on the banks of the Tweed. When the carriage drew up at the front door a crowd of wildly barking dogs, large and small, rushed out followed by the figure of the limping man, their host, wearing a tight black jacket and his black and white checked trousers. The French officers warmed towards him because he was smiling in hospitable welcome. Though some of them were men of rank and good family, the gentry of Melrose had studiously avoided them. This was the first time a gentleman's door had been opened even to Colonel Berton in friendship.

The lady of the house did not put in an appearance and it was an all-male dinner, but no less splendid for that. The vast dining table in a cosily firelit, panelled room was covered with a thick, cream-coloured linen cloth and set with dishes of silver and fine French china painted all over with roses. A troop of curious servants carried in course after course – soup, fish, fowl, mutton, cheeses and thin-crusted pies of apple and pear. The wine too flowed freely, a fine dark claret that shimmered like purple velvet in their glasses. Even Blaize, who was the least amenable of the group, seemed mellowed by the affability of their host.

They toasted each other; they toasted peace; and when Scott toasted the King of England he immediately followed it with a toast to Napoleon. At the mention of their emperor's name a solemn hush fell and the men in their patched uniforms stood up and raised their glasses to their lips.

16

When they sat down again Scott said, 'Your emperor is a very remarkable man. I must admit to having a great admiration for him.'

The colonel nodded his grey head. 'I don't think I ever knew a man with such a powerful intellect. Even as a lad, it was obvious he would have a great career in front of him.'

The Shirra leaned forward in his seat, his blue eyes gleaming with interest.

'We're told so many terrible things about him. They would have us believe he's got horns. Is it true about his temper and his lust? His enemies make him sound like the devil incarnate. They say he smells . . .'

The fumes of the wine that had filled Blaize's head cleared suddenly, reawakening his disillusionment and bitterness. He spoke up angrily. 'That's a lie. He takes a hot bath every day, which is more than can be said for his enemies.'

'Ah, it's our flute-playing friend,' said Scott, smiling at Blaize. 'With your family background I didn't expect you to be in favour of a Revolutionary like Napoleon.'

This was an accusation Blaize had heard before.

'I'm in favour of the Revolution and so was my family. I'd follow the Emperor anywhere. It's my greatest grief that I'm here in captivity while his armies are marching all over Europe.'

Scott teasingly pushed the decanter towards Blaize. 'Tell us about Napoleon, my friend. Is he made like other men? Is it true that he can satisfy ten women in a day? Is he really endowed like a bull?'

Blaize challenged Scott, 'So there is a reason why you brought us here – was it to pick our brains about our Emperor?'

With that he pushed back his chair and left the room, striding past a group of gaping servants who had come rushing from the kitchen at the sound of raised voices. Without looking back he burst through the front door and disappeared into the darkness where a few flakes of snow were falling. It was bitterly cold. His memory of

17

the journey to Abbotsford told him he should turn left to reach Melrose, but instead he deliberately turned right and strode off into the night. Blaize was making his long-dreamed-of escape, without a map, without money, without warm clothing and completely without premeditation.

When he had been missing for five days, Colonel Berton, who was responsible for the prisoners adhering to their promise to stay within the loosely drawn boundaries of their confinement, reported his escape to the official who came every week to pay their boarding and feeding fees and distribute money sent to individual prisoners from France via Coutts Bank.

'A man has gone missing,' said the colonel with shame in his voice. 'I've reported his escape to the town's law officers and they're out looking for him. A reward has been posted for his return.'

'He won't get far in this weather,' said the official, for the town square was by now almost thigh-deep with the snow which had not stopped falling since the night of Scott's dinner party. Berton agreed and shook his head sadly, for it was his private fear that Blaize, for whom he felt sympathy in spite of his rebelliousness, was dead of exposure on the windswept hills that fringed the horizon to the south. He would never be able to find his way through them in the bitter blizzards that whirled over their heights.

By the time another ten days had passed all the Frenchmen gave their missing comrade up for dead but one morning the snow began to melt and the sun shone again. Looking up in gratitude towards the Eildons, Jacques suddenly spied two men climbing down the slope of the nearest hill. Shading his eyes with his hand, he made out that one was a grey-haired shepherd in a home-spun cloak, carrying a tall crook – and the other was Blaize, very thin and pale but safe and, of course, unchastened. He and his captor were on good terms and when the old shepherd handed him over to the town policeman,

18

they shook hands and parted with words of mutual respect.

'There's a reward of ten shillings for handing in this man,' said the officer to the shepherd. 'If you wait, I'll get it for you.'

'I dinna want your money,' the old man replied with dignity. 'Keep it. I brought him back because our countries are at war and it was my duty. I don't want any money for that. He's a good fellow, don't be too hard on him. If I was in his shoes, I'd try to get back home too.'

The colonel, summoned from his lodgings by Jacques, regarded Blaize with a disappointed look.

'You were on parole, on your word of honour. You broke it. They could send you back to Valleyfield or even to the hulks in Woolwich and you know what that would be like. Don't you realize how fortunate we are to be here? If people like you break our trust, it's harder for everyone else, our confinement becomes more strict.'

Blaize was unapologetic. 'I'm a soldier. I want to get back to the fighting.'

'And how do you intend to do that? I wouldn't mind you trying to escape if you made a good job of it. But you bungled it, my friend. That reflects badly on us as well.'

This barb hurt and Blaize flushed angrily. 'I didn't have time to plan it, I was angry at that man asking about Napoleon . . . I suspected his reasons. So I just walked off and the snow beat me. I hid in a hut in the hills till that old man found me.'

Berton shook his head sadly. 'I'll do what I can to intercede with the authorities for you. I'll ask them to give you another chance.'

'Don't bother, because I'll try to get away again,' said Blaize. 'I have to try again.'

'Don't tell me things like that,' replied the colonel. 'Just make sure that if you do try again, you organize it better.'

Berton's intercession was successful and because the authorities did not want to have the trouble of sending an escort for Blaize through the winter blizzards, his punishment for escaping was two months' imprisonment in the little cell in the basement of the town hall followed by another month of house arrest under the colonel's supervision.

Christmas passed, followed by a bitter January and then, with the coming of February, spring warmth began to creep across the barren countryside, the skies lightened and the days lengthened. But Blaize, emerging from his cell, seemed to be in the grip of a profound depression. His flute lay unplayed in his room, his food was returned half eaten, and Jacques worried about his friend.

By early March the land was basking in soft sunshine, lambs appeared on the slopes of the three hills, buds swelled on the branches of the bare trees and the air smelt fresh and invigorating. There was the feeling of optimism that spring always brings to the people of the northern hemisphere.

One sunny morning Jacques announced to Blaize, 'There's a party of us going out in a waggon to build a wall for a landowner about two miles away. Put on your jacket and come with us. You won't have to work if you don't want to, but it's a chance to get out into the country.'

When there was no reply he strode across to the chair and shook Blaize by the shoulders. 'Get up, you fool. You're deliberately killing yourself. What good will that do for France? Get up, I won't stop shaking you till you do.' The body beneath his hands swung back and forward as if stuffed with straw, so the blond-bearded giant drew back his hand and struck the other man on the cheek.

'You'll get up even if I have to beat you into it,' he shouted.

This time there was a response. A light of anger shone in the brown eyes that looked back at him, so Jacques shook Blaize again.

'Get up and fight me, get up and hit me!' he challenged as he stuck out his fists.

It was surprising that a man who had taken no exercise for more than three months and had eaten only scraps of food could throw such a punch. It exploded onto Jacques' chin and knocked him out cold. When he came too, lying on the floor of the bedroom, Blaize was sponging his face with a wet cloth and actually laughing.

'You went down like a pole-axed bear. How surprised you looked!'

Rubbing his jaw, Jacques sat up. 'You might have been a little more gentle, friend. You could have broken my jaw. But it's all right, I'm only stunned. Come on, help me up.'

When he was standing shakily on his feet, he shook his head slowly and then asked again, 'Are you coming on the wall-building party?'

Blaize, leaning against the wall, replied, 'I wouldn't mind getting out but I don't want to build a wall for some landowner. I'm not a labourer.'

Jacques' reply was, 'Neither am I, but I want out of this town and here's a good opportunity. There's ten men going and none of us are labourers. Bring the flute. You can provide the musical accompaniment while we work.'

Because he was ashamed of his surliness and for having hit his friend so hard, Blaize pocketed the flute and, shrugging on his jacket, followed Jacques out of the room.

Jane, March 1813

She stood stock still, trying to hide her fear, both hands suddenly rigid at the sides of her white apron and the bunch of snowdrops she had been gathering drifting to the ground. Without speaking the strangely dressed man walked out of the shadows of the coppice and came towards her, then, bending one knee, he gathered up the drifted blossoms. Her eyes were fixed on him in terror as he handed the snowdrops back to her.

'We call them *perce-neige*, what is your name for them?' he said in a strange accent.

With a swallow to hide the tremor in her voice, she replied, 'They're snowdrops but my mother calls them Fair Maids of February . . . They're a little late this year.'

He smiled at her. 'That's a lovely name. They're beautiful. I've never seen so many growing together, it's like a sea of white down there under the trees.'

Her heart had leaped into her throat when she first noticed him standing half hidden behind the cluster of young spruce trees in the corner of the wood. It was the scarlet of his jacket she saw first, then the tarnished braid that festooned his shoulders and the gleaming golden buttons on his breast.

She wondered if she should scream for help or gather up her skirts and run away as fast as she could go. This had to be one of those French prisoners she had heard about – perhaps he had a knife, perhaps he wanted to kill or rape her. But as he smiled, her fear stilled a little and, following his pointing hand, she turned her head in the black straw hat and looked at the carpet of snow-drops spreading as far as she could see under the silver grey trunks of the beech trees. He was right, they *were* beautiful. Every year she thought of them as a miracle, a presage of the coming summer, a promise of sunny days and happy laughter, an assurance that the heavy labour of winter time would finish. When she walked among them she tried to place her heavy boots in the gaps between the clusters of flowers but sometimes it was impossible not to step on them, there were so many.

'The monks planted them,' she told the man in the fancy jacket with its loops of braid.

'The monks? What monks? Are they still here?'

'No, of course not.' She smiled too now, feeling more confident. 'They used to live here. Just behind this wood there's an old abbey. I live there now with my family.'

'Another abbey? Like the one in Melrose?'

'Not so big. It's half ruined really. The monks went away a long time ago.'

He was amused that the girl had obviously been so scared at the sight of him. She was rather unusual-looking herself, like an olden times dairy maid, in a large, face-shading black hat tied down with a cotton headsquare and a yellow and black striped skirt, hitched up to show her ankles and feet in heavy boots.

'What's your name?'

His question was sudden and unexpected and, recovering her confidence, she glared at him haughtily. 'Why do you want to know?'

'I just wondered. My name is Blaize Chardenel, I'm a Frenchman, a prisoner of war.' His tone was bitter again.

She gave a laugh of recogniton. 'Oh, you're the one that ran away. It was my uncle, my mother's brother, who brought you back. He told us about you, he said you looked like the Prince of Darkness.'

The coincidence amused him. 'The old shepherd is your uncle? I liked him, he was a good man.'

She nodded. 'Yes, he is. He said he was sorry that he had to bring you back but we're at war, you know. He liked you too in spite of the way you look.'

Blaize laughed. 'That's good. I can't help how I look, can I?'

She was pleased at the transformation laughter brought

to his face and thought that she had never seen anyone so handsome or so striking.

Blaize Chardenel was so tall, so elegant, so straight-shouldered. His skin was a golden colour and his glossy dark brown hair, which was almost as long as a girl's, curled on his neck. It was his face however that arrested her most of all for it was a mobile face with strong eyebrows over intense brown eyes and a wry mouth that seemed to change its expression with every word he said. He could look sarcastic and cruel one moment, romantic and melting the next. The Prince of Darkness indeed.

'What's your name?' he asked again, and she relented this time.

'It's Jane, Jane Cannon.'

He put out a hand and touched the edge of her coarse working apron. 'Why are you dressed like a dairy maid? Why do you wear that strange hat?'

She flushed. 'It's not strange. I'm a bondager and this is a bondager's hat.'

His eyes showed his surprise. 'A bondager? You mean you're a slave?'

She visibly bristled. 'Don't be silly, of course I'm not a slave. I work on the land with a team of other girls and I'm bonded – promised – to work for a year in the same place. But I'm lucky because my bond is with my father. Some of the other girls are bonded to strangers and that's not so good.'

He stood back and looked at her. This tall, straight, proud girl with the freckled skin was a female farm labourer but she looked very respectable as well as strong and resourceful, not a woman to be treated lightly.

He reflected that no woman could be more different to Marie, his dark-haired, pretty little wife back home in Arles. She could not even dig a garden, far less work in a field. The girl was watching him carefully with eyes of cornflower blue that matched the spring sky, and he sensed that she was afraid of his reaction to hearing what she did for a living, so he said, 'Forgive me, I've never

24

heard of bondagers before. Why are you gathering snow-drops? Is that part of your work?'

'No, of course not. I should really be feeding the sheep, they're lambing now, but my father lets me come here to gather snowdrops for my mother. She loves them and later in the year she makes medicines out of the bulbs.'

Blaize's interest was well wakened now.

'Once again you surprise me. I've never heard of snow-drops being used as medicine. What is it for?'

'She gives it to people with chest complaints. It makes them stronger. The monks brought the snowdrops here from France to make their medicines and some of the old receipts have been passed down. You see, one of my father's ancestors was the last monk to live here in the abbey – that's why we're called Cannon . . .'

'Is your mother a herbalist?'

'No, she's a howdie.'

'That's another word I don't know. What's a howdie?'

She looked pityingly at him. 'You don't know much, do you? The howdie's a midwife and a healer. She treats people who are sick and can't afford to go to the apothe-cary or the surgeon. My mother's better than they are anyway, and people come to her from all over the countryside. I'll have to get back to the field but I wanted to take her a bunch of snowdrops first.'

'I'll help you,' he offered and, bending down, started to gather fistfuls of the delicate flowers.

The broken gable end of the abbey church peeped over an ancient yew with a trunk so thick that three men could not link arms round it. The stone of the ruined buildings was a soft salmon pink and where the sun glinted on the broken walls they shimmered as if dusted with silver and gold.

He paused in surprise when they turned a corner of the path beneath the trees and were faced with the cavern of the roofless building. The only sound that broke the silence was the rapturous singing of birds in the trees.

'It's lovely,' he said softly, as if to himself. Then he stepped forward and stood beneath the arch of the great

25

doorway, looking up at the clusters of weather-eroded rosettes that ran round it.

She stood quietly beside him, pleased at his reaction. 'I love it. I was born here, you know. It always makes me wonder what it was like when the monks were here.'

'It's splendid,' said Blaize, gesturing up to the expanse of blue sky that arched between the ruined walls. 'In fact I think it's probably more splendid as a ruin with the sky as its roof. Churches can sometimes be depressing places.'

Without speaking they walked up what had once been the main aisle of the abbey church, littered now with massive carved stones from the fallen roof and spire. He followed her as she picked her way to a broad stone staircase on the right-hand side that rose up to a stout wooden door halfway up a smoothly dressed wall. She pointed ahead. 'We go up that stair, that's where I live.'

Inside the room behind the heavy, iron-studded door it was dim because there was only one small window, and it was darkened by the branches of the ancient yew outside. Blaize blinked to clear his eyes of the acrid sting of smoke from a fire that was burning in a huge, ornately carved fireplace. Alice, Jane's mother, sleeves rolled back over her forearms, was kneading dough at a deal table in the middle of the floor. He saw that she had handed down her strong frame to her daughter.

Surprised at having a visitor, she stood staring at Blaize, her hands covered with flour.

Jane explained, 'Mother, this is the Frenchman Uncle Tom found on the hill, I met him walking in the woods down by the river.'

The older woman looked hard at Blaize. 'You've not run away again, have you?'

He shook his head. 'Not this time. I came over from Melrose with a party to help build a wall over there . . .' He gestured westwards to where he knew his friends were working under the direction of a red-faced land-owner and his sullen steward.

'For Mr Glendinning? He's building a wall now?' The woman and the girl looked at each other anxiously.

26

'Yes, he wants to enclose his estate, he said. In France we're pulling down estate walls. Here you're building them up.'

The woman made a sound that could have implied either agreement or disapproval as she turned to a wall dresser to pick up a large blue and white jug.

'You'd like some buttermilk?' she asked, and without waiting for his reply poured out a cupful and handed it to him.

He was starving and accepted it gratefully. Pulling snowdrops had proved hungry work.

For the first time in months he felt happy, hungry and vigorous. This magically peaceful place where the only sounds were birdsong was having a therapeutic effect on him.

'Your daughter says you're a healer,' he said, handing back the empty cup.

Alice smiled sweetly. 'Oh, I wouldn't say that. I make up cordials and draughts for local folk or for their animals if they're sick. My mother did it before me and her mother before her.'

'So your recipes are old? You use herbs?'

'Yes, herbs and other things as well. If it helps people it makes me happy. It's good to help.'

Blaize looked at Jane, who was putting the snowdrops into a large earthenware jug.

'Does your daughter make medicines as well?'

'Jane helps, she picks it up the same way as I did. But you've got to have the power – you only know if you've got it when you start. Jane's got to go to the fields now because her father has to have a bondager to share his work.'

Blaize was curious. 'I'd never heard of bondagers before today . . . is it summer work?'

Both women laughed ruefully.

'I wish it was,' said Jane. 'No, I'm out in all weathers and in the winter it can be very cold and wet. If you saw me with the straw ropes round my legs and the mud up to my waist, you wouldn't think I was a dairymaid.'

27

'We all work for Mr Glendinning in the big house where you're making your wall,' explained Alice. 'He owns the farm. His steward hires the hinds and he won't take on a man unless he has a woman to work with him — just like my brother, the shepherd, has to have a dog.'

'And my mother has to work in the fields at harvest time for this house,' said Jane. 'That's our rent – mother's harvest work.'

Blaize looked round the big room and as his eyes became accustomed to the dimness, he could see that it had a fine arched stone roof with carved columns, and masterly rosettes at the top of each column. One of the rosettes was a wreath of holly, another a deeply carved rose, and then a lovely open sunflower that brought back memories of French fields in summertime. Whoever carved that sunflower must have been a Frenchman, he thought.

'But I thought you said your family had lived here for centuries. Is it not your own home? Does this place too belong to that man with the red face?' he asked Jane.

Alice replied, 'My husband's family have lived here a long time, ever since the last monks left. But they've always been tenants. Until a couple of years ago we farmed about thirty acres of the land round about for ourselves, but when Glendinning bought the big house, he took back all the lands of the tenant farmers to make his spread into one big place.

'So now we don't farm on our own any more – we're labourers and we've got to make our bargain with Glendinning every year. If he wanted he could turn us out at term time, but so far it's been all right because my husband is a strong man and a good worker and we've got a strong son and a hard-working daughter. We're a good bargain for a farmer.'

Jane's face was sad as she listened to her mother. This was obviously a topic that deeply concerned all the members of the family.

'We wouldn't want to leave here,' she told Blaize with an anxious note in her voice. 'I was born here. My father was born here and his father before him. It never seemed to matter who the old abbey belonged to – we lived here and paid our rent and we were left in peace. But now everything's changed. Some of our neighbours who were tenants too have lost their land and they've had to go away. Some went to Canada! I couldn't bear to go away from here.' She shuddered at the thought.

Her mother became very brisk, returning to the kneading of the dough.

'Don't you worry about it, lassie. It won't happen and if you don't want to leave here, you'd better get back to the fields. That steward'll be watching who's working and you'll catch it if he finds you're not there.'

The girl rushed away, grabbing a piece of cheese as she went.

When she'd gone her mother said to Blaize, 'She worries a lot about us leaving this place. I try to keep her mind off it. Come on, I can see you're hungry. Sit down and I'll feed you and then you'd better get back to work as well.'

As he ate he talked to her, telling her about his capture in Spain and about his longing to get back to the war. He asked about her life and about her family and for an hour or more they exchanged opinions and information. This made a bond between them. He found he admired the woman as much as he had admired her brother, the shepherd. When they parted, they were friends.

Jacques was greatly relieved to see Blaize coming up the path towards the working party.

'I thought you'd bolted again,' he said, wiping his brow with his vast forearm. 'I'm glad to see you back. Where have you been?'

Blaize was a different man to the one who had grudgingly accompanied the working party that morning. His face was changed, his step lighter, his back straight again.

'I met a family who live in a ruined church down there,' he said, pointing over his shoulder. 'It's like a

29

secret hiding place . . . a sort of fairyland. I'm not sure I didn't dream it.'

Jacques roared with laughter. 'You've met a woman, I knew you would. You're just as human as the rest of us after all.'

'I'll come with you again today,' Blaize offered the next time a wall-building party was being made up, and when they got to Charterhall House he said to Jacques, 'When lunchtime comes, I'll take you across to the abbey and introduce you to the woman there. She's a healer and would enjoy talking to you about medicines.'

Alice liked Jacques very much and invited both of the Frenchmen to visit the abbey house any time they were at Charterhall. She also introduced them to her husband, Adam, an upright, solemn, grey-haired man who resembled his brother-in-law the shepherd who had brought Blaize back from the hills. Like the old shepherd too, Jane's father had a deep respect for book learning, and had he been born in another class of society, would have made a scholar and a savant. His hunger for knowledge, unsatisfied by his brief schooling to the age of twelve, still burned strongly after years of labouring in the fields and he passed this hunger on to his children, to his daughter as well as his son. At night, when work was finished, the family sat round their majestic hearth and took turns reading to each other from the books of devotion they had collected over the years. They told Blaize and Jacques about their evenings round the fire, but the Frenchmen were never able to join them then because they had to be back in their lodgings by sundown and could not risk breaking their parole.

Alice, her husband and her children grew to like the handsome Frenchmen and to respect them for their fervent loyalty to the Emperor Napoleon. When they heard accounts of the war and Boney's evil ways from people who had access to newspapers, the Cannon family were able to take the more outrageous of those tales with a pinch of salt.

Jacques teased Blaize about his devotion to the people who lived in the ruined abbey.

'It's that girl, don't deny it. She's a fine big girl, as tall as you, and she's the marrying age. You make a magnificent couple. That's why you don't need to slip down to Nanny's like the rest of us.'

'Don't be stupid. The girl's just a friend. Anyway her mother told me she's spoken for in marriage by a local lad and I'm a married man, don't forget that.'

Marie's letters, written on fragile paper in her childish hand, came from time to time, full of gossip and details of her outings with her sisters or the last embroidery she had finished. He read them quickly and thrust them aside – not impatiently, but because they brought back the image of his wife to him. She was small and pretty in the way he thought women should be, pale-skinned and tiny-featured, with delicate hands and dainty feet.

He did not want her to be clever or well read, for he had always found sufficient mental stimulus among his male friends and did not seek a wife who wished to discuss his work or matters of intellectual weight. Marie's music, her watercolour painting, her sewing and her continual domestic warfare with the servants was sufficient as far as her husband was concerned.

The enforced chastity of captivity did not worry him either. His spirits had been depressed for so long that the need for a woman was low in his priorities. The other prisoners, including Jacques, openly patronized a trio of amateur prostitutes who had set up thriving businesses in Melrose. Nanny Pawston was the favourite among them because she was the youngest and the lustiest, the wife of a soldier who was away fighting for Wellington in the Peninsula where so many of Nanny's clients had been captured, perhaps by her husband's regiment. She often passed Blaize in the town's high street, flirting her eyes and her skirts at him as she went by for he, the most handsome of the captives, was a challenge to her. He had never risen to her bait. In truth, if Blaize had been looking for a woman he would not have looked at Nanny and neither would he have looked at Jane, who was too strong, too unflirtatious and reserved, not sufficiently skilled in the arts of coquetry for him. He regarded her with almost as much awe as he regarded her mother. It completely escaped his notice that when he appeared in the abbey house, she flushed scarlet and her hands trembled with excitement at the sight of him.

They were cutting hay one morning in late June, bending low with flashing sickles over the tall grass with its bounty of pink clover, yellow-hearted daisies and purple vetch.

'There's your Frenchie over there,' teased Maggie Maxton, the prettiest, cheekiest member of the gang of eight bondagers. 'He's waiting for you. I fancy you'll be off to France when this war's over, Janey.'

Jane's heart thudded in her ribs as she lifted her head and saw Blaize standing beneath the hedge at the side of the field. His jacket was slung over one shoulder and he was wearing a white open-necked shirt that showed the strong sinews of his neck and the lines of his straight shoulderbones. The hand she raised to wave to him shook slightly with the strength of her emotion and she dreaded the sharp-eyed Maggie seeing how she felt. He was gazing at the bondagers and she wondered if he were comparing her to the other women in the field, for they made a romantic-looking group in their hats decorated with flowers or love tokens, their print blouses and striped skirts. But there were many of them far prettier than Jane herself – little Maggie, for example with the dark-fringed, doll-like eyes that she rolled with such devastating effect at the local lads. How Jane wished she could look like that and be able to make Blaize smile at her the way all the boys smiled at Maggie.

She knew that her terrible, heart-wrenching love for this Frenchman was futile, for he had told her mother about his wife in France. But though her love was useless and unreturned, that did not stop it burning painfully inside her. Thoughts of Blaize kept her awake at night.

She went to work every morning wondering if she would see him that day. And when he did appear, the sky miraculously lightened even on the dullest days. He brought the sunshine with him.

As she walked across the hay field towards him she knew that her man, Jock Hepburn, was watching her. She could see his red-haired figure among the men loading haycarts near the field gate and the intensity of his stance told her that he was burning with jealousy. Poor Jock, they had been promised in marriage for the past two years and in her bondager's hat she wore the double looped love token of straw that he had made for her last autumn. Jock always made her feel protective, for though he was large and strong, he was a vulnerable soul. His mother was Big Agnes, the forewoman of the bondagers, a massive woman with forearms like a blacksmith's and a face so weatherbeaten that in summer it looked as if her nose was made of copper.

Agnes Hepburn had never married and the identity of Jock's father was a secret she kept to herself, but people said that one of the hinds she was bonded to when she was very young had forced himself on her, raped her in fact. She was very bitter and scathing about men – all of them that was except her Jock and a few of the men, including Adam Cannon who was her close friend, with whom she worked.

Jock was twenty-one, two years older than Jane, a large, gentle giant of a man with a ruddy face and red hair. She thought that when he was old he would look exactly like her father, and loved him for that. Unlike Adam Cannon, however, Jock was ambitious and dreamed of getting his own farm one day. 'When we get married you'll be mistress in your own house, you won't have to work in the fields to pay the rent. You'll have a servant girl and people will touch their hats to you,' he often told her, explaining why the wedding would not take place until he had more money saved up.

She did not mind waiting, for she had not been ready to marry and settle down even before Blaize turned up.

Anyway, she didn't believe that Jock's dreams would ever come true. They would never achieve landowning status and when he talked about it, she smiled and put her fingers on his weatherbeaten face, saying, 'Don't work too hard, Jock, life goes past and you'll never know it's happened.'

Then Blaize walked out of the wood and took her heart. For the first time she knew what it was like to be devastatingly, painfully in love. She would have gone away with the Frenchman if he had not a penny – providing he really wanted her. But of course he did not, and she had the pain of that to suffer.

He grinned when she walked up to him, and held out a bunch of pink campions to her. 'Put them in your hat,' he said, 'they'll look well against black.'

She accepted the flowers, glancing anxiously over her shoulder to see if the steward had noticed her taking time off from the hay cutting. 'I can't stay talking to you, but I'm glad you came today,' she said. 'I wish you'd go over to the abbey and have a look at my mother. She's not well and she won't tell me what's wrong with her. Perhaps she'll tell you.'

'I'll go there now,' said Blaize. 'They won't miss me from the wall gang. You come when it's your break. How long do you get today?'

'We get two hours – they need that time to rest the horses,' Jane told him wryly.

He walked through the coppice where they had first met, the green velvet of the sward beneath the silver-barked beech trees carpeted now with bluebells instead of snowdrops, and as always his heart rose when he saw the ragged parapet of the abbey wall above the yew tree. Every time he came here he felt as if he'd walked into another world.

Alice did not hear him walking across the soft grass of the yard for she was sitting on a hard wooden chair beneath a line of pear trees trained along the cloister wall and she was asleep, her head drooping in the sun while the bees from her carefully tended hives droned round her. In sleep her face looked yellow and strained, and Blaize felt a tug of concern in his heart at the sight of her.

He gently touched her limp hand and she woke with a start.

'I've come for one of our good talks,' he said and she smiled at him, but her smile was weary.

'Sit down, I'll get you some ale,' she said and struggled to rise from her chair.

He held her back. 'No, sit still, I'll fetch it myself. You look tired. Let me look after you for a change.'

It did not take long to discover what was wrong with Alice. Indeed she was very matter of fact about what ailed her. In a resigned, matter of fact tone she told him, 'I've seen it often enough in other women – the lumps in my breasts, the pains, the bleeding, the sickness. My mother died of it and there was nothing she could do. I'm dying of it too but I don't want to worry Jane, she's so tender-hearted.'

'I was afraid it might be something like that.' Blaize slumped down on his heels at the side of her chair. He knew she would not appreciate him pretending to make light of what she said. 'How long do you think it will take?' he asked.

She shrugged. 'By winter, or at the latest by early spring – when the snowdrops come again. It should be over by then. Will you help them? They'll need your help.'

'I'll help them and I'll help you. Have you any laudanum?'

'I've poppy juice, that's what I give other people.'

'I'll get you something better from Jacques. You won't suffer, I promise you. Leave it to me.'

She put out a work-hardened hand and laid the rough fingers on his wrist. 'I trust you,' she said.

When Blaize asked Jacques for laudanum, his face expressed consternation.

'But you're better. You are a changed man. You're not going to take laudanum are you?'

'Of course not. It's not for me. It's for Alice in the

abbey. She's dying from the wasting disease and she has much pain. I want to help her.'

Jacques looked sad. 'I didn't think she looked well. So many of the women here have that. I've never seen so many. Is it too far gone for hope?'

'She says it is and I trust her judgement.'

'Perhaps I could come and have a look at her. I've treated many cases and sometimes they last much longer than doctors expect.'

'That would be good. Come with me tomorrow, she's expecting me.'

The howdie and the French surgeon trusted each other. He held her hand and felt the beat of her heart. 'You're a strong woman,' he told her. 'You can fight this.'

But she shook her head. 'No, I don't want to. I don't want to be like my mother who fought and fought till she was screaming in agony at the end. I want to die quickly. I want to die with dignity.' The two men looked at her and neither could think of an argument against that. She was a woman who embodied dignity.

'Then I'll help you die when the time comes,' promised Jacques, and that was enough. For the rest of the afternoon the three of them sat laughing and talking beneath the pear trees in the sun, drinking her home-brewed beer from pottery mugs and talking about other things. Just before the Frenchmen were preparing to leave, there was a rustling of silken skirts on the steps behind them and when they turned, they saw a small, dark-haired girl in a full-skirted blue dress coming down from the ruined church aisle. She was carrying a basket covered with a white cloth and she was smiling.

'Oh, it's Miss Christian from the big house,' said Alice, introducing the girl to the French prisoners. 'She's the daughter of Mr Glendinning, the man you're building the wall for. You'd better get back to work or she'll tell her father about you.'

The girl laughed. 'Don't tease, Alice, of course I won't tell. I think father's stupid to want to build such a huge

36

wall anyway. I don't want to be cut off from the outside world.'

As she spoke her eyes caught the eyes of Jacques and for a moment everyone in the small group felt the electric shock of understanding that passed between the two strangers.

Standing up, he took her hand and led her to the chair beside Alice. 'Sit down, Miss Christian, it's so lovely here in the sun.'

The colour rose in her face and she sat, spreading out her pretty skirts. 'Yes, isn't this a lovely place? The monks knew where to build, didn't they? You said they planted those trees, didn't they, Alice?'

'Well, they've been here as long as any of us can remember and they were bearing fruit when my husband's grandparents were alive,' Alice said.

Christian looked at Jacques again and told him, 'The pears are beautiful, soft and sweet. No one around has fruit like them. They say the trees came from France.'

'Like us,' said Jacques, with a guffaw. 'All the best things come from France.'

Christian giggled and looked up at him from beneath her long eyelashes. In that instant they fell in love.

When the enthusiasm of the wall-building party began to wear off, they were chivvied back into action by Jacques and Blaize, both of whom did not want to lose the opportunity of returning to Charterhall with its twin attractions in the mansion house and the ruined abbey.

Work was never going on for long before Christian rode up on her neat black cob or driving in her shining governess car. She would pause and lean down to talk to Jacques, who was as excited as a boy after she left.

Once or twice, when she did not come, he would be anxious and short-tempered with his workmates and asked Blaize to find out from the family in the abbey if they knew what had prevented her from visiting him.

Christian and Jane had become friends although the difference in their stations of life meant that the friendship had to be concealed from her father. Christian, a motherless girl, enjoyed visiting Alice in the abbey, and often walked back from these visits with Jane, talking about the things that concerned young women of their age.

She was very curious about Jane's engagement to Jock – when would they be marrying? Where would they live?

'I don't want to think about a wedding now,' said Jane. 'My mother's sick. If anything happens to her, I'll be needed at home to look after my father and brother. Jock understands. He says he'll wait.'

She did not tell Christian or anyone else that she was not eager to marry because her heart was by now entirely given over to the unattainable Blaize. He still came to the abbey several times a week, and as she watched him comforting her mother, her love for him deepened even more. He had completely forgotten his misery and hatred of confinement now that he had something else to occupy his mind.

Christian glanced at Jane's sombre face and said, 'Perhaps you've noticed how much I like Jacques. And he likes me too, I know that. He's asked me to marry him and he wants to come to speak to my father. I wonder what Papa will say?'

Jane had her doubts about this, for Mr Glendinning was the worst sort of mindless patriot, a loud bellower against Boney, and she could foresee that Jacques would have a hard time convincing him that a Frenchman, an enemy, even one who was a surgeon from a respectable family, was a good prospect for the hand of his daughter. Christian also had a brother who would not take a tolerant view of her wanting to marry a Frenchman either. Like his father he adopted conventional attitudes and, though he had no intention of risking his own neck in the fighting, could sound as belligerent and anti-French as the most fearsome fighting man.

'When's he coming to ask your father?' she asked.

'Soon, very soon, when I think the time's right,' said Christian, who was under no illusion about how easy her father would be to win over. But she held a trump card. Her father doted on her and was continually anxious about the state of her health. Like her mother, Christian Glendinning was a consumptive – the dread disease had killed her mother shortly after she was born – and her childhood had been plagued with outbreaks of feverish illness, some of which had looked like being her last. But since they had come to live at Charterhall, Alice had been treating Christian with various potions and cordials which seemed to have worked and set her on her feet again. There had been no recurrence of the disease for the last two years, and now everyone hoped that she was cured for she was a pink-cheeked and healthy-looking eighteen-year-old. From time to time, however, if she became too excited or upset, her cough would start again and old Glendinning would fly into a panic. He would do anything rather than upset Christian.

It was a magnificent summer that year and during the first two weeks of August the sun shone brilliantly so that the corn ripened golden in the fields, giving promise of an early and abundant harvest. Farm people all seemed to take a rest just before the harvest ripened, preparing themselves for the rigours ahead, and it was during this time that the French prisoners in Melrose decided to hold a fête to celebrate Napoleon's birthday on the fifteenth of the month.

There was to be music, and stalls selling the things that the men had spent the winter making – straw hats, ships carved out of bone, toys, paintings, intricately designed boxes with decorations made from straw. Many of the men did not receive any money from France and the sale of these gew-gaws gave them some money in their pockets.

All the prisoners were very excited about the fête and invited local people who had become their friends. One of the Frenchmen, a rich merchant's son from Bordeaux whose father sent him the princely sum of one hundred livres a month, announced that he would pay for a dinner to be laid on after the fête, to which each prisoner could invite a friend. Jacques invited Christian and Blaize asked if any of the Cannons would like to come as his guest.

Adam Cannon refused. 'I'm not a one for fêtes,' he said, and his shy son standing behind him nodded his head in agreement. They would have felt awkward and out of place at a gathering with people they considered to be their social superiors. But Jane longed to go and her mother saw the disappointment on the girl's face at her father's words.

She said, 'Well, I wouldn't mind going but this pain's worse and I don't think I could stand up very long. What about taking Jane as your guest, Blaize? She'd like to go to the fête and she could come back here before the dinner if she wanted, but since Miss Christian's going, she might be able to come back with her.'

He thought that was a good idea. It was a nice way of repaying the family for all their kindness to him so he said eagerly, 'Yes, Christian's going in her governess cart. Her father won't go, of course, but he said she could if she took her aunt along as chaperone. She'll bring Jane as well. Leave it to me, I'll organize it.'

Jock did not want Jane to go to the French celebration but she told him that she was only attending to keep Christian company. 'She can't go unless her aunt and I go with her and I know she wants to. She likes a party, does Miss Christian.'

If he thought it unlikely that Old Glendinning would want his daughter to go to the fête with one of his bondagers, Jock said nothing. He knew there was no point in trying to stop Jane doing something she had set her heart on.

The old packman knelt down on the stone paving of the abbey aisle and slowly untied his bundle, carefully laying out things for Jane and Alice to look at. Jane had known him since she was a child and, when she was small, had been very frightened of him in his black clothes and with the enormous hat pulled down low over his face. Now that she was grown up however she recognized him to be harmless, just an unwashed old man who carried gossip from house to house and farm to farm around their corner of the Borderland. He was their local newspaper really, because he called in every month or so, full of stories about who had married, who had died and who had given birth to a baby, usually out of wedlock according to him.

'You're going to the French party for Boney's birthday, they tell me,' he said to Jane. 'You'll be needing a grand frock for that.'

She looked at his dirt-engrained face and wondered how she could bear to wear anything that came out of his greasy sack, but when he stepped back and displayed his stock, her breath was caught in her throat because there, on the top of the pile, was the exact piece of material she had dreamed of. It was pale green satin with a soft sheen and she knew that it would look magnificent on her.

Alice saw her eyes on the material and glanced at the packman, who had also noticed which piece attracted the girl.

'That's a piece of cloth fit for a lady,' he said. 'You'd look like the Queen of Sheba in that. But it's not cheap. It's a shilling and sixpence a yard.'

A bondager's wage was eightpence a day and when she heard the price, Jane's face fell. She needed at least five yards. Where was she going to find seven shillings and sixpence? Even her father did not earn that in a week.

The other materials were plain cottons sprigged with flowers, like the pieces the Cannon family usually bought to make Jane's headcloths or her print blouses. She could not go to the fête in a dress made of that.

'I don't think I'll go to the party after all,' she said suddenly, standing back from the packman's display.

Alice looked surprised. 'Why not? You were very keen this morning.'

'Oh, it's going to take too long to make a dress and

I don't know anybody over there in Melrose. I'd feel awkward.'

'There's a lot of folk going,' wheedled the packman. 'The family from the farm up the hill will be there and so will Miss Christian. I've just sold her a fine piece of lace to make a stole.'

Jane walked towards the door. 'I can't go,' she said.

Alice looked at the packman. 'What price did you say that green material is?' she asked.

'One shilling and sixpence a yard, but I'd let you have it for one and threepence if the lassie really wants it,' was the reply.

'I'll take it,' said Alice. 'Just wait here till I get the money.' She disappeared into the house, where Jane heard her rattling about, taking coins out of the hiding place in an old stone jar on the mantelpiece.

She rushed in after her mother and said, 'Don't waste your money on me, Mother. I don't want to go, really.'

Alice turned in the shadows near the window and Jane saw that she looked very tired. 'But I want you to go and I want you to have that green dress. I'll help you make it up. You'll be as fine as any lady there – but Jane, remember that you're playing with fire. Just remember that.'

Where the road narrowed at the old gateway of the town, Blaize and Jacques waited in the doorway of an alehouse and when Christian's governess cart came briskly round the bend, they stepped forward to greet their guests. Jacques seized the bridle of the pony while Blaize put out a hand to help the women down.

Christian, soft and feminine in pale blue satin with her lace stole over her shoulders, stepped down first. Then her sour-faced aunt in black alpaca that must have felt hot and stuffy on the warm August day, bustled down carrying various wrappers and parasols in case Christian was too hot or too cold. It was when he put out a hand to help the last passenger out that Blaize started with a surprise which he could do nothing to conceal. He had never seen Jane dressed in anything but her bondager costume and when he thought of her, he saw her as a rural seventeenth-century milkmaid in the voluminous striped skirt, white apron, heavy boots and face-shading hat over the patterned cloth which always concealed her hair. He had never seen her bareheaded and today she was transformed, like a character from a fairy tale. The dress she and her mother had stitched together was made of cheap material but it was in a deep shade of sea green that made a bold contrast with her golden hair, and its low-cut neck showed her fine shoulders and the tops of her milky breasts to their best advantage. The folds of satin loosely draped her tall body, hinting at the points of her hip bones and the soft swell of her belly. It was the glorious hair that fascinated him most of all, however. It was very thick, piled up on her head but with softly waving tendrils that had already escaped at the sides of her cheeks and down the back of her neck.

Tucked into a comb behind her ear was one of the sweetly scented, tightly furled white roses that grew beside the ancient graves in Charterhall abbey grounds.

He bowed gravely as if to a queen, and equally gravely she stepped on to the cobbled street. Without speaking, she took his arm and they followed the others up the little hill to the square where lines of stalls were set out and crowds of people were wandering about. Flags were strung from house to house and a group of musicians was already playing on a dais outside the Masonic Rooms in the high street.

As Jane turned the corner, her hand gently resting on Blaize's arm, she gave a gasp of surprise and delight at the sight.

'Oh, I'm so glad you asked me,' she told him with a dazzling smile lightening her face.

'I'm so glad you could come,' he replied in his most courtly manner, his surprise at her transformation still evident. He felt as if he were escorting a stranger to the party.

It was so easy to see that Jacques and Christian were

deeply in love. They never left each other's sides all after-noon and looked lovingly into each other's eyes, whispering softly. When the dancing began they took the floor together as if they were unaware of anything except the other person. Each touch of the hand, each brush of the skirt seemed to have an electric effect on them. They caused a good deal of head-shaking gossip among the other guests.

When some of the townswomen had seen Jane arrive they had tut-tutted among themselves at the unseemliness of farm women being invited to the party. They knew who she was because from time to time, or on fair days, she went into town to do her shopping. Jane however was unaware of their disapproval for she was glowing, sparkling, carried away with the delight of the fête. In her green gown, with her hair loosely tumbling, she made a majestic figure and more than one man stared at her with frank and open admiration. Her escort however looked stunned, and as several old beldames of the town watched, he put out a finger and gently touched one of the freckles on Jane's cheek. She flushed at the touch of his hand.

'You are – how do you say – *tache de rousseur,*' he said softly. '*Tache de son* – with the sunshine. I've never seen you without that big hat and the headscarf before.'

'You mean I'm freckled. That's why I wear the scarf and the hat. You can't work outside and not be freckled, you know. I hate those freckles. I've got them all over – even in places that the sun never touches.' She sounded defensive.

He laughed. 'But they are magnificent, they make you look as if you are golden. You look like the goddess Juno. I'm sure she was freckled too.'

'I've tried everything to get rid of them – I rub myself with rosemary oil and ointment made from cowslip flowers, but nothing works. I hate those freckles. I wish I had a milky-white skin like Christian's.'

They both looked across the square to where Christian

44

and Jacques were dancing, their eyes fixed on each other's face.

Blaize stood up and took her hand. 'Don't worry. You're a very different kind of woman. Let us dance, too. Do you like dancing?'

'Oh yes, I like dancing. At least I can do that like other women,' she said.

A local country air was being played and the dancers held hands, turning in time to the beat, smiling into each other's faces and bowing now and then, advancing and retreating in stately measure. Blaize and Jane danced in perfect unison, as if they had rehearsed it and as he looked into her face, he felt himself drawn deeply into the eyes which today seemed to have taken on the aquamarine colour of her gown. He saw that the irises were, like her skin, flecked with little golden dashes. She was a goddess. Why had he never noticed that before?

She in turn stared back at him, every nerve in her body alert to the touch of his hand. She felt the blood beating through him and in unconcealed fascination she greedily drank in every part of his face – the high cheekbones, the deep sardonic grooves at the sides of his mouth, the tender curl of the hair on his neck.

Then their eyes met and everything became very solemn, the music was muffled by the beating of their hearts. Like two people in a trance they stared at each other and when the dancing finished they stood awkwardly apart as if embarrassed at being caught in an unseemly show of private emotion.

Neither of them spoke and when they returned to the table to join Jacques and Christian, it was time for the toast to the Emperor. All the Frenchmen stood gravely up, the gathering darkness of the evening making them look magnificent in their old uniforms, and raised their glasses high. Then, still standing, they sang the 'Marseillaise'. Though the guests did not join in, they were deeply impressed by the solemnity and genuine emotion of their hosts. That reminder of the difference between them, the knowledge that in spite of good fellowship, the French and the British were still at war, that in Europe their armies were battling bloodily against each other, brought the night's festivities to an end. Christian's party returned to the alehouse yard where the pony was patiently waiting in a straw-filled stall and Jacques reharnessed it while Blaize pulled on the shafts of the cart and buckled up the leather traces. Then the women drove off into the velvet darkness waving and calling farewell. Their magic night was over.

Blaize did not visit the abbey for a week although every day she looked for him. Christian came over to the abbey to tell Alice that Jacques had asked Mr Glendinning for her hand in marriage and the big house was full of the noise of shouting, of coming and going and family arguments. In spite of her apparent frailty she was a doughty fighter, and it was obvious that in time she would wear her father down. Jacques, she pointed out, was a surgeon and who needed a surgeon as a husband more than she did? He was as rich as the Glendinnings, with a considerable property in France. His family was older and more distinguished than hers.

At the end of the week her father reluctantly gave his consent, but the couple had to agree to wait until the war was over. According to his newspaper, the *Kelso Chronicle*, that would not be too long, for events on the Continent definitely going the way of the Allies now. Boney would soon be beaten and when peace came, they could be married.

The harvest was in full swing while this was happening and the bondager gang was working frantically till late at night, till the moon rose high in the night sky and the owls flitted around the hedgerows. They cut the corn, tied it up into sheaves and threw them with pitchforks up on to the high-piled harvest waggons. Even at midnight they were still hard at it and would go on working under the light of the harvest moon until the early hours of the morning.

Christian came out with some servants from the big

house with pitchers of beer and a jug of whisky for the men and found Alice in a corner of the field, bending painfully down and winding lengths of twine round the heavy-headed swatches of corn that the reapers had left behind.

'Oh Alice, you shouldn't be out here working. You've not been well. Go home this minute,' said the girl.

Alice raised a weary face, the lines on it deeply etched by the moon's silver beams.

'Miss Christian, you ken fine that I can't go home. I've got to work at harvest time for our house. It's part of our bargain, it's our rent. If I don't work, we could lose the house.'

'Rubbish. I wouldn't allow it. Go home this minute and I'll tell the steward I sent you.'

'You mustn't interfere. It's not right. It's not fair on the others. Just leave me be. This field is nearly finished and I'll go home then.' Her voice was cracked and wavering.

Forgetting her own happiness, Christian ran across the field to where her father's steward was supervising the loading of the carts.

'You've got to let Alice go home,' she ordered him. 'She's not well.'

'She's one of the best workers, we can't do without her. It's going to take every hand we have to clear this field tonight. You mind your own business, Miss Christian, and let me mind mine.'

The girl stared round at the faces of the men watching her. They were blank and impassive. Among them she saw Adam Cannon and his son. Even they were not going to protest on Alice's behalf, they could not afford to.

'But she's ill,' she protested.

'She's still working, that's all I know,' said the steward. 'Harvests won't wait for anybody. That lassie over there had a baby yesterday but she's back at work today.' He pointed to the figure of a bondager at the far side of the hay waggon. She was tossing sheaves of corn up into the air on the point of a pitchfork.

Christian's astonishment showed in her face. 'She had a baby yesterday?'

The steward smiled, showing dirty, broken teeth. 'They're not like well-born ladies, Miss, they're not like you.'

When the harvest was finished everyone was almost too weary to talk but it had been one of the best harvests for years, and both Glendinning and his steward were jubilant. Not a drop of rain had fallen during the two weeks of harvesting and now the bins were full of winnowed corn and the yard full of stacks, stoutly built and covered with plaited straw to withstand the hardest winter winds.

On Saturday night, Mr Glendinning was giving his workers a kirn, a harvest supper and dance, in the big barn. Even the most tired was infused with new energy at the news. Christian came to the abbey to tell the Cannons about the party and she was so excited that two round spots of red burned in the middle of her cheeks and beads of perspiration dotted her upper lip. She kept wiping them away as she talked and complained about the oppressive heat.

'Father says that the weather's going to break soon, there'll be a storm any day now. I hope it waits till after the kirn.'

Jane listened to the once-again repeated story of the long-fought-for engagement with a smile on her face but pain in her heart. She felt guilty for envying Christian. Blaize had not even bothered to come to see her in spite of the way she thought he had felt when they danced together in Melrose.

'Will Jacques be at the kirn?' she asked.

'Oh no, unfortunately not,' said Christian. 'He's not allowed to go outside the town after eight at night, you know. He wants to come but he can't get here.'

1813 – GOOD HARVEST – GOOD CHEER . . . Jock was making a huge placard to be hung at the end of the barn during the kirn. He spelt out the words with leaves, branches of berries and flowers and when it was finished it was a brave sight. Jane stood in the open door and watched him at work, his face serious as he painstakingly sorted out the materials he had collected early that morning. Since he was a little boy, Jock had made the harvest banner. It was his annual artistic expression and each year he tried to surpass himself.

She clapped her hands. 'It's your best yet, Jock,' she called to him. 'It's really lovely.'

He turned to her and grinned broadly, an unusual thing for him these days because his expression had recently been generally gloomy.

This was not a time for gloom however, this was a time for taking a rest, for looking back on labour and giving thanks for an abundant harvest. Even the people who would receive no financial benefit from this year's generous bounty were rejoicing. Their work would be safe at least for another year at Charterhall.

The barn, built of the same neatly dressed sandstone blocks as the abbey and probably plundered from its ruins, was swept out and decorated for the kirn.

Barrels of porter, benches and tables filled half of the floor space. The other half was cleared and dusted with chalk for the dancing that would follow the feast.

Charlie Glendinning sat at the top table, face afire, with his son, young Charlie, on one side and his daughter Christian on the other. He was drunk before the kirn started and during the proceedings kept banging a pewter mug on the table top and shouting in a slurred roar, 'Everybody have a drink, Everybody drink to the harvest. It's the best for years.'

Three musicians were tuning up their fiddles outside the doorway when the Cannon family arrived, and as the oldest fiddler caught sight of Alice and Jane he said, 'You'll give us a song tonight, ladies? We'll play your special songs for you.'

'I'm not much good at singing now,' said Alice, 'but Jane here'll sing. She's better than me.'

'You were the best singer I've ever heard,' said the

49

fiddler. 'I'll never forget how you sang at my brother's wedding. It brought tears to every eye in the room.'

Alice was pleased. 'Oh, that was long ago,' she said, but she was still smiling as she sat down at her place in the middle of a long bench.

Jane looked at her mother with love and admiration. The strong body was thin and stooped now, and sometimes Alice audibly caught her breath with pain. But she never complained so the family usually managed to deceive themselves that death had been defeated. They told themselves that, miraculously, Alice was going to live longer than anyone had guessed when she first became ill. Jacques was taking a keen interest in her and persisted in trying a variety of medicines and treatments. His latest notion was to confine Alice to a strict diet of milk, eggs and vegetables, instead of the normal labourer's fare of oatmeal porridge and salt meat. Though she lost weight on it, her energy seemed to have returned.

As she thought gratefully about Jacques' solicitude for her mother, Jane's mind reverted to Blaize. He had not been over to see Alice for more than two weeks. Why had he abandoned them? Was it her fault? Had she been too forward with him at Napoleon's birthday party? Had she shown too clearly how much she loved him? The pain burned in her heart and, as if to deny it, she turned to Jock who was sitting on her right and gave him a most brilliant smile, taking his hand as she did so.

'I meant it when I said the banner this year is the best you've ever done. It's like a big painting of flowers. Where did you get them all?'

He grinned happily again. 'Miss Christian told the gardeners to give me the run of the garden. She's in grand form these days now that she's going to marry the Frenchman.'

Jane looked over the row of heads at Christian, febrile with excitement in her white silk gown.

For a chilling second a feeling of terrible grief swept over the watching girl. It scared her badly because she had experienced moments of foreboding like this before.

50

Once, when her grandmother was visiting, she had known that the old woman would die very soon and indeed she died the following week. Another time, even more frightening, on a misty autumn evening she had looked out of the window in the abbey and seen a silent procession with a coffin passing beneath the old yew tree. But there had been no funeral that day and what she saw was a presagement. She was terrified at her powers when three days later the old schoolmaster, who had been kind and encouraging to all the local children, died and was buried in the abbey grounds.

She told no one of her uncanny and unwanted powers, and when she felt them take her over, she tried to rationalize them away. Tonight however she could not drive away the terrible grief she felt at the sight of Christian.

The revellers ate, they drank, they danced and they sang. Soon even Jane, her head swimming from the strong ale, forgot her troubles and in response to the cries of the crowd, agreed to give them a song. They all whistled and clapped as she walked towards the group of musicians and stood gravely beside them, adjusting the folds of her skirt with her hands and nervously clearing her throat. When she had told the men what songs she would sing, she threw back her fine head and launched into music in a clear, thrilling soprano.

She knew the sort of songs her audience liked for she had grown up hearing her mother sing them. They liked the sad old dirges mourning the men lost in Border wars against the English, and she sang of sorrow and the devastation of humble homes. She sang the songs of exile and the songs that spoke of the love all Borderers feel for their secluded, landlocked countryside. When she responded to the urgings of the audience to sing a song called 'My Peggy', she poured extra feeling into it . . .

'Love never more shall give me pain,
My fancy's fixed on thee,
Nor ever maid my heart shall gain,
My Peggy, if thou dee.

If fate shall tear thee from my heart,
How shall I lonely stray.
In dreary dreams the night I'll waste,
In sighs, the silent day.
I ne'er can so much virtue find, nor such perfection
    see,
Then I'll renounce all womankind, my Peggy, after
    thee.'

Her father, thinking of the sick wife at his side, wiped his eyes with his hand as his daughter's power of music stirred his heart. Then, embarrassed, he looked away from her towards the doorway and saw that a group of men were standing in the shadows, listening in silence.

Adam Cannon took a second look. Was that not Blaize, the Frenchman, muffled up in a plaid and wearing a blue shepherd's bonnet? He blinked but when he looked again the figure had vanished. It could only have been a trick of the light, he thought.

Jane finished her recital in gayer mood with the traditional song that ended all convivial parties, 'Guid Night and Joy be wi' Ye A'. As the last notes died away, her audience began to straggle off home in a happy frame of mind. Satisfied, she walked across the floor towards Jock, whose face was burning red. He looked as if he were drunk, an unusual thing for him, because he was normally very sober. He staggered to his feet when he saw her coming and threw an arm round her shoulders.

'It's a braw night,' he whispered in her ear. 'Come with me to the stackyard, Jane.'

The smell of whisky on his breath repelled her and she drew away from him, a recoil that did not go unnoticed.

'Oh, Jane,' he groaned, 'what's happened to you? You won't even give me a kiss these days.'

She felt great pity for him and forced herself to turn her head and peck him lightly on the lips. 'There, I've kissed you,' she said lightly, but he was not satisfied.

'Marry me, Jane, marry me. We've waited too long. I

want to marry you now,' he implored, but she knew that it was all too late.

'Go home, Jock,' she said firmly. 'You're a little bit drunk and you'll feel different in the morning.'

She watched him reeling off towards the bothy cottage that he shared with his mother, and her heart was sore. At one time, only a few months ago, she would have married Jock but now she knew that it would never happen.

Alone and lonely, she walked out of the farm court-yard, leaving behind in the barn the last revellers, men and women lying across the table tops with their heads among the empty ale pots. Her father and mother had gone home already and her brother was nowhere to be seen. Probably, she thought, he'd be sporting in the hay shed with one of the bondagers. She knew which girls would not be averse to a bit of sport like that on a kirn night and she didn't blame them. With such a moon, with the air sultry and heavy with the smell of newly threshed corn, with the fumes of the porter she'd drunk stirring her brain, she would like to sport in the hay too – with the right man.

The outline of the abbey buildings could be seen rising above the trees and she wondered if she'd hear the monks singing tonight. Moonlit nights were the best time to hear them.

She paused in the middle of the flight of worn old steps that led to the cloister yard and waited, head cocked and listening, but there was no monkish chanting tonight. Then suddenly a tall, dark figure stepped out of the shadows and grasped her arm. A scream rose in her throat but she quelled it when she saw that the face beneath the slouched shepherd's bonnet was Blaize's.

'I heard you singing in the barn,' he whispered in a choked sort of voice. 'I didn't know you could sing like that.'

'You didn't think I could dance either,' she whispered back with a little laugh, suddenly madly happy but unable to still her racing heartbeat. He drew her into a little alcove where the old monks had once kept their books and held her close.

She laid her head on his chest and whispered, 'You shouldn't be out. You've broken your curfew.'

'I know. I had to come. I wanted to see you. I borrowed this plaid and bonnet from a man in the alehouse. He said I looked like a Border shepherd in it.'

He was proud of his disguise and indeed he could pass as a local in the darkness of the night. They stood closely together, not speaking, only enjoying the physical nearness, the delight of being together. His grasp on her was loose, as if he were sure she would not want to break away.

She sighed deeply and broke the silence between them by saying, 'Why have you not been near us for so long? I thought you'd abandoned us.'

'I couldn't come. I'm a married man, you know I'm a married man, Jane.'

She nodded. 'I know that. It doesn't make any difference to me.'

He shook his head. 'Listen, you must understand. My wife's in France and I'm fond of her but I haven't really missed her since I was taken prisoner. And now, this has happened – ' He bent his head and very carefully kissed her on the lips. She felt as if she were about to die with happiness. He smelt of lemon grass and rosemary, and her stomach lurched with desire as he touched her.

After what seemed like hours of kissing, he raised his head again and said, 'I've never been so obsessed by a woman before. I think about you all the time, ever since the fête . . . I'm going mad for you but I'm married, and so I thought I'd better stay away. But I couldn't, Jane. I just couldn't.'

She took his face between her hands and kissed him to still his words. 'I'm glad you didn't stay away,' she told him.

He gripped her tighter now, speaking urgently into her ear. 'I love you. I love you. I must have loved you for months but I didn't know it. Tonight when I heard you singing I knew that I'd die for you, I'd kill for you. I never believed such a thing could happen to me – I've always been so rational.'

She was silent in his arms, listening to his voice, to its cadences and the strange accent that she had grown to love so much. She remembered the first time she saw him, when she thought him the Prince of Darkness, and then with a thrill of wickedness she threw her arms round his neck saying, 'I love you too. I've loved you since the day I saw you in the snowdrop wood. I don't give a fig if you're married.'

They did not speak much after that but kissed and kissed, some of their kisses deep and clinging, others soft and light like butterflies landing on parted lips. He kissed her ears and down her neck; she felt his hands slipping down to her breasts where he caressed her rigid nipples so gently that he almost stopped her heart with longing and desire.

Suddenly he stepped away from her and gently pulled her dress back to cover her naked breasts.

'I can't do this. I can't betray you and your family like this. For God's sake go home, girl, and stop enchanting me.'

But she did not listen. With her eyes shining she took his arm as if he were a child and pulled him out into the middle of the smooth, grass-covered cloister yard. He walked with her like a man in a dream while, still gently pulling, she led him through the arched gateway into a long green meadow that marked where the monks' road had run up to the ruined gatehouse.

It was as flat as a dancing floor and, as the similarity struck her, she laughed and swung him off in dance, all the time singing softly to him like an enchantress. Eyes fixed on each other's faces, they danced under the moon, with her singing as they bowed and curtsied, advanced and retired. Each time he put his hand out to touch her the charge of energy between them grew stronger. It was as if they were joined together by invisible strings, as one stepped back, the other stepped forward and never did they stop staring into each other's eyes. She was still singing as they danced into the wood and lay down together very slowly on the carpet of soft springy moss beneath the beech trees. There, in the silver light of the moon, with the smell of moss in their nostrils and the rustling sounds of midnight woodlands filling their ears, they made love without protesting and without promising anything. There was no need. They knew that they would love each other for ever.

Blaize watched his woman going out in the gang of bondagers to sow the earth with winter corn, scattering the seed far and wide as she walked, strewing it in generous handfuls like Persephone. As she walked the field he waited at the gate, and when the forewoman allowed the girls to stop for their morning break of cold beer and a crust of bread, she came across to him and he took her hand.

'I made this for you,' he said, and tried to tuck into the brim of her hat a little garland of rosehips and purple elderberries that he had picked on his three-mile walk from Melrose to Charterhall.

He was surprised when she drew back and would not let him fix the garland to the hat brim, saying, 'Oh, Blaize, not those, don't put those on me. They're unlucky. They're from the boon tree, that's the tree of the witches.' She was pointing at the deep purple elderberries and there was genuine fear in her face.

He laughed and said, 'You do amuse me, Jane. You have all those ancient beliefs that must have come down from the pagans but you're meant to be a good Christian. You go to church every Sunday, don't you?'

She nodded and said, 'Sometimes we go twice. But it doesn't do to ignore the old ways. My mother'll tell you that.'

In fact Jacques had already told him that many of Alice's cures were part magic. She believed that if you rubbed affected parts of a patient's body with a special

56

kind of stone or hung an ancient blue bead round their neck, they would get better. 'The funny thing is that sometimes they do,' the French doctor had said.

Now Jane was telling him that anyone who picked even a leaf from the elder tree should first ask permission from the witch who lived in it.

'You didn't ask, did you?' she said.

'I didn't know I had to ask,' he replied with a laugh, but he threw the garland away.

He had been in the Borders for over a year and now he was in a different frame of mind, more prepared to appreciate the staggering beauty of the countryside around him, prepared to marvel at the myriad colours of the dying beech leaves as they drifted to the ground and covered the earth with a Persian carpet of red, gold and brown. He watched with delight as the huge horses dragged their ploughs up and down the sloping fields, turning the blood-red soil beneath their harrows, followed by skeins of black and grey pee-wits with their haunting cries of 'Go back, go back!'

He no longer wanted to escape. The love he felt for Jane kept him captive more securely than all the chains and prohibitions governments could lay on him.

He went to see her every day, and waited for her coming home in the gathering dusk so that they could snatch a short time together before the curfew called him back to Melrose. He waded the ford in the river below her home and dreaded the winter floods which would cut him off from her. Then he would have to make a four-mile detour over the only bridge in the district across the Tweed at Leaderfoot in order to visit her.

One grey December day the women were working in the cattle sheds when he arrived and he was shocked when he saw the condition they were in as they stepped outside at the end of their day's toil. Their legs and arms were wound round with thick ropes of straw to protect them from the wet and the cold but, worse than that, they were covered in dung. Their skirts up to the waist were sodden with it and their boots so heavily caked that no leather showed.

'My God,' he said, standing well away from her so as not to be overwhelmed with the smell, 'that is a terrible job for a woman. Why do the men not clear out the cattle sheds?'

Big Agnes, who was walking behind Jane, said gruffly, 'They won't. Men refuse to do the job. They say it's women's work. They're clever, it's the worst job of the year but we have to do it.'

There were tears in Jane's eyes when she saw how shocked he was. 'I didn't want you to see me like this,' she said brokenly as he walked back to the abbey with her. 'I hate being so filthy and smelling so bad. It's loathsome.'

He stopped her with his hand and took her in his arms, careless of the smell. 'I love you. I hate to see you doing this work but believe me, when this war's over, I'll take you away from this. You'll never have to get dirty again.'

In the abbey, Alice, creeping like a sick snail now, had a huge tub of hot water waiting on the hearth for her daughter for she knew what the day's work would have been. She started in surprise when she saw Blaize, with his scarlet jacket all streaked down the front with slime and muck.

'Oh, your lovely jacket!' she said. 'What a mess you've made of it. Give it to me, I'll clean it for you.'

He took it off and handed it to her but he still smelt bad. Seeing him looking ruefully at the stained sleeves of his shirt where he had held her, Jane laughed.

'Look, this is a big tub, there's room in it for two,' she told him.

Alice had withdrawn to another room, so the girl and the soldier stripped off their clothes and climbed into the wooden tub in front of the fire.

There, with the flames dancing before them, they washed each other clean but they did not speak or kiss for fear of Alice hearing them. It was the most erotic thing that he had ever done.

*

Alice's life was slipping away fast. Blaize had come to respect her more than any older woman he had ever met and now he despaired when he realized that she had stopped fighting the malignancy that was eating her away. Soon she could only lie passively in a huge bed in her alcove room, watching the grey winter clouds through the little window opposite her eyes.

'Have the swallows gone?' she asked her daughter one day.

'Oh yes, Mother, they went many weeks ago.'

'I won't see them back. You must look after your father. Your brother'll soon be married and he can look after himself.'

There was no use protesting for they both knew that what she said was true. Jane held her mother's hand as Alice went on, 'Blaize is a good man. He loves you very much, I can see that and I'm happy about it though I'm sorry for Jock. What will happen when the war ends?'

'He'll have to go back to France but he says he'll come back for me when he's told his wife. He'll come back and stay here, perhaps. I don't want to leave this place, you know I love it here.'

Her mother turned her head on the pillow. 'Oh, this enchanted country. It holds us, it never lets us go. We can't breathe easy anywhere else. They say it's fairyland and perhaps we're all under a spell.'

'It feels like fairyland. When I look out at the Eildon hills I feel they're protecting us somehow. I'd never feel easy in my mind if I couldn't see them.'

Alice's eyes sought out the shapes of the hills through her window.

'I know, I feel the same. An old woman once told me that King Arthur's buried in the middle hill. I wonder if it's true.'

She died a few days before Christmas when the earth was so frozen that it took a long time for her husband and son to dig her grave. The mourners included Blaize and Jacques, but Christian, whose hacking cough was worse these days, stayed in the abbey house with Jane while the ceremony was going on outside the window. After the ceremony, Jane's brother announced that he was going to join the army and was setting off for Berwick to enlist.

'I don't want to be a landless labourer all my life, and I know that if I stay here much longer, this place will get me too, like it's got everyone else in our family,' he told his father and sister. They did not try to stop him going.

Jacques and Christian walked back to the big house, the blond Frenchman's arm supporting the frail girl. Jane had not seen her friend for some weeks and was surprised at how ill she looked.

'Is Christian sick again?' she asked Blaize.

He nodded. 'She's spitting blood. Jacques is beside himself with worry. He's trying to persuade her father to allow them to marry as soon as possible. He seems to think that by marrying her, he can protect her from the illness.'

But Charlie Glendinning never gave his consent. While the January winds were howling through the bare trees around the big house, Christian's illness took a turn for the worse. She drifted out of life effortlessly, like a child. Sometimes it seemed she was rallying, but there would be a relapse, another haemorrhage, and she would be worse. Jacques was like a caged lion, raging against fate, powerless to stop the stealthy disease. All his medicine, all his knowledge could do nothing to turn aside the inevitable.

The pretty, fragile girl died on a sunny February morning when the first snowdrops were shining on the banks. She simply sighed and smiled, and died in her lover's arms.

Her funeral, like Alice's, was in the abbey but her resting place was in her family's large, ornate crypt.

The skies were grey as they laid her to rest. Jane, at the back of the little crowd, shivered as she watched Blaize standing ramrod straight beside a wretched-looking Jacques. Then suddenly the sun shafted down through a break in the clouds, slanting over the broken abbey wall and lighting up her lover's face. He looked as if he were standing in the beam of some heavenly light, and she gave a gasp of terror.

'Oh no, no, no,' she cried aloud in terrible grief, and ran from the aisle with her hands over her face.

When he came to comfort her later she let him believe that she had been weeping for Christian. She did not dare admit that she was mortally afraid for him because when the sun shone on his face she remembered the old superstition that whoever the sun shines on at a funeral will be the next to die.

The news from Europe was old by the time it reached the more remote corners of Britain. A few people in the Borders bought the *Kelso Chronicle* or one of the Edinburgh news sheets which were sent down a day late on the carrier's cart, but as each copy cost sixpence only the rich could afford such luxuries. The poorer people read them later or simply had items of news passed on to them verbally.

Melrose heard about Napoleon's defeat in Russia three months after it happened. But delight swiftly changed to despondency in the autumn of 1813 with the news of his victory at Dresden, a victory which made the prisoners of war strut through the town's streets with their heads proudly high. But they were to be abashed again in the spring of 1814 when the news came through that the Allied armies had invaded France.

Then the unthinkable happened – the Allies were in Paris. Finally, on 14 April Napoleon signed a deed of abdication at Fontainebleau. That bit of news passed round like wildfire by word of mouth and long before the newspapers were circulating the official reports, victory celebrations had begun. The bitterness of defeat for the French prisoners was sweetened by the knowledge that the long war was at an end. They would be going home soon.

Blaize and Jane did not bother to hide the fact that they were lovers, but they were not the only couple in the same state, for many others had broken down the walls of hostility between antagonists and had fallen in love. There had already been a few marriages between local girls and Frenchmen and, of course, there were many illegitimate children born who would pass French blood down to their descendants. When Blaize heard the news of Bonaparte's abdication and the end of the war, the deliverance he had longed for no longer seemed sweet, for he was in another kind of bondage.

Three of the prisoners had decided not to go home at all and they married their sweethearts, but Blaize did not have that option open to him. He had to be repatriated to France whether he wanted to go or not. If he tried to escape, it would be regarded as running away from captivity and he would be caught and punished in the same way as when he took off for the hills. Jane wanted to hide him but he refused to allow her to do so because a fine of twenty pounds was levied on anyone providing shelter for a runaway prisoner – and prisoner he still was until he was re-landed in France.

Arrangements were made by the Transport Office to ship the prisoners out, and the town was anxious to have some sort of party to mark the ending of their long relationship with the French.

Many friendships had been formed and the strangers had brought a new sophistication, a breath of the outside world, to Melrose. There were private parties every night and finally the prisoners gave their last concert in the theatre they had converted from a hay shed. Blaize and Jane did not join in the celebrations, for their coming separation weighed heavily on them.

At the beginning of May she suspected that she was carrying Blaize's child. This was something she had longed for but now her delight was mixed with sadness. By the time her child was born, where would its father be?

They could make love in the woods again now that the winter had ended and she lay in his arms, worrying about what would happen when he went back to his own country where his wife was waiting.

'How will you tell your wife about us?' she asked him.

He was worried too. 'I'll tell her immediately. That's why I'm going back. I promise you that I'll not live with Marie again. I'll tell her and then I'll leave. When I've arranged everything, I'll come back for you and the baby.'

'But surely she'll make trouble? You can't just walk in and say you're leaving her. You're Papists, aren't you? Your marriages last for ever. In my religion it's fairly common for people to live apart if they don't get on, but not in yours.'

'That's true. She'll be angry but I'll make a settlement for her. I don't have a religion – I gave up the church long ago. But Marie does, and there's no question of dissolving the marriage. You and I will have to live together without marrying. People do it all the time. It's not so rare.'

It was arranged that the prisoners should leave Melrose in two batches. The first contingent marched out in May, so anxious were the authorities to be rid of them. They looked martial as they strode round the square in what was left of their uniforms, mixed now with articles of local apparel, and they sang the 'Marseillaise' as they swung off down the rutted road heading for Berwick-on-Tweed. Many of the people watching them wept, for they were losing friends and lovers. The French had transformed the life and outlook of the sleepy little town.

Blaize volunteered to wait with the second party. Colonel Berton, grey and old now, and Jacques who cared little whether he went or stayed now that Christian was dead, also stayed behind to organize the last affairs of the French. At the end of the month they were told that 10 June had been set as the date for their departure.

When this news arrived he left his lodgings and walked swiftly to the abbey.

He climbed the stair to the house, which felt deserted and empty without Alice. He came out again and sat in the sun on the steps where he had often sat with her, waiting for Jane to come back from her labours.

Soon he saw her walking slowly through the roofless aisle, her head hanging low in tiredness beneath the shady hat. She looked pale and he wanted to rescue her from the life of unremitting toil that she was forced to lead. When she saw him, she smiled and climbed the steps towards him, to sit on the top step at his side. She knew he had something to tell her.

'It's bad news?' she asked.

'We're to leave in three days' time. I have to go.'

She gently put out one hand to grasp his. 'I love you,' she whispered. 'I don't know what I'll do without you.'

The pain of parting burned in him like an unquenched fire. He hugged her to him and said urgently, 'I love you too. I love you so much that I can't bear to leave. I've been sitting here thinking about it and I've decided to run away. If I hide out for a time they'll give up looking for me. When peace comes, who cares about a runaway Frenchman?'

She shook her head. 'They've ordered you to go. They've said that anyone who tries to escape will be treated as a runaway. Everyone round here knows you now and if you were seen, you'd be reported.'

'Damn it, at least I'd have a few more days with you. I've had enough of obeying orders.'

That night he defied the curfew and stayed with her in the abbey house. They lay together in Alice's bed and whispered words of love. Neither of them slept.

When the first light of morning came through the little window, she said, 'It's five o'clock. I've got to get up. We've got to be in the hayfield by six.'

He groaned and put his hands to his face. 'Stay here with me, don't go.'

'I must go. I'm bonded to go. My father would suffer if I didn't go.'

Silently she slipped round the room, dressed in her working clothes and cut bread for her father, who had slept that night in the hay shed so that Blaize and Jane could be undisturbed.

'I'll stay hidden here. I'm not going back,' Blaize told her as she went out into the chill of the early morning.

He was reading some of Alice's old herbal recipes when there were steps on the stone stairway outside the door. It opened and Jacques stood there. He had lost weight since Christian died and looked sad and thin, but today some of his old energy had returned to him.

'Get your coat on. When you didn't come back last night we knew what you're trying to do. But you've got to come with me. The colonel sent me to get you.'

'I'm staying here,' said Blaize.

'Don't be a fool. If you stay and let this family hide you, they'll suffer as much as you when you're found. They'll be prosecuted for sheltering a fugitive. You know you've got to return to France. Be sensible, once you've sorted out your affairs you can come back for her. But you've got to go now.'

He'd known it all along, really. Together the two men went to the hayfield and Blaize walked across to Jane in the middle of the group of women and took her in his arms, uncaring of the scandalized faces of the others. Any open show of emotion outraged their Scottish souls.

She kissed him and clung to him, weeping. There was no need to explain what had happened for she too had known that their parting must come.

He left her with the words, 'I'll come back. I promise you I'll come back. Never doubt me, no matter what happens. I love you. Trust me.'

'I'll speak to the steward and get you a day off,' said Adam, but Jane could not bring herself to go to Melrose to watch Blaize march away. He was walking to Berwick in the company of Jacques and a handful of other men who had been left behind from the first batch of prisoners. The colonel, who was growing old and frail, was given a horse to ride by a tradesman friend in the town, for the walk to Berwick, a good thirty-five miles, would have been too much for the old man.

Mounted on this grey horse, he saluted the small crowd that came to see him leave and took a last look at Melrose. Each of the ancient thatched houses that led up the high street to the square had a small knot of people in its doorway, waving the colonel off. He had been a popular man. He made a short speech thanking the 'canny' people of Melrose for their kindness to the French. It was a good time to use some of his collection of local words . . . 'I'll aye mind you guid folk . . .' he told them before pulling on the reins of his horse and riding off through the narrow vennel that led to the east.

In Charterhall that morning, Jane was inconsolable. Every now and again she stared up at the sun, trying to calculate the time and wondering where Blaize would be. It was a fine day and not too warm, so his journey would not be too arduous.

When she thought of him, tears rose to her eyes and her throat tightened in pain. By dinner time, when the work halted for a couple of hours, she was shaking and unable to stop the tears flowing unchecked. Her father regarded her with concern.

'Oh lassie, you should have gone to see him off. The steward said you could and nobody would have missed you.'

'I couldn't, I thought I'd die if I had to watch him going away. But oh, how much I want to have a last look at him now,' she sobbed.

Without another word Adam Cannon walked off across the field and spoke to another labourer who was leaning on his fork in the shade.

When he came back, he told Jane, 'Go home and get on your best dress. Jake's brother Benny has a cart and he'll take you to Berwick. Just go, I'll be responsible for letting you off work.'

'But father,' she gasped, 'Berwick's so far away. Will I get there in time?'

'If you go now, you will,' he told her.

She'd never been farther than five or six miles from Charterhall in her entire life. To travel over thirty miles seemed as hazardous and daring as going to Africa. Like the other people working on the land around her, she had little idea of distance and thought that America was about the same number of miles away as Glasgow, so hazy was her idea of travel.

Her father was more matter of fact, however, and he said, 'Remember, he's walking, you'll be riding and Benny's got a fast wee pony. You'll get there in time if you go *now*.'

Benny, a slow-spoken, lethargic giant of a man, was difficult to infuse with her sense of urgency. He pottered around harnessing up his pony and it was nearly three o'clock when they finally trotted out of the yard. She knew that Blaize's party had left Melrose at about eight o'clock that morning but she had no idea when the boat would sail from Berwick. She did not even know for sure if it would sail that day. Her father had told her that, allowing for rests, a walking man would probably reach Berwick by late afternoon, however, and she was determined not to miss him.

'Oh hurry, Benny, hurry, I've got to see him before he goes,' she gasped, clinging on to the bar of the cart as they spanked along the road.

'I'm hurrying,' said Benny, shifting his chewing tobacco from one cheek to the other. 'The pony's going as fast as it can and it canna' go any faster.'

'When do you think we'll get to Berwick?' she asked.

Benny shrugged. 'That depends. We might lose a wheel or the pony might cast a shoe – that'd hold us up. The road can be bad in bits but it's been dry for the past week so there won't be any flooding – perhaps in three hours?'

'Do try to hurry,' she told him, 'I'm terribly worried in case we miss him.'

'You're in a state right enough,' agreed Benny. 'You're in a bigger state than China.'

She was not too sure what he meant by that but sensed

that she would be well advised to say no more about making good time. Though it was the first time she had ever been on the turnpike road to the east, she had no eyes for the sights they passed on the way. They were following the river Tweed on its course to the sea and as they spanked along, they went through a succession of pretty little villages, but these held little interest for her. Every time they came to a village that was a bit bigger than the others, she hopefully asked Benny, 'Is this Berwick?' and he'd laugh.

'Don't be daft, lassie. Berwick's a big place.'

It was almost evening when they came down the sloping hill from the Berwickshire plain and saw the blue expanse of the North Sea spread out before them. The sight of it made her gasp in astonishment. Then she saw the spires and houses of the grey town stretching along the point at the mouth of the river and the little round-arched bridge that took the road over to it.

It looked enormous to her and she gasped in amazement at the sight. 'It's as big as London,' she said, her eyes round.

'Oh aye, it is that,' agreed Benny, who had never seen London, who had in fact never even been to Edinburgh, but who was not prepared to admit that. His idea of a metropolis was Berwick-on-Tweed — nothing could be bigger or more bustling than the prosperous port that served the south-eastern corner of Scotland.

She leaned forward in the jolting cart and gazed down at the crowded harbour and at the lines of tall-masted ships drawn up in the wide estuary. Was Blaize already on one of those? Had she missed him after all?

Fortunately Benny knew his way to the harbour side and his pony trotted surefooted down the steep cobbled street to the quays where everything was a confusion of shouting and hustle, with men running around among crates, boxes and bundles while sailors with tarred pigtails, lounging on corners, eyed tousle-haired Jane with appreciation as she climbed down from Benny's cart.

68

'Going some place, Missus?' asked one bold-faced man.

'I'm looking for the ship that's taking the French prisoners away.'

'Oh, the Frenchies? They're going out on one of their own ships. It's moored over there.'

He pointed with a dirty, tattooed hand to the end of the quay where a tall schooner was tied up.

She thanked him and ran along the stone-slabbed jetty towards it. When she reached its high wooden sides, she shouted up to a man leaning on the deck rail.

'Is this the ship that's taking the Frenchmen to Boulogne?'

He threw out his hands in a gesture of incomprehension.

She remembered a little of the French that Blaize had tried to teach her . . . '*À Boulogne? Les prisonniers?*'

The man nodded vigorously in agreement . . . '*Oui, à Boulogne,*' he shouted back.

'Blaize Chardenel, find Blaize Chardenel,' she called up to him, 'A soldier – *un soldat* – of the Hussars.'

The man on the deck consulted another who came curiously over. 'Chardenel? Hussar?' They called down to her and she nodded eagerly. '*Un moment,*' said one, and disappeared.

It did not take long before he was back with Blaize, who looked over the rail suspiciously.

When he saw Jane his face lit up and he threw out his arms. 'Jane, wait, wait, I'm coming down,' he called.

They hugged each other on the quay while the watching sailors shouted encouragement and words of bawdy advice.

'Are you coming with me?' he asked. 'I'll get you aboard. The captain's an old friend of Jacques. He was his captain on the privateer in the war, he'd take you with no questions asked.'

'No, no,' she shook her head. 'You know I can't go. I've just come to say goodbye to you. I couldn't let you go without seeing you again.'

His face showed his disappointment but she kissed him again and said, 'I thought I'd die if I didn't see you, Blaize . . .'

He clutched her to him and muttered, 'Thank God you did. I was sick with longing for you too. Oh Jane, come with me. You've come so far, don't go back now.'

'I can't, you know I can't. There's my father – and my home. I can't just go away to France without a word.'

'Sometimes I think Charterhall means more to you than I do,' he said bitterly. 'You're wedded to your abbey. You're enchanted, Jane. If you're ever going to live your own life, you must break free.'

But again she shook her head. 'No, it's not that. I'll wait for you there and one day you'll come back for me. When the baby's born, I'll go with you then. But first you've got to tell your wife and make up your mind that you really want me. If you still do, then I'll go with you.'

It had never occurred to him that she was so afraid of what would happen when he got back to France, so sure was he about how he felt himself.

He held her to him and whispered, 'Of course I really want you. Haven't I told you often enough? I've never wanted anything or anyone in my life as much as I want you. Can't you believe that?'

'But what about your wife? What if when you go home you fall in love with her again?'

'I won't!' He was angry now. 'I've told you. I know my own mind. I'm not a foolish boy. You must believe me. If you asked me to kill myself now, here on this quay, I'd do it for you.'

She put her arms round him and kissed him tenderly. 'Oh, I believe you. I'll never doubt you. I'm sure you love me. Goodbye, my darling.'

There was a noise of shouting and clattering from the deck above and someone shouted down to Blaize to get aboard, they were preparing to leave. She could see the conflict on his face, she could see that he wanted to stay with her but she gently pushed him towards the rope ladder that swung down from the ship's side, and stood

70

back as he climbed swiftly up it. But he had only gone up three or four rungs before he leaped down again and stripped off his Hussar's jacket.

He handed it to her with the words, 'This will keep you warm on the journey home and it will always remind you of me. I've kept it carefully all these years, I've been so proud of it but now I'm giving it to you as an earnest that I'll come back.'

The Borderers believe that it is unlucky to watch a loved one out of sight because that means you will never see them again. She was keenly aware of this superstition but deliberately thrust it aside as a primitive fear, for she knew how Blaize would laugh at her if he knew about it. She stood alone on the quay, waving at his departing ship and clutching to her breast his uniform jacket, now and again pressing the fading cloth to her face and breathing in the smell of him from its folds. The stately ship swung round in the tide and headed for the open sea, with the wind filling its magnificent range of sails. She heard the strange creak of the canvas and the groan of the ropes as it sailed away from her and she was almost blinded with tears. The figure of Blaize stood in the stern, waving his arms at her as it sailed off into the distance. The last sight she had of him was the white blur of his shirt and his long arms waving above his head.

With his jacket slung over her shoulders and the tears running down her cheeks, she went back to the alehouse where Benny was refreshing himself for the return trip and, without speaking, they set off on the long journey home.

'Is it no' awful shaming to be having a baby and no man?' Maggie Maxton, who was to marry one of her many suitors in three weeks' time, stood in the hay shed and looked critically at Jane's bulky body coming in from the farmyard. She had always disliked Jane, who was too stuck up for her own good. Thought herself something, did Jane Cannon, and now she'd got her comeuppance.

Jane did not care whether Maggie liked her or not, for

it was raining and they had been called back out of the fields. They'd only be paid for a half day's work – that concerned her a good deal more, for she needed every penny she could get now that the baby was so near. Yet she was mildly surprised at Maggie's question. Illegitimacy was not uncommon among bondagers and Maggie had been lucky not to have conceived already herself.

'I don't think so. We'd have been married if we could have,' she replied.

Maggie dimpled. 'A love bairn! He's back to his wife now, is he, your bonny Frenchman? I can't say I blame you, he was a grand man, like a big stallion.' She giggled at her own effrontery but she enjoyed getting in a dig at Jane.

'The last I heard he was in Paris and was going down to Arles – that was in July,' Jane said, determined not to rise to Maggie's taunts.

A note from Blaize, enclosed in a letter which Colonel Berton sent to his friend the Melrose lawyer, had found its way to Jane. She cherished every word and carried it around with her until the paper almost wore away.

'July? That was over four months ago. Haven't you heard since?' quizzed Maggie cruelly.

Jane shook her head. It did worry her that there had been no news, but she was sure he'd write when he was able. She did not want to write to him though she had his address in Arles. She did not want to do anything that would cause him trouble while he was breaking the news to his wife.

Maggie was a mean little minx though, she rubbed salt in the wound. 'Well, that's the last you'll see of him. Aren't you going to marry poor Jock Hepburn now and give your bairn a name?'

A feeling of shock swept over Jane and she flushed scarlet. Maggie was a loose-moraled girl who had been with many men before she captured the innocent Bob. Yet here she was, in the near safety of marriage, adopting an attitude of outrage because another woman, a virgin

72

when she slept with Blaize, was having an illegitimate baby. Jane reacted vehemently.

'I think it would be a lot more immoral to marry a man and foist someone else's bairn on him than not to marry and bring it up on your own,' she said stiffly.

'Immoral is it? Well, we'll see what the minister says about immoral, won't we, when you take your bairn to the kirk to be christened.' Maggie was enjoying herself.

Her belly and back were aching dully when she got back to the abbey that night and she sat down on her mother's favourite chair, spreading her legs wide. Her father was on the other side of the fireplace, patiently polishing her boots for the next day.

'I wish my mother was alive to help me have this bairn,' she suddenly said, and he looked up at her with a worried frown which showed her that the same thought had occurred to him.

'Who's going to act as howdie for me?' she asked.

'Don't worry, I've been thinking about that. Big Agnes has delivered a lot of babies in the fields and I'll go for her if you need help. But you've seen your mother do it, haven't you? You've some idea of what to do?' he replied soothingly.

She nodded. 'Yes, I've seen it done. We have to boil water and you'll have to cut the cord for me when the baby's out. Like you do for lambs, Father.' Seeing her mother help other women through their labour was not the same as being faced with labour herself, she thought privately.

'We'll manage, my love,' he said consolingly, and patted her lightly on the shoulder.

Early one morning she went into labour and her father was wakened by the sound of agonized grunting from her box bed. When he pulled back the curtain he found her crouching on all fours like an animal, her face covered with sweat. Wordlessly she waved him away and pulled the curtain back again.

It was a Sunday, so he could rush out to the farm to

73

feed his pair of horses and rush back again to be with her. Then he took up his vigil, sitting outside the door listening to the terrible noises she was making. His wife had never endured such agonies and he was worried for his girl.

About dinnertime he heard her screaming and, panic stricken, rushed inside. Her face was ashen white and her hair hung down, wet with the sweat of her exertions. This time she was standing up, hanging on to the bedpost.

'I can't deliver it, I can't deliver it, Father. You'll have to go and get Big Agnes.'

In a frenzy he ran off and met Agnes and a group of other bondagers coming back from church in their Sunday best.

Agnes saw the worry on his face at once and asked anxiously, 'What's the matter, Adam?'

'Oh Agnes, it's Jane, she's in labour and she says she can't deliver the baby.'

Agnes liked Jane and had forgiven her for abandoning Jock. These things happened, she had told him. The girl has just fallen in love . . .

Now she rallied to the rescue. 'My God, just hold on a minute and I'll come with you,' she told Adam.

When she'd changed into her old clothes, they ran back to the abbey house together.

The big woman was kind-hearted and she shook her head at the sight of Jane, for she could see at once what was wrong.

'It's a breach,' she told Adam, 'we'll have to try to turn it.'

Jane's father went white as he thought of the many times he had struggled to pull a breach presentation calf or foal from its mother. He thought of how they tied ropes to the tiny body and hauled it out into the light while the mothers screamed in agony. Not that for his Jane, surely?

Big Agnes saw his consternation. 'You go away and get some logs chopped or something. We'll need a big

74

fire. I'll do it, I've done it before but . . .' Her voice trailed away.

'But what?'

'But the mother died.'

He sank on to the wooden settle by the fire and put his head in his hands. 'I'll have to go and get the doctor.'

'You'll have to go to Melrose then,' she reminded him. 'That'll take an hour or more and she can't hang on much longer. I'll do what I can for her while you're away.'

He ran out of the abbey without putting on his jacket, a white-haired old man running as if pursued by the devil.

Jane never forgot the two hours she and Agnes fought for the baby. The big woman was gentle, in spite of her coarse appearance, and with both hands she grappled inside Jane till she managed eventually to grab hold of the child. 'Hold on, lassie, hold on,' she grunted, and with a terrible heave, she pulled it into life.

In agony Jane fell back on to the tumbled, blood-soaked covers and it took a few moments before she realized that her newborn child was silent. There had been no cry of life as it entered the world. Her pain was so agonizing that she could not move, but she whispered, 'Is it dead, Agnes?'

Agnes stood in the window with the bundle in her arms. 'I don't know. It's very weak – it's a wee lassie, Janey.'

'Give her to me,' said Jane and held out her arms, into which Agnes laid the pathetic little bundle wrapped in a bloody sheet. As the doctor came in with Adam both women were crying over what they thought was a corpse when suddenly the infant shuddered, flexed her tiny legs and gave her first cry, a feeble little peep like the mewling of a kitten.

Aylie, December 1814

'What name are you going to give her?' Adam asked the first time he saw the baby.

Jane surprised him when she said, 'Alouette. It means lark. Blaize once said that I sang like an *alouette*. I'll call her that.'

No one but Jane could pronounce it of course so they called her Aylie.

She was a small, white-faced child who frightened the kind heart of Big Agnes. She preferred babies to be fat and rosy. On the second day after her birth, Jane was back on the farm with her precious child wrapped up in a shawl and tied tight against her heart.

'You'll not send her out in this cold,' Agnes warned the steward. 'That bairn's not strong. The cold wind would kill it and you wouldn't want that on your conscience, would you?'

The steward blustered. 'We've got work to do, we don't have time to worry about bondagers' bastards.' But he was intimidated by Big Agnes' eye and when the work was being handed out, he told Jane to stay in the barn and cut turnips for the sheep.

Fortunately for Aylie, her mother was strong. The milk flowed abundantly in her breasts and in spite of everyone's fears, the child prospered.

By the time the post runner brought the letter from France, even gloomy Big Agnes was beginning to hope that Jane's bairn would live.

The runner in his blue coat with the brass buttons searched round Charterhall looking for Jane so that she could pay the charge on her letter. It cost one shilling, but she would have paid every penny she possessed to take it from the runner's hand.

Standing in the barn, she ripped off the seal and read it eagerly. Blaize had only learned of the baby's birth more than a month after it happened because he had been away from home. His reaction was everything she desired, however:

At last I'm a father! I feel so proud, as if no one else has ever been a father before. I think the name Alouette is lovely for the baby, perhaps she will be able to sing like a lark too. Is she small? She can't be, with such a magnificent mother. How I long to hold and kiss her – and even more to hold and kiss you, my Jane. I long for you, I think of you, every day. I have told Marie and now we are organizing a division of our property. I suspect she prefers celibacy to marriage. Her main concern is: Who is going to have the house and the carriage horses?

I will be with you in the summer. One day, when you're out in that big hayfield with your hat shading your freckles from the sun, I'll come up beside you and put my arms round you. Oh Jane, how I love you.

She read and re-read the letter, then she sat down on a pile of hay and suckled her child, who grabbed with her tiny fists at the blue thread Jane wore tied loosely round her neck. All nursing mothers in the Borders wore those threads, she did not know why, but it was the custom and as always she followed the old ways.

Big Agnes came into the barn with a load of turnips and Jane told her that she'd had a letter from Blaize.

'He says he'll be back in the summer,' she said joyfully.

'I'm glad to hear that, because yesterday I heard Glendinning telling the steward that he's planning to build a new stableyard – and he's going to use the stone from the abbey for the buildings. You might be losing your house, Janey,' was Agnes' reply.

The shock made the breath catch in Jane's throat. 'But he can't pull down our abbey. He can't, he can't . . .'

'He owns it, lass. Using the stone saves him buying new stuff. He'll use your abbey for a quarry.'

She kept this news from her father because she feared it would worry him, but a few days later she saw by his face that he had heard the rumour too.

'They're planning to use the abbey stone for building over at the big house,' he told her.

'Can't anybody stop them?' she asked.

'No, it's Glendinning's property, he can do what he likes with it,' Adam said resignedly.

She stared around their cosy home with tears in her eyes. 'But it's been like this since the monks left. Look at all those lovely carved stones, and all those wee stairways, even the old doors are just as they left them. You know they sing in the choir at night when the moon's full, Father. How can the ghosts go on singing if he pulls it all down?'

'They're just spirits. We're people, and it's more to the point to ask where we'll go when he pulls it down,' was Adam's bitter reply.

His daughter was suddenly frantic with terror. 'But we can't leave here. Blaize won't know where to find me if we leave here. I've got to stay in the abbey, Father. He's coming back for me.'

The old man soothed her. 'Sit down, girl, it's not happened yet. We'll worry about it when it does.'

About a month later Glendinning's steward came to the abbey to give them notice to quit. Coincidentally that was the same day as a lawyer rode out from Melrose to inform Jane that a money order for the sum of fifty pounds had come for her from France. It was sent by Blaize.

This was a fortune to people like the Cannons, but her surprise and pleasure were spoiled by the cruel realization that they could no longer stay in their old home.

'But where are we to go?' she demanded of the steward. 'Have you another house to offer us?'

He looked shifty and said, 'You'd better see Mr Glendinning about that,' and he rode off in a hurry.

If such a thing was possible, Jane's anxiety increased. She suspected that if Glendinning was not offering them another house, that could mean that he was planning not to offer them work. When she shared her fears with her father, he pulled on his jacket to go round to the big house and see their employer.

Glendinning was eating his supper and kept the hind waiting for almost an hour, but eventually he sent the serving girl out to tell the old man to come in. He and his boorish son were sitting at a lavishly covered table spread with the remains of their meal.

His first words were friendly. 'Sit down, Cannon, you're getting on and must need a seat. The heavy work must be hard for you now. How old are you anyway?'

Adam Cannon sat awkwardly on a sabre-legged chair and fixed his blue eyes on Glendinning. 'I'm sixty next year, but I'm as fit as a man ten years younger.'

'Oh, I'm sure you are but for how long? For how long?' replied Glendinning, 'And what's happened to that son of yours? Where's he gone?'

'He went to Berwick to join the army. They've sent him to Bengal.'

Glendinning and his son looked at each other with raised eyebrows. 'India? My word, that's a long way away.'

Adam said nothing and Glendinning was forced to carry on speaking. 'You'll have heard about my plan to build a new stableyard. The one we've got is a ramshackle mess. The house needs a good stable. We'll be using the stone from the abbey for it.'

The hind made no objection. 'So I've heard,' he said.

The silence hung between them, heavy with meaning, and Glendinning felt anger rising in him. He was the landowner, he was the employer, he did not have to explain to this man why he no longer needed him on the farm, but there was a dignity and composure about Adam Cannon that demanded respect.

'You'll not be able for heavy work much longer and your son's off now. Jane's a good enough worker but that bairn's taking up a lot of her time and the other bondagers won't let the steward send her into the field when the weather's bad. That's nonsense, you know. We're not running some sort of poor's house here. At the next hiring fair I'll be looking for a hind that can give me more working hands from one house, so we'll not be needing you any more after the term.'

Adam Cannon was too proud to beg. He'd worked on Charterhall all his life. His father and grandfather before him, all his ancestors back to the Middle Ages had lived and worked there. None of them ever had to go to a hiring fair to stand in line for a job. He was a proud man who'd farmed his own acres, paid his rent and raised his family decently and now, when he was old, he was being turned out of the home that was his as much as it was Glendinning's.

Proudly he turned on his heel and walked from the room. With a determined stride he followed the path down to the river and stood looking into the weir where fat spawning salmon gathered every year. When he was a boy, all the local people could take a salmon now and again but since men like Glendinning owned the river, anyone taking a salmon risked going to prison for poaching.

With a bitter expression he stood watching the slow-running, brown-flecked water for a long time and then, when it was dark, he went back to the abbey house and told Jane the terrible news.

Hard eyed, Jane stood with crossed arms watching the men taking down a part of an old wall which bore delicately carved traceries branching like trees across the dark red stone.

'Where's that going?' she asked.

'It's for the front of the groom's house, it'll look real bonny,' said the foreman who was supervising the removal of the stones.

'It looked bonnier where it was,' the angry girl replied, and turned on her heel to walk away.

The peace of the abbey was shattered daily by the noise of the gang of labourers who had moved in as soon as the better weather began. They demolished walls and grubbed out fallen pieces of carved stone which horses dragged off in carts across the meadow to where the rising buildings of a large stable block for housing riding horses, carriage horses and the new carriages could be seen. It was far superior, better built and more water tight than any of the houses the working people inhabited.

Jane's impotent fury increased all through the spring days. Glendinning had relented slightly and told Adam that his services would be retained till next spring term, but then they would definitely be no longer required at Charterhall. They worked as hard as ever, for it was a matter of pride not to shirk their duties even when they were burning up with resentment and a sense of injustice. Besides, they needed letters of reference from Glendinning if they were to find another position.

Jane was playing with her baby on the cloister steps one Sunday afternoon when Jock came through the arched doorway and sat silently down beside her.

'You're looking sad, Jane,' he said gently, tickling the baby's legs with a piece of feathery grass.

She looked at him with gratitude and admiration. He had never reproached her for abandoning him for Blaize, but had taken it with silent dignity.

'I am sad,' she replied, 'I can't bear the idea of leaving here. I love Charterhall abbey. It's part of me.'

Jock looked around at the old walls that shone salmon pink in the rays of the dying sun. 'It's a sin when you've all worked so hard for that man,' he said. 'But don't you worry, Jane, you and your father'll find another job, a better one.'

She shook her head. Her worries sat heavily on her. Her father was visibly failing, as if the spirit was going out of him with every stone that was dragged away from the abbey. His strength was failing. It was noticeable that he had to stop frequently to draw laboured breaths when working, and he was no longer able to carry the massive loads he once shouldered without thinking.

'Adam's not the man he was,' she told Jock, 'and it won't be easy for me to find a good place because of the baby . . . Farmers don't want bondagers with bairns.'

'Are you still waiting for your Frenchman coming back?' Jock asked tentatively.

She did not speak but stared past him at the long green meadow beside the wood and nodded her head silently.

Jock looked downcast and she realized that he still hoped she would come back to him in the end.

'You mustn't wait for me, Jock. If I don't marry Blaize I won't marry anybody.'

'I can see you love him, far more than you ever loved me,' he told her. 'I remember seeing you with him, you never looked like that for me. It fair broke my heart but I don't blame you, Jane. I know what it's like to love somebody. You just can't help it, can you?'

'No, you just can't help it,' agreed Jane.

Haymaking had come and gone without Blaize and if Jane was anxious she hid her anxiety beneath the other urgent concerns that took up her day. The labourers had cleaned a good deal of the abbey site but they left the nave and the old dormer house in which she and her father lived with the baby.

'You can't start here,' she warned the gang foreman one bright morning. 'It's our house till next term time.'

'And on that very day he'll be in pulling it down,' said Glendinning's son, who had ridden out to inspect the work.

Jane turned her large, angry eyes on him and stared for a long time without speaking. Her gaze disturbed the young man. He pulled the reins and was about to swing the horse round when she called in a clear voice, 'I see something coming for you, Mr Glendinning. You might not be here at term time.'

The young man flushed scarlet with anger and fear. 'You'd better not threaten me, you whore, you with your

Frenchman's bastard,' he shouted, and urging his horse into a canter, burst through the gaping crowd of men and disappeared among the graveyard trees.

When the corn was ripened again Jane, her growing baby still tied to her side, was out in the fields with her sickle. All the time she was cutting and stooking the sheaves of corn, she thought about Blaize. A perpetual worry niggled away in her mind. It was not that she feared he had betrayed her. She trusted him implicitly and was secure in the knowledge of his love, but something else made her mortally afraid for him. As she worked, she could not stop her mind persistently returning to the memory of the shaft of light shining on his face at Christian's funeral. When it made her shudder, she impatiently thrust a hand over her face, wiping away the sweat with the corner of the cloth she wore tied over her hair. 'Don't be a fool,' she told herself, 'there were lots of other people at that funeral who'll probably die before Blaize does.'

On the night of the 1815 harvest kirn Jane and Adam Cannon stayed at home. They heard the sounds of revelry coming from the direction of the big barn and it awoke her memories of other harvest celebrations. Her memories of making love with Blaize were vivid and painful but she deliberately put them out of her mind, bustling about looking after the baby and trying to cheer her dispirited father.

It was as if he could divine her secret thoughts for he suddenly asked, 'When he comes, what'll you do?' They both knew who he was talking about.

She stared out of the window at the meadow where they had danced together – bathed now, as then, in silvery moonlight.

'I don't know. Perhaps we'll settle down and live near here.'

Adam shook his head. 'You wouldn't go back to France with him because of me, would you? But lassie, I could stay on my own. I wouldn't be lonely.'

'Don't you worry, I won't leave you. We'll think of

something else,' she told him, slipping an affectionate arm round his shoulders.

The harvest celebrations had an unexpected ending. It was a warm night and after the feasting and the singing were finished, young Glendinning and a group of other men, all drunk, went down to the river to bathe in the salmon cauld. They splashed about naked and shouting in the light of the moon but when they climbed back on the bank again, one of their number was missing. Glendinning's son and heir had disappeared in his own stretch of river, a stretch known for its sullen and dangerous currents. His body was not found for more than a week but in the end it was washed up at Berwick and carried back home to Charterhall on a farm cart.

Tongues wagged furiously in the district and everyone was talking about how Jane Cannon had foreseen the death of young Glendinning. As the tale went from mouth to mouth, it was embroidered and embellished until everyone believed that she had not only forecast a violent end for the young man but had seen him sinking down through black water.

'She's got the sight, that lassie, oh aye, she's got the sight. It's better not to cross her,' said the chatterers, drawing back as the girl passed by.

When Adam Cannon went into Melrose in the middle of September to make inquiries about jobs that were likely to become vacant the following year, he heard the first news of the battle of Waterloo which had taken place on 18 June.

An old man in the King's Arms told him, 'Thon deevil Boney escaped from Elba and started all the fighting up again. But our chaps have beaten the hell out of him at a place called Waterloo. The newspapers say the war's really over this time. Boney's given himself up to our sailors and they're going to shoot him.'

From his shepherd brother-in-law, a less bellicose informant, he heard more details of Waterloo. 'Do you mind thon Colonel Berton, the old chap with the grey hair who was the head of the prisoners here? Well, folk are saying he was killed at Waterloo fighting for Bonaparte again. Poor old soul, he should have given up making war at his age. When he left here he didn't look strong enough to get to Berwick.'

Adam took this news home to Jane and when she heard it, a terrible chill spread from her heart throughout her entire body.

'Oh, not the colonel, the kind old colonel Blaize admired so much! How could he be killed in battle! What happened? How did Bonaparte get out of Elba?' she asked her father.

He shrugged. 'I don't know. That's all they said in Melrose. The newspapers said that Napoleon's been on the loose since March and when he landed in France all his old soldiers rallied to him again. He must be quite a man, that Bonaparte, for men to follow him that way.'

The French had been fighting since March! Blaize sent her fifty pounds at the beginning of that month – oh, surely he had not rejoined his Emperor? But she remembered only too well how he admired Bonaparte, how reverently he talked of him as if the man were a sort of god. He respected the Emperor more than any other man alive and she knew that if Blaize was asked to rejoin the Imperial army, he would do it.

She could hardly force herself to ask the next question, but she had to know. 'Did they mention anybody else from Melrose being killed at Waterloo?'

But her father, giving her an understanding look, shook his head. 'Don't worry, Jane, they only talked about old Colonel Berton. That's all they knew about. If there was anyone else we know who was killed, they'd have heard, I don't doubt it.' Neither of them mentioned Blaize's name.

Then another thought struck her. 'What would happen to the men who survived the battle? Would they be taken prisoner again?' she asked.

Her father shook his head. 'I don't think our side would bother. No, they say France is well and truly beaten this time so they'd just let them go home. If they do shoot Boney there'll be nobody to make them want to fight any more and even those Frenchmen need a leader.'

The news reassured her in a way. If Blaize had gone off to fight, his plans for return would have been set back. That's why he'd missed the haymaking season but she'd wait for him. She'd wait for ever if necessary . . .

In the years that followed the Napoleonic Wars, agriculture and the farming people were to go through a period of great hardship. Not only were wages low but expenses were high and families had to choose between putting clothes on their children's backs and shoes on their feet, or feeding them. As for sending them to school, few labouring families could afford the handful of coppers a week that it cost to have a child taught to read and write in one of the little village schoolrooms. Yet as a class they had a deep respect for learning – it was the only way for the cleverest among them to escape the back-breaking toil that was their daily lot. The dream of any mother or father with a clever son was to be able to send him to university and then into the church. In fact many clever boys from poor homes in Scotland did fulfil this dream but it took hard work, dedication and much privation, not only for the young men but for all the rest of their families as well, before they could do so.

Like their social superiors, however, most labourers' families thought that educating girls was a waste of time and money. A girl was destined to marry and even after marriage she was regarded as little more than a working animal, hardly superior to the beasts of the field.

Strong or feeble, clever or simple, they went to work by the age of twelve and when they lifted their heads up from their toil and watched their well-born sisters walking in flower-filled gardens or riding by in carriages with silken parasols over their heads, they regarded them with a lack of envy, a sense of wonder and feeling of apartness like African natives watching white missionaries.

It was ill luck that Adam Cannon had to go looking for a new place at such a time of depression. His friends and fellow tenant farmers, the few who were left, could not afford to offer him work. They needed younger men with big families to occupy their farm cottages. The more hands that came out of one house the better. Old Adam with his unmarried daughter and her baby was not a good bargain, and it made him feel ashamed to have to ask for help. But it was necessary to find a place before the March hiring fair in Earlston. His proud soul revolted at the idea of having to stand like an animal in a market waiting to be picked out by some man with money.

But no job came. Jock Hepburn came to the abbey house to repeat his request that Jane should marry him. He pressed his suit with a little gentle blackmail, giving her the reminder that he would be able to offer her and her father a home, for he still had his job and his cottage with Glendinning.

Jane's mobile face showed that she appreciated this point. She was worried about her father, who was daily slipping into more profound despair as his efforts to find work failed.

When Jock left, however, Adam roughly told her not to turn back on the road she had set herself. 'If you don't love Jock, don't marry him for my sake. If you believe your man will come back, trust him and wait.'

He clinched his argument with a lie. 'Anyway, I've had an offer of a place at Earlston, so we don't need his help.'

So Jane turned Jock down, telling him once again how much she respected him but that there was no love in her heart for him, not the love she knew she was capable of feeling. 'We'll always be friends, but I'd like to see you married to some woman who'll love you for yourself, not just because you gave her a roof over her head,' she said sadly.

The job and house in Earlston did not materialize, of course, and Adam's spirits grew lower and lower. He was obsessed with the fear of having to turn to the parish for help — for he knew how grudgingly charity was handed out to paupers. He tortured himself with the thought that without him round her neck, Jane would have her fifty pounds from Blaize all to herself, as well as a better chance of a job. She could hire herself out as a housemaid perhaps, and then she wouldn't have to labour in the fields. Big Agnes, or one of the other farm women, would take in her baby to foster.

Besides, if Jane was alone and Blaize came back, she would be able to go off with him to a better life without worrying about her father.

He took to wandering the fields and woods alone, saying goodbye to the hidden corners he'd known since boyhood. Every time he forded the river it murmured seductively to him and he stood in it with the foaming spume bubbling round his boots, wondering what young Glendinning felt when the Tweed water closed over his head for the last time. It wouldn't be a bad death.

Then he looked up, dizzied from his contemplation of the rushing current, and saw the majestic beech trees standing sentinel along the stark red riverbanks that rose up steep like guardian walls. He watched the shy herons stalking in the shallows, stilt legged and beady eyed as they scanned the pools for unsuspecting fish. He turned his white head to follow the flight of a skein of ducks and smiled at the sound of their flapping wings. He was drinking in every sight and sound of a scene which had always delighted him.

One night when the river was rushing down blood red in its first autumn flood, he told Jane he was going to search for firewood.

'Don't worry. I might come home the long way round. Go to bed if I'm not back.'

When he reached the riverbank the sound of the rushing torrent, wrenching and tearing wildly at the banks, delighted him because he knew that once in, there would be no chance of fighting for his life or swimming to safety. Smiling as simply and innocently as a child, he slipped off the bank into the cold water. His beloved river treated him kindly. It did not carry his body down to Berwick to be examined by curious strangers but washed him up only a mile from home, and left him floating, arms outspread, in a side eddy, pinned back from the main stream by a large tree branch.

In the morning when he did not emerge from his tiny bed closet, Jane went looking for him. Distraught, she alerted the other labourers and they formed a search party. It was Jock Hepburn who found him floating gently in the river.

The burying place of the Cannons was marked by a lopsided, lichen-covered stone with a curly-haired, trumpet-blowing angel carved on it. No names were decipherable now, for the inscriptions had all worn away long ago and the stone had sunk gently into the earth till it was half covered with mossy earth so that the angel looked as if she were rising resurrected out of the ground.

When Jane's father was buried beside his wife, her predominant feeling was gratitude that he never had to face the agony of leaving the abbey house. Mr Swanston, the minister from Earlston who conducted the ceremony, had agreed to bury Adam in consecrated ground because everyone told him that the old man must have slipped and fallen into the river in the darkness. It was an accident, they all said, Adam Cannon was far too sensible a man to even consider suicide.

Only Jane, who had witnessed her father's growing depression, knew the truth, but she kept her own counsel.

At the end of the burial ceremony she stopped the minister on his way back to his gig and asked him, 'Mr Swanston, if I bring my baby to your church will you christen her for me?'

He was a thin, pinched man with red-rimmed eyes and a nose that permanently dripped. His sermons were long and hectoring and he tended to take himself very seriously indeed. Now he looked on the girl with the child held close to her heart, disfavour and disapproval in his eyes.

'That child's a bastard, isn't it?' he asked.

Shaken, she nodded. 'I suppose she is – legally. Her father and I aren't married. He's married already, you see.'

Swanston reeled in shock. 'How could you tell me that? You're a fornicator, an adulterer! And you ask me to christen the child of your unholy union? Have some sense, girl. I wouldn't allow a child like that in God's house.'

She stepped back with a look of disbelief on her face. The Cannons had perhaps not been as fervent in their church attendance as some of the farm servants who would attend services three times on Sundays, but they were a God-fearing, good-living family and it had never occurred to her that the minister would refuse to christen Aylie. Without a word, she turned on her heel and walked away from him, hating his pious face and his sanctimonious voice. 'I'll never go into his church again,' she swore to herself.

In mid March, Jane with Aylie in her arms walked the three miles along the twisting road to Earlston where the hiring fair was held. She left the abbey house early in the morning when a cruel wind was howling down from the hills with cutting rain in its breath, and she shivered in misery each time she turned a corner into open ground and its teeth bit into her.

She wore her bondager costume because it was necessary to show prospective employers the sort of job she was able to do and also because she knew that the outfit made her look strong and capable. Her grey and yellow striped overskirt stuck out over layers of stiffly starched petticoats – and a thick flannel one as well. The big straw hat had been newly varnished with black japanning and in the brim she tucked a few early daffodils, a brave gesture against the bitter weather. A pink flowered headscarf tied the hat down against the strong wind and it matched her print blouse which showed beneath her father's old black jacket. On top of all she wore a tightly wound black woollen shawl into which she wrapped her pink-cheeked baby.

Aylie was her greatest pride, for the child was always happy, smiling and eager for an outing. Today, in spite of the cold, she stared out from her cosy nest, laughing in delight each time they passed some lambs clustered round their mothers or startled a rabbit or a gloriously gleaming pheasant from under the bare-branched hedgerows.

It was still only seven o'clock and half dark when Jane took up her stance in the cobbled square of the town. Behind her loomed the red sandstone bulk of the recently built Corn Exchange where crowds of farmers were already gathering. Through the open door of the Red Lion Inn next door, sounds of shouting and revelry could be heard, for the drinking had begun before dawn.

Jane stationed herself on a corner and the wind whipped round her legs as she stood trying to ignore the curious eyes that were turned in her direction. Though she did not know everyone there, they all knew her or at least had heard of her . . . 'That's Adam Cannon's lassie . . . the one wi' the Frenchman's bairn.'

Heads were shaken and tongues were clicked in disapproval or in dismay at the death of her father, for Adam had been a well-respected man and his death had shocked the community. How could he slip into the river like that, they asked each other? He knew the river well because he'd lived beside it all his life. He was not a drinker so there was no excuse that he had lost his footing while under the influence. What a terrible pity! It was decent of the minister to give him a Christian burial.

By eight o'clock there was a dense crowd in the square. Shepherds stood in groups, each man holding his horn-handled crook, the symbol of his trade. Carters brandished whips with long cruel thongs; grooms carried riding crops; ploughmen and hinds had wisps of straw in their hats or carried pitchforks. Some of the people seeking work were bent and grey headed while others were little more than children. Near Jane, a fresh-faced and eager boy of not more than twelve years of age was smiling eagerly at each farmer who passed him by. As time passed, his eagerness began to wear off and dejection took over . . .

'Don't worry, someone's sure to take you, you're a nice-looking boy,' she whispered to him in encouragement.

'There's not a lot of work for half yins now,' he said, 'they want a full-grown man. But my father's dead and there's only me to help my mother and the other bairns in the house.'

'How many of you are there?'

He looked sad. 'There's six of us and the baby's only a year old. If I don't get work we'll have to go on the parish.'

She felt ashamed at feeling pity for herself. At least she still had her nest egg tucked away safely. The parish was at least a year off for her. Aylie, who had fallen asleep in her mother's arms, woke up and began to whimper softly, for she needed feeding.

An older woman in the bondager costume who had been standing apart from the rest came up to Jane and said, 'If you want to feed your bairn, go into the inn, they've a room there that they'll let you use. The landlady's a decent woman. Say Meggie Andrews sent you.'

The girl looked at the ruddy-faced woman and smiled. She could see that her costume, though clean, was much patched, and the brim of her hat was frayed though it, like her own, had been freshly lacquered.

'Are you looking for a place too?' she asked.

The woman nodded.

'Aye, I am that. My husband died last year and I need some place to live and some money coming in. My lassie's over there, she wants a place in a house because she can't bear the idea of working in the fields. She's a very delicate lassie.'

She nodded across to a sweet-faced girl of about thirteen dressed in a grey gown with a white apron, for she was offering herself as a maid of all work in a farmer's household.

'She's so pretty,' said Jane in admiration.

'Oh aye,' said the girl's mother with a sad note in her voice, 'she's too pretty. The pretty girls don't get hired by farmers' wives, or if they do, they often find themselves in trouble. I'm trying to make sure she gets a good house. I know most of the folk who come here, you see. My man worked as a shepherd on a farm not far away, and my father was there before him. I've lived here for thirty years. If somebody offers for you, I'll tip you the wink too. Some of them sound plausible enough but it's a different story once you've taken their shilling.'

The inn was poky and smelled strongly of beer but the landlady was friendly and she ushered Jane into a back parlour where she could breastfeed Aylie in front of a roaring fire.

As she was buttoning up her dress and preparing to return to the square, the landlady came back in with a pot of ale and thrust it into her hand, saying, 'Feeding mothers need nourishment. Take it, it's a present. I had to stand in hiring fairs myself once and I know what it's like. My, but that's a bonny bairn you've got there.'

In baby worship, the two women looked down at Aylie kicking on the hearthrug and Jane smiled, for she thought her daughter was the loveliest child ever born and it delighted her when other people commented on her beauty. Her own hated freckles had not appeared on the baby's soft white skin. In the infant features she saw a look of the handsome father – the long, eloquent mouth, the frank and open eyes. She wanted nothing of herself to come out in her daughter because she did not value her own beauty, thinking herself too large, too freckled and too blonde. Blaize's Gallic looks were what she most admired.

Back in the square, most of the farmers had made their bargains with the shepherds, hinds and carters and now it was the turn of the hired hinds to rush about finding themselves bondagers because each man had to supply a

93

woman to work alongside him, in accordance with the bargain he'd made with his new employer. Strong-looking young women were besieged with offers and Jane was pleased to see three or four men haggling round her friend Meggie, whose daughter too seemed to have found work because she was standing beside her mother smiling proudly.

With her baby in the crook of her arm, Jane took up her stance again beside the little group and the young boy paused beside her to say, 'I got a place. I'm all fixed up. I hope you get some place too, soon.' In a little while the attention of some of the wandering men switched to her for she made a striking sight.

The first man to speak was a long-faced man of about forty whose smile looked false. 'You're a strong-looking lassie, what's your terms?' he asked her.

She was flummoxed by this for she hadn't worked out what she should ask. Her father had always made the bargain with Glendinning.

'Where will you be working?' she asked, and he named a farm she knew to be on the other side of the village of St Boswells. Then she asked a question which caused several eavesdroppers to look at her in surprise. 'Can you see the Eildons from there? I won't work in any place that doesn't have a view of the Eildons.'

The man laughed. 'Oh aye, you see them well enough, the farm stands right on the edge of the farthest Eildon. Our sheep graze on it.'

Before she committed herself, Jane looked across at Meggie and saw her new friend gently shaking her head in warning.

'No thank you,' she said firmly, trusting Meggie's judgement. 'I don't think I want to work with you.'

With a curse, the man walked away, shouting back over his shoulder, 'You and your bastard bairn might find it harder than you think to get a place, Miss high and mighty Cannon.'

The morning wore on and Jane was still standing alone, for the sight of Aylie caused approaching hinds to turn on their heel and walk away. She was growing desperate when Jock Hepburn came up and stood looking at her, his eyes vulnerable with longing.

'I hate to see you standing here like this. Let me hire you, Jane, come with me as my bondager. I'm needing a lassie.'

'You're not. I know fine you're staying on at Charterhall and your mother's your bondager. What would she do if you hired somebody else? You can't afford two bondagers.'

'She'd find a job in her own right. She's one of the best bondagers in the district, you know that. She's even a grand hand with the horses.'

'I won't have her making way for me. She doesn't want to leave Charterhall any more than I do. Besides I can't come and stay in the house with you, Jock. You know what people would say and I'm not going to marry you. It'd only mean pain for you. You've got to forget me. You must.'

Jock looked sad but her reaction did not really surprise him. 'I can't. I'll never forget you. But if you won't work for me, I'll find you someone who'll treat you well. Just wait here.'

In less than five minutes he was back, bringing with him a red-faced older man in a checked suit who exhaled a strong smell of whisky into the cold air. He grinned and looked at Jane with frank admiration in his eyes.

Then he said to Jock, 'My word, Hepburn, that's a grand lassie. She'll make a great worker. I don't mind the bairn, my wife'll take it in with our ain.'

Jane was doubtful about agreeing to a bargain with him but Jock assured her it was all right and even Meggie was nodding away in agreement over the old man's shoulder. So she took the man's arles, the customary shilling which he pressed into her hand on the sealing of their bargain, and then she found herself bound to work as a bondager with Archie Turnbull for a year. He agreed to pay her ten pence on the days the farmer wanted her labour; to keep her in his house; provide her with food and, a generous gesture, also provide food for her daughter. The farm where he was going to work was called Maryfield and it was situated on the slope of the Black Hill, directly facing her beloved Eildons. From the farmyard, he told her, she could even see the trees that embowered her old home, Charterhall abbey.

The traditional day for farm servants moving from one job to another was 12 May, and on the night before moving day, Jane could not sleep. Rising at about two o'clock in the morning, she pulled a shawl over her nightgown and went outside to wander round the grounds of her beloved home. It was once again quiet and peaceful and the trees were growing back over the fallen walls, because after the death of young Glendinning quarrying at the abbey had ceased and the old landowner completed his stable block with new stone.

In spite of his depredations there was still a lot of the original abbey buildings left. She wandered around, examining every nook and cranny in the light of the full moon, anxious to imprint the memory of them on her mind. It was a magnificent night, the moon shone like a huge silver coin in the middle of the sky and there was not a sound except the occasional swoop and screech of a hunting owl.

Suddenly she was infused with energy and rushed back into the house to pack her most precious possessions into an old brass-bound chest. Carefully she laid in a bundle of ancient and cracking vellum manuscripts, some of them illuminated with paintings like jewels down the margins, intricate coloured drawings which her father had told her were the work of the monks of Charterhall. If only he could decipher the Latin, he said, he would know the history of the abbey. She also hid Alice's herbal books; a couple of big silver spoons and an elegant silver chalice that had been in the family possession since the abbey fell into ruin. She thought about hiding Blaize's jacket in the trunk too but instead laid it on top of her sleeping baby. She believed that no evil spirit would harm

96

a child if it slept under something that belonged to its father.

Then she heaved the trunk out of the house, down the stairs and across the cloister yard to a dark corner of the old gateway tower where there was a hidden cellar that only the Cannon family knew about and to which they owned the only key. In the days of Border wars, when raiders came, they used to hide there till trouble passed. Because it had not been used for years, the cellar door was now almost hidden by trees and tangled ivy. That hiding place, though she did not know it, had once been a cell for penitent monks, and in it she now secreted her trunk of treasures, pulling the ivy back carefully when she was finished.

She was tired and was walking slowly back through the grass-floored nave when the singing began – cold, clear voices were rising and falling in a medieval chant from somewhere above her head.

It was an ethereal, icy cold sound that stopped her in her tracks but, strangely, did not make her afraid. She had heard it once before when she was a little girl and it had not frightened her then either. She stood still, clutching the shawl round her shoulders, and listened to the voices of men dead for hundreds of years rising to the heavens in a contrapuntal chant. They were singing words which she did not understand but she was transported by the purity and glory of their voices. She knew that the monks of the abbey were granting her a last privilege. They were sending her on her way with proof of the secret of the place she loved so much.

It was also local custom that new employers send a cart to transport a worker's belongings to their new home, and early next morning Jane and Aylie were wakened by the sound of wheels outside the window. It was a carter from Maryfield, come to take her away from Charterhall. When she showed him what had to be moved, he looked surprised, for there were only one trunk and a bundle of bedding.

'You haven't a lot. Where's the rest of your stuff? They said you'd have a houseful to move.'

She shook her head. 'I gave most of it away.'

She had given away most of the bits of furniture and tools. The secret of the hidden trunk she would keep to herself.

Maryfield was a large farm about three miles from Charterhall, set above fertile daisy-covered meadows that stretched along one bank of the river Leader and with sheep pastures that extended well up the scree slopes of the Black Hill. It was farmed by a good-humoured, lazy gentleman called Colonel Scroggie whose only interest in life was fox hunting, a pursuit he enthusiastically followed over the surrounding hills and coppices behind his own pack of foxhounds.

The Colonel's stable was full of highly bred hunters and his house was the resort of roistering hunting cronies who drank port as if it were water and hurray-ed and halloo-ed well into the early hours of the morning whenever the Colonel gave a supper party.

Their employer's good spirits and joie de vivre was passed on to the people who worked for him and his farm toun was a happy place. Jane, who had only ever worked at Charterhall, felt the different atmosphere the moment the cart swung round the corner of the farm road and a line of workers' cottages came into view. Groups of men and women were standing around gossiping and laughing. Obviously none of the people here lived in mortal dread of their farm steward as they did at Charterhall.

Old Archie and his red-cheeked wife Bertha were busy moving into their new home, which was the last cottage in a row of seven. They were happily shouting at each other, cuffing their children and tripping over animals on their way to and fro from another cart, piled so high with possessions that it looked in danger of capsizing. Jane was amazed to see that Bertha was resplendent in a huge hat with a tall white ostrich feather nodding in its band.

When she saw Jane staring at her glorious headgear, Bertha laughed and said, 'You're admiring my flitting hat. I keep it for moving days and never put it on any other time. It makes me feel grand and proud sitting up on top of our things with my feather bobbing about.'

Archie grinned when he saw Jane climbing down from her cart. 'Come on over here, lassie,' he shouted, 'and help me with this box of hens. You take them into the back yard and untie their legs.'

Jane did not like the fierce way hens could peck at her hands and she drew back slightly.

Archie reassured her, 'They'll no' peck you. They're as tame as wee doves. My, they're so tame that on flitting days they lie on their backs with their legs up in the air for me to tie them thegither.'

Everyone laughed at this and a man in the crowd said, 'You must have done a lot of flitting, Archie, if your hens are like that. Does no place ever suit you?'

Bertha replied, 'Oh, he likes wandering about does my man, but this time we're going to stay put. I'm tired of packing up every flitting day. I'm not going to let him move again.'

Archie had indeed been a wanderer, going from farm to farm throughout the Borders. He'd even worked in Northumberland, people said, when discussing the extent of Archie's travelling. But now that he was growing older he was happy to find himself a comfortable berth at Maryfield, which had the reputation of being the best place to work for a good thirty miles.

On her first night in the farm, after all the work of settling in was completed, Jane sat at the cottage door with the others and heard the tales about her new employer, Colonel Scroggie.

'He's a real gentleman is the Colonel,' said a woman with a clutch of children clinging to her skirt. 'I've been here ten years and in all that time I've never heard of him being unfair to anyone. He'll not stand for his workers being abused, no steward of his would ever dare raise a stick to a worker.'

The others nodded in agreement. They knew only too well that there were places where women as well as men had been beaten to the ground by stick-wielding stewards.

'Do you mind that time last autumn when the Colonel heard about Richardson down the road at Cleughfoot using two bondager women to pull a plough because one of his horses was sick?' asked a young man lounging with his back against the cottage wall.

The motherly woman nodded vigorously in agreement. 'Aye and he went down there with his face bright red and he told Richardson, "Don't you let me hear of you using women as draught animals again or I'll be round with my horsewhip." One of the women's my cousin and she told me what the Colonel said. Richardson was fair affronted.'

The listeners sucked in their breath with appreciation. 'He's a real gentleman is the Colonel,' they all agreed.

Jane climbed the ladder to her shake-down bed on the loft floor of the little cottage, feeling happier than she had been for a very long time. She was going to be well treated by Archie and Bertha who had given her and Aylie a good supper and shown them loving kindness.

When she lay down on the straw-filled mattress and closed her eyes, her mind as always wandered back to Blaize . . . Where is he tonight? she wondered.

She gave no hint to the outside world how bitterly unhappy she was at not having heard from him for over a year, and there were times when she asked herself if she had been wrong to trust him. Was Blaize untrue? Had he returned to France and conveniently forgotten her and Aylie? But then she remembered their days and nights together; she remembered how they clung together on the jetty at Berwick and she knew it was wrong to mistrust him.

'I *know* I'll hear from him again,' she whispered, laying one hand on the Hussar's jacket that covered the sleeping child by her side. Then she fell asleep.

*

Jane was deeply grateful to Jock for having found her such a happy place with Archie and Bertha. She had heard enough stories of the miseries of bondagers' lives not to appreciate her situation even though Bertha's children were noisy day and night and the cooking was very rough and ready. Her food was abundant and ungrudged and she was treated well, not like many other women in her position who had to live with grudging hinds who tried to skimp on every bit of food, or with a man who cheated them of their wages and assumed that the terms of bondage included the woman sharing his bed as well as his work in the fields.

The only fault that Archie could be said to have was that every Saturday night he got happily drunk and fell into bed beside an equally merry Bertha to make enthusiastic and noisy love. On Sunday morning, with sore heads and solemn faces, they forced themselves up, and after they'd done their tasks around the farm, they dressed in their best black and walked their protesting children to the church in Earlston. In spite of frequent invitations Jane refused to accompany them because she could never forgive the minister for his refusal to christen Aylie.

When she told Bertha her reason for not going to church, the hind's wife looked solemn and asked, 'But does it not worry you that the bairn's not been baptized?'

Jane nodded. 'Yes, it does, very much. All my family were churchgoers . . . I worry that if anything were to happen to her, she'd go to Hell.'

Bertha clicked her tongue in commiseration. 'I don't believe bairns go to Hell just because the minister's not splashed water on them, but if it does worry you, I'll christen her. Anybody can baptize a bairn, you know. They say Mary Queen of Scots baptized the daughter of her serving woman. I'm no queen but I'll baptize Aylie.'

And next Sunday afternoon she did, solemnly dipping her fingers into her best china bowl and incanting the words of the baptism service which she had memorized while watching the minister performing the same function that morning for a baby born within wedlock. When she

101

handed back the crying little girl, who had not liked cold water being trickled over her face, she said, 'It's good she's greetin', it means she's driven out the devil.'

Jane felt safe now, less anxious that Aylie would be snatched away from her by evil spirits or fairies – along with her other superstitions, she had a strong belief in the little people.

Three or four years of working at Maryfield passed and she grew less miserable inside. She often paused in her work to stare out across the fields at her beloved Eildon hills, and one day realized, with an uplifting of the heart, that in spite of her secret sorrow and longing for Blaize, she was happy most of the time. Her beloved Borderland was holding her safe, sheltering her and Aylie beneath the folds of the hills, hills which had moods like people, sometimes smiling and soft, other times threatening and forbidding but always magical, awe-inspiring and reassuring.

In the summer when she was thirty, Jock came over the hill and, standing stiffly in the cottage garden, asked her again to marry him.

'Your Frenchman's not coming back, Jane. He's been gone ten years. Marry me now and I'll give you and the bairn a good home. I've been offered the tenancy of a farm down there beside Merton' – he pointed to the east – 'and I'm going to take it. You know I've always said I'd have my own place one day. It has a nice wee house and forty acres of good land. There's a lot of hard work to be done and I'm needing a good woman to help me. It's a new start for both of us.'

She looked with affection at his resolute face and sturdy frame. He would succeed, she could see that now. She had immense respect for Jock – but she still did not love him.

'Oh, I'm so glad for you. It's what you wanted. But I can't marry you. I wouldn't ten years ago and I can't now. I'm still not sure that I won't hear from Blaize again. I'm certain he meant to come back, nothing anyone says

102

ever makes me doubt him. There must be a very good reason why he hasn't come back and I'm sure that one day I'll find out what it was.'

Jock shrugged. He'd expected that, really. 'Well, I'm needing a wife and I won't ask you again. If you won't marry me, I'm going to ask somebody else. But I'll always be your friend. If there's ever any time you need help, Jane, you've only got to ask me.'

She kissed his cheek and sent him back home with a heavy heart, for he felt as sorry for Jane and Aylie as for himself. They deserved more than the life of a bondager and her bairn.

A month later he married Flora, a shy, sweet-faced girl, the daughter of the head groom in Charterhall stables. Jane went to the wedding and in spite of herself, felt a twinge of envy when she saw the joy on the face of the bride as she danced with her sturdy and respectable new husband.

Big Agnes, growing wrinkled and grey now, put her arm round Jane's shoulders and whispered, 'Cheer up, lass. I'd have liked you as a daughter but it wasn't to be. Take care you don't waste your life waiting for something that doesn't happen.'

There was a strong and loving bond between Jane and Aylie – they were more like friends than mother and child, for Jane treated her daughter as a confidante, telling her the secret things that occupied her mind and hiding nothing from her. Every Sunday, instead of going to church like the other farm workers, they walked the three miles back to Charterhall and wandered through the abbey grounds. Though it was only a few years since the place had been lived in, trees and bushes had taken it over, climbing over the ruins, pushing their way up between tumbled stones. In the burying ground the grave-stones leaned at even more perilous angles and the old pear trees along the cloister wall had sprouted in all directions for want of pruning.

Old Glendinning had been stricken with apoplexy and

lived on in his gloomy house, attended by unfeeling servants. His plans to clear the abbey ruins were totally abandoned for he no longer cared what happened to the place and did not have the power of speech to issue any more orders.

So they were unmolested on their visits back to Jane's old home. With her daughter she always went up to the first floor of the chapter house but Glendinning's workmen had removed the roof and the stone floor now shone like wet silk after rain, was covered with snow in winter, or felt hot underfoot during the summer months.

The carved bosses of sunflower, rose and holly on the tops of the columns were still there however and she would cup her hands lovingly round them as she showed them to the little girl and told her stories about the men who had carved them hundreds of years before. She told Aylie about the ghostly singing that she had heard in the choir and about the secret cell beneath the gatehouse tower. The cell frightened the child because it was so cold and damp, but once they were inside and her mother lit a taper, she was entranced at the display of Jane's treasures which were still safe in their brass-bound trunk. She would stand beside a little window shaped like a cannon ball and show the child the illuminated manuscript and sheafs of notes and recipes that had belonged to her grandmother, the healer. But the bit of the afternoon Aylie loved best was when her mother told her about Blaize, about how she first saw him among the snowdrops and how he hid in the cloister, all dressed up like a shepherd in a plaid and bonnet.

If anyone ever saw them there, they were never interrupted. Old Glendinning was in a wicker chair in his sitting room, fed by maids who hated his slobbering and put to bed at night by an uncaring man servant who systematically stole from him. The business of the farm was run by the steward, who believed that Jane Cannon had put a curse on the Glendinning family. Even when he knew she was wandering around the abbey grounds, he was afraid to stop her for fear she put the evil eye on him too.

The child was growing up to be a slim and elegant girl, very lady-like looking, wide-shouldered like her father and with his intelligent, searching face. Her hair was almost as blonde as Jane's and gently curling. To her mother's relief she had no freckles, not even over the bridge of her nose in summertime.

One autumn Sunday in 1825 they went to the abbey as usual and were walking through the burying ground on their way to the ruined house when Jane stopped in her tracks like a startled animal.

'There's someone over there, in the aisle beside the big graves,' she whispered to Aylie.

The child's eyes looked where her mother pointed and saw the bulky figure of a man in a black suit and a tall hat standing before an imposing-looking headstone. He was wiping his eyes with a large handkerchief.

'Poor thing, he's crying,' she whispered back.

'He's at Christian's grave, he must be crying for her,' said Jane. Christian's brother was buried there too but she did not imagine that anyone could be crying for him.

Mother and daughter advanced towards the stranger, and when they grew close Jane gestured to Aylie to hide herself behind a pillar while she spied on the weeping man more closely.

After a few seconds, without speaking to a wondering Aylie, she stepped out into full view to ask in a strangely trembling voice, 'Oh, is it you Jacques? Is it really you come back after all this time?'

The stranger lifted his head and stared at her. The golden beard had gone and so had the dashing earrings. Now he was a soberly dressed, respectable, middle-aged man in a broadcloth coat and expensive-looking boots. A tall hat was held under his arm and he had laid a bunch of flowers on the stone slab at his feet.

He stared in surprise and then, after a few seconds, he threw out both arms with a cry. 'It's Blaize's Jane. What a miracle, it's you Jane! I've been looking everywhere for you but in the big house they said you'd gone away long ago.'

They rushed together and he hugged her to him, like the friendly bear he once had seemed to be. While they embraced he wept openly and she cried too, so rackingly that she barely heard him as he explained.

'I came back to see my Christian's grave. I've never forgotten her, you know. Life is so cruel. You and I have both suffered loss, my dear.'

At this she stiffened and stepped slightly away from him. 'Loss? What do you mean?'

'But you must know about Blaize. Surely you know . . . You must have heard about Waterloo.'

She shook her head, fear on her face. 'I heard there was a battle. I hoped he wasn't in it.'

Jacques took her hands. 'Oh, my dear, he was killed there, fighting for Napoleon. I wasn't with him when he fell but a friend of mine was. It was very swift, a soldier's death, my dear.'

Jane reeled and put her hands up to her face, gasping, 'Oh, Jacques, that's what I've been afraid of ever since I heard about the battle. I knew he'd go back to fight – he would go if Bonaparte needed him. Oh my God, he *was* going to be the next to die. I knew that when I saw him at Christian's funeral!'

Frightened, Aylie rushed up to comfort her weeping mother and glared at the man who was bringing such devastating news. She had not heard everything that was said but she could tell from her mother's face and voice that it was very important and very sad.

'Blaize died a soldier's death,' Jacques repeated very slowly to the child, 'at Waterloo.'

Jane said, 'I knew something terrible had happened to him but I never really let myself believe it. I kept thinking he'd come back one day . . . I kept on hoping.'

She was not fully aware of what she was saying and, sensing this, Jacques took her arm and led her across to the old stairs where they had sat so often in the past.

'You must have known that he would come back if he

106

were still alive. He loved you, Jane. He longed to come back to you but when the Emperor landed from Elba, Blaize was nearby and he felt he had to join him again. Napoleon had that effect on the men who knew him. Blaize thought they'd win and it would all be over in a few weeks . . . I felt the same. I left my home in Brittany to fight as well. We never thought any of us would die in the attempt. When Blaize and I met again he told me about his dreams of the day he'd come back for you, how he'd see you in the hayfield and run across to you. . . . He talked about it all the time.'

'What about his wife?' Jane asked, dry-mouthed. 'Did he mention his wife?'

'He'd told her about you. They'd organized things. She kept his house and he was to pay her an income. She wasn't happy to see him go but Blaize was not a man to argue with, she realized that he meant what he said. No man ever loved anyone more than he loved you. Didn't you get a letter? His wife promised me she'd write to tell you what had happened.'

She shook her head. 'No letter. I wrote to his address in Arles once or twice. I was so sure he wouldn't just forget about us.'

'That's true, he didn't. He loved you and he longed to see his baby. Is this the child?'

They both regarded Aylie, who stood looking anxious, clinging to her mother's arm. Jane nodded.

'That's our daughter. I called her Alouette but no one here can say it so we call her Aylie.'

She put an arm round the girl and introduced her to Jacques. 'This gentleman was a friend of your father's.'

Aylie started to weep; the highly charged emotion of the meeting had touched her tender heart. Since she was tiny she had been told by her mother of the day her handsome dashing father, in another scarlet jacket like the one they treasured, would march into the cottage and take them both in his arms. She knew how much her mother longed for this to happen and now she was weeping in pity for her.

Seeing her sorrow, the big man knelt down beside her and said gently, 'Don't cry. Your father was a very fine man. He was my friend. When I look at you I see him again, for you look very like him. He'd be so very proud of you.'

Aylie, 1826

When she was twelve years old Aylie looked like a long-legged filly with an alert, startled head and wide eyes which gave her an animal elegance. She was a kind child with a great love of animals which had shown itself early, for even when she was very young Jane had found it impossible to restrain her from cuddling snarling puppies, picking up spitting kittens or bringing hedgehogs into the house from the cottage garden. None of these animals, even the most savage that would have attacked anyone else who handled them, ever turned on Aylie. She even won the confidence of wild birds so that they would flutter down and take crumbs from her hand.

Children loved her too and as soon as she was old enough to be given responsibility, she walked over to the Hepburns' farmhouse to help Jock's wife Flora with their baby son, Sandy. She became his unofficial nursemaid and looked after him for Flora who was delicate, and after Sandy's birth suffered frequent miscarriages. Sandy was to be their only surviving child and he was doted on not only by his parents but by Aylie and Jane as well, for he was a sweet-natured little boy with an enchanting wide grin and loving ways.

When she was well enough to go out, Flora often took Sandy and Aylie to the stables at Charterhall, which were ruled with a rod of iron by her father, the head groom. There Aylie fell under the enchantment of the horse. The carriage and riding horses that fidgeted and fretted in the palatial boxes of the rebuilt stableyard fascinated her. Because of old Glendinning's disability they were worked very little, so when they were taken out for exercise they cavorted, kicked and bucked all over the paddocks like dervishes. She thought she had never seen anything more lovely or more exciting than those prancing horses.

Sometimes Flora's father would find the girl standing on tiptoe to peer through the bars of one of the boxes, whispering to the horse inside till even the most suspicious and ill-tempered of them turned and came over to snuffle with open nostrils at her face.

One morning as she watched the horses being rubbed down with twists of straw, she told Flora's father, 'Oh, I'd love to ride a horse. I wouldn't be frightened.'

He looked at her skinny little body and said, 'I've no doubt you could, lass. Come on, I'll put you up on old Tusker. He's the quietest of the lot and he won't hurt you.'

She felt like a queen when she was perched on Tusker's soft bare back, her hands twisted among the coarse hair of his mane while one of the boys led her round the stable paddock. After the short ride was over she laid her face down on Tusker's neck and breathed in the smell of him. 'Oh, doesn't he smell wonderful,' she sighed in delight.

Her twelfth birthday was due just after Christmas and she knew that when it came she would have to start working. On her last day at school she looked around the little schoolroom with sorrow in her heart, for though it was only a poky, mud-floored room in a tumbledown cottage, stifling hot in summer and damp and chill as an igloo in winter, she had been happy there. Now it was time to leave the old pedagogue who taught the children from the farms round about – at least those children whose parents could find a penny a week to pay for them to learn the basic rudiments of reading, writing and arithmetic. Most of the pupils left when they reached the age of twelve but it was the old schoolmaster's proud and justified boast that none of his pupils went into the world without basic learning, and their careful copperplate handwriting bore testimony to his teaching methods. When Aylie told the teacher that her schooling must finish and she was going out to work, he looked sadly at her and shook his head. Her quickness and eagerness to learn had made her satisfying to teach and, because he knew the story of her parentage, he could not help wondering what her life would have been like if she had been fathered by Blaize in France.

But this child, who could have been a good scholar, was the daughter of a bondager, destined to labour in the fields like her mother. As he bade her farewell he said something of this and she stared at him with a disturbing look in her eyes.

'But no matter where I was born, I'm still me! I have to go out to work but I have my own thoughts, don't I? I'm as good as anybody else.'

He had to agree for he was a poor man's son himself, though like many of his class he was over-reverent to the upper classes and convinced of their total superiority. 'But, Aylie,' he told her, 'there's not going to be the chances for you. You'll have to accept your place in society, that's what I mean.'

She bent her head and did not reply, leaving the schoolmaster with the disturbing thought that he had said something very wrong to her.

Colonel Arthur Pelham Scroggie was not a native-born Borderer but an Englishman who had gone out to India as a young ensign before the turn of the century and served in the army of the East India Company. He was one of the few who survived to come home again with a modest fortune which allowed him to retire to a part of Britain as unlike Madras as possible. He chose the Borders with its northern climate of short summers and long winters, its landscape full of trees and slowly meandering rivers because there he could pursue his passion for horses and hunting the fox without necessarily expending vast sums like huntin' gentlemen who aspired to their own packs of hounds in sporting counties farther south.

The Colonel was a widower. His wife, the daughter of a fellow officer, had succumbed to the Indian climate

111

when she was only twenty-five, leaving him with one daughter named Madeleine – a large, noisy, bouncing girl who tried hard to live up to her father's expectations.

And these were considerable – at least from Madeleine's point of view. First of all he expected that she capture a suitable husband 'with wool on his back' – which meant he should be possessed of a fortune greater than the Colonel's. Madeleine was no beauty but she was the Colonel's only daughter, a minor heiress with land to her name and, as such, highly sought after by the sons of dynastic-minded gentlemen farmers.

She might have to take her choice from the sons of Johnny-Come-Latelys but she would not be left on the shelf.

Her father's other requirement however – and the one that was nearest to his heart – was more difficult to fulfil. He wanted Madeleine to ride out beside him, stirrup to stirrup, a dashing lady after hounds. He wanted Madeleine to lead the field on the fine, but high-mettled, horses he bought for her. He wanted her to outride all the other followers of his hounds – except himself of course.

He forgot that he had learned his rough riding by going pell mell after jackal through the dry-bedded nullahs and stony plains of southern India. He expected his daughter to match him fence for fence when her only schooling ground had been the soft paddocks that enclosed their house at Maryfield. He never took into account the notion that Madeleine might be less bloodthirsty and more careful of her own neck than he was. For poor Madeleine, in spite of all her cheerful bluster, was timid in her heart and the thing she hated most in the world was fox hunting. The thing she hated second most was the horse.

In her expensive habit with its full black skirt worn over gleaming top boots and a shiny top hat tied round with a flowing band of crêpe, she looked the daughter the Colonel craved, but her heart was not in it.

When she went to bed at night she folded her hands and prayed that soon some kind man would marry her and take her away from Maryfield. She longed for the day when she would walk up the aisle to become the bride of some indolent gentleman, and she fully intended to dedicate the rest of her life to lying on chaise longues eating sweetmeats. If she lived long enough to get married, that was.

In the meantime she had to pretend for her father's sake that she enjoyed a day's hunting as much as he did. On frosty mornings when her father, in his scarlet coat, came bellowing into breakfast and informed her that they were off to draw the hill covert or to ride over to another gentleman's estate to raise a fox in his moss – which, she remembered with a sinking heart, was reputed to be bottomless – she acted out bloodthirsty enthusiasm. Madeleine had missed her true vocation. She should have been an actress.

Her father came into the dining room one day looking extraordinarily well pleased with himself.

'I've just bought you a grand little horse, Madeleine,' he informed her, rubbing his hands in glee. 'A dealer from Kelso brought it over. You wait till you see it. Your eyes will pop out, gel.'

Madeleine toyed with her game pie and forced an expression of delight on to her face. She knew the Colonel could never resist a good-looking horse. Even though its temper was atrociously bad, he would buy it for its appearance and breeding alone and then expect someone else to ride it, for he never threw a leg over the wild ones himself, pleading old age as his excuse.

'Hurry up, finish eating,' he ordered, 'and come out to the yard and see this horse. I've never seen a better. Its sire was Prince Leopold, the Duke of York's Derby winner in 1816 . . .'

Madeleine felt sick with fear. A good-looking blood horse bred from a Derby winner that arrived in the Colonel's stables as a bargain from a Kelso dealer was very bad news indeed. The horse was a lissom, red-nostrilled chestnut mare who fidgeted and sweated as she was led around the cobbled yard. It did not matter to the Colonel that his new acquisition laid back her ears and bared her teeth every time anyone went near her or lashed out with her hooves at the slightest noise, she was going to make this season's mount for Madeleine.

'She's a bit high-spirited but you like them like that, don't you?' he said to his daughter who, he often boasted, could ride anything. 'You'll look wonderful on this little mare.' Madeleine looked round the yard for the dealer who had brought this horror into her life but he had pocketed the Colonel's money and fled before the old man had time to change his mind.

The first time she was thrown up on to its back, Madeleine lasted five minutes before the mare dumped her unceremoniously on to the ground. The second time it reared up and tried to scrape her off against the stable wall as soon as her bottom touched the saddle. The third time it bolted and carried her ten times round the paddock before she could stop it by sawing frantically at its mouth.

In tears, with mud on her face and a rip in her riding skirt, she told her father, 'I *will not* ride that mare. I hate her, she's vicious and she has a mouth like iron.'

The Colonel could not believe his ears. 'Don't be silly, old gel, she's a beautiful animal. I've never seen a better-looking mare and her father was . . .' he tried to reassure her.

'I don't care if her father was Napoleon himself. I'm not going to ride her. I'm afraid of her, Father.'

He was really shocked. 'Afraid? You can't be! If you're afraid of a horse, the animal knows it. You've got to ride her to prove to yourself that you're not afraid. Come on, get up again and get over your fear. That's the only way.'

'But I *am* afraid. I'm terrified. I know that horse will kill me,' Madeleine wept, and ran into the house.

The head groom at Maryfield was a gypsy called Gilbert Kennedy, a dapper, dark-skinned man who had a wonderful way with horses. He sympathized with Miss Madeleine because he had always known how she fought to conquer her fear of horses when the Colonel forced

114

her on to greater and greater feats of daring. Without asking the Colonel's permission, Kennedy led the mare into the stable and bedded her down. He was not going to join the Colonel in persuading the girl to do something she dreaded.

Later the same day when the Colonel ordered him to saddle up the horse again for Madeleine, Kennedy improvised. 'I'm afraid the mare's going a little short in her left fore, sir,' he lied, 'I'll have to put a poultice on her leg and she can't go out today.'

'Short in her left fore!' the Colonel was highly disturbed at the news. 'Bring her out, Kennedy, and let me see.'

The mare, going perfectly sound, was trotted up and down the yard, but Kennedy persisted, pointing and saying, 'Look, sir, you can see she's going short, look at that, yes, there she goes, oh yes, she's lame all right,' until the Colonel allowed himself to be persuaded that his eyes were deceiving him. Not wanting to admit to failing to see when a horse was lame, he agreed with Kennedy and Madeleine was granted a reprieve.

She was not fooled by Kennedy's ruse, however, and hung back after her father left the stables to say, 'Thank you, Kennedy. I know the mare's perfectly sound but I'll be forced to ride her tomorrow and I'll be just as scared then.'

'Don't you worry, I'll take the steam out of her, I'll tire her out before you've got to get up on her, Miss,' promised Kennedy. 'I'll get someone to ride her into the ground.'

Jane had been slow to find her daughter a job because she could not bear the idea of sending her away from home, so during the next couple of months Aylie had hung around the stables, begging rides. Gilbert Kennedy recognized Aylie's enthusiasm, and allowed her to help with the horses. That was how she came to witness the drama between the Colonel and Madeleine. When Gilbert made his promise to Madeleine, Aylie knew this was her opportunity.

Madeleine's new mare was little over fourteen hands high and light-boned, but all the stable lads were heavily built, so that if the mare behaved well with them, she could well turn wild when a lighter rider went on her back. By rights it would be safest for her to grow used to a woman rider before letting Madeleine try her out again.

'Let me ride that mare. Please let me try. If she throws me off, I won't worry. I'm not scared of her,' Aylie pleaded with Kennedy.

The groom looked reflectively at the girl. She was just a little thing, a child, but he'd seen her handling some of the most vicious horses in the stable with calmness and authority, and he'd promised poor Miss Madeleine that he'd quieten the horse down. It was worth a try.

'All right, we'll take her out into the back paddock. Mind, if anything happens to you, it's your ain fault.'

As the mare was being saddled Kennedy's conscience pained him, but when Aylie stepped up to the horse and gently began to fondle her ears, he began to relax. This child was without fear of any kind and though the mare drew back her lips and rolled her eyes, Aylie persisted, whispering in a soft murmur that brought the animal's ears forward in an attempt to listen to what was being said to her. They stood together, the mare with her head down listening to the girl and the girl concentrating entirely on winning the animal's confidence.

After a bit she turned and said to Kennedy, 'It's all right now. Can you give me a leg up?'

She rode with her thick skirt kirtled up, showing her thin legs in the woollen stockings and heavy boy's boots that she'd worn on her walks to and from school. Her seat in the saddle was light but confident and her little hands looked capable as she gripped the reins with gently hooked fingers.

'Take a tight hold of her when you get into the field,' Kennedy warned, 'she's going to try to bolt with you.'

Then he opened the gate into the paddock and stood aside to let them pass.

The mare knew they expected her to bolt so she walked slowly out into the field and then began to buck. She tried everything to dislodge the girl on her twisting, writhing, plunging back but Aylie clung like a limpet, bottom firmly down and hands close to the horse's neck. Her thin spine twisted and turned and her long hair burst from its ribbon and flowed out behind her as, giving up bucking, the mare took off. It reared, shuddered, galloped and jumped but the girl stayed on and eventually her will predominated over that of the horse until they were cantering in tight circles round and round, back and forward with the assembled stable staff applauding enthusiastically.

Kennedy sent a message to old Archie to ask his bondager Jane if she would come to see him.

When Jane came into the yard she asked Kennedy suspiciously, 'What do you want? My lassie tells me she's been riding that wild horse of Miss Madeleine's. Can't Miss Madeleine ride it herself?'

Kennedy was, like all gypsies, an able liar. 'She's not very well and the mare needs exercising, but it's a wee animal and it can't carry a big man. Your lassie's a good jockey and I heard she's left the school and needs a job. I'll take her on here in the stables for a few months. I'll give her a half yin's wage, sixpence a day, and she can live at home with you if she rides the mare for me.'

'But it's not a job for a lassie,' said Jane with doubt in her voice. 'Women never work with horses, and how do I know she'll be safe?'

Kennedy reassured her. 'Take my word, Missus, she'll be fine. I just want her to ride the mare round every day before Miss Madeleine goes hunting. She's a great wee rider.'

Because the mother's anxiety still showed, Kennedy leaned towards Jane and said with awe in his voice, 'Your

117

bairn's a wizard on a horse. I've never seen anything like it in a lassie before.'

The following years were halcyon times for Aylie. Jane was glad that her daughter was so happy working in the Maryfield stables and though her dreams for Aylie might have been different, it pleased her that the girl was not being forced to work as a maid or take up the back-breaking toil of a bondager.

Because she was not a member of the bondager gang, Aylie did not have to be dressed in the same uniform as her mother but went to work in a dark grey drugget skirt, boots and a thick jacket. In cold weather she wrapped her head in a printed headscarf.

Aylie felt no fear and horses went smoothly for her, so smoothly that as he watched them cantering round the paddock, Gilbert felt it a great pity that the Colonel could not see how well Madeleine's mare looked when it was being properly ridden.

At first Aylie rode astride like a boy, but when she grew taller and her figure began to round out, Gilbert felt this was indelicate and he taught her to ride side saddle, which made her look even more magnificent on a horse.

Maryfield was a happy place with the easygoing Colonel as its master. So long as his hounds were running well and his horses sound, he never complained and turned a blind eye when Gilbert occasionally brought in a horse from his dealing friends, put Aylie up on it in the paddock to show its paces over fences, and made a fast sale to one of the Colonel's friends.

Apart from the time she spent with the horses, summer Saturday evenings at Maryfield were what Aylie loved best because then all the people from the cottages would gather at the nearby crossroads with the workers from nearby farms. A few of the men played fiddles and melodeons while couples danced in the dust. The lane was fringed with flowers, white meadowsweet with its heavenly scent; pink campions; tall daisies with pure white petals and yellow hearts; creeping purple vetch beneath the tangled bushes of pink-flowering dog rose. This was the backdrop to their balls, as fine a setting as any chandelier-hung ballroom as far as they were concerned. Romances flourished in the warm summer evenings while the jigs were played and old men and women, looking on with smiles on their worn faces, remembered the times when they too danced with lightness in their feet and hope in their hearts. The tunes they danced to were very old, 'The Shepherd's Rant', a stately minuet that turned the dancers into elegant figures from a bygone age, and 'The Scotch Bonnet' which sent them stamping and shouting up and down in hectic glee.

Jane rarely danced, though when she did she moved with a stately elegance that impressed her daughter. Aylie, who loved dancing, was on her feet for every tune, a wildly stepping little tomboy with an intense face and flowing hair. One late evening when the dancing was all but finished, Gilbert turned up in a group of men.

One of them was younger than the others, a flashing-eyed youth with a red handkerchief knotted round his neck and his jacket slung over one shoulder. This bold-looking boy, a gypsy from the darkness of his hair and skin, danced with all the pretty girls – though not with little Aylie – and as she watched him she thought that he was the most dashing-looking man she had ever seen.

Though he was not a great deal older than she was herself, he had the air of a man with much experience, a dangerous air that thrilled her in much the same way as the feeling of a nervous horse prancing under her.

'Who was that boy with Gilbert?' she asked her mother as they walked home in the gathering darkness.

'Which boy?' asked Jane.

'The one with the black hair and the red neckerchief.'

Jane sounded disapproving. 'Oh, *that* gypsy boy. It was Hugh Kennedy, Gilbert's son. The one who buys and sells horses, they tell me.'

Aylie was silent for a bit and then she asked, 'Was my father's hair that colour?'

Jane was genuinely shocked. 'Of course not. It was brown, dark brown, very glossy, and it waved. It was long and he'd never get it cut.'

'Was it the same colour as Hugh Kennedy's?' Aylie persisted.

'Hugh Kennedy's? No, of course it wasn't. Hugh Kennedy's hair is blue-black like a crow's wing and it looks as if he puts goose grease on it.'

'All gypsies have that sort of hair, at least all the ones I know,' said Aylie.

Jane drew herself up proudly. 'Your father wasn't a gypsy. He was an aristocrat and he looked it. He was a gentleman! And the less you know about gypsies the better, my girl, because none of them are to be trusted.'

'Gilbert's all right,' said her daughter and Jane had to agree.

'Well, yes, but he's not like the rest of them. At least he's got a job and sticks to it. Most of the others just wander around, doing this and that. That son of his, Hugh, works in the summer with labouring gangs at the harvest or the potato picking but the rest of the time he deals in horses and what he does in the winter is anyone's guess. They say he's involved with the smugglers.'

She couldn't have said anything that interested her daughter more and she regretted it as soon as the words were out of her mouth because Aylie stared back at her round-eyed. 'Involved with the smugglers? How romantic!'

On Sundays Aylie and her mother still went to the Charterhall cellar and pored over Alice's notebooks, for Jane was becoming more and more interested in her mother's old cures. When some of her neighbours in the farm cottages became sick, she started to treat them and her fame as a healer spread as her mother's had done before her. There were still people who were in awe of her as a witch but this reputation seemed to make her cures even more effective. In fact many of her treatments did smack of witchcraft for when a patient suffered from toothache she wrote a special charm on a piece of paper and hung it round the sufferer's neck. Her favourite cure for madness or derangement of the mind was to rub the affected person's forehead with a smooth slab of ivory and to ease the pains of childbirth she rubbed the labouring woman's belly with an old stone, called a toad-stone, which was really a piece of fossil fish eaten through with holes like a scrap of ancient cheese.

Aylie loved the sound of the Colonel's hounds, especially when they were out on the hill. Then their baying was like music in her ears and she felt her blood rise when she heard it. She often watched from the top of a gate as the hounds made their music among the gorse and the scarlet-coated riders streamed after them in glorious pursuit. Her eyes shone at the thought of joining in, but then she would remember: I'm only a servant.

But the Colonel had noticed Aylie, for he knew an equestrian genius when he saw one. 'That girl's a natural,' he said to Kennedy one day as they stood watching Aylie schooling Madeleine's recalcitrant mare. By now the Colonel regretted his impetuous purchase and wanted to be rid of her, but before she could be sold she had to be seen performing well on the hunting field.

'If Madeleine could ride the mare as well as that girl, we'd have an offer for her in no time,' he told Kennedy.

'You'd get a buyer quick enough if the wee lassie rode it to hounds,' suggested the groom.

The Colonel laughed at this but a couple of days later he brought up the subject again. 'Could that girl take the mare out hunting, do you think?'

Kennedy shrugged. 'You're the master, you can let people ride after your hounds or turn them away. She's a nice-looking girl and if we got her dressed up she wouldn't look like a bondager's bairn.'

They gave her an old habit of Madeleine's which was far too large, but she and Jane stitched and tucked away at it till it fitted.

Early in the morning of the meet, a maid came out of

the big house with a shiny top hat in a box and handed it to Gilbert, who carefully fitted it on Aylie's head. Then he tied a pristine white stock round her neck and stood back to survey his handiwork. She looked every inch the lady.

When she saw herself – or at least bits of herself – in the broken shard of mirror on the saddle room wall, she could not help staring in astonished admiration. The shiny black boots on her legs delighted her, the feel of the soft white gloves over her fingers made her soul cry out in joy, and when she mounted the mare and spread the generous skirt over her lap she felt magnificent.

'You look real fine,' said Gilbert.

As the stable boys chorused their agreement, she saw Gilbert's son, the dark-haired dancer, standing at the saddle room door and watching her with a peculiarly arresting stare. As she turned the horse and rode out of the yard after the Colonel and his whippers in, the gypsy boy suddenly smiled at her and she noticed how white and regular his teeth were, and how bold his eyes.

But she soon forgot even him. She forgot everything in the excitement of the chase. They ran well that day, yelling through the coverts and bursting out of the bracken in full cry. When the hounds eventually made a kill, she was the only woman up with the leaders, mud-splashed and panting but looking as beautiful as Diana.

Her bones ached as she rode into the yard and she felt so stiff from the headlong ride that when she flung herself out of the saddle, she staggered. Now she felt like Cinderella when the ball was over. She was a stable girl again.

Humming softly, she worked over the tired horse, soothing her and rubbing her down gently, cleaning the mud off her flanks and finally giving her a steaming-hot bran mash. Finally she hauled a bucket of water into the box and closed the door, shooting home its big bolt.

At that instant she heard a noise in the box next door and realized that she was not alone, for in the dimness she could see the figure of a man sitting on a pile of horse blankets.

'My word, aren't you a grand-looking lady,' he said in a softly teasing tone, 'but they tell me you're only a bondager's bairn.'

She bristled. She hated being called a bondager's bairn. 'So what? My mother's a bondager but that doesn't mean I'm some sort of animal, does it? Your father's a groom, what does that make you?'

He laughed and came out of the box into the passageway. In doing so he passed a hand over the muzzle of the listening mare and she noticed that he unconsciously made this gesture with the same sort of tender affection as she would have done herself.

'One to you. Of course it doesn't matter,' he agreed. 'I just think you look very fine. I like a fine-looking girl. You've heard the song "The Lady and the Gypsy", haven't you?'

She looked at him harder. It was easy to tell this man was a gypsy, but it was not only his swarthy skin and curling dark hair that gave him away, it was his effrontery as well.

He introduced himself. 'I'm Gilbert Kennedy's son. My name's Hugh.'

'I know who you are,' she said, sweeping past him, 'and if you don't mind I've got to go and get changed out of all this finery into a bondager bairn's clothes again.'

Madeleine's suitor was brought to the point of proposing in the summer of 1830 and their marriage was set for that autumn, after the harvest had been gathered in and before her father's new hunting season began.

The ceremony and a lavish reception for guests from all over the country was to be at Maryfield. On the night before the wedding, the Colonel threw a party for all the servants and workers on the estate. Tables covered with food and bottles were set out in the barn and a fiddle band was hired to provide the music.

They ate and they drank; they toasted the bride and groom and most of all they toasted their favourite, the Colonel, who sat beaming at the top table. Then they all

123

danced. Aylie, sitting with her mother at the back of the barn, was astonished to see Hugh Kennedy, who should by rights not have been there at all, walk up to the top table and proffer his hand to Madeleine. She looked astonished but on such an occasion she could not refuse to dance with him, though both her father and her insipid blond groom looked thoroughly disapproving of his cheek.

The couple took the floor – Madeleine large, blonde and highly coloured like one of the cream-filled puddings that the Maryfield cook had provided for the feast; Hugh needle-sharp, dark-haired, brown-skinned and dangerous. It was obvious that by asking the bride to dance he was making a point and everyone in the barn, including his mortified father, knew it.

Poor Madeleine, not a sensitive woman, knew she was being used. But she kept her dignity and when the music stopped she curtsied stiffly before he handed her back to the top table. He walked back to his own seat with a smile, and Aylie heard her mother take a sharp intake of breath. She remembered Jane's warning words: 'Gypsies are dangerous.'

The trouble was that, after her adventures on the hunting field, Aylie had acquired a taste for danger and when Hugh came up to ask her to dance she leapt to her feet eagerly – too eagerly, her mother thought.

Hugh was a wonderful dancer, nimble on his feet and bold with his eyes, and he made Aylie feel like a woman, and a desirable woman too. She forgot her still knobbly knees and skinny arms; she forgot her lack of a decent bust and her boyish hips; her childish awkwardness fell away when she was in his arms.

As he released her from the spell after the last bar of music he held on to her hand for a brief moment and said, 'You're almost as good on the dance floor as you are on a horse. You're a funny little thing, aren't you?'

'I'm not so little,' she said defensively, drawing herself up to her full five foot five inches, and he laughed, showing his magnificent teeth.

'I'll come back for you when you've grown up then,' he said, and disappeared into the throng.

With the marriage and departure of Madeleine, the Colonel grew even more lax and indulgent in his manner of treating his servants. The house more or less ran itself; the butler helped himself to the Colonel's port and the maids grew fat on the cook's dishes. In the stables Gilbert was more master than his employer, and when the Colonel was looking for a second whip in the winter of 1832, he suggested that there was no need to bring in another man when they had Aylie.

This time there was no objection from Colonel Scroggie. His only stipulation was that she could not be kitted out in a pink coat. She was to dress like a lady in order to avoid scandal.

On a cold, dull day in December two years later Aylie, on a fidgety grey gelding, was scrambling after the Colonel over the most slippery slope of the Black Hill. They had been hunting the pack for over an hour and hadn't yet managed to raise a scent, for the wind was high and any traces a fox left behind were blown away very quickly.

'We'll draw that covert down there, there's sometimes a fox in it,' he shouted back to her, gesturing with his whip hand at a clump of trees below them. She collected her reins and, holding the horse in tight, for it tended to be loose footed, slid rather than walked down the slope. The Colonel was waiting for her at the bottom.

'You go to the far side and keep a watch,' he instructed, 'I'll hunt them from the back.'

None of the other hunt followers had managed to keep up with them and they were on their own, with the questing hounds rushing to and fro in search of a scent.

The Colonel urged them into the patch of scrubby trees while Aylie cantered round to the back of the covert, where she sat easily in the saddle waiting for them to re-emerge. Within a very short time she was rewarded for,

125

heads down and baying, the hounds burst out almost under her nose after a flying red streak, Mr Fox. In full cry, headed by old Warrior, the hounds took off across the slope of the nearest field and disappeared over the horizon. Rising in her saddle and giving a shrill scream, Aylie swung her horse round and followed them at full gallop, her blood up.

It was a good scent and the fox was only just in front of the hounds as they ran on for over two miles, baying savagely as they went. Aylie, jubilant, rode on their tails and when she glanced over her shoulder she could see the Colonel on his big bay closing in on her fast. By the time they reached a big hedge that marked the main road, they were riding shoulder to shoulder. When the Colonel's horse saw the size of the obstacle, however, he suddenly turned his head, stuck in his toes and refused to take it.

His rider, mortified and scarlet in the face, laid into the horse with his whip while calling to Aylie, 'You set your horse at it. He'll follow you over.'

The hedge was high and Aylie knew that on the other side was a deep, water-filled ditch. It would be necessary to make the horse spread itself wide to get across it. Purposefully she wheeled the grey to the right, rode a short way back across the field and then, with deliberation, swung round again in a canter, gathering the horse together as she set it at the hedge. Both she and the horse knew that they were risking their necks and she was only too aware of the huge effort that was necessary. Her urgency communicated itself to her mount as, heads down, they raced towards the hedge that looked bigger and bigger the closer it got. In the final approach she felt the animal gather itself together under her legs, change its stride on the approach and then launch itself bravely into the sky. Not for the first time she was awed by the boldness and bravery of a horse and after what seemed like an eternity, they landed safely on the other side. The horse slid on to its belly in the mud but Aylie clung to its neck and kept her seat. They were over! They'd made it!

Jubilantly grinning, she looked back over her shoulder and saw the girth-ringed belly of the Colonel's horse rising into the air. Then as she watched, it buckled at the knees on landing and fell on its side; she saw the anguished expression on the Colonel's face as he hit the ground and she heard the terrible thump and groan as the wind was driven out of the horse's belly.

Under her horrified stare, they lay still on the grass, sprawled with legs in all directions and heads lolling. The chase and the baying hounds were forgotten as she turned her horse to gallop back to where the Colonel lay like a red-coated rag doll on the muddy bank.

The death of Colonel Scroggie meant the end of the good days for everyone on Maryfield. Safe in her elegant mansion on the other side of the country, Madeleine was anxious to be rid of her Borders property quickly, and it was sold to a hard-eyed farmer who gave all the workers their notice. It was reckoned to be a bad move to retain old staff when a property changed hands because they were always sunk in old ways and the people at Maryfield had enjoyed the good life too long, said the farmers round about. It was time they got back to real work and hard living.

Archie and Bertha, downcast, packed up their things once again and prepared to take themselves off to the poor's house. They were growing grey now; all their children had left home and they had saved nothing from their years of toil. They knew they were too old to find another place. Jane, anguished, faced up to the fact that she would have to go to another hiring fair. The memory of her only experience at Earlston was still vivid and painful.

Aylie was simply confused. She did not know what was happening and she was so traumatized by the memory of the Colonel's dead body beside his mortally injured horse

127

that she could no longer ride, far less face another head-long chase after hounds.

Once again moving day was to be 12 May, but before that they all had to find other places. Where were they to go?

Aylie had never stood at a hiring fair but she had heard her mother's story often enough. Fair day always seemed to be cold and wet, and this year was no exception for it was raining and the wind was howling just as fiercely as it had on the day Jane first went there. Jane looked bent and ill. She was going to be old soon, her daughter realized for the first time, and the thought gave her a frisson of terror. She could not envisage a life without her mother.

She noticed that Jane's hands, once so slender and adroit, were now swollen and red. They had been giving her much pain, which she tried unsuccessfully to hide from her daughter but, more successfully, from anyone who might be prepared to offer her a position.

Farming was better that year, the economy was on the rise and there had been a good harvest, so farmers had money to spend.

Once again the Red Lion Inn was crowded, and even before nine o'clock drunk men could be seen sprawling along the horseshoe-shaped benches in the public bar, singing, cursing or muttering to themselves.

Jane still stuck to her original specification for a post; it had to be on a place from where she could see the Eildons. Though she was offered work in various places, for she made an impressive figure as she stood like a tall pine tree in the square, she turned them all down. Eventually a middle-aged man in a brown smock came up and asked her terms. When she told him, he appeared satisfied and said, 'I've been hired for Lilybank, it's changing hands this coming term. Will you come there as my bondager?'

She looked hard at him. 'You're not needing a wife?'

He shook his head.

'I'll not share your bed, you know.'

He shook his head again. 'That's all right. It won't be necessary.'

'In that case, I'll take your job.'

The main reason she'd agreed was because Lilybank was the next farm to Charterhall.

Jane shouldered her way through the crowds in Earlston square, looking for her daughter. All around her were excited groups of men and women, standing chattering in the middle of the square or clustered around lines of stalls selling bits of pottery, squares of jaw-clamping toffee, gingerbread and sugar-plum cake. She rushed past squatting peddlers displaying swatches of brightly coloured material, Kerseymere shawls and bundles of multi-coloured ribbons. One of them was the old peddler who had sold her the sea-green material for her gown, and though she nodded and smiled to him, she did not stop.

There were labourers offering roughly carved dolls and spinning tops that they had made during their meagre leisure hours to the other farm workers trailing around the fair with gaggles of children. An Aunt Sally stall with grinning heads waiting to be knocked down by muscle-armed rustics was doing brisk business. She was held up by a throng of people listening to a loud-voiced busker yelling out the attractions on show inside his flag-hung tent: 'Come in, come, pay your threepence and see the bearded woman, the two-headed calf and' – dramatic pause – 'the mermaid's baby. It was born with fins instead of arms, folks!'

People jostled past her with their coins held out, but even if she had been interested in the display, which she was not, Jane wouldn't have stopped because she had to find Aylie. She searched through the tight-packed throng in the hall and was heading for the Red Lion when, outside the bar door, she found Aylie talking to Gilbert Kennedy. Her depression seemed to have been lifted and her eyes were bright and her face once again alive and youthful because of the excitement of the occasion.

Jane grasped her arm gently and said, 'I've got a place,

it's at Lilybank on the other side of Charterhall. Do you want me to try to get you fixed up there as well? They might still be looking for more bondagers.'

Aylie smiled at her mother. 'Oh, I'm glad you're fixed up, Ma. Lilybank marches with the Hepburns' place on the other side, doesn't it? You'll be with all your old friends. Don't worry about me, Gilbert here was just telling me about a job at a place near Jeddart.'

'Jeddart!' gasped Jane.

Local people always named the town of Jedburgh as Jeddart. Though it was only about fifteen miles away, Aylie might as well have told her mother that she was planning to go to London.

The girl knew the reason for her mother's consternation. 'Don't worry, it's on *this* side of Jeddart. I won't be so far away. Anyway I mightn't take it, I've got to speak to the steward first.'

She did not tell her mother that she felt a great need to move out of the tight five-mile radius in which she had lived her life. She wanted to be independent and no longer Jane Cannon's bairn, as everyone at Maryfield knew her. Like so many young people since time began, she longed to see more of the world and, for her, going to Jedburgh was almost as adventurous as someone else with a wider horizon setting sail for Canada.

When Gilbert had told her about the possible job and added, 'My son Hugh thought you might like it over there. It's grand open country on the top of the hills and he knows some of the people on the farm,' that made her eager to seal the bargain even though, when she spoke to the farm steward, she found him a surly and unfriendly man. She saw doubts on Gilbert's face as well, but she ignored them.

The steward's terms seemed fair – the farmer needed a girl to work half the time on the land and the other half in the house. He'd pay tenpence a day for land work and she'd get her keep and three pounds a year for house duties. She accepted his shilling arles and agreed to start at Myreheugh on the moving day in May.

*

The place was well named. The farmhouse huddled defensively in a muddy hollow beside an old humpbacked bridge that carried the ancient Roman road of Dere Street over to the Cheviot Hills. A chill wind seemed to blow all the time at Myreheugh, even when the skies were blue, and it was a grim-looking place, the atmosphere not lightened by the fact that the faces of the people working there were withdrawn and reserved as if, like the house and the farm, they were deeply suspicious of strangers.

With her small trunk Aylie arrived on the carter's waggon and was told by a hard-faced old cook that she had to sleep in the servants' room in an attic over the kitchen where the cook herself and the housemaid, Phemie Anderson, also slept.

Aylie heaved her trunk up the narrow stair and was surprised at how small the attic was, hardly bigger than a hen coop and filled by a bed with scanty coverings.

'I don't have to share the bed, do I?' she asked when she came back into the kitchen.

The cook placed her red fists on her hips and demanded, 'What's wrong with sharing a bed? Phemie and me are clean.'

'I don't want to share a bed,' said Aylie firmly. 'I'll sleep on the floor if necessary.'

'Then you do that,' was the cook's reply. 'It's probably what you're used to.'

Phemie came in during this exchange and listened silently to the two women arguing. She was about the same age as Aylie, but completely different in appearance for she was a white-faced, hunted-looking girl who started in fright every time anyone spoke to her and whose white-lashed, red-rimmed eyes seemed to be perpetually in danger of overflowing with tears. Her only claim to beauty was a long fall of straight yellow hair that she slowly combed out every night before going to sleep.

That night Phemie and the cook, Meg Mather, slept together in the double bed while Aylie was bedded down on a pile of clothes beneath a little window through which a vicious draught howled. She lay on the lumpy bedding and regretted her eagerness to leave her mother, for the atmosphere in Myreheugh had been overall so hostile that she felt bitterly sorry she had not listened to Jane and checked out what the place was like before she agreed to work there. Why had Hugh Kennedy said she'd like it? He must have been playing one of his jokes, like the night he asked Madeleine to dance. Her heart burned with resentment. Just let him wait till she saw him again!

The mistress, a grim-looking minister's daughter who felt that by marrying a farmer she had lowered herself socially, spent most of her waking hours in a parlour jam packed with heavy furniture and gloomy paintings of her ancestors. There she brooded like a solitary malevolent owl, only making occasional swoops on the servants, tweaking their cheeks and upbraiding them in uncompromising terms. Nothing they did ever seemed to please her. She was a miserable woman with no children and few friends, so carriages never came rolling down the Myreheugh road with callers as they used to do at Maryfield. There were none of the cheerful comings and goings that Aylie had been used to.

She observed the domestic life of her employers with dismay and very soon realized that all exchanges between husband and wife were short and peremptory, made only for the sake of the listening servants. She was sure that when they were alone, they never spoke to each other at all, and each seemed to hold irreconcilable grievances against the other.

What was the biggest disappointment was that Phemie, a girl of her own age with whom she had hoped to become friendly, only spoke to her when it was absolutely necessary. Annoyed by this, Aylie turned on her when they were alone in the farmyard and said abruptly, 'You don't have much to say, do you? I've never seen you before. Where's your home?'

The reaction was as if she had asked some taboo question, for the girl shot an anguished and suspicious glance at her before replying, 'I'm from Bowden.'

'Do you come from a farm place over there?' Aylie knew most of the working people in that district through hunting round it with the Colonel.

'No, my father's the tailor there,' said Phemie.

Like all Borderers, Aylie was pleased as soon as she could place a stranger. She relaxed a little and grinned. 'Oh, I know him. He used to come up to Maryfield for orders when I was there with my mother. That was my last place.'

She remembered the old tailor, as white-faced and frail-looking as his daughter, who came to the farm cottages and sat cross-legged on a table while he sewed away at the cloth his customers had chosen. He only worked for men of course, women made their own clothes, but his tailoring was famous round about because it was always immaculate. Gilbert Kennedy, who like most head grooms was excessively dressy and fastidious about his clothes, had once said that suits made by Anderson rivalled in cut any the Colonel brought up from London. She repeated this compliment to his daughter and the strange girl smiled at last. She seemed pleased that Aylie thought well of her father.

They had walked around the corner of the cow byre and out of sight of the kitchen window, so Aylie put the metal scoop into the hen-food bucket and sat on the edge of the stone water trough, prepared to chat.

She asked Phemie, 'Come on, you can tell me. What's this place like? I'm beginning to wish I'd never come here. Nobody talks to you.'

The other girl did not sit down beside her but glanced back over her shoulder in a frightened way as if she were afraid to be caught slacking. 'It's the mistress, she's always picking fault. Servants never stay with her more than six months or a year,' she whispered.

'How long have you been here?' Aylie asked.

Phemie looked harried. 'This'll be my third year, but the master's a cousin of my father. That's why I came.'

Aylie was horrified. 'Three years in this place! You could leave and get another hiring. There's plenty of places for girls with experience of housework, or you could be a bondager like my mother. After only one day of house work, I think field work's better. At least you're out in the open and you're independent. Your time off's your own. It's better fun too. Women on the land aye have plenty of jokes and company. I'll be off next hiring day, I can tell you.'

Phemie was fidgeting, plainly anxious to get back to work. 'I can't leave here, my father wouldn't let me. He thinks it better for me to work for a relation than to a stranger. Little does he know!'

Her words were bitter and her face as haggard as an old woman's. She looked as if she did not get enough to eat. Aylie felt a sudden welling up of sympathy for this miserable girl.

'Well, if the mistress is a bitch, what's the boss like?' she wanted to know.

At this question Phemie seemed to fly into a panic and the words rushed from her. 'Oh, keep away from him. He's my second cousin but he's an awful man. Just keep out of his sight as much as you can.' It sounded like a heartfelt warning.

Anything previously experienced by Aylie or told to her by her mother did not prepare her for Myreheugh. She had heard the usual labourers' horror stories about farmers who held back wages; who raised sticks to workers; who cheated on their annual fixed allowances of potatoes or milk. She'd heard about men and women having to work in the fields when they were ill or till they were dropping with exhaustion, but she had never encountered such indifference to human feelings as she met with at Myreheugh.

The farmer — a fat, waddling man with a mottled, heavily veined face and mean pig-like eyes — never addressed anyone except in a hectoring shout. Many times she saw him bring his heavy metal-tipped stick down on the back of the hinds and orra men. A halfwit boy who could do nothing to defend himself was one of his favourite targets.

The boy's mother, a bent, grey-haired bondager, stood by silently and watched her son being beaten, her eyes like those of a helpless wounded animal.

'Why don't you stop him beating your laddie? He's doing no harm, he's just a bit slow,' Aylie protested to the woman one morning after a particularly vicious attack by the farmer on the boy.

The old woman shook her head at the girl. 'Look at me, lassie. I'm an old woman and he's not right in the head. Where would we ever get another place? Nobody would want us. If we didn't stay here, it would be the poor's house or we'd starve.'

There were eight other bondagers on the farm and they all worked silently with their heads down and spared no time for gossip. Everyone was anxious to get the work over as quickly as possible and spare themselves from their employer's wrath. At Myreheugh there were no Saturday night dances, no fiddle or melodeon playing, no cheerful meetings or singsongs in each other's cottages. The people were perpetually sunk in poverty and despondency, for their employer docked money off their wages for jobs he said were badly done, and there were many weeks when they ended up with less money than it took to feed themselves. The hovel-like cottages had holes in the thatches and no glass in the windows, which had to be stuffed with rags to keep out the perpetual wind.

They were full of starved-looking children who never went to school and downtrodden wives who bitterly resented having to find food for a bondager as well as for the other hungry mouths beneath their roofs.

Aylie was lucky. She got fed in the kitchen on the scraps from her employers' table and she slept on a watertight floor. To her relief the bulk of her work was out of doors and because she was strong and able, she came in for little criticism. In fact, she sometimes felt as if the farmer was favouring her and that made her uneasy. From time to time he stopped to talk to her, his little eyes glinting and his wet, red mouth half open as he stared at her. He made her feel tainted and she always drew her shawl carefully over her breasts before she stopped to answer him.

'Watch him, he's mad for the lassies,' warned an old hind who had eventually befriended the girl when he realized he had known her grandfather.

'I'm watching him very carefully,' she agreed.

She had been at Myreheugh for two months, and a very long time it seemed, when Hugh Kennedy arrived riding an eye-rolling, rangy black horse. He was looking very dashing in a battered cocked hat with a feather and a coat with embossed brass buttons which must once have graced the back of a gentleman.

When he saw Aylie in the field with the other women he grinned and waved his whip to her. It was break time so she could go over to speak to him without fear of reprimand.

She grabbed his stirrup iron to stop him riding off, and said accusingly, 'Why did you get me this place? It's awful. The farmer and his wife are horrible people. I'm afraid of them both.'

He leaned down teasingly towards her and said, 'Come on, don't tell me that! You're not afraid of anything. I know you. Don't you worry about old Myreheugh. He won't try anything on with you because if he does, Hugh Kennedy'll get him.'

Then the farmer came waddling out of the house and held up a hand, gesturing to Hugh to go across to him, but the gypsy sat proudly on his horse, staring boldly over without deference at the fat man. He was forced to walk across the mud to stand at the horse's shoulder. As he came up, he gestured to Aylie to leave so she could not hear what was being said between them, but she watched closely and eventually saw Hugh's shoulders rise in a cheeky shrug. Then he raised his hand in a mock salute and with a loud laugh, rode off.

The mother of the halfwitted boy asked Aylie, 'Do you know young Kennedy?'

The girl nodded, 'Yes, I know him, I used to work with his father.'

'Oh, I ken Gilbert too, he's not like his son. That's a dangerous one. Some folk say he'll end on the gallows. He's into everything.'

'He's into everything . . .' The words rang in Aylie's ears as she worked at cleaning what seemed to be acres of muck out of the big cowshed. It was the filthiest task on the farm and she was glad to have something other than the smell to occupy her mind. She went over the short meeting with Hugh Kennedy. How did he get a horse like that? It was a blood horse, worth a bit of money, yet he was only a labourer like herself. And why was he not out working like all the other labourers? Where was he working anyway? She realized that she knew little about him but that his appeal, the feeling of adventure that he gave off, acted on her as a linseed trail did to a hound. She had to follow it and no amount of warning would put her off.

They were unable to work because of the rain when he came the next time. All the bondagers were huddled into the hay shed watching the rain teeming down and turning the dirty yard to a sea of mud. The women's depression was intensified by the knowledge that until it stopped and they were able to go back to the fields, there would be no pay for them.

Aylie, who was saving in order to take a nest egg home to her mother as the only bonus from this dreadful year, sat with her clenched fists supporting her head in the battered and discoloured straw hat. There was no incentive at Myreheugh to keep herself smart or spend money on black japanning for her bonnet.

Then, through the grey sheets of rain, came Hugh Kennedy on a different but equally flashy horse. He jumped off and, leading it by the reins, came into the shed to sit beside her on the hay, letting the horse nuzzle his pockets for a titbit. The terrible memory of the Colonel's death was beginning to recede for Aylie and

137

her love of horses came sweeping over her as strong as ever when she stroked the velvety muzzle and let the soft, tentative lips search over the palm of her hand.

'I came to tell you that there's a meeting up in the schoolroom tonight,' said Hugh, 'I wondered if you'd want to go.'

She was surprised and interested. 'What's it about?'

His voice was low as he replied, 'It's about forming a union, there's a lot of talking going on and some people are going to speak against the bondage system. I thought you might be interested.'

She was very interested. Her experiences since she left Maryfield had taught her that the conditions of labouring people, especially labouring women, were an insult to human dignity. Now from first-hand experience she knew women who were downtrodden and allowed themselves to be treated like animals by their hinds in order to keep a job; she knew others who were forced to share the hind's bed while his bitter wife slept in the next room with her children. She knew women who lived in an atmosphere of sheer hell because of the jealousies, justified or otherwise, of the hind's wife. Aylie's own proud spirit hated the idea that any of those indignities might be forced on her or her beloved mother. So far they had been lucky, but how long would their luck last? Now she knew that there were few Colonel Scroggies in her world. People like her and Jane needed work and they had no bargaining power at all, for once they signed or made their cross on a bond, they were literally the property of the man they'd signed themselves away to for a year. To break it was to bring down on yourself a lifetime of unemployment.

'I'll go,' she said with decision.

'It starts at seven o'clock,' Hugh told her.

He said nothing about meeting her there or even if he was going himself. When she told Phemie that she was going out to a meeting about the union campaign, the other girl was shocked.

'You'd better not, word'll get out if you're seen there.

138

You won't get another job so easily if you're a troublemaker.'

Phemie had gradually come to speak openly to Aylie and to relax when she was with her but there was still something hidden and secret about her that she would not divulge.

'I'm not a troublemaker. I'm only going to listen to what's said. Why don't you come too?'

Aylie's colour was high and she was excited at the prospect of her outing, but Phemie refused to go, making a variety of feeble excuses.

'Then I'll come back and tell you what goes on,' said Aylie.

Later that night she went out into the rain with her shawl drawn up over her head and a layer of sacking across her shoulders. In spite of its protection she was soaking when she reached the little schoolroom about a mile and a half away. To her surprise it was packed full of people she had never seen before. They were mostly men – only two or three women could be seen among the throng – and the workers at Myreheugh were represented only by Aylie herself. There was no sign of Hugh.

She sat on a bench at the back of the dark room and gazed around. The first thing that struck her was that everyone looked angry.

Their anger reflected the mood of the whole Borders during 1835 because the much-vaunted Reform Bill of 1832, in spite of everyone's high hopes, had done nothing for the labouring classes. Even after the new legislation was enacted and the franchise was extended, only one man in eight in Scotland had the vote. The rest remained disenfranchised landless labourers or industrial workers who were dominated by employers all eagerly intent on improving their social status and making themselves rich, rich, rich.

Yet, because the Scots had a reverence for learning, there were among them many men of the mould of Adam Cannon and his brother-in-law Tom Armstrong, as politically conscious, intelligent and well read as the men who denied them a vote. Most of the hinds on Border farms could read and write and many of them made up songs and poetry with a fluency which would have won them acclaim in other societies. These were the men who were furiously angry. Their women, on the other hand, had so few expectations that they were rarely disappointed.

The anger of some families took them off the land which they loved but where they had no prospects except to slave for the rest of their lives. They went to the growing industrial towns of the district where emergent woollen and cloth mills were turning out rolls of cloth to be sent south. The Borderers had long been known for their skill at weaving but till the early nineteenth century it had been a cottage industry, centred in small villages. Now it was concentrated in two or three towns where mill owners built new buildings and installed new machinery powered most efficiently by the swiftly running Border rivers. One day there would be work aplenty, for women as well as for men.

Yet although those who went to the town earned more money and were free of the feudalism that had ruled their lives, amid the noise of the clattering mills they still dreamed of the fields and the lonely hills. They were a rural people, bred from a race that had always lived on the land and did not take kindly to being penned up from the early morning mill whistle to the end of the shift at nightfall.

Others, more adventurous, were driven by their disappointment after 1832 to go abroad. In this way the most dynamic people removed themselves from the scene, leaving the more timid and acquiescent behind.

Ships sailed every day out of Greenock for Canada and America with their quota of emigrant Borderers, men and women weeping at the pain of leaving their cottages and farmsteads. Their homes were lonely and abandoned, crumbling into piles of stones, the haunt of ravens and foxes. Eventually only spring snowdrops or rose bushes with sweetly scented flowers clambering round broken

140

stone lintels in summertime marked what had once been a garden. The pain of leaving their homeland gave rise to the songs of nostalgia and longing that exiled Borderers – and emigrant Scots everywhere – sang with such feeling.

Those who remained behind discussed the news that filtered slowly through to them and they suffered silently under their sense of impotence. Like the patient, plodding horses so many of them drove over the land, they were weighed down by the demands of employers and over that, by the feudal dominance that was exercised in the entire Borderland by the gentry – dukes, lords and earls who knew without question that they were not like other men. They expected that their slightest whim would be gratified by people who, in many cases, shared their ancestry of thieving Border reivers. But no one dared to say that a duke's ancestors had only been more unprincipled, more savage rogues than the ancestors of those who touched their forelocks to him.

From her seat Aylie watched the crowd and listened to their talk. Though no one actually said it, the main strain of complaint was that they had been denied the rights of other men; they felt as good as anyone else but equality was officially denied them.

The muttering and murmuring was growing when, from a door that connected with the schoolmaster's but-and-ben, Hugh appeared with another two men. He stood silently for a few seconds surveying the gathering and this was a Hugh she had never seen before. Now his dark face looked determined and it made his alien gypsy blood very evident. Then he spoke . . .

'There's no use you all just grumbling and groaning,' he said in a loud voice. 'There's no good making speeches to each other and drawing up useless petitions. In the south they've taken up their cudgels, they've rioted, they're out breaking windows, they've even dragged dukes off their horses . . .'

The crowd gasped at the enormity of that idea!

'That's what *we* want to do. We want to show that we've been treated like dogs for too long. We're labourers, at the mercy of the men who hire us and we trust to luck that they'll be men with a sense of fair play and honesty. But you know and I know that they're not all like that.

'There's many rogues among them, men who cheat us and swindle us, who treat us with less consideration than they treat their dogs and horses. Don't stand for it. Fight back. If we were all to stop working, we'd have better wages pretty soon. If we were to stop working the bondage system wouldn't last. Who among you doesn't think it a sin for a man to have to find a bondager to work in the fields with him? He has to pay her wages, he has to keep a stranger woman in his house, because without her he can't get a job. That way farmers get two pairs of hands for the price of one!'

An old woman in the middle of the crowd raised her voice at this. 'It's just as bad for us bondagers. We don't like it either. We'd rather be free to make our own bargains with the farmers but the way it is now we're cheated and ill treated by two masters.'

But the audience were men and they had little time for women's complaints. Some of them shouted the old woman down.

Hugh went on, raising his voice above the uproar, 'Don't worry, old woman, if the bondage was done away with you could make your own bargains. What we want to make sure is that the farmers and the landowners know how we feel about bondage and about many other things. We want decent housing; we want decent wages; we want decent working hours.

'They keep us out in the fields till after midnight at harvest time without extra pay – and if the farmer sends out a bottle of whisky to the men to make them work harder, they cheer him! He should be paying for the hours they work, not numbing their minds with whisky. And look at the houses you all live in. The pigs in their styes and the cows in the byres have better cover against the weather. Their roofs don't leak; their walls keep out

142

the winds – yet your houses are neither watertight nor windproof. Don't stand for it. Fight back.'

An old man called, 'And how do you suggest we fight back, gypsy?'

Hugh's black eyes were flashing. 'Don't work, lean on your hoes and your spades. Don't harness your horses in the morning. If you all do that, the farmers will have to make things better. They can't and won't work the land on their own. And if that doesn't work, there are other things we can do – you know that as well as me. They've done it in the south.'

But the crowd was unconvinced. One man yelled out, 'Aye, and they've gone to Botany Bay for their trouble!'

Everyone had grumbles but they were timid and afraid. Aylie sat still in her seat as the meeting broke up and she heard people saying to each other as they left, 'And who'll feed my bairns if I've no money coming in? What's to stop the farmer going out and hiring another man? Where would I be then without a house or a penny in my pocket?'

What she had heard was a revelation to Aylie. It summed up everything she had dimly felt throughout her childhood and adolescence: the perception of the differences imposed on people by their class; the realization of the lack of hope for betterment that afflicted the people she knew. Even her mother, the woman she most admired in the world, was an acquiescent bond slave, tied to her toil without hope of anything better. In time, Aylie would be the same – unless, unless, unless what? She could not visualize any alternative.

She remembered the well-off men and women she had seen while hunting the Colonel's horses. They had the same bodies as the men and women with whom she worked but their lives were so different that they could have been the inhabitants of another world. If they got wet or cold while out with the hounds, they went home to hot baths and attentive servants. They had no perception of what it was like to be wet, cold and hungry day after day after day. If they endured bad weather while

143

hunting, that was sport to them, but they did not know what it was to face the cutting wind and driving rain in order to earn enough money to put a basic meal in your belly; to sleep crowded together on hay-filled mattresses covered with threadbare blankets.

Hugh's speech had fired her, he had wakened her up to the injustices around her. She felt as angry and as desperate as he had looked when he stood addressing the crowd. Then he had been transformed from the teasing, idle gypsy into something else, a man with a purpose. He had made one convert to his cause.

She was the last person left in the room and as he glanced across at her, he was struck by the animation of her face.

I don't want this, he told himself. I don't want to have anything to do with her. I've got too much to do.

The first time he saw her she was only a child coping with a difficult horse, and even then her face had caught his attention because it was so alive and vibrant. Tonight he saw that though she had been soaked by the rain and her clothes were plain she did not look like a bondager but a high-born lady, the lady he had teased her about being when he met her in the stables in Maryfield.

He could not resist calling out to her in his old teasing way, 'Come on, little lady, come down here and tell me what you thought about our meeting.'

She gathered her rough, mud-hemmed skirt in one hand and stepped between the benches. 'I thought you were marvellous,' she said, 'but you know you'll never get them to do anything. I hope you know that.'

'Would you do anything if you could?' Her intensity struck home with him. He could see he had impressed her.

'I'd do anything I could. I think the way many of us live is foul. I think we're fools to put up with it.'

He was completely the teasing gypsy again, head on one side, confident and very male. 'Foul, fools . . . good words, I'll remember them next time. Come on, it's dark and raining. I'll see you get back to Myreheugh without falling into a bog.'

Of course he had a horse, he never seemed to go anywhere without a horse. It was tied up in the school-master's byre and when he climbed into the saddle, he put down a hand for her to climb up behind him. It was good to be on a horse again and she sat on the crupper with her arms wrapped tightly round his waist. Then the two of them took off at a hard canter which rapidly developed into a gallop.

They sped through the darkness and she clung close to him, feeling the muscles of his back beneath her own body. He was wildly conscious of her too, and as if to deny his feelings he began to whoop and yell like a madman as they tore along the rutted road and eventually into the yard of Myreheugh. Then with an upraising of his hand, he reined in the sweating horse. When he handed her down to the ground, he lightly printed a kiss on her lips with one of his fingers.

'One day you'll be quite a woman,' he told her. 'Don't forget what you heard tonight. We're going to fight them.'

Again he disappeared out of her life for many weeks but she was too abstracted by work and other worries to brood about it much. She had gone home to see her mother the Sunday after listening to Hugh speak and was concerned to realize how much pain Jane was suffering from what she called the rhematicks in her hands. Aylie took them in her own and gently caressed them. They were covered with the fingerless woollen gloves that her mother had taken to wearing all the time.

'Do you wear those pokies on your hands every day, even when it's sunny and warm?' she asked.

Jane nodded and silently peeled off the pokies, holding out her hands towards her daughter. They were misshapen and horribly swollen, each finger joint red and almost visibly throbbing.

Aylie was full of pity for her mother's pain. 'Oh, how they must hurt you! Oh, Mam, they're so swollen.'

Jane's hands lay in hers, trustfully like the hands of a child, and Jane nodded. 'Yes, they're sore. But it's worse when the weather's cold or when it's raining.'

Aylie looked at the enlarged knuckle joints and the paper-thin skin. She could almost feel the throbbing pain of it herself. 'Have you done anything about it?' she asked.

Her mother grimaced. 'I'm not much of a recommendation for my own cures, am I? I'm trying out some of my mother's recipes. She prescribed onion wine . . . in her notes she said it makes people live a long time, but it doesn't help my hands. I've tried drinking pansy water but you have to take a lot of it, several pints a day, and wild pansies are hard to find round here. The best thing I've found is dried meadowsweet because it helps to kill the pain, especially at night when it stops me sleeping.'

Aylie remembered Hugh's impassioned speech about the rigours of labouring life and she said angrily, 'You shouldn't have to work so hard. You should be living a quieter life, not going out in the cold and the wet. That's for young people like me.'

Jane gave her lovely giggle. 'Oh, bairn, I'm not ancient, you know. I'm just forty-one. But I know that I can't go on in the fields much longer. The pain and the swelling is in my knees and my feet too, now. Soon I'll not be able to bend, perhaps not be able to walk very far.'

The girl was terrified by this information. 'Oh Mam, what're you going to do?'

'You know Jock Hepburn? He wanted to marry me when I was young but I wouldn't have him. Well, he says he'll take me on as a servant in his house. I like his wife and his bairn and it wouldn't be hard work, but I'm not going to presume on Jock's old love for me and I don't want Flora to feel jealous. No, I've decided to set myself up as a howdie and a healer like my mother was. There's plenty of people come to me for cures and I'm getting better at it all the time. I'm going to do that, Aylie.'

This sounded like a good idea except for one thing.

Aylie asked the question that came first to her mind: 'But where will you live? You'll need a house.'

Jane smiled. 'I've thought of that too. I'm going back to live in Charterhall.'

'In Charterhall? But will they let you? Old Glendinning's still alive, isn't he? You'll have to ask permission to live there.'

Jane drew herself up proudly. 'Does a Cannon of Charterhall have to ask permission to live there? We were in Charterhall before the Glendinnings ever heard of the place. Besides, the old man's dead. He died a few weeks ago and they say his heir's a nephew who lives in London and won't be coming up here very often. No, I'm just going to move in and see if anybody tries to shift me. I don't think they will somehow.'

'Tell me what's wrong. I know something's worrying you,' Aylie pleaded with Phemie as they worked together in the dairy, churning away at a large wooden tub of buttermilk which was taking an inordinately long time to set. The weather was thundery, which explained the milk's reluctance, Aylie knew. She wished she could remember the charm her mother used to chant over slow-to-set butter, but all that came to mind were the first words of the incantation: 'Brownie, brownie tak tent wi' me . . .' And obviously those were not enough.

Phemie drooped languidly at her side, face whiter than before and eyes anguished. For several nights now Aylie had heard muffled sobs coming from the bed where the other girl and the cook slept. It was not the cook who was crying, for she slept in snoring oblivion and never heard anything. Generous helpings of the mistress' brandy made her sleep deep.

'There's nothing wrong,' said Phemie, leaning back against the marble slab of the dairy shelf as if she were in danger of fainting. She was obviously lying.

'Then why do you cry yourself to sleep every night?' asked Aylie.

147

'I don't, you must have been dreaming. Oh, Aylie, don't speak about it, will you? Don't tell anyone.'

'Tell anyone what? Why don't you tell me what's wrong, Phemie?'

But the other girl just put her hands over her eyes and sobbed, 'Oh leave me alone. Don't ask so many questions.' Then she turned and ran from the dairy.

She was ill, decided Aylie, she was in the grip of one of those wasting diseases that carried off so many people with Phemie's waxy-white skin and thin frame. Girls who worked on the land, though they had to endure hard conditions, did not suffer from the ravages of consumption as much as those who were shut up indoors.

She ran after her friend and said, 'Would you like me to ask my mother for a medicine for you?'

To her surprise Phemie became instantly defensive. 'There's nothing wrong with me. What sort of medicine could your mother give me?'

Aylie soothed her. 'Any sort you like – you tell me what ails you and my mother'll be able to treat it. I'm sure she will.'

A mixture of emotions showed on Phemie's face – doubt, hope and finally the old suspicious despair again. 'There's no medicine can help me, I'll just have to get better in my own way.'

Her weakness did not escape the eagle eye of the mistress, who continually scolded the girl and threatened to send her home to her father.

'He'll not be too glad to have you back. He was keen enough for us to take you,' she threatened.

Phemie hung her head, pleading, 'Oh, don't send me home, Mistress. Please don't send me home.'

Her reprieve was accompanied by a slap on the face from the tight-lipped, bullying woman and an admonition to pull herself together if she did not want to be sent away.

'Why don't you want to go home? Any place must be better than this hole. When my bond is up, I'm going,' Aylie told her friend that night as they sat together on

148

the orchard wall and watched iridescent mayflies dancing over the surface of the burn that ran past the house.

Phemie turned on her angrily. 'Oh, stop bothering me, Aylie Cannon. You think you know everything but you don't know anything at all, do you?' She looked accusingly at her friend. 'You've been lucky. You've been brought up by a mother who loves you, you don't know anything.'

Aylie bridled. At twenty she thought herself very worldly wise. She and her mother had no secrets from each other and she had not been brought up in the atmosphere of mystery and ignorance that other girls suffered. Many times she'd had to explain menstruation or the mysteries of childbirth to girls who had no idea of the facts of life, for Jane had talked to her daughter as an equal from her earliest years and was unusual in that she always enlightened the child on any question she cared to ask.

'Don't be silly. I bet I know more about things than you do,' she replied defensively.

'You don't. I can tell you that. You just don't.' Phemie laughed a strange bitter laugh.

Angrily Aylie turned away from her and stared out towards the hills. On the horizon she could just make out the tops of the triple peaks of her mother's beloved Eildons. At their foot Jane would be preparing for the night in Charterhall where she had moved into the little cell, transforming it into a home. Aylie could imagine her spreading Blaize's coat on top of her bed, boiling a can of water on the fire in the primitive fireplace that filled the place with smoke when she lit it. Jock Hepburn had manufactured a chimney to stick out through a hole in the wall but it coped with only half the smoke.

The love she felt for her mother softened the girl's heart so much that she forgot her resentment against Phemie and turning back again, put an arm round her waist.

'You sound as if you know some terrible things,' she comforted her.

At this Phemie sobbed heart-brokenly and through the racking sound of her grief, she asked Aylie, 'Can't you guess why I don't want to go home? Can't you guess why I'd do anything rather than be sent back to my father?'

A presagement of terrible knowledge made Aylie feel suddenly cold. She shook her head. 'No, I can't . . .'

'Then I'll tell you.' Phemie sat up straight on the wall and looked at her friend. Her face was hard and bitter. 'My father treats me like a wife. My mother died when I was seven years old and ever since then he's slept with me, he's used me as his wife. I couldn't do anything to stop him. And I can never tell anyone about it because I know they'd blame me. Oh, I feel so guilty.'

Aylie felt sick. She remembered the mild-mannered old tailor, who was treated with such deference by the cottager women. Many a widow had set her cap at him but they said he was so devoted to the memory of his dead wife that he'd never marry again. She thought of the times he had sat on the table in Archie's cottage and sewed while she watched the swiftly flying needle with admiration. Yet this man had done such terrible things to his daughter!

She cuddled the weeping girl for comfort. 'Oh, poor Phemie. You're not to blame. It's your father who's committed a mortal sin. You should go and tell the minister.'

Phemie raised her tearstained face. 'Would he believe me? I tell you he wouldn't. My father's a church elder, a respected man. Anyway I couldn't bear to talk about it, I couldn't bear to tell people what's happened. You're the only person I've ever told. And even if they did believe me, what would happen to him? They'd send him to prison, wouldn't they? He's my father after all. I couldn't do that to my own father . . .'

'Then if you won't do anything about it, you must try to forget it because thinking about it all the time is making you ill. You're looking terrible. Just remember you're safe here. He can't get at you now. You've got to

150

try to start a new life for yourself. Just do what the mistress tells you and she'll keep you on.'

With an abrupt movement Phemie jumped down from the wall and walked off, but before she disappeared among the orchard trees she turned her head, face anguished, and called back to Aylie, 'I was right. You don't understand. I knew you wouldn't understand.'

The first day of August, the day of the big Lammas Fair at Melrose, was one of the few holidays farm workers got in the year. Aylie was up at first light, hanging out of the attic window and watching wreaths of mist rising up from the bed of the burn.

'It's going to be fine, it's going to be a hot day,' she cried in delight, but the other two occupants of the maids' room only groaned.

'Keep quiet, you,' grunted the cook. 'We don't have to get up for another hour. You'll waken them with your din.'

Aylie went over to Phemie and shook her gently by the shoulder. 'Get up, Phemie. Let's get all our jobs done early and then you can come with me to the fair. I'm meeting my mother there.'

She did not add that she was also hoping to meet Hugh, whom she had not seen since the night in the schoolroom. Sometimes, if she woke early in the morning, she lay in bed and luxuriated in the memory of what it felt like to ride with her arms round his waist and her face pressed against his back. She shuddered in ecstasy at the memory, going over and over every second of their ride together.

'I don't want to go to the fair,' said Phemie. 'As soon as I've done my work, I'm coming back to bed. I don't feel very well.'

'But you can't miss the fair!'

Lammas Fair days were the highlights of Aylie's life. She loved the crowds and the noise, the side shows and the rings of carefully groomed animals that were hung over by vying farmers and shepherds. She loved to see the peddlers displaying their wares, the men trotting out horses for sale and the gypsies telling fortunes.

'I'm not going.' Phemie sounded determined.

It struck Aylie that she was afraid she might meet her father at the fair. He would almost certainly be there. So she knelt down at Phemie's side of the bed and whispered into her ear, 'I'll stay with you all day, nobody'll get near you. I promise I'll not leave you for a minute.'

But Phemie turned her face into the pillow and though her voice came back muffled, it was even more determined. 'I'm not going to the Fair and that's that.'

Jane was waiting for her daughter in Melrose square and they embraced affectionately.

'You're getting so tall,' said the mother, holding the girl away from her and admiring the new print dress and the way she had coiled up her abundant hair. Her own hair was still thick but its brilliance was fading, like the draining of colour from autumn leaves.

Aylie took her mother's gloved hands in hers and held them palm up. 'Oh, Mam, you're still wearing those pokies even on a hot day like this. Are the hands still giving you pain?'

'A bit, but today they're fine. They're always not so bad when it's warm. I wear the pokies because I think they look so ugly, so red and swollen. I used to have such nice hands.'

'Bondagers don't have nice hands for long,' said Aylie sadly, and threw her arms round her mother's neck to give her another kiss.

Together they climbed the steep road to where the fair spread out over the slope of the nearest Eildon. There were hundreds of people milling around and many of them knew Jane, stopping to speak to her or touching their hats with respect when she passed. She was a Cannon, the daughter of Alice Armstrong, and now honoured also in her own right as a successful healer and a skilled midwife. As always Aylie felt proud to be walking with her stately mother through the throng.

They stopped at a stall where men were throwing balls at a battered line of cut-out heads, but when Jane realized that the heads with their cockaded hats were meant to represent Frenchmen she turned away her face. They paused beside peddlers who had spread their wares out on the grass, and Jane bought a length of lace while Aylie tried to make up her mind between a piece of printed cotton that would make a good headcloth or a bundle of multi-coloured ribbons out of which she could make a favour.

In the end she opted for the ribbons and, purchases completed, mother and daughter climbed on up the hill. At one tent the same loud-voiced man who had busked at Earlston was trying to attract people in to look at a pair of dead Siamese twins, and Aylie and Jane shuddered, agreeing that was something they did not want to see. They did pay a few pennies however to go into the big marquee where the gardeners from the big houses round about were displaying their best produce, especially flowers in huge bunches that filled the hot air under the canvas with heavenly scents. The smell of cloves from carnations and musk from roses filled their nostrils as they exclaimed in wonder over the bouquets and the size of the mammoth vegetables. It had been a good growing summer and, if the rain held off, promised to be another successful harvest.

They were almost ready to sit down and spread out the food Jane had brought on the grass when they saw the old tailor, Phemie's father, in the distance. He was heading towards them and Jane paused to speak to him but Aylie hung back, sullen faced.

When he went on his way, her mother said, 'Why were you so rude to him? He's the father of that girl you work with and you've known him all your life.'

Aylie looked at her mother. Could she risk telling her?

'Mam, he's not as good a man as everybody thinks.'

'What do you mean?'

'Well, his daughter talked to me about her father the other day and – he's not as good as he seems, that's all.'

Jane had keen eyes and now she fixed them on her daughter. 'What did she tell you?'

'She said he sleeps with her. That he's slept with her since she was seven years old.' They were whispering now, leaning towards each other as they sat on the grass.

The news, as Aylie had expected, astonished and repelled her mother, but to her relief she saw that Jane was not disbelieving.

A look of infinite pity came on to Jane's face as she said, 'Oh, poor lassie, what a terrible thing. I'd never have guessed it.'

'She won't tell anyone,' offered Aylie.

'Just as well. She'd stir up a hornet's nest for herself and for him if she did,' was the reply. 'Oh, poor lassie, poor, poor lassie. But she's well away from him now, isn't she? She doesn't go home, does she?'

Aylie shook her head. 'Never. She hasn't been home for years, she never leaves Myreheugh. I wanted her to come with me today but she refused. I can understand why, I suppose – she knew he'd be here. She hates him.'

The mother and daughter sat in silence staring at the happy crowd around them. Little children ran from group to group, dogs barked, men shouted, buskers incited the crowd to spend money. Farther up the hill a dentist was pulling teeth on top of an open waggon. They could see people climbing into the chair he had tied down to the waggon floor and opening their mouths for his terrible pincers. The pain of their toothache must have been truly terrible to suffer his ministrations to get rid of it, Aylie thought.

Then she saw Hugh, coming through the crowd towards her and flaunting a girl on his arm. He was wearing his coat with the shining buttons and a pair of tight white buckskin trousers, and as usual she thought he looked magnificent. The girl who clung to him was a bold-eyed, full-lipped hussy with a ribboned straw hat on the back of her head and a very low-necked dress. She was laughing loudly and looked drunk.

As soon as she saw Hugh, Aylie swiftly turned her

154

head away, but he had been seeking her out and came over to stand beside them with a broad smile on his face. It was obvious he'd been drinking too. Bending down, he struck out a hand in greeting to her mother.

'You're Aylie's mam,' he said. 'Do you remember me? I'm Gilbert Kennedy's son.'

Jane took his hand gingerly. 'Where's your father now? Has he a good place?'

'Oh, aye, it's a grand place with a gentleman near Yetholm.'

'That's where you come from, isn't it?' Jane said.

He nodded, with a grin, saying, 'Yes, all the gypsies come from Yetholm. That's our native place.'

Then he turned to Aylie and asked, 'Are you enjoying yourself, my wee wildcat?'

At this the girl on his arm pouted and pressed herself against him so that he turned and gave her a quick kiss. When the couple wandered off into the crowd, Jane looked at her daughter's face and, with a pang, saw the pain there.

'He's a real gypsy that one,' she said soothingly. 'They're not to be trusted, the gypsies.'

Aylie could not understand him. Why had he deliberately come to flaunt the girl in front of her? Why had he sought her out? It was almost as if he were playing some game, either with her or himself. He was so strange. One moment he was a womanizing ruffian whom she thoroughly disliked, and the next a man she would follow to the ends of the earth. She could not understand it and her heart felt heavy with the pain of trying to work it out.

During the harvesting Aylie fell into her bed every night, too exhausted even to rub her sore legs and arms with the harvesters' embrocation her mother had made up for her from a mixture of vinegar, turpentine, powdered camphor and egg. Sleep overtook her as soon as her head touched the pillow and she was startled into wakefulness each morning by the sound of the foreman's shouts breaking into her sleep. She was even too tired to dream about Hugh.

On the fifth morning of the harvest she felt so stiff that she could hardly rise. It was still dark when she staggered towards the door but in the dim light she saw the figure of Phemie curled up in bed with her knees drawn up towards her chin. There was an expression of pain on the girl's face and the greyness of her cheek against the yellowed pillow cover startled Aylie.

Phemie turned her head and whispered, 'I wish you could stay with me today.'

Aylie paused, one hand raised to the hat which she was tying on her head.

'I wish I could, but I can't. I've got to be in the field before six. But I'll try to come back and see you at break time.'

Phemie did not answer but turned her head away again.

Soon afterwards the cook got up, swearing and stumbling around as she dressed herself.

'Don't leave me, Mrs Mather,' whispered Phemie. 'I'm not well.'

The old woman looked malevolently towards the girl. 'You're never well! What's wrong with you now? You'd better stir yourself or Missus'll be up here with a stick for your back.'

Phemie's voice was feeble. 'I'm sick. Really sick. Please tell Missus that I can't get up.'

The cook recoiled in fear. 'What's wrong? Is it a fever?'

The girl's head shook slightly. 'I don't know. I'm ill. My stomach hurts. Please stay with me, don't leave me, please don't leave me.'

She reached out one white arm towards the old woman but the cook stood back from her, refusing to touch her, fearing contagion. Then she slammed out of the room, leaving the sick girl alone.

When she complained to the mistress in the kitchen that Phemie was ill and could not leave her bed, the reaction, as she had expected, was fury.

'That girl's useless. We need all the help we can get at harvest time! I don't know why the master keeps her on. She's a lazy, idle slut. You go up and tell her to get up and come down here this instant.'

When the cook returned to the bedroom Phemie was lying, eyes wide open and face distorted with pain. Even a woman as unsympathetic as she knew that something was very far wrong with the girl.

'She's really sick, I think, Madam,' she told her employer back in the kitchen. 'Perhaps we ought to fetch a doctor.'

The mistress was parsimonious and she saw no need to waste money on a maid. 'Nonsense, there's no need to go to that expense. If she's ill we'll leave her for a few hours and then you can take a look at her again.'

The next time the cook went upstairs Phemie was crying. When she saw the figure standing in the doorway she reached out with both arms and cried, 'Oh stay with me, please don't leave me, stay with me.'

But the cook banged the door shut and cried out, 'I can't stay with you. I've got work to do.'

Because she had promised Phemie that she would come back to see her during the day, Aylie ran into the farm-house at twelve o'clock but was told by the cook that she was not to go upstairs.

'Phemie's asleep, don't disturb her. If you try to go up there, I'll report you to the mistress,' she ordered.

Feeling uneasy, the girl went back to the fields and in the house, the grumbling cook was preparing the supper alone when there was a piercing scream from the room above her head. She was stood stock still in front of her cooking range, wondering what to do, when Phemie came rushing down the rickety ladder. Her face was wild and her nightgown was covered with bloodstains. Without speaking to the cook she rushed over to the dresser where she seized a carving knife from the rack and ran back up the little ladder again.

Her eyes rolling in terror, the cook stood aghast, unable to speak, and as soon as Phemie disappeared she ran into the main part of the house to fetch the mistress. Together, very tentatively, the women climbed the stair to the bedroom. Everything was very quiet up there now and they popped their heads carefully through the door to see Phemie lying amid tumbled covers on the blood-marked bed, her arms and legs outstretched and eyes staring at the ceiling.

'My God, I think she's had a bairn,' whispered the cook in horror.

The mistress, tight-lipped, advanced towards the bed and lifted the bloodstained knife from where it lay on the floor.

'What have you done with it?' she asked the girl, but there was no reply. Phemie just kept on staring upwards. The woman was even more abrupt the second time she asked. Leaning down, she shook the girl's arm. 'Tell me what you've done with it? Where is it, you little whore?'

Phemie seemed to be stricken dumb. Her eyes never left the ceiling and her arms hung limp at the sides of the bed. Tears ran down her cheeks though there was no sound of sobbing.

The mistress told the cook, 'Here, take the knife. We've got to find it. She's had a baby all right.'

Together they went round the little room, throwing back bedding, turning out the only cupboard and throwing out the clothes that were folded up on the shelves – but to no avail. Then the cook knelt down and lifted up the drooping bedcovers to look under the bed. She stayed stooped for a moment and then she stood up, her face more grim. 'It's down there, Missus, and I think it's dead.'

The mistress bent down too and stared beneath the bed. When she stood up she told the cook, 'Fetch my husband. Tell him to go for a constable. She's cut its throat.'

Aylie was on the top of a corn rick, building up the sheaves that the other women tossed up to her, when she saw a trap coming spanking up the lane with two men in it. Less than an hour later it left again and what looked like a body was lying on the floor of the trap between the men.

It was dark by the time she got back to the farmhouse where the cook was excitedly waiting for her, breath heavy with whisky and face flushed because she had rich gossip to impart.

'Oh my, have you heard the news? Phemie had a bairn in my bed this afternoon – and then she cut its throat,' she whispered hoarsely into Aylie's ear as the girl sat down at the kitchen table and began to ease off her working boots.

A cold chill seized Aylie's heart. She couldn't believe what she was hearing and asked, 'What, what did you say?'

'Are you deaf? That whey-faced bitch, your friend Phemie, had a bairn, a wee laddie, and she cut its throat with one of my knives from the kitchen. She got it when I wasn't looking. I found the bairn under the bed. You should have heard the mistress!'

'Where's Phemie now?' Aylie asked.

'She's where she belongs, in the jail. The constables came and took her away. What a fuss she made, yelling and howling like a dog. They had to tie her up like a chicken.'

'Oh, poor Phemie, what a terrible thing. She must have been out of her mind. Oh, I wish I'd been here to help her.'

The cook stood back, outraged. 'You help her! You'd want to help the murderer of her own bairn. You'd better not let the mistress hear you saying that.'

Aylie too looked angry and she stood up abruptly, asking, 'Where's the mistress now? I want to speak to her.'

The cook sounded pious: 'Poor soul, she's had a terrible day, she's in the parlour but she'll not speak to the likes of you. Poor woman, she's had a terrible shock.'

Meg Mather, who normally could say no good of her employer, was now thoroughly on her side. But Aylie was not in the mood to listen or to sympathize with either of them. She swung out of the kitchen into the dark passage, and on into regions she had never penetrated before to the sitting room where the mistress sat with her embroidery frame beneath the portraits of her family.

'What do *you* want?' the woman asked in disbelief when she saw the bondager standing in the doorway in her stocking feet.

'I want to know where they've taken Phemie,' Aylie said.

The mistress sounded well satisfied as she replied, 'They've taken her to Jedburgh of course, to the jail. She'll have to go on trial for killing her child.'

The girl eyed her coldly and demanded, 'Didn't anybody think to ask her why she did it?'

The insolence of this girl was beyond belief but her directness made it impossible not to answer her.

'No, of course not, why should we? The sight of the poor dead body of the wee baby was enough.'

Aylie came farther into the room and shouted, 'That girl was abused by her own father. She was terrified of men. She wouldn't know what was happening to her when she had that baby, didn't you give her any sympathy, didn't you ask her who was responsible?'

The woman at the fireside stood up, a gaunt, austere figure. 'Get out. You get out of here this minute. If you're making insinuations I'll see to it that you end up in the same place as she is. Just get out this instant.'

Aylie was as furious as she. 'Don't you want to help her? She's a woman like you, she needs your help. Don't you want to know who was responsible for the child she killed? Don't you realize she was so mad with fear that she wouldn't know what to do?'

The mistress summoned up enough strength to push the girl back into the passage. 'The court'll decide what happens to her, not me and certainly not you,' she shouted back through the closed door.

*

All the workers on the farm relished the happening as an event to brighten up the boring round of their lives. They gossiped about it constantly, speculating about who had fathered Phemie's child.

'She's been here for three years, she never left the place, so it must be someone on the farm,' said one of the other bondagers to Aylie.

Aylie kept to herself Phemie's terrible story, and she discounted the possibility of the old tailor being the child's father because Phemie had hidden from him all the time she worked at Myreheugh. Some man must be responsible – but who?

Phemie never went out, never flirted, never hung around the stackyard in the evenings like other girls did, and there was no weekend dancing to the melodeon at Myreheugh to entice her out.

In her bed at night Aylie lay with her arms above her head, staring at the moon through the dirty window glass, and wondering, wondering about Phemie until it became an obsession with her.

The Myreheugh kirn was a muted affair, just really an excuse for everyone to get drunk on the last night of the harvest. She was too dejected to enjoy it and sat in a corner huddled up in a brown shawl like a wet sparrow, watching the drinking going on. Men and women were pouring Myreheugh's whisky over their throats as if it were the last drink they'd ever have.

One of the young hinds came to sit beside her and said, 'You're looking very sad. What's the matter?'

She shrugged. 'I keep thinking about Phemie. She was my friend, you see, and I wonder what's going to happen to her.'

He was matter of fact. 'She'll go to prison. She killed her bairn and they won't let her off that. You can't do anything to help her now.'

'But I could have helped her if I'd known. I could have stopped her killing it. Women have bastard bairns all the time and nobody thinks anything of it.'

'It's too late to think of things like that now,' said

the man, standing up because he was put off by Aylie's depression. 'Come on and have a drink.'

But she shook her head. 'No, I don't want to. But tell me something. Does anyone have any idea who fathered Phemie's child? It must be somebody here.'

He glanced over his shoulder at the table where the boss and his wife were sitting. 'Well, it wouldn't be the first time a maid here has fallen in the family way, but it's the first time it's turned out like this. I don't think you'd have to look very far for the father.' And his eyes went over to the farmer who was drinking as much as his workers.

Aylie followed his gaze and then stared at him with disbelief. 'Not him? It couldn't be him? If it was, he wouldn't have let them take her away like that, would he?'

'Wouldn't he?' rejoined the hind, and walked off to find a more cheerful companion.

Disconsolate, she wandered out of the barn to the yard, where she saw a group of young men crowded round the water trough. They were yelling and shouting, and going up behind them she saw that they were teasing the poor daftie, the halfwitted son of the old bondager.

'Daftie, daftie,' they were chanting, 'the boss says you're the father of thon bairn that had its throat cut. Did you tup the housemaid, daftie? Do you even ken what to do with a lassie?'

The halfwitted boy stood among them giggling, looking from face to face, not knowing whether to be pleased or made afraid by their attentions.

'Come on, tell us what you did. Show us,' said a big, florid boy who drove a pair of horses and drank up all his wages every month. He was more than half drunk now.

'I dinna ken,' mumbled the halfwit, still giggling, 'I canna say.'

'You can, you can show us, come on, give us a show,' and the blond giant reached out a hand and pulled down the halfwit boy's tattered trousers, exposing his flaccid genitalia to the crowd. The boy tried to cover himself with his hands and his face flushed red, but the other lads howled and jeered in delight.

'Did you do it with that, daftie? My you're a lad after all. Come on, show us what you did to her . . .' cried the big boy.

The halfwit giggled, flattered now, thinking they were approving of him in some way.

'Take your hand away, come on, show us your dagger,' yelled his tormentor and wrestled with him.

Then, like a thunderbolt, another figure rushed past Aylie and into the crowd, shouting, 'Let him be, he's no idea what's going on. Let him alone or I'll duck you all in the panni!'

The saviour was Hugh Kennedy, looking so angry and so fierce that the blond bully backed away from him.

'Aw, come on, Hughie, it was only a joke. We were just having a bit of fun,' he whined.

'Then have it with someone else, not with him. Have it with someone who knows what's going on.' And to the halfwitted boy he said, 'Put your trousers back on, Willie, and go home to your mother.' Then he put an arm round the confused boy's shoulders and led him away from his tormentors, with Aylie following.

When Hugh opened the door of the bondager's cottage and pushed the boy inside, Aylie stepped up behind him and said, 'I saw all that. I think you were very kind.'

'Kind?' He looked annoyed. 'I wasn't kind. I just can't stand to see anybody hurting a dog or a horse or making fun of a daftie.'

She shrugged. 'I still think it was kind of you.'

He grinned at her. 'Well at least I'm in your good books, little lady. Where's your mam tonight? Not here is she? She looks after you like a tiger does your mam.'

Again Aylie was surprised at the way he could switch from being nice to being nasty.

'Don't talk nonsense, my mother trusts me.'

'Then she's sillier than she looks,' was the reply. 'Would she trust you to dance with me?'

163

This was a challenge. 'Of course she would.'

'Then come on, they're playing a reel now. Come on into the barn and we'll have a dance.'

They danced like adversaries, stamping, advancing and retreating, challenging each other in time to the music. They vied with each other, preening themselves like peacocks, and each time their eyes met they gave back defiance.

When the music stopped he held on to her hand and looked at her with something like respect in his dark eyes. 'I always remember how you looked on a horse. I wonder if you'd treat a man like you treated your horses,' he asked.

'I always treated horses well,' she replied.

'That's what I mean,' he laughed, showing his magnificent white teeth and throwing back his strong neck with the thick sinews that gave some hint of the immense physical strength he possessed.

He walked her back to the farmhouse and when they reached the back door, she suddenly turned to him and said, 'Did you hear about my friend Phemie?'

He nodded. 'Yes, I heard. Poor lassie. What's so wrong about having a bastard?'

She suddenly decided to tell him. 'It wasn't that so much. She was out of her mind with terror. And she thought that they'd send her back home if they found the baby – she must have thought she'd get rid of it. Turn the clock back, you know.'

The whites of his eyes glittered like ivory in the moonlight as he listened to her. 'Why was she so keen to stay here? From what you tell me it's not such a great place.'

'Her home was worse. Her father abused her.'

'He hit her?'

'Worse than that, he slept with her.'

He drew in his breath with a hiss and said, 'The old devil, sitting stitching away with a face like a soor ploom and him a church elder too.' For a second she thought he was going to laugh. If he did, she'd never speak to him again – but he did not laugh and instead became even more sober looking. 'Poor lassie. She always looked hunted, like a hare in wet grass,' he said.

It was a wonderful simile, for Phemie did indeed look like a wet, dejected animal.

Aylie spoke rapidly: 'I want to go to see her. I want to speak to her. You could help me. No one'll go near her except me. She's got no friends.'

'But she's over in Jeddart, isn't she? How're you going to get there?'

'You could lend me your horse. You've always got a horse. If you lend me your horse, I'll go there on Sunday and see her. I promise I'll bring it back sound.'

He nodded. 'All right, I'll lend you a horse and I'm sure you'll bring it back sound. There's nobody I'd trust more with a horse than you, and gypsies don't lend horses to just anybody.'

The news that Jane Cannon had moved back into Charterhall spread fast, and the steward – the same man who used to order her around in the fields – went marching down to the ruins to put her out.

When he broke through the thicket of hawthorn bushes which now surrounded the abbey ruins, he saw her digging up a little patch of ground in a southern facing corner behind a tumbledown wall.

'Hey, you're trespassing,' he shouted across a deep grass-covered moat which had been the monks' main drain and watercourse.

She stared back at him defiantly.

'I'm not. The Cannons were here before any Glendinnings. Nobody ever comes near this place except for a few burials in the graveyard over there. I'm not doing any harm. I'm going to stay and God help anyone who tries to move me.'

He did not make any attempt to cross the ditch but blustered in an ineffectual way. When he saw that if she were to be removed it would have to be done by force, he withdrew, making threatening noises. She noticed with wry amusement that he was afraid to come close enough for her to fix him directly with her eyes. Her old reputation was still working for her and she would not have been above putting a curse on him to frighten the man away. Though she had no real belief in her power to bring ill luck to anyone, and would not have wanted to use it even if she did possess such a power, there were times when fear of her was a great advantage.

If the steward chose to believe that she was a witch, she would play the part.

Over the first few months she lived in Charterhall, the man came back now and again to shout threateningly at her but his shouts were half hearted and soon he gave up.

The first time Charterhall's new owner came to look around the place however, the steward was apprehensive of his reaction to having a squatter in the abbey ruins. The heir, a lean, languid Englishman who seemed to think that everything in Scotland was primitive and amusing, walked round the estate swinging a malacca cane and gazing about with haughty disdain, but when he came to the abbey ruins he brightened a little. 'How picturesque,' he drawled. 'Quite romantic really . . .'

The steward told him how Old Glendinning had began to remove the stones of the ruins but had lost interest before the job was finished. Did he want them to start again?

The new owner shook his head. 'Oh no, don't bother, leave it the way it is. It's quite a feature of the park.'

Emboldened by this the steward confessed that a woman, a witch he said, lived in one of the abbey cellars and, to his surprise, the heir was openly delighted.

'Our own hermit, what? *Very* romantic. Down south people used to pay hermits to live in their grottos, I've got one for nothing. I'd like to see her.'

Jane was sitting in the sun at her cell door shelling peas when he and the steward took up their position on the moat bank to observe her.

The heir was slightly disappointed. 'She's very clean

looking, not very savage really, is she? But never mind, let her be. I don't suppose she'll make any trouble.'

The growing stiffness and pain in her hands and legs made field work impossible, but Jane was quite comfortably off because many people came walking through the woods to her solitary home seeking cures and advice on their health. She recultivated the old herb garden, and on a pillar in the middle of it a friendly mason chipped out a carving of a rose with two buds which was the ancient sign of the herbalist. The long-neglected herbs, planted by her ancestors, revived under her loving hands and she used them to concoct the recipes in Alice's manuscripts. Many cures were attributed to her and though she often felt that the patient's belief was as much a factor in recovery as the powers of the plants, she was proud of her knowledge and expertise.

She had many friends and her life was not lonely because almost every day someone came to see her. The most important of them were still Jock Hepburn and his wife, Flora. Their son Sandy was growing into a fine, strong boy and he too often arrived at the abbey with presents of food or invitations to dinner at the farmhouse, occasions Jane enjoyed because she would sit at the table with Big Agnes, in her eighties now, and reminisce about the old days when they both worked as bondagers at Charterhall.

As he had always hoped, Jock was growing prosperous through hard work and acumen, and his home reflected this growing prosperity. He went to Melrose and bought a piano on which Flora learned to play the old Scots songs, and after their convivial dinners Jane sang to her accompaniment. It was the first piano in the district and on the nights that Jane and Flora gave their impromptu concerts, workers from Jock's farm would gather in the garden and listen through the open window, marvelling at the wonderful music. Her voice was still capable of casting the same spell over her audience as it had over the audience in the kirn long ago.

One afternoon she was painfully bending over her

neatly tended herbs when she heard a noise and looked up to see Hugh Kennedy standing on the paved path. She stared at him but not in a welcoming way because she distrusted his gypsy impudence and flashy appearance. She had heard too much – about his wayward behaviour with women; about the poaching for which he had been hauled before the sheriff more than once; and especially about his espousal of radical politics – for her to like him much. The biggest fear she had, however, was the interest she sensed he had in her daughter. Hugh Kennedy was not the sort of man she dreamed of for Aylie. A well-set-up farmer was the husband her daughter should have, not a gypsy who was always on the run from the law.

Her hostility was, however, wasted on him because he stepped cheekily into the garden and squatted down on a log beside the bed of sweetly smelling thyme.

'I was just passing by and took a deek in to ask if you'd like a wee salmon for your supper. I put it in a bucket of panni at your door.'

'Was it poached?' she asked abruptly.

He laughed unabashed and she had to admit that he gave off a strange animal magnetism that would attract women.

'Who did salmon belong to before rich men started buying up riverbanks? They belonged to people like you and me. You're a trespasser here, a bit of a lawbreaker yourself. I didn't expect you to be so fussy,' he told her.

She had to smile at that. 'I'm not too law-abiding, it's true,' she agreed, 'and I like a bit of salmon now and then.'

'Then eat it with my good wishes,' he told her, rising to his feet and turning as if to go. But after he had taken a couple of steps, he said over his shoulder, 'Oh, yes, Aylie asked me to tell you that she'll be over to see you on Sunday.'

This news did not please her because it meant he'd been seeing her daughter. She stood up to her full height. 'You take your salmon away, I don't want it. And get out of here before I chase you out,' she said shortly.

She heard him laughing as he went off down the ruined aisle. When she returned to her cell at night, the salmon, neatly gutted, was in the bucket of water by her door.

The cell above the gatehouse entrance was as tiny as a dog kennel and very dark. The only time light got in was when the jailer swung open the heavily studded door to push some food in to Phemie or summon her out for yet another session of questioning by men with clean linen and pale hands who had little sympathy with her problems.

When she heard the sound of approaching feet, she did not raise her head and did not see Aylie being shown in by the jailer.

The first she knew of her visitor was when the girl knelt down beside her and threw her arms round the bent shoulders.

'Oh Phemie, why didn't you tell me? I'd have tried to help you.'

Phemie raised her blonde head and stared unblinkingly at Aylie. 'You couldn't help me. Nobody could. I kept thinking it would go away. I kept thinking it would never happen . . .'

Aylie squatted on the floor at her friend's side and whispered so that the listening jailer couldn't hear, 'But didn't you realize? Didn't you understand you were pregnant?'

Phemie shook her head. 'I've never had regular bleedings. It never happened before and it could have, often enough. When the baby was born I just hated it . . . the horrible little wrinkled thing.'

Aylie took her hand gently and asked, 'It wasn't your father's, so whose baby was it? You can tell me, Phemie. I won't say anything to anybody.'

'I tried to tell you but you didn't understand. Surely you see it now? The farmer's the father of that bairn. My father *sold* me to him!'

Aylie's face showed her astonishment. 'Old Myreheugh? Didn't his wife know?'

169

Phemie just sounded tired. 'Oh, Aylie, even if she did would she ever let on?'

Jane was up early on the Sunday morning preparing for Aylie's visit. She made curds, her daughter's favourite dish, and then walked a couple of miles to a cottage where she knew a woman kept a cow, to buy thick yellow cream to pour over them. But as the day passed and there was no sign of Aylie, Jane's spirits sank. Had that Hugh Kennedy been playing a trick on her, she wondered?

It was late afternoon when she saw a horse and rider ford the river and come cantering across the long meadow towards the abbey. The rider set the horse at the moat and it leaped bravely, just missing the top and floundering with threshing legs to mount the slope. It was Aylie on the horse's back, sitting astride because Hugh had forgotten to bring a side saddle, and her hair was loose and tangled over her shoulders.

She looked as if she had ridden for a long way at breakneck pace. When she came closer her mother saw that she was exhausted and her eyes were red-rimmed as if she had been weeping.

In the cloister yard she leaped from the horse, dropped its reins and ran towards her mother.

'Oh Mam,' she cried, 'oh, Mam, it's been so terrible! Oh Mam, I need to talk to you.'

Jane held the girl to her, cradling her head with both hands.

'My cushie doo,' she whispered soothingly. 'What's wrong, what's happened?'

'It's Phemie, I've been to see Phemie. They'll send her to prison. It's so unfair!'

The news of Phemie murdering her baby had not yet reached Charterhall so Jane was surprised at her daughter's anguish. 'Phemie, that's the girl who works in the house with you . . . What's happened to her? Why's she going to prison?'

In tears Aylie burst out with the story of Phemie's baby and its murder while Jane continued to hold her in a comforting embrace. As she wept, Aylie said, 'I should have stayed with her. She wouldn't have killed it if I'd been there. Now she's going to prison!'

'Ssh, ssh,' soothed the mother while the girl went on, pouring out the sad story, telling about the tailor and his daughter and what she had seen when she went to visit Phemie in Jedburgh jail.

'Oh, what a terrible place! She's shut up in a cell all on her own in the gatehouse beside the abbey. She cries all the time and she won't eat anything. They think she's gone mad – her father told her he hopes they send her to Bedlam but she's not mad. She talked to me . . . She has to talk to someone. I asked her who the father is and, you'll never guess – it's the farmer. It's the man I work for, that horrible, horrible man who's busy pretending he knows nothing about it and won't lift a finger to help Phemie. It's his brother who sits on the bench in Jeddart and he'll be the one who's got to decide what's to happen to her but Myreheugh won't do anything to help her, not even have a word with his own brother!'

Jane was not surprised for she had been one of the labouring classes too long not to be aware of the ways of the masters. 'You mustn't be too upset. They won't be cruel to her and she did commit murder, you have to admit that.'

'But Mam, she was desperate, she didn't know what she was doing. If you could only see her, she's like a poor wee animal, maddened by fear. Oh, she's such a timid girl. Going to prison will be the end of her.'

Aylie wept, inconsolable, while her mother, feeling helpless, held her close.

When the sobs began to lessen, Jane said soothingly, 'Come on inside and have something to eat. What about that horse? You'd better tie it up and let it graze in the meadow. Where did you get it anyway? Is it from the farm?'

Aylie shook her head. 'No, of course not. Hugh Kennedy lent it to me. It's a great horse – fast and brave.

I'll rub it down and feed it before I head back to Myreheugh.'

They tied it up with a long rope so that it could graze in the meadow grass and when they were finished, Jane broached the subject that was worrying her even more than Phemie. 'Do you see much of Kennedy's son? He's not good company for a girl like you.'

As soon as the words were out of her mouth, she regretted them for Aylie stiffened at her side. 'Oh, don't you start, Mam. Just because he speaks his mind, lots of people don't like him. He won't stand for the things the rest of us stand for, that's why.'

'They say he's a troublemaker, one of those wreckers and thatch burners.' Jane had heard plenty of tales about Hugh.

'He believes in every man being equal but he isn't a wrecker or a thatch burner,' defended Aylie.

'I've heard tell that he's one of the Boomer men . . .' said Jane.

This was a new one to Aylie. 'Boomer men? What are they?'

Her mother shrugged. 'They're smugglers. They go back and forth to Boulmer on the Northumberland coast – local people call it Boomer and that's how the smugglers get their name. Lots of wild young lads take up the smuggling and he's one of them, I've heard. If the excise men get him, it'll be worse than Jedburgh jail for him.'

'Boomer men . . .' Slowly Aylie turned over the words. 'I've never heard of them. But he could be a smuggler, I suppose, he always seems to have money – and horses – but he only works at odd jobs.'

'Gypsies like him always have money and it doesn't do to ask where it comes from. Oh, keep away from him, lassie. Gypsies are bad for people who aren't the same as them. Let gypsies stay with gypsies is what I say.'

On the slow ride back to Myreheugh, Aylie turned over what her mother had said. So Hugh was a smuggler, one of the Boomer men. She was not as shocked as Jane had hoped she would be, in fact she was intrigued. If he

172

was a smuggler, a rebel against authority, he was even more fascinating as far as she was concerned.

Phemie lay in her cell for three weeks before her final appearance before the magistrates. On the morning this was due to take place, a woman came to help her wash and dress. She was a kind woman who combed the girl's hair gently and whispered, 'Don't be frightened, trust in the Lord and He will help you.'

'Will He?' Phemie looked desperate. 'Why should He help me? No one else does.'

The court was crowded but as she was led to the little box above the crowd, she recognized some faces – her father was there, sober and respectable-looking in his best black suit. She looked down at him with loathing. It was all his fault this had happened. The farmer and his grim wife sat together on the front benches, both of them avoiding looking at the girl as she was led in. The presiding magistrate looked exactly like his brother and she shuddered at the sight of him.

The proceedings went by in a sort of dream. They asked her questions. They asked if she had really cut her baby's throat and she nodded her head.

'Yes, yes, I cut its throat with one of the knives from the kitchen.'

'Why did you kill your baby?' was the next question.

She dropped her eyes to her hands and furrowed her brow, trying very hard to remember why she had killed the child, but no idea came.

It was as if that horrible day had been lived by someone else. All she could remember was her unreasoning terror.

'I don't know really, but it looked so ugly and it made such funny noises,' she finally said.

The judge and the lawyers conferred. Huge books were dragged out and their pages turned. The court was adjourned and she was taken back to her cell. Then in the afternoon they came for her again and, like a wild animal flushed from undergrowth, she blinked as she was led into the bright sunlit courtroom. She did not seem to understand what the judge was saying when he told her that she was a wicked girl, the killer of an innocent child, and that she had to pay the penalty of her crime.

'You will serve five years' hard labour in the prison for women in Edinburgh,' he pronounced, and the court gave back a rustle of approval at this sentence.

Only one dissented. She stood up in the middle of the court and began to shout: 'You can't do that! You can't send her away for five years! Why don't you ask her who the father of her baby is? Why should he get off scot free while she goes to prison? Why don't you ask your brother who's the father . . .?'

It was Aylie and she was pointing directly at the farmer whose face was flushed to port-wine red and whose mouth was opening and shutting like a stranded fish's, till it appeared to the onlookers that he was about to have an apoplectic fit.

Aylie was still shouting when two court officials bore down on her and hustled her out of the courtroom, down the steep stairs into the town square. Shaking her violently, they threw her on to the steps of the market cross and were about to lift her up and shake her again when a group of men came down the court stairway behind them. The new arrivals were all gypsies and they looked very threatening.

'Leave the girl alone,' said Hugh Kennedy. 'Let go of her. Go back into the court and let her be. She won't make any more noise.'

Then he lifted Aylie up and said, 'You went a bit too far that time. You could've gone to jail with your friend for shouting too much. Come on, I don't think they're going to have you back at Myreheugh, so I'll take you home to your mother.'

Jane had known this was the day of Phemie's trial and she could not conceal the relief on her face when she saw Aylie coming up the track riding pillion behind Hugh Kennedy on his black horse. She said no word of reproach nor did she worry that Aylie had lost her job, but bustled about getting them something to eat.

'I'll have a word with Jock,' she said eventually. 'He could be needing an extra girl for summer work. One of his bondagers died last month and they'll be needing someone else. They'll take you, I think.'

Aylie looked at Hugh. Was he going to say anything to stop her taking this job? But he held his tongue so she nodded her head and said, 'All right, Mam, you can tell Jock I'll do it if he wants me.'

'That gypsy's courting you,' Jane told her daughter one winter night after Hugh Kennedy had arrived with a huge bundle of firewood held across the pommel of his saddle and put it down at their door. Her fears were confirmed when she saw a flush rise in Aylie's cheeks.

'Oh Mam, he isn't. He hardly ever comes near me and when he does all he talks to me about is horses.'

'He's courting you none the less. He's stalking you as craftily as he stalks all those hares and pheasants he catches. Watch out for him. I wouldn't want to see you having to go from house to house selling tin pots and clothes pegs.'

'Oh, I'd never do that. Anyway he's not like the other gypsy men. He's got ambition . . .' Aylie protested.

Jane snorted slightly. 'I've heard how his ambition takes him, wandering around the place stirring up people against their masters. He should get himself down to London if he wants to start a revolution.'

It never struck her that Blaize had been a soldier in the army of Revolution. She saw his war as something quite different and resignedly accepted that French ideas of liberty did not apply to people like her and the labourers who lived and worked around her.

As she walked to Jock's farm next morning in the frosty dawn, Aylie reflected on what her mother had said. She knew full well the reputation of gypsy men for drunkenness, ill treating their women and for dishonesty, but Hugh, she was sure, was something different. His father, Gilbert, was an honourable and well respected man who had always held down a job, and her memory

175

of an incandescent Hugh vainly urging the farm labourers in the schoolhouse to better themselves, still stayed vividly in her mind. What he had said that night had struck a note in her, he awoke all her latent feelings – not of resentment exactly – but of awareness of the inequalities of life. She was an intelligent girl who chafed at the restraints of life as a bondager, for even though she was lucky enough at the moment to be working in a good place, what assurance did she have that it would last?

'I might as well be a sheep or a cow, I'm as powerless and as trusting as they are. Even horses are better off than women in this life,' she told herself, kicking loose stones in front of her with her enormous, hobnailed boots as she walked. What would it be like, she suddenly wondered, to walk in dainty satin shoes? What did it feel like not to have to rise before dawn every day?

As far as Jane's warning about Hugh courting her was concerned, Aylie was unconvinced. She had seen him only three times since the day at Jedburgh, and that was several months ago. If he was courting her, he was a very dilatory lover.

The ploughing finished and within days a thick blanket of snow covered the ground. There was little work for the farm people so they were put to indoor tasks tidying up the sheds and the yard. Jock was a good employer and did not think it fair to lay his people off without wages if he could help it.

The reflection from the snow outside the barn door dazzled Aylie as she helped with the draught horses, crooning to them as she forked over the straw of their bedding. If the snow did not melt soon, she thought, they'd be as frisky as colts when the time came to take them out again. As she worked she glanced out at the snow through the open door and remembered how she used to play in it as a child, throwing snowballs and making long glassy slides down the bank at the side of the lane. She was only twenty-one years old but child-hood and games seemed very far away.

The door creaked further open and a dark figure in a long greatcoat stood silhouetted against the light in the doorway. Hugh's voice said, 'You must have time on your hands with all this snow. How do you fancy an outing?'

She slowly leaned on her fork and stared at him. 'Where to?' Her voice was cold because he had not been to see her for almost six weeks.

'What about Coldstream?'

'What's on there? It's a long way to go in this weather.'

'I've got a nice wee pony with a gig out there. We could be at Coldstream in a couple of hours.'

'I'm not going to Coldstream in this weather. How's your pony going to get over the roads?'

'Well, the mail coach is getting through and if it gets through, so will I. We'll go on the high road. Get your shawl and come to Coldstream with me, Aylie.'

It was the way he almost whispered her name that made her stomach turn over. He was putting her under his old spell again and though she tried to fight it, her protest grew fainter.

'But why should I want to go to Coldstream?'

He came right into the stable and put his arms round her, pressing her against the thick serge of his shawl-collared coat. 'We'll go to Coldstream and get old Patie Mudie to marry us. I'm in a marrying mood today.'

She felt she had gone mad as she sat beside him in the gig, watching the adroit way he handled the reins and cracked the whip over the head of the trotting pony.

'I can't get married like this,' she protested, spreading her hands out over the thick material of her working skirt and sacking apron and indicating her heavy boots. He hadn't even been prepared to wait while she changed out of her working clothes.

'Of course you can. The bondager costume suits you, especially that hat. Tie it down with your headcloth so the wind doesn't have it off your head. I don't want a bare-headed bride,' he laughed.

'I can't get married without telling my mother,' was her next protest.

'Of course you can. She'd only try to stop you,' he replied. 'But she'll get used to it. It's best just to go back and tell her it's been done.'

'But we don't know much about each other, do we? She might think we're marrying in haste and you know what they say about that. Why should I marry you anyway when you've never courted me properly? You only come to see me now and again . . .'

He turned his head towards her and looked her straight in the eyes.

'I know enough about you to want to marry you. And it's not in haste. I've thought about you ever since you were that wee lassie in Maryfield stable. Do you remember? I tried putting you out of my mind but you kept getting back in. Believe me, I didn't want to get married at first.

'I stayed away because I was trying to fight you off – but you've got me, Aylie Cannon, and you're never going to get rid of me now.'

She remembered every single time she had ever seen him, including the day at the fair when he had that bold-eyed girl on his arm.

'But what about your other girls? What about that one you went to the Lammas Fair with?'

He laughed, his eyes crinkling at the corners. 'She worried you, did she? That was me trying to put you off. Oh, she was just a diversion. I want *you* for a wife.'

They made good progress because, as they travelled eastwards, a thaw came creeping in from the coast. She knew she was going to do it – she'd known that from the moment he asked her – but she was not going to make it easy for him.

Coldstream was growing closer and she could see the little town clinging to the north bank of the river Tweed as they came along the road from Kelso towards it. Using his whip as a pointer, Hugh showed her the wide arched

178

bridge over the river that marked the boundary with England.

'The place Patie marries people is at the end of the bridge,' he said.

'I don't think I should do it,' she said. 'After all, I don't even know how you earn your living.'

He shot a glance at her. 'But you must have heard.'

'My mother says you're a poacher and that you're one of the Boomer men.'

'She's well informed, your mother, for a woman who lives in a hermit's cell.'

'Are you really a smuggler, Hugh?'

'Would it make a difference if I said I was?'

They were in the main street now, heading for the little inn at the end of the bridge. Then she laughed.

'No, I don't suppose it would,' she told him, shaking her head.

Everywhere Hugh Kennedy went people knew him and greeted him by name. In the inn at the end of the bridge, an old man behind the rough bar shouted out at the sight of him.

'What're you after in this weather, Kennedy?' he asked jovially, pouring dark porter into a pewter mug.

'I'm after Patie Mudie. I'm getting married today,' said Hugh, lifting the mug and handing it to Aylie.

The other men in the bar gave a cheer. 'A wedding! You'll have to put up the drinks then,' and one ran out of the inn door, shouting back over his shoulder, 'I'll fetch Patie before the lassie changes her mind.'

Patie Mudie was a grave-faced man who could have passed for a churchman, so solemn was his demeanour and so dark his clothes. He was immensely tall, with very long arms that made him look like a monkey Aylie had once seen in a cage at the fair. The lugubriousness of his expression as he surveyed the bridal pair reminded her of the monkey's face as well.

'It'll cost you half a guinea,' were his first words to Hugh, and when the coin was handed over he bit it with his yellow teeth to see if it was counterfeit. 'You canna be too sure,' he solemnly informed the bride as he did this.

They were told to stand up together in the middle of the bar-room floor, watched by the smiling drinkers and a few women from the kitchens who came crowding in to see the fun. They made a handsome pair as they held hands and Patie chanted his formula over them, ending with 'I declare you to be man and wife before God and in the sight of man.'

The crowd cheered but Hugh and Aylie were deaf to the noise. Like people in a dream they dropped hands, stepped close together and for the first time he kissed her – very gently. At the touch of his lips and his breath on her face, she felt the strength leaving her entire body. There was no doubt left in her now. She had done the right thing.

'Is that it?' she softly asked when he released her from his arms. Then to Patie she said, 'Are you sure this marriage is legal?'

Patie was incensed at her doubt. 'Of course it's legal. I've married hundreds of couples. It's as legal as any ceremony done by a preacher. I'm a professional man, I'll have you know.'

He produced a slip of paper which was filled in with their names, dated and handed over for them to sign. Aylie wrote her name and gave Hugh the pen but he looked at it with a red flush rising in his face. 'I can't write,' he said to her.

She took his hand in hers and said, 'Don't worry, I'll guide your hand,' and with her helping him they wrote his name on the marriage lines.

Patie was pleased when everything was done and he had a mug of porter in his hand. 'There, that's your proof,' he told her when he handed the marriage paper to her.

They walked out of the inn like people in a trance and Hugh said, 'Before we go back, I want to buy you a wedding favour.'

There was a little shop selling cloth and ribbons tucked

180

away in the corner of the high street, and the old woman who came bustling through from the back premises when the bell over her front door rang out was smiling and friendly. She seemed to guess that they were newly wed and was happy for them.

'I want a wedding favour for my wife,' said Hugh, reaching into his pocket for some money.

The shop woman looked at Aylie's radiant face and asked, 'What sort of favour would you like?'

Hugh had obviously been thinking about this and he answered for Aylie, 'I want a white flower for her, something made of satin.'

'I've just the thing,' she said and from a drawer behind the counter she took a curving spray of white satin roses which she held out to Aylie.

'Oh, they're lovely, so lovely,' whispered the girl and took them gently in her mittened hands. The roses looked exotic and out of place against her working clothes but Hugh took them from her and gently pinned them into the brim of her black hat and then stood back, looking at her.

'You're the most beautiful woman in the world,' he said with fierce and infinite feeling. Then throwing some money down on the counter, and without waiting for change, he led Aylie back to the waiting gig.

As they trotted out of Coldstream he said, 'We'll go back by Yetholm. I want you to meet my people.'

'But what about my mother? She'll be worried if I don't go home tonight,' she protested.

'Oh, the news that you've run off with the gypsy will have got to her by now. Don't worry about that,' he told her, and turned the gig over a humpbacked bridge heading for the south.

The cottage of Hannah Fa' his mother – gypsy women, like many bondager women, kept their maiden names after marriage – was a hovel. She shared it with her mother and the place was like a cowshed, filthy, unfurnished and stinking with the smell of the foul tobacco

181

the two women smoked constantly in dirty clay pipes. When Hugh strode in with Aylie they were sitting side by side before a fire in the middle of the floor. Over it hung a blackened cooking pot that was giving up a steady hiss of steam and smelt as if they were cooking something unmentionable.

Neither of the women looked surprised and stared at the girl with expressionless black eyes which told her that they had heard about her and liked her as little as her mother liked Hugh – even less in fact.

Both women spoke roughly to Hugh in a strange language, Romany she supposed, and though she guessed that they were perfectly able to speak ordinary Scots, they refused to do so in front of her. She never heard either of them say a single word she could understand because when she was there they stuck resolutely to their own incomprehensible tongue.

Hugh was embarrassed by their reaction to his new wife. 'We'll have to stay here tonight and then I'll take you back to your mother tomorrow,' he said. 'We'll sleep on the floor but pay no heed to them, they don't like strangers.'

At this the oldest woman spat noisily into the fire and the flames crackled spitefully up the chimney to the blackened beams of the roof.

After they ate some of the horrible stew from the blackened pot, Aylie lay in the crook of her new husband's arm, watching the flickering flames and thinking that they were having a very odd bridal night. The two evil crones had no intention of going to sleep or leaving them in peace and they crouched whispering over the fire till it seemed to her that they were busy casting evil spells against her. Soon, however, sleep overtook her and he held her close till morning came.

Jane received the news of the wedding with a grim face.

'I hope you did all the right things; I hope you carried a nosegay of herbs to drive away the devil and had a silver coin in the heel of your shoe,' she said to her daughter.

'Oh Mam, that's all old rubbish, all witchcraft. People don't do things like that now,' Aylie protested.

Jane shook her head. 'Well, they should,' she said before turning on Hugh, who was silently watching the mother and daughter. She glared at him and said, 'Will you look after my daughter, young Kennedy? Will you look after her truly?'

His face was as grim as hers when he replied, 'I love Aylie, I really love her. You can feel safe about that. I'd never do anything to hurt her. She's in my heart . . .' And he put a clenched fist on his chest in an expressive gesture that allayed some of Jane's fears about his suitability as a husband. She remembered only too well the power of love and could not bring herself to argue against it.

Before he came to take her to Coldstream, he had found them a place to live in one of the abandoned farmhouses that dotted the Bowmont Valley a few miles outside the hidden village of Yetholm, which local people said guarded its isolation because it was inhabited by two kinds of outcasts – gypsies and smugglers.

The valley was a lonely and empty place, peopled only by sheep belonging to a nearby grazier and dotted by a few isolated farmhouses left empty by families who had emigrated to Canada in the early years of the century.

The house Hugh had taken over and repaired was huddled down behind a man-high drystone dyke, a strong protection against the driving wind and snow that swept up the valley in winter time.

When she stepped inside her own front door for the first time, Aylie was surprised at the size of the house. It was like a mansion compared to the cottages in which she had lived her life, for there were two main rooms downstairs and another two rooms above with tiny windows staring out at the hills that closed in around them like the rim of a bowl. Hugh had made the place watertight and built a brick oven beside the open kitchen hearth, so it was a snug hideaway. Outside there was a line of old stone sheds and byres where they would keep a cow, a pig and, of course, their horses.

His father, old Gilbert, was waiting in the house for them to arrive and he embraced her warmly. 'My word, I'm glad he had the sense to pick you for a wife,' he told her. 'You're the best woman on a horse I've ever seen in my life and I've seen a few. I'm going to give you a wedding present, I'm going to tell you the Horseman's Word!'

He caught hold of her head and whispered in her ear . . . 'Belthazar, Melchior, Achitophel . . . Guard it well, never write it down. Not many people have the word and some would kill to get it.'

She was suitably impressed because the Horseman's Word was a closely guarded secret. Those who did not have the secret regarded it as a joke but the initiates firmly believed that knowledge of the words gave them power over the most intractable horses. It had to be passed on by someone with the power, and the knowledge was guarded jealously by the gypsies. Fathers told the 'word' to their eldest sons – but usually to no one else.

All spring and summer Hugh stayed at home with her, and when they needed money he took occasional jobs on neighbouring farms, helping with the sowing, then with the shearing, the hay making and finally the harvesting. He gave her his wages which she buried beneath the earthen floor of the kitchen in an old stone crock. Living cost them little because they cultivated their garden and augmented their diet with vegetables brought from the farms where Hugh worked and fish or game he poached from the nearby moors and rivers.

They were blissfully happy, like two children in paradise. One of their greatest joys was to go together to every local fair, riding out in the early morning mounted on two good horses, to spend the day among the stalls and sideshows, greeting old friends and making new ones. Marriage had made Aylie blossom into a lovely, proudlooking woman and her happiness showed in her face.

Her eyes were full of her dashing, handsome husband and she espoused all his causes with fervour.

He had never been taught to read or write – in fact he had never gone to school at all – but he had needle-sharp intelligence and could absorb information more quickly than anyone she had ever met. In the evenings, they sat together in one big chair by their fireside and she read to him till the candle guttered down in the brass candlestick. Then they went up to bed, to lie close and deep on their down-stuffed pillows, under a thick quilt. Their lovemaking was ecstatic and as the months passed she grew more and more adroit in the art of pleasing them both in bed.

'You're a witch like your mother,' he whispered to her as they lay naked and close together after their fury of passion subsided.

She thought this innocent life would never end but when autumn came, when the rosehips and brambles glowed like jewels in the hedgerows and mists drifted like melancholy ghosts up their valley, he told her about the smuggling trade.

From time to time, they had ridden out together at night to attend meetings where he spoke about the fight for better conditions for farm workers, though never as fervently as he had done in the Myreheugh schoolroom. The audiences, usually small and predominantly male, would nod and agree with what he said but no one was ever moved to the same level of indignation as Hugh.

When he sensed that his audience were backing away from him and were too timid to answer his plea that they form unions and organize themselves against their employers, scorn crept into his words. Aylie, who knew him so well, could see it burning in his dark eyes and hear it echoing bitterly in his voice. He knew he was preaching a lost cause.

One night, as they left a particularly lukewarm gathering, he said to her, 'I'm giving this up. The people round here are too scared to stand up for themselves. You mark my words, Aylie, when the rest of the country is free, the Borderers'll still be touching their forelocks to the masters. I'm sticking to smuggling from now on.'

She stared across at him, fear gripping her heart. 'Smuggling, what do you mean? It's dangerous, Hugh, you might get caught.'

He laughed. 'I've not been caught yet, lass, and I've been smuggling since I was ten years old.'

He never spoke at a meeting again and she grieved because she knew that the enormous energy and rage which possessed him had to be channelled into something else, and she worried about where it would take them.

In early November he came into their kitchen one evening accompanied by a large, ferocious-looking white dog. It had tiny, piglike eyes set in a wedge-shaped skull and its head moved from side to side as if it were trying to size up everything and everyone in the room.

'My God, Hugh, what's that?' she gasped, recoiling from the slobbering beast. She liked dogs but this one struck her as being particularly ugly and dangerous.

He laughed. 'Don't be scared, it looks worse than it is. It's a bull terrier, doesn't it look fierce?'

'What do we want a dog like that for? We've got two collies already and one of them's due to have pups any day now. We've plenty of dogs.'

'Oh, I've got a use for Nelson, haven't I, old man?' he said and bent to fondle the animal's ears with a grin on his face. She could tell that he already knew what the use was.

'What are you going to do?' she demanded, hands on her hips, and he laughed again.

'Nelson and I are going smuggling.'

All during the following week there was a great deal of coming and going at their isolated home. Hugh brought in four new horses and he trotted them out, putting them through their paces for the men who drifted into the yard as the evenings closed in. For a short time she hoped he was only trying to sell the horses but that was not the case, he was showing them off.

One of the most frequent visitors was a half gypsy

186

called Charlie Eckford who was a blacksmith in a tiny hamlet between their house and Yetholm. He was as fiery and wild as her husband and almost as impressive to look at, for he was massively built – burly as an ox, with muscles like knotted ropes in his arms.

Like Hugh, Charlie was a radical who violently preached the cause of workers' revolution. He was an educated man who greedily soaked up information from any newspapers he could lay his hands on and he passed it all on to Hugh. They agreed in their disillusionment about the attitudes of his more accepting contemporaries.

'The fools, they should be organizing themselves, not bending their heads and taking what's handed out to them. They should want more, they should demand more. For God's sake, we're as good as any man, aren't we Hughie? Good as any man!'

'And better, much better than most!' Hugh always replied to this plea from Charlie.

She knew they were planning some nefarious expedition and it was no surprise when he told her, 'Aylie, I'm going away for a couple of days down over the Border. Will you be all right here or do you want to go and stay with your mother?'

She looked round from the fireplace where she was raising bread on the top of the oven and said without hesitation, 'I'll stay here, Hugh. If anyone saw me at Charterhall, they'd wonder why. You know how tongues can wag. No, I'll be all right. Nobody ever comes up here and if they do I'll pretend you're out on the hills.'

He was delighted at the way she was taking it, and gave her a kiss.

But she struggled out of his grasp and said, 'You'd better tell me exactly what you're doing. What are you smuggling anyway?'

'Charlie and I have decided that we ought to get into the trade in a bigger way . . . we've been at it off and on for years but in a small way, and always for other people. We just carried the stuff over the Border. But now we're going to make money for ourselves, we're going to take whisky down to Boulmer. There's a Frenchman called Daniel Fleury who comes over from France with brandy and tobacco and he'll take all the whisky we can carry down to him. If we can't change our lives one way, we can change them another! We'll get rich, Aylie, you'll have a silk gown yet.'

She sat down at the kitchen table and said, 'So that's why you've been getting new horses?'

Hugh nodded. 'And that's why I got Nelson. He'll run with us as protection against nosy excise men.'

She looked at the slobbering dog. 'But he's so gentle, what could he do?'

Hugh laughed. 'Nothing, I suppose, but he looks damned wicked, you've got to admit that. All the big gangs have dogs running with them.'

Aylie was disturbed. 'I hope you know what you're doing. What if you get caught?'

He stood up and went over to the fire, where he leant an arm along the mantelpiece, staring back at her defiantly.

'I won't get caught. I'll make sure of that. I know these moors like the back of my hand. My grandfather, old Matt, used to take me out with him when he did a bit of smuggling so I know old gypsy routes across the hills that no one else knows. We'll take our stuff to Boulmer and bring more back. No one will be any the wiser.'

The magnitude of the undertaking suddenly appalled her. It was not a jape any longer.

'I'm afraid for you,' she said simply and he came across to put his arms round her waist, nuzzling at her hair.

'Don't be afraid, my dearest heart. I'm doing it to give us a better life, you and me. We'll have money in our pockets and a gig for you to drive in. You won't ever have to slave in the fields again or go in fear of a farmer. I've told you, if we can't win pride and independence one way, we'll win it another.'

The two men in Aylie's kitchen were laughing and joking

as if they were going to a fair and not on a nefarious trip, fraught with danger.

For the past two weeks Hugh had been filling the hayloft with ankers of whisky bought from some of the many illicit stills that were scattered over the lonely hills. Now he and Charlie were bringing them down and rolling them over the yard so that they could be tied to the sides of their four packhorses. Each man was to ride one horse and lead two others, an undertaking that required expert horsemanship.

'Why do the English want to buy our whisky? Haven't they any of their own down there?' she asked as she watched the neat little barrels being heaved on to the backs of the horses.

'Oh aye, Aylie, they've whisky all right but they pay duty on it. It's half as cheap for them to buy it from us, whisky's a real money maker. We'll take part of our money in brandy and sell it at another profit when we get back,' said Charlie, who was rolling the barrels around as if they were acorn shells.

'I'm worried about you both. I won't sleep a wink till you get back,' she told him and he laughed his deep laugh.

'Don't you worry about us, we'll be fine. My grand-father's folk were reivers and it runs in my blood to go out raiding at night.'

She looked across the stable to where her husband was tieing a load on to another horse's back. His anticipation and energy almost made him shine in the shadows. It also ran in his blood, she knew, to relish dangerous trips under the light of the moon, and there was nothing she could do to stop him. Even Nelson seemed to be infected with the excitement of the occasion and to know what was required of him, for he sat grinning in the doorway waiting for the cavalcade to leave.

'Take care,' she whispered as she kissed Hugh just before the mounted men clattered out of the yard. She felt as if time had been turned back. Women in the Borders had been sending their men off at night on dangerous raids like this for centuries. 'I wish I could come with you.'

He leaned down from the saddle to tell her, 'I wish you were too. Perhaps next time.'

They were away for two days and on the morning of the third day, she heard sounds in the yard at about three o'clock. Still in her night clothes, clutching a blanket over her shoulders, she ran out, heedless of the chill air, to see a jubilant Hugh leaping from the back of his tired horse and running towards her with his arms in the air.

He was more exhilarated than she had ever seen him and he swung her off her feet, whirling her round in the air as he cried out, 'We did it Aylie, we did it! We sold everything at a good price and brought back lots of brandy. My, that Frenchman Fleury's a real lad!'

The profit they made from the trip was the equivalent of six months' wages for labouring in the fields. As Hugh counted it all out on their kitchen table she realized that her husband's way of life was now to be that of a full-time smuggler. The days of hiring himself out with farming gangs was finished.

'If you go on doing this long enough, you're almost sure to be caught,' she protested.

'I won't get caught. Besides, lots of people are doing it, far more than folk ever know. There's a minister at Coldstream who goes back and forward into England with a sheep's bladder full of whisky in his lum hat!' he laughed.

'A bladder full of whisky's not so bad as eight ankers of the stuff,' she pointed out. 'If they catch him, they'll probably let him off with a fine. If they catch you and Charlie, they'll send you to prison.'

Her mind went back to Phemie in the prison in Edinburgh. Being shut up like that would kill Hugh. The thought chilled her blood and anxiously she took his hand. 'Oh Hugh, we don't need so much money. We've been so happy living up here and we've everything we want. You get plenty of work and dealing in the horses brings in a bit. Don't go riding out again.'

His face darkened. 'You don't understand, Aylie, it's not just the money . . . it's more than that. It's the danger and the fact that you're cocking a snook at the bastards. Besides how else would we get so much money as we've earned by two nights on the trail? Next time, we're going to take more. Next time we'll do even better.'

They quarrelled for the first time and she flounced off on one of the ponies to visit her mother and allow both of their tempers time to cool down.

Jane's cell was always damp in the winter and even the charcoal brazier burning alongside her little fireplace failed to take the chill out of it.

'Oh, Mam, you shouldn't be living here in this weather. Come back and stay with me till spring comes,' said Aylie, saddened by the evidence of her mother's growing stiffness.

'Of course not,' was the robust reply. 'I wouldn't live a week away from here. Besides, how would the people who need my medicines find me up there in the Bowmont Water? They get sick more in the bad weather than they do in good, you know.'

Her voice was sad, however, and her daughter could see that there was something else on her mind.

'What's wrong. Are you ill, Mam?' she asked.

'I'm no worse than I was. No, I'm not ill.'

'What's wrong then? I know there's something. I can read you like a book.'

'Well, I've been wondering how to tell you this but I was up at the Hepburns' last week and that old tailor was there . . . you know, Phemie's father.'

Aylie shuddered. 'Oh him, I can't bear to think of him.'

Jane nodded in sympathy. 'I know. Anyway he was speaking about Phemie to Flora Hepburn. She's in the Calton jail in Edinburgh and he was saying that she's gone very strange . . . raving and breaking things in her cell. Sometimes she's so bad that they've got to tie her up to keep her quiet.'

Aylie sank her face in her hands, she could hardly bear

191

to think of her friend's suffering in prison. Phemie had been such a strange girl, it was difficult to be friendly with her, but her misery and terrible plight moved Aylie's heart unbearably. To be shut away from the sky, the trees, the birds and the lovely rolling hills . . . how terrible!

When she reached home again, she sought out Hugh in the stables and threw her arms round him. 'I'm sorry we fought. I know you're quite capable of looking after yourself – but I can't help worrying . . .'

He held her close and kissed her gently. 'I'm sorry too. I shouldn't have been so short with you. You're looking very sad, what happened at Charterhall? Is your mam sick?'

She shook her head. 'It's not that. She was telling me about Phemie – you remember, the girl who killed her bairn. She's in the Calton jail in Edinburgh and she's gone a bit funny in the head.'

Hugh was sombre. 'I don't blame the lassie. The Calton jail's a terrible dungeon, I've heard.'

'Oh, I wish I could go to see her,' Aylie said sadly, and her husband stood back in sudden decision.

'Right, you can! I've never been to Edinburgh and they say it's a grand place. What do you say we take a trip there before my next trip down to Boulmer? We've got the money.'

She gasped in genuine amazement. 'Us go to Edinburgh?' It seemed as remote as America. 'Oh, we couldn't do that. How would we get there? It's too far to ride in one day.'

'Nonsense, we don't need to ride it. No, what we'll do, you and I, is take the mail coach. We'll catch it in Jeddart and ride all the way to Edinburgh like gentry.'

It was just after dawn when the olive green mail coach drew up in front of Jedburgh's Spread Eagle Hotel. Embarking passengers gathered at its door, saying farewell to the friends who had come to see them off, and

192

new arrivals wandered into the hotel, rubbing the sleep out of their eyes.

Shouting ostlers were hoisting bags and boxes up on to the railed-in section of the roof and other men from the hotel stables were unharnessing the sweating, tired horses and putting six fresh ones in their place.

Aylie and Hugh bought outside tickets – for one shilling and sixpence each – which entitled them to a seat on the roof among the baggage. In bad weather it would have been a miserable ride but the day promised to be clear and dry, and Hugh said they would have a better view of the countryside than the people cooped up close together inside.

Then off they went, the six strong horses galloping flat out and the post boy sounding his horn in gay abandon as they flew along. Aylie had not had such a thrill since she went hunting with Colonel Scroggie.

They followed the old Roman road from Jedburgh to St Boswells. It was deeply rutted and in places the stone slabs laid down by the Roman builders could still be seen, deeply engraved with the ruts made by their wheels.

The mail stopped first at Earlston, in the yard of the Red Lion Hotel, where the horses were swiftly changed, and once more they were off. From now on it was country that Aylie did not know and she leaned forward, clinging tightly to the rail, taking in every detail of the landscape.

As it flashed past her in an unending panorama, she was struck by its tranquil beauty, by the majesty of the hills, the mysterious depths of the woods and the twisting Leader river, high with water now, cutting its way between banks of blood-red earth. This magic fairyland was her native country, and seeing it spread before her, she could fully understand her mother's passion for it.

The next change of horses was in the huge stableyard of the Carfraemill Inn where the passengers were able to alight and refresh themselves in the taproom. Spirits were rising now that they were getting near Edinburgh and even the post boy's horn sounded gay and cheeky as they

193

sped up the steep road that led to Soutra, the summit of the bastion of hills that guarded the Borderland from the north. The wheels of the coach were throwing up sharp stones and lurching into deep ruts in its headlong pace but Hugh and Aylie, alone on the roof, clung to each other and yelled like banshees in delight.

Their cries abruptly ceased when they reached the crown of the hill and saw, spread in front of them, the awe-inspiring panorama of the Lothians. The coach stopped to give the horses a breather and they sat in silence staring around them, totally transfixed by the view. It was a bright, clear day and they could see for miles ... To the north was the jagged silhouette of Arthur's Seat and the misty spires of Edinburgh's churches, all guarded by the castle perched high on its outcrop of rock. Beyond that was the silver sheen of the Forth estuary and the hills of Fife. Towards the east spread the blue waters of the North Sea, dotted here and there with fishing boats, and westwards spread the towering line of the Pentland Hills. Aylie gulped in astonishment at the sight and felt that the whole world lay before her, spread out in its majesty.

Even Hugh was impressed as he gazed around and with a sharp intake of breath, he whispered, 'My word, isn't that grand!' Then putting out his arm, he gathered his silent wife to him.

It was afternoon when they disembarked from their rooftop seats, stiff legged and chilled but eager to see as much as they could of this bustling city where the people on the streets paid no attention to them. They were accustomed to being greeted as they walked along, to knowing every face, and now they felt as if they had landed in another world. The crowds pushing past wore different clothes to the people at home and they even spoke a different language. Aylie could not imagine how their daily lives were led.

The coach had put them down outside a large theatre that faced across to the elegant façade of an imposing building. Roads seemed to lead off in every direction. To

194

their left and their right were streets lined with tall tenement houses. From almost every window women were leaning, screeching over the windowsills, high above the heads of passers-by. On all four corners of the square were alehouses that sent the malty smell of beer out into the streets.

They were lost so Hugh stopped a passer-by to ask, 'Where's the Calton jail?'

The stranger grinned knowingly. 'Oh, you're after the prison? It's over there to your right, go alang the bridge and when you look up you'll see it. You canna miss it.'

He was right. The massive bulk of the jail looked like a fortress, standing grimly on the top of a steep rockface. From the barred windows they could see tattered bits of cloth fluttering in the breeze and sometimes a white face staring out between the iron struts.

Aylie shuddered at the sight. 'Oh, what a terrible place. Imagine being shut up in there for five years.'

Hugh's face too was solemn. 'You might as well be dead,' he said feelingly.

Both of them were children of the open air, they needed space to live and were already beginning to realize that city life would not suit them.

A man in a snuff-stained uniform stood in the gatehouse and he was very abrupt. 'You can't come in here. No visitors are allowed.' He glared at the two country bumpkins who had the effrontery to ask to speak to a prisoner.

Aylie put on her most winsome face and pleaded, 'But we've come all the way from Jedburgh. We want to see my friend Phemie Anderson.'

Winsomeness did not work with him. 'This isn't Jedburgh. This is Edinburgh and we do things different here. We don't let folk go wandering around our prison. Your friend'll be in the women's prison anyway, and it's over there.' He pointed to the left where they could see another block of buildings and yet another gate.

'But you'll not get to see her, not unless you've got a

letter or you're official visitors.' His tone indicated that he was perfectly well aware they were very unofficial.

The gatekeeper on the women's prison was just as rude.

When he saw the disappointment on his wife's face, Hugh knew what was needed. Like a conjurer, he produced a handful of silver and pressed it into the man's hand. 'See what can be done,' he asked.

The jailer's attitude changed as soon as he got the money, which he slipped quickly into his pocket. 'Wait here. I'll speak to the chief wardress.'

In a short time he was back. 'What was the name of the prisoner you wanted to see again?'

'Phemie Anderson.'

'What's she in for?'

'She cut the throat of her baby,' said Hugh.

'Oh, then she's a long-termer. That's going to be hard. Most of them are kept in solitary confinement. Is she doing hard labour?'

Aylie well remembered the judge's voice sentencing Phemie to hard labour and she nodded. 'Yes, she is.'

'In that case you're in luck. They're just ending their work for the day,' said the jailer. 'They'll be coming out of the treadmill shed over there any minute. If you stand here, you'll see her, but don't try to speak to her. She's not allowed to talk and if she does she gets extra punishment.'

The young people looked at each other aghast but stood where they were told until a straggling line of women came slowly out of the shed door and walked one after the other across the courtyard. They were all dressed in dark gowns with broad yellow arrows painted on the material. Their heads were covered with tightly tied white caps and round their waists they wore long white aprons. Each woman walked with her head down and her hands folded in front of her apron, but as they passed, Aylie saw their eyes sliding towards the watchers at the gate. Some eyes were watchful, some hopeful, some resentful or completely mad. Phemie was almost past before Aylie recognized her, for she had grown as thin as a skeleton and her face was drawn and parchment white like the face of an old woman.

She looked directly at Aylie and a flash of recognition lit in her eyes, but only for a split second. Immediately it was replaced by blank indifference.

Aylie took a step forward but Hugh put a warning hand on her arm, whispering, 'Stand still, you'll get her into trouble.'

She did as she was told but the tears were running down her face as the column of prisoners disappeared through a heavily barred door.

The jailer saw her distress. 'Don't cry, the woman jailer says your friend's getting better. She's not so violent now, just a bit distracted in her mind, if you see what I mean. She's very religious, always praying. They think she's repented for what she did.'

'What do they make her work at every day? She's not a very strong girl,' Aylie asked, fearful for Phemie.

'The women work at the treadmill, they pedal it for eight hours a day. That's their punishment,' she was told.

'What do you mean, pedal it? What does it make?' asked Aylie.

The jailer shrugged as if they were a pair of ignorant rustics. 'Nothing, it doesn't make anything. They just sit and pedal it. That's their hard labour. It keeps them out of trouble.'

Both of them were sombrely silent as they walked off into the city in search of lodgings for the night.

Edinburgh now seemed hostile and alien, no longer the place of enchantment it had seemed when viewed from the top of Soutra hill. Though they were well accustomed to muddy farmyards and cow byres, the filth and smell of its streets repelled them. They recoiled from the reeling drunkenness of men on the pavements and drew back from the importuning beggars. Aylie stared around and wondered how men and women could live in a place where there were no trees and no flowers. City life was definitely not for her.

197

They spent a sad night in a shabby lodging house on the High Street and she was still sunk in depression when they mounted the mail coach to go home again next morning. From her seat on the coach roof, she never even turned round to get a last sight of the city as they headed back to the Borderland.

Smuggling was a winter trade. It needed darkness for its cover; it needed bitter nights when no prying eyes were likely to be abroad; it needed the secrecy of empty moors and lonely roads. The Boomer men only rode out between late October and early March, so when spring came Captain Midnight's cutter was no longer to be seen sailing past Seahouses and Hugh put his packhorses out to grass. Nelson lay sleeping in a sunny corner of the yard, and Hugh and Aylie went out to spend their money. Hugh had made five trips that winter and for the last three he recruited his cousin Abel, a shy youth of about seventeen, to join him and Charlie in the Boomer runs. The money had come rolling in and now, dressed in their best, Hugh and Aylie visited all the fairs and festivities of the Borders. They never went back to Yetholm to see Hugh's mother but they paid calls on Gilbert Kennedy in his immaculately kept stableyard and, most often, on Jane.

When she went to see her mother Aylie delighted in taking along unexpected presents – toffee in a twist of paper bought from a peddler met on the way; a bunch of flowers plucked from the hedgerow; a fairing figure made out of thick earthenware. Jane was pleased to see the obvious happiness and prosperity of her daughter and when Aylie confided that the only shadow in her life was her failure to conceive a child, she set herself to the task of preparing an elixir that would solve the problem.

The specific used by Alice in cases of infertility was sage juice, taken daily, and as she prepared a bottleful for Aylie, Jane reflected that its value would probably only be in easing her daughter's mind. They were both healthy young people and when the time was right, they would have their child, of that she was sure.

She asked no questions about how they had suddenly become so flush with money and Aylie volunteered no explanations. Though Jane had her suspicions it was better not to know the truth, she decided.

The summer of 1837 was the happiest of Aylie's life. The sun seemed to shine every day and she luxuriated in its warmth like an opening flower. On the hottest days she and Hugh went down to the Bowmont Water that ran near their house and bathed naked, confident that no one could come up their track without Nelson warning them first. They splashed like children in the crystal water, laughing and pushing each other into the pools fringed by tall flag irises, then they lay down on the springy grass, cushioned upon sweet-smelling wild thyme, and made love before falling asleep in each other's arms, only waking when the golden orb of the sun sank below the rim of the tallest hill that stood guardian over their hidden valley. Their skins glowed berry brown with health and it seemed to them that this blissful happiness would never end.

On 1 August they went again to Melrose's Lammas Fair, bigger than ever this year, and riotously noisy with the shouts of stallholders and hustlers trying to induce the drifting crowds to spend their money.

Many of the people in the fair crowd knew them and stopped to talk with them, casting admiring eyes on Aylie who looked very handsome in a blue print dress and a large pale-cream straw bonnet with blue satin ribbons. They met Jock Hepburn and his family, and Aylie was pleased to see how tall and strong young Sandy was growing. For his part, Sandy looked at her as if she were a goddess, remembering that when he was small she had looked after him.

'Do you remember us playing hide and seek in the woods at Charterhall when you were a wee boy?' she asked him teasingly and he blushed scarlet, the red tide rising up to the bushy ginger hair that was so like his father's.

'Yes, I remember,' he mumbled, staring awkwardly at his feet for he was at the age when boys fall deeply, painfully in love – and the object of this boy's love for a long time was to be the unattainable Aylie.

Gilbert Kennedy was at the fair, and they found him in the centre of a ring of dapper grooms. He was proudly boasting about a fine pair of horses his master had recently bought and which had pulled the carriage all the way from Yetholm to Melrose in record time.

When Hugh and Aylie joined the group, his father put his arm round Aylie and said to his friends, 'This laddie of mine's a grand horseman but his wife's even better. Aylie's got the finest hands of anybody I've ever seen on a horse – don't ever stop working with horses, Aylie. Don't get too grand a lady for that.'

She laughed and shook her head. 'I'll never be too grand for horses, Gilbert. I love them as much as you do.'

'Do you still remember the words I taught you?' he asked her. 'You might need them one day.'

Hugh snorted. 'Oh, you and the Horseman's Word, it's a lot of nonsense. You can either make horses work for you or you can't. You don't need special words to make it happen.'

Gilbert flashed his dark eyes at his son. 'You're wrong. You can say what you like but I know they work. Come on, Aylie, whisper them to me so's I know you haven't forgotten them . . .'

Laughing, she cupped a hand round her mouth and whispered softly in Gilbert's ear, 'Balthazar, Melchior and Achitophel . . .'

His face was solemn as he listened and when she was finished, he straighted up and said, 'Good, you've not forgotten. Tell the words to your children, Aylie, and to no one else. They're gypsy words and they should be kept by gypsy folk. I only told you because of your gift.'

The mention of children cast a shadow over Aylie's

face and seeing this, Hugh grabbed her hand and led her away. 'Come on, I'll take you to get a drink. It's very hot.'

The ale tent was packed with people and they had to shoulder their way through. In the middle of the sweating throng, Hugh was stopped by a fat, freckled hand on his shoulder.

A coarse voice said, 'Hey gypsy, you're getting a bit big for your boots, aren't you?' The speaker was the farmer from Myreheugh, the father of Phemie's baby.

Hugh arrogantly shrugged the hand off his shoulder and glared at the speaker. 'What would you know about the size of my boots?' he asked defiantly.

'Just what I hear. They tell me you're one of the Midnight Men these days . . .'

'I've heard the same of you,' said Hugh, 'except you don't ride out. You wait at home and send others out to do the riding for you.'

The farmer's face darkened. He was obviously well on the way to being drunk. 'You're a cheeky young pup. But listen to me and listen well. I don't want any of you gypsies horning into my business. Take a warning, don't go running down to Boulmer again or you might find yourself in trouble next time.'

'When I want your advice, I'll ask for it,' said Hugh, and pushed on through the crowd.

Aylie, following behind him, was shaken by the encounter. The sight of the Myreheugh farmer brought back memories of Phemie and the miserable time she had while working on his land.

'I hate that man,' she said shakily when they were out in the open again. 'What did he mean by speaking to you like that?'

'He thinks he's got the smuggling trade tied up round here. He's in it with his brother – the one that sits on the bench – and they've had everything their own way for years. He puts up the money and hires people to do the runs for him. Then he takes the profit. That's how I started, taking loads down for him, and he's mad now that I'm setting up on my own. He thinks he should be in charge of all the smuggling trade that goes in and out of the district and till I started, he was.'

The girl shivered. 'But people like him have got power behind them, haven't they? Oh Hugh, perhaps you should stop now that you've made a bit of money. Perhaps we should stick to horse dealing.'

He looked proud and defiant. 'There's no way I'm going to stop. Certainly not because that rat of a man threatens me. He'd think he'd scared me off! I'll see *him* off, I'm younger than he is and cleverer. Anyway I know that Daniel Fleury would rather deal with me than with him. His whisky's often watered and Captain Midnight's no fool. You wait, Aylie, I'll be King Smuggler round here yet.'

When October came, the crab apple trees along the road that led to their house were heavy with fruit and the old peddler walked under them to pay his last call of the year. In Aylie's warm kitchen with the tabby cat sleeping on the hearthrug, he spread out his enticing wares – laces and ribbons, pins and needles, lengths of material and a couple of shawls with red and blue Persian patterns on them, and she made a few purchases.

When he was rewrapping his bundle, he said, 'You were at Myreheugh when the lassie killed her bairn, weren't you?'

She nodded. 'Yes, I was. She was my friend.'

'Then you'll be sad about what's happened to her,' said the peddler.

'What's that? I heard she'd gone a bit strange in the head. Is she worse?'

The old man pulled on his coat and said, 'Oh aye, much worse. She's dead.'

Aylie gasped and leant back against the table top. 'Oh, did they kill her in that awful prison? Did they work her to death?'

'No, she killed herself. She tore up her apron into strips

202

and hanged herself from the window bars. I heard the story from her father yesterday.'

Aylie was furious. 'That's awful, I can't bear to think of it.'

'Oh well, she's out of it now,' said the peddler and disappeared through the door.

When Aylie told Hugh about Phemie she stormed in rage, 'He said "She's out of it now!" Yes, she's out of it and her bairn's out of it but her wicked father and that man who fathered her baby are still in it and very safe. The people who shut her up in jail and made her mad are still in it. Everything's rotten, Hugh. You're right. They're all bastards! You're right not to care about their laws.'

A few days later a dark stranger arrived in the yard when Hugh was away and said to her, 'Tell your man that Captain Midnight gets in in five days' time.'

It sounded like a riddle. She looked at the man cautiously and said, 'Captain Midnight? Who's that?'

'Just you tell him what I said,' replied the man, walking off down the road.

When she recounted his words to Hugh, he was delighted. 'Captain Midnight, that's what they call the Frenchman Daniel Fleury. It means the season's on again. He'll be coming in with a load from the Low Countries. I'll have to get busy and get my whisky together.'

She followed him across the yard and said, 'I'd like to ride with you this time. It would be better than waiting at home.'

He gazed at her over his horse's back and replied, 'You'd be capable of it, that's for sure. You're better on a horse than any of the others – better than me, in fact. But it's a long way and it's tough.'

'Take me with you, Hugh,' she pleaded and to her delight he nodded his head after only a moment's reflection.

'All right. I might. It means we can take another pair of packhorses. Our trip will be even better than last time. Don't tell your mother though Aylie, keep it to yourself.'

There was plenty of whisky to buy, for Hugh offered a better price than Myreheugh and the hayloft soon filled up with barrels, so many that it was going to be a problem to get rid of them.

'We're going to take a chance, we'll take them all down to Boomer. With Aylie riding and Abel too, that'll be eight packhorses,' he decided.

But two days before they were due to start out, a horse he was shoeing kicked Charlie and broke his leg. He couldn't ride on the smuggling trip so another man had to be found. Hugh went to Yetholm and came back with a sly-eyed man called Josey whom Aylie distrusted on sight – there was something shifty about him that put her on her guard at once. Josey was to go on the next trip to Boulmer, said Hugh, in spite of the fact that he was a coarse, unskilful rider. He could only cope with one packhorse but he was the only man available.

Josey was very curious, always asking questions. Where did they get their whisky, he asked Aylie and she sent him away with a short 'I don't know'.

'What route are we taking?' he asked Hugh and in a distracted way, he was told the line across country that they always used. Hugh was very taken up with a new horse he had just bought himself, a truly magnificent dark bay stallion called Jupiter who stood seventeen hands high and was reputed to be descended from the Barbary Arab. Jupiter had come from Newmarket where he had won several races, but the gentleman who brought him north could not ride him and was glad to get rid of him for as much as he had paid – one hundred pounds.

Then, on the day before they were due to leave for Boulmer, Hugh went out and came back with a new mare for Aylie, a deep-chested, strong-boned dapple grey who looked as if she too could bear a line of racehorses. The secret of how much money Hugh was spending on these horses was kept from his wife, for he knew that if she ever found out what he had paid for Jupiter, she would have thought he had taken leave of his senses.

Aylie was still careful with money and buried what she

could prise out of her husband's hands in her stone crock beneath the floor. The crock was almost full of coins now and she planned to give some of it to her mother when the stiffness in her hands made it impossible for her to go on working.

Jane rarely complained but Aylie knew that there were many days when her pains were so acute that even her most effective medicines failed to muffle them.

In the end however their trip had to be postponed because in the night the snow came sweeping over the hills and the storm raged for more than a week, blanketing everything in white and sweeping shepherds and their flocks to their deaths in the muffling drifts. With the ankers of whisky piled up in the hayloft, Aylie was afraid that some snooper would report them to the excise men. No one in their right mind would ever believe that two people needed so much liquor to get through the winter. It would take ten years to drink it all.

Each morning Hugh stood in the doorway, staring out anxiously, searching for signs of a change in the weather. But everything was in the icy grip of winter, and day after day the sky stayed the same dull pewter colour.

'It'll have to break soon,' he told Aylie every morning. 'We're missing a lot of trade by this weather. When it does thaw, we'll have to get all of the stuff out of here fast.'

When the thaw came however Charlie's leg had still not healed, so they were forced to take Josey with them. Hugh told him to be ready for riding out that night, but later that day they found that Josey had disappeared.

Abel went looking for him and came back to say that he had not been seen in Yetholm. 'I reckon he lost his nerve,' he said scornfully. 'He's a coward is Josey.'

'Damn him, just when I need him. I can't get anyone else now because I don't want people to know when we're going out. The excise men have been around asking questions and you've got to know who you can trust,' cursed Hugh.

Aylie was still burning with the resentment that had

seized her when she heard about Phemie's death, and if she had any doubts at all about going on the expedition it was because she had missed two periods and was starting to allow herself to hope that she might at last be pregnant. This was not the time to tell Hugh, she decided, or he might stop her taking part. She'd keep the information to herself and when they got back from their smuggling trip, she'd break the wonderful news to him. She had no fears that the long ride down into England would be bad for her. She was well used to being in the saddle.

The moon was full as they filed out of the yard, Nelson running alongside. While they plodded along she glanced at Hugh and her heart went out to him in love because of the boldness of the bones of his cheeks and high-bridged nose. His face shone like the helmet of a knight, burnished with silver.

He grinned at her and said, 'Now you know why we like going out under the moon. It's a magic feeling, isn't it?'

To a stranger she would have looked like a young boy because she was riding astride, dressed in a pair of men's trousers and a long greatcoat that swept over the horse's back behind her. Her hair was tucked into a woollen cap pulled well down over her brows and in her belt was a small knife in a leather scabbard. Through all the long ride her heart was singing wildly and there was no thought of sleep as she stared around her at the expanse over which they passed. The horses plodded slowly along, startled now and again by the rustling of a fox or a badger in the dried bracken and heather that fringed the narrow sheep trails they were following. Hugh took his bearings from some internal compass and the others followed him silently, making little conversation – and when they did, not raising their voices above a whisper. For three hours they passed no houses, but at about two o'clock Hugh pointed ahead and she saw the lights of a building in the distance.

When they drew closer she saw that it was a rough

stone house with a low thatched roof. A trickle of smoke was coming from its chimney.

'She's waiting for us. I sent her a message,' said Hugh.

'What is that house?' she asked.

'It's an alehouse. The smugglers use it a lot because the widow woman who keeps it knows how to keep her mouth closed. We'll stop in there to rest the horses and have a meal. She's a good woman is Maggie.'

There was a painted board stuck up over the door announcing 'Meg Swinton, Ales and Porter'. Inside the single room a fire was burning in the hearth and a plump motherly woman was sitting in a rocking chair with a sleeping cat on her lap.

She beamed in welcome when she saw Hugh and gave him a warm hug. 'It's grand to see you, lad. I thought the snow would stop you but I should have known you'd get through.'

She looked quizzically at Aylie. 'Who's the laddie?'

Hugh laughed. 'It's not a laddie, Meg. It's my wife. Take off your hat, Aylie, and let Meg see what I'm saying is true.'

When Aylie's hair tumbled out of the hat, Meg laughed again and said, 'My word, you're a game one, but it would have to be a game one that married my Hughie, wouldn't it?'

She fed them and they rested in front of the fire for an hour before it was time to remount and head off again. By the time dawn broke Aylie caught her first sight of the slate-grey sea far below them. Even from that distance she could see a furious spume breaking over the rocks and it looked bitterly cold.

'We're nearly there,' Hugh told her, 'it's not much farther. Are you tired?'

She shook her head. 'No, I'm not tired. When do we get to Boulmer?'

'Oh, in about three hours. We've got to by-pass Alnwick because the folk there'll be getting up soon but when we're on the flat ground it's an easy canter to

Boulmer village and no one will stop us. They're used to the riders going by.'

The path twisted sharply down a steep valley side, shaded by pine trees, and at one of the bends a young boy with a sheepdog was standing. When they came up on him he called out, 'He's at the Fishing Boat Inn. It's quite safe, there's no excise men around.'

'How do they get away with this so easily?' she wondered aloud.

Hugh laughed as he told her, 'The Frenchman has it all organized. Some of the excise men take his money and the ones who don't are too afraid of him to make things difficult. You wait till you see him, he's a tough character.'

It was not often that Hugh admired other men and her curiosity about Captain Midnight was sharpened.

The village was a stretch of little cottages sitting sideways on to the sea and the Fishing Boat Inn was in the middle of them, at the end of a rough stone pier that jutted into the boiling waves. Moored out beyond the harbour bar, she saw a little cutter. They pushed open the door and found the inn full of smoke and very noisy in spite of the early hour. Men were crowded into the room, sitting at long benches along the walls and drinking out of metal tankards. Hugh and Aylie paused, looking around, and Hugh nudged her, indicating a tall man in a blue coat who was leaning against a wall near the dirty window.

'That's him, that's Captain Midnight.'

His profile was towards them and the first thing that struck her was that even when his face was in repose he seemed to be smiling, for the curving deep lines at the sides of his mouth made him look humorous and amused. His nose had been badly broken at one time for there was a hump on its bridge and it twisted sharply to one side. He was clean shaven and his hair was fair and very curly. From his mouth hung a long, thin black cheroot, the smoke of which curled slowly up to the ceiling. When

208

he turned to see who had arrived, she also noticed that he was wearing golden earrings.

He looked pleased to see Hugh. 'It's the gypsy!' he exclaimed in a strange accent. 'Come in, gypsy, what have you brought for me tonight?'

His eyes ran over Aylie in an interested way and he smiled at her. 'You're a little young to be one of the moonlight boys,' he said laughingly.

Hugh was delighted at the sensation his wife was making. 'This isn't a boy, this is my wife, Aylie,' he said again, bringing her proudly forward.

Captain Midnight removed his cheroot from his mouth in surprise. 'A woman smuggler! I thought you were a boy. Forgive me, Madame.' He took her hand, bending over it in an elegant gesture, and she blushed scarlet, thinking that he was laughing at her but in a way she did not mind, for his dancing eyes made her want to laugh too.

Daniel Fleury, the French smuggler, was famous all down the Northumberland coast. He had been making the trip across the North Sea in his neat little cutter, *L'Esperance*, for ten years and when he said that he would arrive on a certain day, you could be sure that he would keep his word. He was a magnificent seaman, a daring smuggler and above all a fair dealer, who never attempted to cheat or short sell anyone who dealt with him and so his name was highly respected by everyone who dealt in contraband, either as a buyer or a seller. If brandy came from Captain Midnight, it was good brandy, never watered down or adulterated.

The novelty of dealing with a woman amused him, so when he came to settle up with Hugh, he gave him a good bargain and said, 'I'll send a messenger to tell you when I'm coming next time. I like your style, you're a man after my own heart.'

Aylie beamed with pride and pleasure at the captain's words and when, seeing her smile, he turned his eyes on her, she blushed again. He made her forget that she was wearing men's clothes under an overcoat many sizes too big for her. He made her feel like a woman, as fresh and as feminine as if she had been dressed in her finest gown. There was something about the Frenchman that made her want to preen herself and step lightly. Was this a peculiar quality of the French, she wondered? Did her father Blaize have the same effect on her mother? She loved Hugh deeply but he had never allowed himself to flirt with her and he had certainly never openly sighed with love for her or courted her with sweet words, though she did not doubt that his feelings towards her were deep and genuine. When he was moved to emotion it was in private, intense moments and he thought it unmanly to show it outside. Her response to Captain Midnight was not lost on Hugh, whose face darkened.

They left Boulmer at sunset and he rode ahead, imposing a spanking pace on them, cantering up the slopes to the moors and not slackening his pace when he reached them.

Puffing at his side, Abel protested, 'Hold on, we're not in a steeplechase, are we? What's the hurry?'

'I want to get to the inn. I'm thirsty. Now we've just got to deliver the brandy and we're finished.' Hugh was surly and sullen-faced. He didn't speak to Aylie at all.

In misery and confusion she rode behind him. Hugh was jealous. He thought she'd made eyes at the Frenchman. How unjust! It was the first time she had evidence of the jealous streak in her husband's nature and she regretted having unwittingly provoked him into showing it.

She rode up alongside him and spoke directly. 'What do you think you're doing treating me like this? I won't stand for it. Who do you think I am?'

'*You* won't stand for it!' He was as furious as she was. 'I won't stand for you bobbing and becking to the Frenchman. If that's what you want you can just get yourself back down to Boulmer and stay there.'

She gasped in anger. 'So that's what's wrong! I thought as much, but I wasn't doing any such thing. Don't be a fool, Hugh, speak to me properly. You know I'd never look at anyone but you.'

He glanced at her obliquely but his face was still sullen. 'We'll talk about it when we get home, Aylie. I don't want to discuss it now,' he said, digging his spurs into the sides of his horse.

She needed every ounce of her energy when they hit the top of the hill called Yealverton Bell and began the long trek over the Cheviots, for the rain turned to sleet that cut through their clothes and made the horses turn their heads aside in pain as its lash cut into their eyes. Abel, at the back of the line, was battling to control his two led horses, who would have turned and dashed back downhill if he had slackened his hold on them. Aylie, in the middle, crouched in her saddle and, whenever one of her charges became restive, muttered Gilbert's magic words to them. There was no way of knowing if they even heard what she was saying however, because the wind was howling so loudly in her ears that when the riders tried to shout words of encouragement to each other the blast carried the sound over their heads.

Will this journey ever end? Will we be found up here on the hills frozen to death? she asked herself and wondered if Hugh was thinking the same thing. She could just make out his figure, sitting well down on his horse, coat collar turned up round his head, which was bound up like hers, in a woollen scarf.

'This is a hard way to make money,' she called out cheerfully to him, but he did not turn round and she could not tell if he had heard her. She wished he would forget his jealousy and talk to her.

Their progress was slow against the bitter wind. At times it threatened to blow the horses off their feet, and they had to tack and turn in a twisting route to take its fury on their flanks. She stared into the darkness and admired the way Hugh always knew which direction to take. He had a sort of sixth sense about it and even on the most starless nights, he could unerringly find his way home over unknown territory. He had once said there

211

was a sort of magnet in his brain that told him which way to go.

'I think the swallows must have the same thing because they always find their way back in the spring,' he told her.

Nelson was running at the side of the line, head down and tongue lolling. He always liked to keep up with Hugh and his white skin made a marker for her in the darkness.

Their first stop was to be the widow's lonely inn and Aylie longed to see its pinpoint of light on the horizon, but hours passed without any sign of it. Her mount stumbled many times and once when she was on the verge of falling asleep with sheer exhaustion, it almost threw her into a water-filled ditch. The shock made her gather herself together, call up new resources and battle on. She tried to imagine what they looked like to a deity in the sky – if there was such a thing, for like her mother she was a sceptic – three lonely figures, each riding a horse and leading two others, across a vast expanse of lonely land on the top of the world.

She was half dead with tiredness when they reached a crossroads in the track, a point where the old Roman road crossed a droving road used by smugglers. There was a ford there, swollen now with water from the melting snow, and the place where it was safe to cross was marked by a thicket of scrubby hazel, rowan and hawthorn trees that grew only to a man's height because of the ferocity of the prevailing winds. They made up for their lack of height by an impenetrable thickness, however, and deep inside their twisted branches sheltered hares and foxes, badgers, voles and frightened birds who peeped out with flashing eyes when the midnight convoys went by.

Hugh's horse was level with the thicket on the bank of the ford when two shots rang out and Aylie, riding behind him, was startled to full alertness by brilliant orange flashes lighting up the sky. Her husband's figure seemed to slump in his saddle and the white shape of Nelson flung itself towards the thicket with terrible snarls. Another loud bang rang out, another orange flash illumined the scene and the brave Nelson lay dead on the bank.

Abel, behind Aylie, let out a blood curdling yell. 'It's the excise men, the excise men!' Letting go of his led horses, he wheeled his mount round and made off southwards. Aylie, caught in the middle, was frozen into immobility for a few seconds and in that time the wind fell and she heard Hugh crying out to her, 'Get away, save yourself. I'll hold them off.'

He straightened up in the saddle and rode straight into the thicket. As he went, he turned his head again towards her and she noticed that he never used her name. 'Get away, damn you, *get away*!'

She dropped the reins of the plunging packhorses which, feeling their freedom, went dashing off in different directions, scattering their loads as they ran. Her own mare was rearing beneath her and she gathered up the reins, dug her heels into its flanks and cleared the ford in one mammoth leap. She galloped up beside Hugh calling, 'I won't leave you. I'll stay.'

Their booted legs were brushing together, the metal stirrups clashing, when he turned his face to her, brandishing his unsheathed knife. 'If you don't go I'll kill you,' he yelled and she knew that he meant it.

The grey mare proved that her looks did not play her false. With her deep chest and good bones she was capable of outlasting other, more refined-looking horses. Head down, she carried Aylie over the roughest ground on the Border, galloping flat out and taking bogs and ditches in her stride. Once a stone wall loomed before them and the girl gathered the horse together, remembering Gilbert's advice long ago on the hunting field when he said that the way to face an impossible jump was to 'throw your heart over to the other side'.

Horse and rider soared into the air and cleared the top by only a couple of inches. Landing on the other side, the gallant mare sank to her knees in a bog but Aylie stayed in the saddle and pulled her back up again. She was in agony from a pain in her side and the mare was staggering on her legs when at last they saw the lights of Meg's inn.

The widow was waiting, face dimly showing in the candlelit little window overlooking the southern slope of the hill. She ran out to open the stable door for Aylie and without asking questions started to pull down hay bales to reveal another secret stable behind them.

'Put her in there. I'll get a scoop of corn and I'll bring some water for her when she cools down a bit.'

When they were finished tending to the horse, the widow led the exhausted girl into the house. 'I'll get you some soup. You're Hugh's wife, aren't you? What's happened?'

The tears began to fall at last and Aylie told about the ambush at the thicket.

Maggie frowned. 'How did they know he was crossing there tonight? I never talked about it to anyone and there's been no smuggling for weeks. Someone must have tipped them off.'

'And they must have got Hugh or he'd have been here by now. Oh, do you think they'll kill him?'

Maggie shook her head. 'No, they'll not do that. They like to have somebody to haul up in court to prove that they're doing their jobs. They'll not kill him if they can help it. I just hope he doesn't kill any of them.'

'What do you mean?' It was a fearful whisper.

'You said he had a knife. If he kills one of them they'll hang him.'

Aylie put her hands over her face. 'Oh my God, I hope he gives himself up.' But in her heart she knew that was an unlikely prospect.

The widow put her to bed and as the girl undressed both women were horrified to see bloodstains marking her clothes. They stared at each other in consternation and Maggie asked, 'Are you cut? Did you hurt yourself?'

Aylie shook her head. She knew that, wild though her ride was, it would not make her bleed.

'I'm pregnant, I think,' she whispered.

'Oh, you poor lassie,' said Maggie, and helped the girl into bed.

In spite of her ministrations, within two hours Aylie miscarried and the older woman carried the minute body away in a bucket.

The noise of people kicking at the locked and barred front door woke her and she struggled to sit up in bed but sank back on the pillows, overpowered by waves of pain.

In the room beneath she could hear Maggie shouting at the intruders ... 'Who do you think you are? What do you want here?'

Men's voices rumbled and she caught a few words – 'two men ... smugglers ... the gypsy ... gone to Jedburgh'.

Then Maggie again, loudly – to warn her, she knew, 'I haven't seen anything. Nobody's been here all night, there's just me and my serving girl and she's upstairs in bed. She's sick.'

Tramp, tramp, tramp came feet up the bare wooden stair and she huddled under the covers in terror. A face looked at her from floor level as a man shoved his head through the trap door that covered the stair well.

'Get up, lassie, till we have a look at you.'

She replied weakly, 'I can't.'

'Get up.' His order was more peremptory this time and she threw back the covers to stagger to her feet.

The sight of her bloodstained nightgown made him flinch, and Maggie shouted up, 'I told you the lassie's sick. If you want to know, she's just lost a bairn.'

Embarrassed, the man withdrew his head and she could hear them muttering below. Then the clank of the bucket handle told her that Maggie was giving the men proof of what she said.

For what seemed like hours they searched the stable and rampaged noisily through the innyard. Eventually however they rode off and when they were well gone,

Maggie came bustling back up the stairs, red-faced and flustered.

'They've gone away. They didn't see your horse, it stayed quiet, thank God. That's a good hiding place.'

'Were they looking for me?' asked Aylie.

'No, they weren't looking for a woman, though they knew there was three in the gang. Of course they think they're all men. They wanted you to get out of bed in case you'd somebody in there with you.'

'Two men, they said they're looking for two men. Does that mean they've got Hugh?'

Maggie looked sad. 'I'm sorry, yes, they've got him. He's been taken to Jedburgh jail. Abel got away. I hope he's got the sense to stay out of the way.'

Aylie leaned back against the pillows and let her tears flow. 'How I wish I could get my hands on whoever it was that told the excise men Hugh was riding out,' she sobbed through clenched teeth.

'You'll find out who that was at his trial, I expect,' said Maggie.

Hugh looked like a man in the grip of serious illness. His skin had lost its healthy glow and even his hair hung lank and lifeless. Yet he had only been in the prison cell for five days. What would he look like, she wondered, if he got a long sentence? She dared not think of anything worse than that happening to him.

With Jane she had ridden over in the carter's waggon to see him and a kind jailer let them into his cell to sit beside him on the wooden bench.

'What are you going to plead?' she asked, gently massaging one of his hands in hers. They talked in whispers so that the jailer could not hear what was said.

'What's the point? They caught me. It doesn't matter what I plead. I don't even know what they're going to charge me with yet. They say I tried to shoot the excise men.'

Aylie's heart chilled at this but she controlled her face so that he would not see her fear.

'But you didn't have a gun. I know that. They were the only people who fired any shots. I was there and I saw that.'

A glimpse of the old Hugh shone through as he glared at her. 'Don't you ever mention that again. I don't want you involved in this. Awful things would happen to you if they knew you were with us.'

He turned to Jane. 'Keep your daughter quiet, good wife, promise you'll make her hold her tongue no matter what happens.'

Jane nodded silently. She was well aware of the consequences for Aylie if the news got out that she had been in the smuggling gang.

Wanting to soothe him, Aylie changed her tack. 'Will the court sit here?' she asked.

'I don't know. Nobody tells me anything, I've just to wait and see. If it's here there's a good chance that Myreheugh's brother'll be on the bench and I don't fancy that. I'm sure it's them that got me put here in the first place.'

'What do you mean?' she asked.

'Well, I've had the time to do a lot of thinking. They were mad at me taking the smuggling trade off them and then that Josey turned up – just at the right time, didn't he? He stuck around till he knew our route and exactly when we were going and then he vanished – but he didn't know you were riding out with us and that's why they've left you alone so far. Promise you won't give anything away. I'd never forgive myself if they got you, Aylie.'

They remanded him in custody and while he was waiting for the circuit judge to come round, Aylie saw him every day because a friend of Gilbert's who lived in Jedburgh took her into his house.

In the cell they sat talking for hours under the eye of the indulgent town jailer and he said how sorry he was to have allowed his jealousy to take him over. Their love for each other during these few days was so intense that Aylie thought she would die from the pain of it. To spare him, she never mentioned the lost baby and instead they

217

talked only of what would happen when he had served his sentence and they could be together again.

'Will you wait? Even if they send me away for years, I'll come back for you, Aylie. I promise you that. Will you wait for me?' he asked her over and over again.

She leant her head on his chest and said, 'I promise with all my heart I'll wait for you, Hugh. Even when I'm an old, old woman, I'll always be yours, I love you so much.' Her heart ached in her breast as if it were made of stone. How long would it be, she wondered, before he was free again? She never once allowed herself to consider the possibility that he might be hanged.

However, others were not so optimistic. One day she overheard a group of people discussing the possibility of Hugh Kennedy suffering the death penalty.

'He shot at the excise men. He's been a bad lad in the past, all that poaching and preaching revolution. It's quite likely that they'll make him swing.'

When she was told that the circuit judge who would hear Hugh's case was much feared for his harsh sentencing, she tried to banish horrible speculations from her mind but in the darkness of the night they haunted her like spectres.

Aylie sat between her mother and Maggie, staring sightlessly at the judge's empty chair. She wished she was able to pray. Jock Hepburn was on Jane's left and Gilbert Kennedy occupied a seat farther along. There was no sign of Hugh's scrawny spectre of a mother.

Then the judge mounted his high seat and wiped his red face with a large silk handkerchief before ordering that the prisoner be led in. Aylie felt her heart lurch and begin to palpitate as Hugh climbed the steps to the prisoner's box. He looked so young, so vulnerable, no longer a rogue, no longer her dashing gypsy. She wanted to rush up to him and throw her arms round him, to protect him from the hard-eyed men who were weighing him up like a beast in a market stall.

The case proceeded without any hitches. He pleaded

not guilty to a charge of attempted murder and, brazenly, not guilty to one of attempting to smuggle excisable goods into Scotland. Then the panoply of the law swept into action. One by one witnesses appeared, some of them people she had never seen before, who swore to having watched Hugh engage in open smuggling; who swore that they had been offered the chance to go with him but because of their rectitude, of course, they had refused. A self-satisfied Josey appeared in the witness box, his hair plastered down on his head and his face as sly as ever. He testified that he had found out when the gypsy's gang was going out and which route it took. This information he had passed on to his employer – the Myreheugh farmer. When it was Myreheugh's time to give evidence, he said that he passed Josey's information on to the excise men.

After all, he said self-righteously, Kennedy was well known to be an agitator, a troublemaker. His kind were best removed from society.

Then the excise men stood up and perjured themselves by swearing that they had stepped out of the thicket unarmed and challenged the smugglers. They had told Kennedy to give up his arms and yield quietly but instead of doing that, he fired on them, shooting his own dog by mistake. They portrayed themselves as innocent, unarmed men who were fired on point blank by a villain determined to kill.

While listening to this evidence, Aylie gave a gasp and was about to step to her feet when both Jane and Maggie took hold of her and forcibly held her down. With one strong hand Maggie also effectively gagged her.

'You'll make it worse for him if you cause a disturbance,' Maggie whispered.

The proceedings dragged on all day and to the worried people in the front row, it seemed that everybody there except themselves was enjoying the spectacle as much as if they were at the theatre. It was not often that they had such a sensational case to listen to, and the gypsy lad was a local hero.

It was late afternoon when the judge suddenly decided to begin his summing up and the jury were admonished to make haste with their verdict if they did not want to spend another day in court.

They filed dutifully out and within five minutes they were back. The foreman, a tenant on one of Myreheugh's brother's properties, said they had agreed their verdict. Hugh Kennedy was guilty of smuggling but – amazingly – not guilty of attempted murder. Aylie never knew who among the local traders and property owners had swung that vote in her husband's favour, but she was eternally grateful.

The judge actually looked disappointed. It was obvious that his fingers had been itching to place the black cap on his tightly curled wig but he was not going to be thwarted too badly. The gypsy had to be made an example of.

'I sentence you to ten years' transportation,' he intoned and as his words boomed sonorously out over the hushed court, Aylie fainted.

'Don't look at me, Aylie, don't look at me!'

Hugh's voice rang out loud and clear as the hustling knot of men came out of the iron-studded door under the round arch that marked the entrance to Jedburgh's Bridewell Jail. Aylie, standing with her mother on the other side of the square, covered her eyes with her hands because she knew his pride was crying out to her. He did not want her to see him being led away in chains. His call however came only a few seconds too late for she had already caught a fleeting glimpse, a glimpse that was to haunt her dreams. His shackled feet could only shuffle along for they were joined together by massive iron links and a third chain led from them up to his manacled hands. At the sight of him, the silent crowd drew in their breath, resentfully angry that one of their own kind was being taken away like that. Shackled, he would travel across oceans to a place from which only horrific tales came back.

Aylie's last sight of her husband was his dark head held high and overtopping the warders in the open cart that was to carry him to Perth prison. She had been told that he would be kept there for about a year, then if he was passed fit, he would be transferred to the prison hulks moored in the Thames estuary at Woolwich. From there his journey to Australia would begin.

Jane tenderly put a hand on Aylie's arm and guided her slowly down Jedburgh's High Street, only too aware of the curious glances of local people who knew that Aylie was the gypsy's wife.

At the corner of the square they were accosted by a spitting black hag who pointed a skinny finger into Aylie's face and hissed, 'It was your fault, you got your hands on my laddie. It was because of you he wanted money. It was to give you silk gowns that he went smuggling . . .' Hugh's gypsy mother, wrapped in a tattered black shawl and incandescent with hatred, cursed and spat on the ground at Aylie's feet and was about to say more before Jane stepped between them.

'Go away, woman, leave her alone. She's broken-hearted, can't you see that?'

The gypsy shouted, 'She'll be worse before this is done, you mark my words,' but it was obvious that, like so many other people, even she was afraid of Jane and she hurried off, still hissing as she went.

Though she knew the gypsy's accusation was untrue, for Hugh had been smuggling before he married her, the meeting shook the girl's fragile composure. Heedless of the watching people she now allowed her tears to flow and she clung to her mother like a child again. 'What'll they do to him, Mam? What'll they do to him?' she sobbed.

'You've just got to have faith in him. He said he'd come back and he's the sort that will, you mark my words, you'll see him again,' said her mother consolingly.

Aylie was to treasure those words like a talisman. Her mother had never let her down, everything Jane had ever told her was true.

*

221

The lonely house in the valley was empty and threatening now. Every room held bitter-sweet memories that wrenched her heart as she walked through them. She realized with a shock that in her absence someone had been in and cleared away anything of value, even the loft was empty of the contraband whisky they'd had to leave behind when they set out fully loaded for Boulmer. She did not know whether Hugh's friends or the excise men had taken it and of course she could not ask. She grubbed with her hands in the corner of the kitchen floor where she hid her crock of money and, miraculously, it was still there. Digging it up, she tipped out the coins and without counting them tied them up safely in her petticoat.

Only one horse was left in the stable, her grey mare with the flowing white tail that Hugh had bought for her and which carried her so well over the midnight moors when she fled from the excise men. Someone had given it food and cleaned its bedding while she was away and she stroked the horse's velvet muzzle.

It whickered softly at the feel of her hand and the pain in her heart broke fully. Leaning her head against its soft neck, she wept racking tears which hurt so badly that she thought her very heart would break. When the agony was wept out, however, she felt strangely cleansed and began to saddle up the mare.

She was leading the horse out of the stable, bolting the door behind her for the last time, when a man stepped forward from the shadows of the hay shed.

His face was solemn as he said, 'I heard your man was sent away yesterday.'

She stared at Daniel Fleury and asked, 'Have you been here long?'

'I heard you crying. I didn't think I should interrupt you. It's good to cry sometimes.' His voice was sympathetic.

'What do you want?'

'I came to ask how you'll manage now that he's gone. Have you any money?'

She frowned. 'Someone's taken away everything I had. But at least they left me this horse. I'll manage.'

'Have you any children?' asked Fleury.

She shook her head. The painful memory of the aborted child had been overlaid by her anguish about Hugh.

'What will you do?' he persisted.

Angrily she turned on him. 'I'll work like all the other lonely women in this countryside. I'll put on my bondager's hat and stand at the hiring fair and then I'll work, day after day, week after week and year after year till he comes back again.'

'Not many transported convicts get back. I've known a few and none of them got back,' Fleury told her.

'My Hugh'll get back,' said Aylie firmly. 'Hugh said he'll come back for me and he will. What do you want anyway? Why have you come here? Was it you who took my whisky?'

He looked disappointed that she should think such a thing of him. 'Of course not, the place was empty when I got here about two hours ago. I was waiting for you. I wanted to ask you to come with me.'

She stared in open astonishment. 'What did you say?'

'I want you to come away with me. You and I would go along together very well, I know.'

'But that's a terrible thing to ask. My man's been sent to prison yesterday and you expect me to pack up and go with you?'

Fleury looked grim. 'I thought you might if you're sensible. He's gone for good, you know. You'll have a lonely and terrible life. I could offer you something better. You deserve it.'

All Aylie's anger disappeared. There was indeed an understanding between this man and herself. She felt no resentment any longer at his offer. Turning her back on him, she pulled tight at the girths of the mare's saddle.

When she turned back again she said in a cool voice, 'Thank you very much for the offer, Captain Fleury, but I'll never leave the Borders till Hugh comes back – and I know he will. Nothing anyone tells me makes me doubt that. I love him and I'll wait for him.'

'I was afraid you'd say that but I had to try,' said Fleury, and walked over to help her on to her horse. As she gathered up the reins he said, 'We'll never meet again, smuggler lady, but I won't forget you. Remember that.' Then he reached into the pocket of his coat and brought out a little bag of jingling coins which he pressed into her hand. 'Take this, you'll need it.'

She withdrew her hand. 'It's kind, but no. I'll manage. I've got some money. Goodbye, Captain Midnight.'

And with that she cantered out of the yard, leaving behind the house where she and Hugh had been so happy.

She went to see Gilbert. 'You must sell this mare for me, but make sure it goes to a good home. It's a good horse,' she told him.

He took the reins from her hands, his dark eyes mournful, and he too asked, 'What'll you do now, lass?'

'I'm going back to work, back to the land. What else is there for me to do? I'll wait for Hugh like he told me to.'

Gilbert also doubted whether he or Aylie would ever see his son again, for he knew that men who were shipped out to Australia usually stayed there and their families rarely heard from them again. They never knew even whether they were alive or dead. But he was careful not to show his doubts to Aylie, for he saw she needed hope to cling to.

It was difficult for her not to despair. She went back to her mother in the abbey, where she helped to make up potions and medicines and delivered them to the cottages of Jane's patients. Everyone greeted her with grave sympathy but a few of them were not too tactful in what they told her. Tales of horrific floggings handed out to transportees; of attempts at escape being punished by hanging; accounts of the privations of the sea voyage; and, worst of all, of the harridans of women prisoners, all prostitutes according to local lore, were recounted to her.

One kindly woman however told her about a relative

224

who had been transported for stealing a sheep and his wife travelled out to Australia to be with him.

'Can women go out on their own?' Aylie asked, wide-eyed.

'If you have the price of a passage,' she was told. 'But they say it's not a place for a decent woman.'

When Aylie told Jane this story, her mother instantly knew what was in her daughter's mind and her face seemed old and frightened.

'But it's so far away, it's a long and dangerous voyage. How do you know Hugh would want you to go out there among all those convicts?' she protested.

Aylie set out for Perth and when the coach arrived at the Salutation Hotel in the middle of the town, she was grey with dust and tiredness but, fortunately, the prison was only a short walk away. Of course the guards refused to let her in.

'I want to send a message to my man,' she explained. 'I want to ask him if I should pay my own way to Australia to be with him when he's transported.'

One of the jailers laughed. 'Dinna waste your money, lassie, just go out and steal some rich man's purse and you'll get there quick enough for free.'

She flashed a pleading look at him. '*Please* take that message to Hugh Kennedy. I'll wait here for his reply.'

She held out a few coins towards him and as he looked at the girl, noticing her youth and tired beauty, sympathy stirred in his heart.

'Keep your money. Wait here and I'll take your message in,' he told her.

After a long time, he came back and told her, 'I've spoken to him. Go and stand under that window over there . . .' He indicated a barred window high on the wall beside the portcullis gate.

When she heard Hugh's voice she felt for a moment as if it had all been a dream and that she would waken up to find him beside her in their deep bed again.

He sounded urgent. 'Aylie, Aylie, don't leave the Borders. Don't go to Australia. Stay near the Eildons and

I'll come back for you, my dearest. I promise I'll come back.'

She knew she had to do as he said and without a backward glance she turned on her heel and walked away.

All Jock Hepburn's years of hard work were paying benefits now. He had sold his smallholding and bought a larger farm with a solid red sandstone house and a collection of snug outbuildings sitting in the middle of three hundred acres of good land. He and Sandy worked from early morning till late at night and made such a good living from Harestanes Farm that envious neighbours said he must have found a cache of gold hidden in his fields.

He extended the farmhouse, adding a front wing with a plaster-ceilinged drawing room to house the piano. Then he built a stableyard for hunters and carriage horses. Jock Hepburn, the bondager's bairn, was on his way to becoming a gentleman farmer.

Aylie spent most of the summer helping him, but when November began she knew she could presume on his kindness no longer and told her mother she was going back to Earlston hiring fair to find herself a place.

The hiring day was fine, and early in the morning Aylie sat on the step of her mother's little cell rubbing a high shine into her working boots. As she polished she remembered how Hugh had once told her that her days as a farm labourer were finished. But fortune had turned and, once again, she was back in the striped skirt and canvas apron of the bondager.

She stood up, pinning the straw hat on top of her crown of hair and called over her shoulder into the dimness behind her, 'How do I look, Mam, do you think someone'll hire me?'

Jane came out carrying Blaize's coat over one arm. 'I'm going to give you something for luck,' she said. 'Hand me over the scissors till I cut off one of your father's buttons for you.'

'Oh, don't cut his coat. You've kept it so fine all these years. Don't cut it for me now.'

'But I want to. I want something of him to go with you. I can't give you the coat but I'll give you one of these braw buttons.'

They polished it proudly and threaded it through a cord to hang around Aylie's neck.

'It'll take care of you,' Jane told her.

'Pride is a sin,' Aylie told herself as she stood alone outside Earlston's Corn Exchange trying not to notice the strolling crowds of men evaluating her with their eyes. Some of them were only interested in her capacity as a worker but others looked at her more lasciviously for she was in the full flower of womanhood and the old-fashioned bondager costume made her an eye-catching sight.

They began approaching her as soon as she took up her stance and after an hour she had three definite offers of work. The men who wanted to hire her as their bondager were all young and offered wages over the normal – elevenpence a day for her if she would go with them.

She knew what questions to ask: 'Have you a wife? How many children are there in your household? Do you guarantee to give me the same food as you eat yourself?'

All those questions had to be asked, for men without wives were more likely to want to sleep with the bondager; to go into a house with a very large family meant that the bondager had to share a bed with children and that there was never any peace. Some men fed bondagers on the same sort of scraps as they threw to their pigs . . .

Eventually she agreed to take the arles of a hind called Fergusson who had a place on a farm not far from Charterhall. He was married and had two small children, and his wife, a timid-looking woman, was with him when he made the bargain with Aylie.

*

227

The best way to survive was not to think too much. If she allowed her mind to dwell on memories, she screamed inside in silent agony. Sometimes her guard slipped and she would recall loving words he had spoken to her; she would remember the feel of his strong-muscled back beneath her hands as they made love or the splash of cold water over her thighs as they frolicked in the shallows of the Bowmont Water like two brown trout that summer long ago. Then she pushed those memories away, for they hurt too much. It was better to concentrate on the work in hand. On wet days, as she bent over her hoe singling out the turnip seedlings, a chill of despair engulfed her heart, but when the sun shone and warmed her back through the cotton blouse, hope would rise again.

Aylie worked hard; she gave a good day's work for her wages and it was galling to realize that she earned far less for working harder than her boss, the hind Fergusson. He proved to be a mean-minded man who sullenly envied and resented his employers, who chafed bitterly but in a two-faced way at the caste system of the farming communities. He felt himself to be superior to the people around him and admired Aylie because she read books and any newspapers she could get her hands on. He talked to her because she had opinions about matters outside the incestuous gossip that occupied the minds of most cottagers.

But his admiration alienated his wife against their bondager. Because he was continually holding her up as a superior woman, the atmosphere in the little cottage where they lived grew tense with antagonism. Mrs Fergusson refused to look Aylie in the eye; replied to her attempts at conversation with sullen grunts; and made snide comments about her clothes and her books behind her back.

'Mrs High-and-Mighty's always got her nose in a book,' Aylie overheard her telling the woman next door one day. 'You wouldn't think her man was a convict out

228

in Australia, the way she goes on. She thinks she's a lady does that one, not a gypsy's doxy.'

It pleased Mrs Fergusson that Aylie never received any letters from Hugh. Because she knew he could not write, she did not expect them but was hurt when the hind's wife sneeringly asked, 'How is it you never get any news from that man of yours? How do you know he's not taken up with another woman away out there in Australia?'

When he was sent to Woolwich, she had wanted to go there too to say goodbye to him, for relatives of prisoners were allowed on the hulks to take farewell of their loved ones – the authorities knew that most convicts never saw their families again.

Gilbert warned her against going however. He told her, 'He doesn't want you to see him down there. We've had a message from him through one of our folk. He wants money because prisoners can buy extra comforts if they've money but he asked to tell you not to try to go down – hulks are hell holes.'

She gave Gilbert all the money she had saved and asked, 'Who's going to take it to him?'

'Abel's going down with it. We can trust Abel,' said Gilbert.

'Then ask him to tell Hugh that I'll be waiting,' she said.

There was something soothing about the way every farming year followed the same course – the spring ploughing and the sowing of the seed; the weeding and singling of the young plants; the shearing and the hay making; the harvest with its glorious sense of completion and then the bitter days of winter when the animals were brought into warm, dark sheds and fed with hay or chopped turnips.

Aylie loved the spring because it brought with it a wonderful feeling of rebirth and as she saw the snow-drops opening in the grass beneath the trees around her mother's hidden little home, she knew that there was one less year to be lived through until she saw Hugh again. The white flowers with their fragile heads bending so elegantly over the spearlike leaves symbolized hope for her and she gathered them in huge bunches, sinking her face among the delicate flowers and inhaling their soft scent in delight. It was a smell that she remembered from childhood and it always made her feel happy and confident that the coming year would bring, if not complete happiness, at least some sort of consolation.

After a year of living with the Fergussons, Aylie could stand the tension in their house no longer and told the hind that when her term of bondage ended, she would be seeking a new position. So once again it was back to the hiring fair and once again she had no trouble in finding offers, for she had earned a reputation as a good worker. This time she was hired for a farm about eight miles away from her mother, but as Jane had been well in the past two years and her rheumaticky hands were not so stiff, it seemed safe to leave her. The new farm where Aylie found herself was a larger establishment with a staff of over thirty workers and in the stables a dozen pair of horses. The farmer recognized her on the first morning she turned out in his gang of bondagers.

'You're the lassie that used to be with Scroggie, aren't you?' he asked. 'You're the one that's such a great hand with horses.'

She nodded and he said, 'I need an extra hand with the horses. Do you think you could do the job?'

'I'm sure I could,' she said.

'Then I'll give you Jed and Bobby,' he replied.

Early morning in November with the sun just breaking through and a white mist hanging like bridal lace over leafless hedges where spiders' webs glittered, strings of pearls for fairy people. Proudly pacing, two by two, a cavalcade of magnificent working horses came swinging out of the cobbled yard and headed for the fields, each giant gleaming with careful grooming and hung around with tinkling harness. The brass trimmings of their high collars and on the sides of their bridles flashed fire in the rays of the watery winter sun. Though she saw this parade every morning, Aylie always caught her breath in wonder and admiration for even on the bitterest days, when driving rain made ploughmen bend before the onslaught, the horses stepped out like monarchs, heads held high.

She was proud of her place at Whitethorn Farm because she was the only woman among the people allowed to drive and look after the horses and now, in the second year she'd been there, she was allowed to plough.

This meant that she rose from her bed at five o'clock each morning and, fighting sleep from her eyes, hurried to the stables before she had as much as a crust of bread in her stomach. The horses came first every time. As she opened the stable door, her nostrils were filled with the warm smell of horses; the smell of sweet hay, of horse embrocation, bran, straw, sweat and horse droppings – as heady to her as French perfume was to other women born in easier circumstances.

Her special charges, Jed and Bobby, were two magnificent bay geldings, each standing more than seventeen hands high so they dwarfed her as Gulliver dwarfed the Lilliputians. She knew that with one swing of their bodies they could pin her to the wall and crush her bones, but she trusted them and they trusted her in return, sensing her love and understanding of them.

Each morning, when she arrived to feed them, they whickered softly in greeting and then stood patiently while she pressed her face lovingly against their bellies and, turning their heads, they breathed softly on her as she went over them with a stiff-bristled dandy brush, standing on tiptoe to sweep her arm down their backs and legs before combing out and braiding their long tails so that they would not get entangled in the plough.

It took an hour to feed and groom the horses to her satisfaction, for the ploughmen all vied with each other for the honour of having the best-turned-out pair. She plaited their manes as well as their tails and tied them up in stiff bows, polished their gleaming skins with a silk handkerchief and then dressed them up in the complicated harness which she had spent the previous evening cleaning. Made of black leather and brass, it was heavy to carry, but she heaved the pieces over the horses' heads, buckling them down till Jed and Bobby, fully caparisoned, looked as grand as the war horses that carried the knights of old into battle.

Every pair of horses had to be in the field by six o'clock and Aylie was never late. In the beginning she found it hard to hold the widespread handles of her plough, to guide it carefully so that the furrows ran straight and true, but she was lucky in having been given well trained horses who knew far more about ploughing than she did. With their heads down they patiently paced up and down the field, turning with exactitude where it was necessary and if the furrows were straight, it was due to them and not to her.

Being a ploughwoman meant that she worked the same hours as her charges, and farmers were always far more careful about the welfare of their horses than they were about people. Starting work at six, the horses were allowed a half hour's rest at breakfast time, nine o'clock. Then they went back to work till eleven o'clock when a rest was taken till almost two in the afternoon. They rarely worked past five-thirty except during the harvest.

If she was quick about feeding and settling them for the evening, Jed and Bobby could be happily chomping at filled haynets by half past six and the rest of the night was her own. Sometimes she went home to see Jane, but more often she stayed in the farm toun because there were another fifteen bondagers on the place and among them she had found friends.

For the first time since she had worked with Phemie she had the pleasure of female companions of her own age. Rosie and May, two other bondagers, teamed up with her and once or twice persuaded her to go with them to the Saturday night dances. Aylie loved dancing and when she heard the music playing, her feet started tapping of their own accord. But after a happy night twirling gaily with red-faced partners who threw her about like a bale of hay, she felt terrible guilt that she had momentarily forgotten her grief at being parted from Hugh.

She spoke about this to Rosie, who snorted.

'Don't be daft, he wouldn't expect you to stay in like a nun all the time, would he? What's wrong with having a dance? How do you know what he's doing? If I know anything about men he won't be without a woman and I don't care how faithful you think he is . . . it's just nature.'

'It's just nature . . .' The words stung her for she knew that as far as Hugh was concerned, they were probably true. His vitality attracted women and there was no point denying it. She started brooding over the possibility of him finding a woman who would replace her in his affections and the thought of it nearly drove her mad. She had never before realized the terrible power of jealousy.

While she was living and working with Fergusson, Aylie had once again become involved in the political ferment that was subterraneously pulsing through the community. In little halls and schoolrooms all over the countryside there were frequent meetings, not rebellious any longer, for people no longer preached sedition or rick burning as they had once done. The meetings now were reasonable (perhaps too reasonable, she secretly thought) attended by people who were anxious to persuade farmers to provide a better way of life for their workers.

Many of the speakers at those meetings were clergymen or farm stewards, men with a foot in both camps, who were anxious not to alienate the powers that prevailed. Agriculture, after having been in a parlous state during the 1830s, was gradually becoming more profitable again and at the same time, workers were drifting off the land, lured away by jobs in the new weaving mills or enticed

233

down south by the railways which had begun to spread their tentacles over the rural countryside. Places which had been isolated since time began found that the building of a railway line joined them up to the outside world. It was the biggest revolution that had ever hit the countryside and it was hard to keep ambitious young men at home when they saw that a train ticket was a passport to another way of life.

They left the land to become soldiers or policemen, or simply to go to the cities to seek their fortunes — which many of them succeeded in doing for they were bred not to be afraid of hard work.

The women left behind on the land found that their labour was more highly regarded than before. It was now not uncommon for a farmer to say that he would rather hire a bondager than a hind, for women worked harder and were more likely to stay in a job. Yet the old system still prevailed; women were not hired in their own right, they had to make their contracts with hinds before they could be hired as a back-up work force. This irked many of them, who knew that they were capable of doing a better job than the hinds who literally owned them during their year of bondage.

Rosie was having trouble with the man to whom she was bonded. He came creeping into her bed at night and when she spoke of it to May and Aylie, May was surprised at her scruples.

'Why don't you let him have his way? It's nothing to you and it'd make your life much easier. Most of the bondager lassies give in — it's easier that way.'

Aylie was surprised at this attitude. 'Do you?' she asked May who laughed, slightly shamefaced.

She said, 'Well, maybe not in this job but I have in the past. If they pester me, I do. The wives are sometimes glad to get them out of their beds and into the bondager's, so *they* don't make any trouble. It means a year without a bairn for them, at least.'

'But what if you have a child? What then?'

Rosie flushed slightly and said defensively, 'My mother was a bondager and she had me in the field. I don't know who my father was.'

May agreed. 'Last year I had a bairn the same way and I gave it to my sister to bring up. I go to see my bairn on Sundays, lots of lassies have bairns like that. There's no shame in it.'

Aylie was anxious to reassure her friends. 'Of course not, I'm a bondager's bairn myself. My mother wasn't married to my father. I'm not accusing you, I just think it's hard not to have any choice . . .'

May interrupted angrily, 'Do any women have choice? My mother had no choice with my father. He just took what he wanted when he wanted it until she died having my sister, her fourteenth bairn. At least if you're a bondager you can get a new place after a year and when you're sleeping with your hind, you've a hold over him. You can threaten to tell his wife or keep him out of your bed till he makes the work easier for you. You're well looked after too in case you up and leave. Oh aye, I'd rather be a bondager than a hind's wife any day.'

Hugh, 1839

Lying in the dark and stinking hold of the convict ship, so unsuitably called the *Eden*, Hugh put one arm over his eyes and concentrated his mind on Aylie. He remembered her hair, so tightly curled and so soft on his fingers; her satin skin; her elegant body and chalice-like waist. The image of her was held in his mind like a holy icon.

Around him in the ship there were nearly three hundred convicts and of these eighty were women – but not women like Aylie, for the convict floozies were tousle-haired and filthy, their bodies scantily wrapped in rags which they discarded one by one as the ship neared the equator. He could look with such dispassion on their naked breasts and wanton eyes that it seemed he had been emasculated by a combination of imprisonment, brutality and his longing for Aylie.

Until the *Eden* reached blue water the convicts stayed shackled together, two by two, and took their exercise walking the decks for the hours of daylight, shuffling along like unwillingly joined Siamese twins. There was no attempt to match up compatible spirits – homosexuals were chained to men who loathed what they stood for; those who longed for stimulating conversation were paired with men little more than congenital idiots. Violence had not been absent from Perth prison but when he reached Woolwich, he looked back on the first part of his imprisonment as a period of refinement. The hulks, moored in the estuary of the Thames, were nothing more than rotting pest houses, tenements of filth and depravity into which men and women were poured while waiting for transportation.

Lesbianism, homosexual rape, beatings up and murder were commonplace among the convicts, over whom towered the authorities, looking on impassively and only intervening when their orders were broken or ignored. Then they resorted to floggings, so brutal and horrible that even men hardened to terrible sights turned their heads away from the lacerated, bleeding backs of those under the lash.

As he lay silent in the darkness, listening to the steady slap, slap of water against the ship's sides, Hugh felt his neighbour turning towards him.

'Are you awake, lad?' came the whisper and he grunted an assent.

'What are you thinking about?' It was always the same question in the middle of the night.

'I'm thinking about my Aylie and wondering what she's doing tonight, how she's managing.'

'I know what my old lady'll be doing. She'll be getting up to feed the kids and the hens – at least I hope that's what she's doing.' The speaker had a thick West Country accent which Hugh had taken some time to understand but he knew there had been a similar difficulty with his own accent for John Parr.

He had been fortunate to find himself united with a compatible man like Parr, who was a countryman with an understanding of animals and who liked a bit of poaching. Chained together, they often lay at night talking about tickling trout in sunlit rivers or stalking the gentry's deer and pheasants in midnight woods. They had been together for six weeks and it had not struck Hugh till now to ask Parr what he had done to earn a sentence of transportation.

'How long are you doing?' he suddenly inquired.

Parr shrugged. 'I've bought fourteen penn'orth, lad. What about you?'

Fourteen years! Trying not to sound thankful, Hugh said, 'I've bought ten.'

There was a long pause and then he asked again, 'What did you get yours for?'

'What do you think?'

Parr was a kind man, that was already obvious. He

237

was not a psychopath or a street villain like so many of the others who lay sleeping, snoring or grinding their teeth and crying out in their dreams, around them. He was also a man of some learning and during their long hours of enforced companionship he had been trying to teach Hugh to read and write.

'Poaching?' Hugh hazarded a guess.

'No, not that, though I've done my bit in my time.'

'Stealing?'

Parr sounded annoyed. 'I've never taken a thing that belonged to another man except for fish or fowl, and I believe that they were put on the earth by the Lord for all men.'

'What did you do then?'

Parr's voice was angry and resentful. 'I tried to form a trade union. I tried to get some labourers like myself to unite in order to better their conditions. They've sent me away from my wife and children for fourteen years for that!'

'They're all bastards,' said Hugh.

'Aye, I suppose they are. Even the men I tried to help are bastards. One of them shopped me, one of my friends who I thought I could trust. He informed on us. And what did they give him? They gave him five guineas and sent him home to drink it.'

Parr, Hugh already knew, was a teetotaller and a deeply religious man, at least he had been both of these things when their voyage started but recently he had begun to question the kindness of his God. Hugh, with his sceptical and irreligious background, had not so many illusions to be so painfully broken as his friend.

'What will you do in Australia?' he whispered. 'Will you try to get home again?'

'I don't think I'll ever see my family again. I told my wife to try to find a kind man who'd look after her. I told her to bring up the chil'ren with love and make sure that none of them grow up wanting to change things . . . They should stick to the paths of righteousness and leave improvement to others. It was trying to help others that got me here.'

'I'm going back when I've done my time. Come what may, Parr, I'm going back for Aylie.'

'They all say that. Oh aye, they all say that but Australia's a long way away, lad, and ten years is a long time . . .'

It took one hundred days before the *Eden* came in sight of Sydney Bay in December 1841. Sydney was the first convict settlement and already a high proportion of the population had descended from convicts or were convicts who had done their time and become free citizens. Some of them, remembering their own suffering, were prepared to look kindly on other convicts but there were others who scorned the new arrivals and saw them only as a source of cheap labour to be exploited to the full. The brutal rigours of life in Sydney outweighed the beauty of the landscape with its strange trees and plants, the azure-coloured sea and vast hinterlands – a land of mystery, full of aboriginal tribes and strange animals.

When they landed Parr and Hugh were separated but before they took farewell of each other, the older man offered to write a letter to Aylie for Hugh.

It said: 'Believe me my hart I love you and long for you. I have landed in Australia but I will come back, wait for me.'

This letter was entrusted to a sympathetic sailor from the *Eden* who took it to England and posted it from Woolwich. Exactly a year after it was written, Aylie read the painfully scrawled words with tears flowing down her cheeks. She cherished every scrape of the pen, folded and refolded the paper and slept with it next to her heart so that she could always feel its folds against her skin.

Hugh's first work was making roads in a chain gang of labourers, all sweating in white suits painted with broad yellow arrows that set them apart from the other people passing along the road. His pride had always been strong, and it was agony to be so marked out and sneered at; to be lumped together with men who had stolen or pimped, cheated or lied, men whom even he, a convict, despised.

They were not all hardened criminals however, and he soon discovered that really bad men did not get transported because most of them ended their careers of crime on the gallows at home. It was the middle-ranking criminal who ended up in Australia, and some of them were only children. Transportees' crimes varied from the trivial – the theft of a stamp or a shilling – to the political like Parr's. Political prisoners were most hated by the guards and the sufferings they had to endure were terrible. Even the best of them were gradually worn down and brutalized by the system in which they found themselves, for to lie and cheat was the only way to survive.

'I've not been an angel in my life but I've found out some tricks out here that I never knew about before,' said an old man sent to Sydney for stealing a horse.

Like Hugh he was of gypsy stock, though unlike him, not pure Romany, and they talked together in their own language which gave them a kind of kinship. The old man had already been ten years in Sydney and he helped the newcomer to learn the ropes of convict life.

Hugh learned the necessity of wearing two faces – one for the officers and jailers who guarded them and another for his fellow convicts. He learned to keep his own counsel; he listened and applied what he heard to making sure his own circumstances were made easier. He learned that there was no justice for convicts. The men who tried to keep on the right side of the authorities were as liable to end up with a flogging as the troublemakers. The first time he was tied to the triangle and awarded fifty lashes it was for looking arrogant when an officer passed by. As the lash descended on his back he knew he must not cry out, no matter how terrible the pain. His silence throughout the ordeal ensured him the reputation of being a hard man, one the others would respect. If he had allowed even one whimper to escape his lips he would have been marked down as a 'sandstone' or a 'crumbler' and singled out for more ill treatment by his peers. So he became a hard man; he learned to step cockily away from the flogging post and swill down the drink of rum laced with tobacco that convicts used to kill the pain.

He learned to sing the convict songs; to bully the weak and join in with the powerful. He learned the solace of getting blind drunk on the rum that was so readily available to the convicts – and on more than one occasion he learned that a hard man enhanced his reputation by grabbing a convict woman and having his way with her. Men who used women, even in the most perfunctory way, were not suspected of being homosexual and therefore not as likely to have homosexual attentions forced on them. The harder your reputation, the more inviolate you became.

He was a strong man; he was a bold man; because he looked both of those things the authorities punished him mercilessly. By the time two years had passed his back was criss-crossed with scar tissue, a badge of acceptability among the other convicts.

But all the time he nurtured his memory of Aylie though he spoke of her to no one, for he felt that allowing her name to pass his lips in the hell of convict life would sully her.

Some convicts attempted to escape but if they took off into the wildness of the country beyond Sydney, they were either recaptured fairly quickly or they died. Some tried to stow away on returning ships but they were usually discovered and the punishment meted out to them was brutal even for that debased place.

Being a realist, Hugh realized that to be sure of seeing his wife again, he would have to serve his time and earn enough money to pay his passage home.

His nickname in the gang was Romany Jem and one day he was approached by a hard-eyed young Londoner who said, 'We're taking off soon, Jem. The big Paddy's coming with me and we're going bushranging. Do you want to come with us?'

There were plenty of tales about runaways who

became bushrangers and harried the up-country settlers. These men earned themselves Robin Hood reputations and there were songs and poems written about them which glamorized their doings and glossed over the fact that they were often brutal murderers.

'I'm tempted,' Hugh said, 'I'm very tempted but if I stick it out here for another eighteen months, I'll get a place as an assigned labourer and then I'll be able to save some money.'

'You'd get plenty of money with us,' said the would-be bushranger.

'But it wouldn't be any good to me, would it? I wouldn't be able to buy myself a passage home.'

'What do you want to go back there for? This is a big, wild country. This is the place to be, a man can roam around here free as air. Back there nothing'll have changed. You'd be back at the bottom of the dunghill.'

'I've got to go back.' Hugh was not prepared to explain why.

'And I thought you were a hard man! You're nothing but a sandstone like the rest. They've broken you, just give up now.' The Londoner was scathing and his scorn burned Hugh's pride but still he would not explain himself. 'I'm going back, that's all,' he said.

The Londoner and his Irish companion got away easily enough but a few months later their bodies were swinging from the gallows beside the prison block as an example to anyone else who thought going bushranging was a way to win permanent freedom.

Hugh won his assigned place and was sent to a farm about ten miles inland where the owner was a freed convict, a brutal man who drove his labourers hard but who appreciated Hugh's skill with animals and the strength that had not yet deserted him in spite of the privations of convict life.

'You stay with me and I'll see you all right,' the boss told him frequently, and his affability lasted as long as Hugh was unable to leave. When he applied for a ticket to live as a freeman, the affability disappeared.

Then every day the boss taunted him, jeered at him, deliberately goaded him.

The other convicts, watching what was happening, were on Hugh's side. 'Don't rise, Jem, he wants you to fight back. He's trying to make you hit him so that he can have you flogged. That way, they won't give you a ticket of leave at the end of the year.'

The strain was terrible for the ex-convict knew very well how to make a proud man's hackles rise. He accused Hugh of homosexuality; he accused him of stealing; he criticized his work; he jeered at his impotent state. Work was piled on to him so that he was often too tired to stagger into the sleeping shed and fell asleep on the ground where he had been working. Food was cut off from him and only scraps passed to him by other convicts prevented his collapse. His strong body became skeletal and there were many times when he was afraid his mind would crack under the strain. He no longer dreamed about Aylie for his nights were full of thoughts of strangling the boss; he could feel his fingers tightening round the man's throat, see his hated eyes pop and listen with relish to the death rattle, but when he awoke he had to bear the insults and injuries without reaction.

The boss beat him without cause until the blood ran down his back, and the more he stood silently enduring the lash, the more the brute laid it on. Of course it had to end, and one day, when the sun was at its highest and men were dropping like flies from exhaustion, Hugh was sent out to the fields to stand in the glare and pick stones out of the soil.

'I'm not going,' he told the leering boss.

'I'm ordering you to go.'

'But I'm not going.' His tone was flat and calm as if he were making an innocuous comment.

The whip was raised and cracked over his head, its tail cutting his cheek.

'You go, you dirty gypsy, when I tell you to go.'

Hugh's fist connected with the man's cheek in a satisfying thud and the boss fell pole-axed, so still that the other convicts thought he was dead and some took the chance to run away. But he was not dead. His jaw was broken but he lived, and when he was on his feet again he jubilantly marched Hugh ten miles on a rope's end to the nearest magistrate with a request that he be returned to the chain gang and flogged.

The magistrate, an unusually enlightened man for that place, looked at the jeering face of the ex-convict and the slumped figure of his roped victim. He knew that the same man had played this trick before. When a good man was about to come up for ticket of leave, he played every dirty trick to prevent him leaving.

The magistrate decided to give Hugh Kennedy a chance and though he returned him to the chain gang it was only to get him away from an employer whom he could not otherwise have left. The chain gang was a respite and when the ticket of leave application came up, it was granted. Hugh Kennedy still had two years of his sentence to serve but he was now able to earn money that would eventually pay his passage home. The trouble was that, after all he had suffered, he seemed to have forgotten what home was like. His cherished memories, the memories that had kept him going through such awful times, were fading.

Aylie, 1844

'I'm getting out of this place. I'm going to London.' Rosie looked defiantly at the faces of her two friends as they were walking back from the turnip field one night.

May paused in the middle of the hedge-lined lane.

'London? Who do you know in London?' The idea of a trip to the metropolis seemed an impossible undertaking.

'Nobody, but a bondager from the farm place my sister works at went down last year and she's doing fine. I'm going to stay with her,' Rosie replied.

'But you'll never get a job in London. Girls never get hired down there if they've been bondagers, they want lassies who've been in service for years, who've got references, letters from ministers and people like that.' Aylie was worried about her friend's rash decision. They had been working together for almost five years now and had grown very close.

'I'm not going to do housework.' Rosie sounded quite definite.

'What else is there to do?'

'My friend lives in Chelsea near the barracks. She'll help me.'

Aylie was determined to get to the bottom of it. 'Doing what?'

'I'm going on the streets.'

The two others turned on Rosie.

'You're mad, you'll get some awful disease. You'll get murdered. You'll go to Hell.' The last threat came from May, a regular church attender who turned up for worship twice on Sundays in her best clothes and sang the hymns loudly.

'Don't be silly,' said an unworried Rosie, 'I'm no virgin. I reckoned it was about time I was getting some money for it, that's all, and the soldiers pay well. I've got to get down there while I've still got some looks left, so don't try to stop me, I'm going.'

When she went, running away in the middle of her bondage, Aylie's only friend left was May, but she too was about to disappear because she was on the verge of marrying a shepherd from a nearby farm. With her friends, especially with the high-spirited Rosie, Aylie had been able to enjoy the girlish pleasures which had not been part of her life as a teenager.

At May's wedding Aylie felt sure that she was the only guest feeling sad. Sitting in the church pew, watching her friend exchanging vows with her steady, reliable shepherd, she thought of Hugh and remembered her own wedding. In her hat she had stuck the white satin roses he had given her then but they were yellowing now and their once tightly curled petals were limp. How long was it since he bought them for her? Wrinkling her brow she counted back – eight years! Sometimes it seemed an eternity and at other times it was as fresh as if it had happened yesterday. Tears stung her eyes as she thought of him so far away and of herself, so lonely and so unfulfilled. May had openly admitted she was marrying because she was pregnant. Soon she would have another child to hold in her arms but Aylie had nothing and, in spite of her innate optimism, it too often seemed she never would.

On her own, she started going to the protest meetings again. They were still arguing about the same things, nothing had been resolved. One night however, in a hall near Galashiels, the chief guest was a woman – tall, thin, white-faced and austere in a high-necked grey dress – who was introduced as Mrs Williamson from Galashiels, the wife of a Church of Scotland minister. She, the audience were told, had worked as a bondager herself before she was married.

Aylie sat forward in her seat, eager with anticipation. Surely at last this would be someone who could appreciate the hardships of a bondager's lot, surely a woman would speak for them.

Mrs Williamson was a good, clear speaker who advocated abolition of the system of the bondage in unequivocal terms. At each pause in her speech, Aylie clapped enthusiastically, but as the burden of the remarks unwound she was disappointed to realize what were Mrs Williamson's reasons for disapproval. She was on the side of the hinds. In passionate tones she recounted the disadvantages of the bondage from a man's point of view – they had the trouble of always finding a woman to work with them or a farmer would never give them a job; their wives and children had to put up with a strange woman in their home, often when money and food were short for the family itself; bondagers were notoriously flighty and fickle, they spent their money on finery which caused resentment with hinds' wives who had no money to spare for themselves. In lowered tones, Mrs Williamson went on, bondagers were often women of low morals ... their presence in a man's household was a temptation to him, a temptation which many of them could not resist. For reasons of morality and Christianity, the bondage system ought to be done away with.

She sat down to a storm of applause but Aylie slumped back on her bench, bitter disappointment filling her heart. Over the feet stamping and hand clapping of the crowd, she heard the chairman ask if there were any questions from the floor and without knowing what she was about to say Aylie stood up, raising her hand to attract his attention.

He beamed paternally at her and invited her to speak. She swallowed nervously and then something inside her made her eloquent, some deep-rooted resentment brought the words to her mouth.

'What Mrs Williamson doesn't say is how bondagers themselves feel. She ignores the fact that we're forced into signing our lives away for a year at a time; we've no choice but to live with a strange family. It's not from choice that we do this, it's for survival. Anyone who's worked on a farm knows the hardships of a bondager's life. We earn our money the hard way for we do a man's work for half the wages. We have no status, too often we're treated as animals and in fact many farmers look after their beasts better than they look after their bondagers. I know women who've delivered their children in barns or under hedges and have had to go back to work next day. I know women who've been forced to sleep with their hinds because they would be driven out of their jobs if they didn't.

'If it is an immoral system, it's not the women who make it so. Mrs Williamson, don't betray us, don't betray your own sex! Speak for us, we need someone who'll do that. I agree the bondage system needs abolishing but not for the reasons you put forward. It needs abolishing because it is unfair to women, it's debasing and uncaring. We need a champion, Mrs Williamson. Remember your own days in the fields and try to sort the wrongs done to your sisters.'

The faces of the platform party were rigid with disapproval as she sat down and a mutter of embarrassment swept the audience. Only one or two brave women dared to clap in agreement and others turned their heads to stare at this woman who had spoken so boldly from the back of the hall. When it became obvious that her interruption was going to be brushed aside as an embarrassment and that nothing was going to be done or said about it, Aylie stood up and left the meeting. But at last she knew what she wanted to do, she wanted to campaign for the abolition of the bondage system. She realized now the surge of energy that Hugh must have felt when he was going around speaking to the labourers about fighting for their rights. Having a cause to fight for was a good reason for living.

Cholera swept the Borders during 1848 and 1849. It started among the gangs of Irish labourers brought in to dig the new railway lines which were beginning to snake across the countryside bringing with them huge changes, the magnitude of which no one could yet comprehend.

In Melrose the labourers and their families died like flies and the bodies were buried communally in a huge ditch at the edge of the abbey burying ground, unmarked by any stone or list of names of the poor bewildered men, women and children who sickened and died within a few hours.

From the town it spread to the larger villages, an insidious infection against which the terrified people had recourse to old-fashioned charms, but too often those failed. Local newspapers kept tally of the numbers who died – fifty deaths in a week were common in places with populations of little over one thousand.

Cholera was no respecter of sex, age or social position. The rich, if they were unable to leave the district, died beside the poor; whole families succumbed and the work-forces of the rising industrial towns were decimated. The only people who were relatively immune from the infection were the agricultural labourers who were not in contact with the sickness and whose open-air life gave them resistance.

The overworked doctors of the district hoped that the onset of winter in 1848 would halt the disease but this proved unfounded. When frost silvered the hedgerows and made the spiders' webs look like lace between the twigs, people were still dying.

Jane was asked for help by frightened people who had lost faith in conventional medicine and were prepared to try her preparations. She brewed her potions and cast her mother's ancient spells but even she was often defeated, although some of her cases did survive through her insistence that they be forced to drink honey and water whether they wanted to or not. Their tightly clamped jaws were forced apart and the liquid poured down closing throats. If the treatment was continued long enough, they had a chance of living.

Her exertions during the time of the sickness made her tired, dog tired. And she was disillusioned by her inability to cope with this killing disease which seemed to face up to her like a personal adversary. Her ancient charms could not combat this new menace brought in by the railways and she thought of the huge black engines – with their shining brass trim and funnels pouring smoke into the atmosphere – as forerunners of an unthinkable future. Her secret Borderland was about to be invaded by the outside world and she hated the idea of its violation.

The fairies would all run away; the monks would no longer chant in Charterhall; the magic dream that had engulfed her beloved countryside since time began would be disrupted.

There were many nights when she climbed down into her little cell ready to die herself with tiredness and disillusion. Yet she continued working, walking into Melrose with her medicines every day and walking home again at night. As time passed her step grew less buoyant, her shoulders drooped and her friends and neighbours noticed how much grey had suddenly appeared in her hair.

In late summer, she realized there was something seriously wrong with her, but the cholera seemed to be dying away at last and she refused to give up. Her chest ached and there were bad pains down her left arm as she staggered home to Charterhall.

'I can't die here,' she muttered to herself as she swayed along the river path, 'I've got to get back to the abbey.'

Her head was swimming and her breath coming in rasping breaths by the time she reached her little home. Once inside she collapsed on the floor, surrounded by her carefully guarded treasures. She lay quietly still and closed her tired eyes. It was just like falling asleep . . .

A woman from the row of cottages on the ridge of the hill overlooking the abbey was concerned that she had not seen Jane for three days and came down to look for her. She found the body lying in the little cell.

'Your mother was smiling,' she told Aylie when she broke the news.

Jane had everything in neat order. It only took one

brass-bound trunk to hold her treasures – Alice's old books, the ink faded to a shadow now; some clothes and of course, Blaize's fine jacket; the silver and the manuscripts; a couple of bits of china, one of them the fairing Hugh and Aylie had given her; a pair of pots in gleaming brass; spare bedding and a patchwork bed cover made by her grandmother. When Aylie closed the door of the cell for the last time she knew that within weeks little dormice and foxes would be rummaging around in it, the whitewashed walls would be stained green with damp and it would soon be forgotten that a woman had lived there, a woman who looked out every morning on to the ruins that she loved so much. The last of the Cannons had left Charterhall.

She was leading Jed and Bobby back to their stables one evening when the steward told her that a gentleman was waiting for her in the yard. Wiping her face with her headcloth, she led the horses into their stalls and went to answer the summons. A dark-suited stranger with a narrow beard running round the edge of his jawbone came forward from the tackroom, extending his hand and, very conscious of her rough clothes and heavy boots, she looked wonderingly at him.

'I'm the lawyer from Melrose,' he told her, 'I've come about your mother's will. I've been looking for you for some time, and finally Mr Hepburn was able to tell me where you were working.'

She was surprised. 'My mother's will? I didn't know she had a will.'

'Oh yes, she came to me some time ago to draw one up. She was a very careful woman. She's left everything to you, of course. It's in the Melrose bank. She's left you three hundred pounds.'

'Three hundred pounds!' Aylie was astonished. How had Jane managed to gather so much money together? The solicitor realized the reason for her surprise.

'She's been saving for years – she lived very frugally as you know but she had many patients . . . I even consulted her myself more than once . . .' He gave a little chuckle at this sally.

Aylie turned solemn eyes on him and said nothing till he was forced to reassume his professional manner. 'The money is deposited in the bank as I have said, and it's yours. I've brought you the will and her bank book so that you can see for yourself.'

In a dream she walked back to the horses in their stable, took up her dandy brush and began rubbing away at Bobby's coat. Three hundred pounds, what would she do with all that money? For a woman who had never earned more than thirteen pounds a year, it was a fortune.

It was a sudden decision. Yes, of course, she would buy herself a cottage, a roof over her head where she would be safe from eviction, safe from being turned out at the whim of an employer.

She'd have to go on working but she could take jobs in the seasonal gangs hired during the busy times of the farming year. She'd still be a farm labourer but she would no longer be in bondage.

Her new home stood at the edge of Charterhall estate in a little hamlet of low-roofed thatched houses with a panoramic view over the spreading Borderland to the south. On fine days she could see the rounded tops of the Cheviot hills that she had ridden over with Hugh. The cottage had a tiny back garden running down to an outdoor lavatory and a pig sty. It cost her fifty pounds and on the day she signed the document which made it hers, she stood in the garden and felt the joy of possession rise in her heart. The earth beneath her feet, right to the core of the world, she thought, belonged to her. Every stone of the rough cottage wall was hers; every flower and herb in the garden; every branch on the two apple trees; every stick of the massive rhubarb plant growing near the pig stye belonged to Aylie Kennedy.

The farmer she worked for did not want to lose her but she could not continue working so far from her new home and was firm in her resolve to leave at the end of her term. The thought of parting with her beloved Jed and Bobby made her sad but when she remembered her cottage and the new life she had planned, that sorrow was swept away by her new concerns.

She was well settled by the summer of 1850. From time to time peddlers came to her door, spreading out their packs of bits and pieces on the whitened doorstep. She was not extravagant but sometimes she would buy a broadsheet, a pamphlet or a twist of lace and always she was eager to hear the news of the world from those itinerants who picked up gossip as they travelled from place to place and passed it on, suitably embroidered like the bits of flashy finery they sold. They brought news of revolutions raging far away – in Italy, in France – there were even outbreaks of sedition in England, they said. People were beginning to stand up for themselves at last, she thought, but in spite of the railways, the Borderland stayed somnolent and indifferent. 'There will never be any revolutions here, what happens outside only causes ripples in our lives,' said Aylie.

One bright afternoon when the rowan tree in her garden was heavy with scarlet berries and there was a sharp nip in the air, she was harvesting potatoes when she heard a rattling at her gate. Thinking it was another peddler, she wiped her hands on her apron and went round to the front of the cottage where a gypsy woman wrapped in the usual dark shawl was standing on her front doorstep. Her heart gave a jump of fear when she saw that it was Hugh's mother, the black-visaged Romany whose high slanting cheekbones showed her origins far more than Hugh or his father, and who looked back at her now with dark, malevolent eyes.

'They told me you were here. I came to ask if you've heard anything about my laddie.'

Aylie silently shook her head. His mother still retained the power to terrify her, such a feeling of evil emanated from the woman.

'He's been away over ten years. It's more than that since they marched him out of Perth jail. Haven't you heard anything?' she demanded.

'No, I had one letter years ago when he first got to Australia – but nothing since.' She hated admitting this, especially to his mother.

'I doubt he's not coming back then,' said the hag, turning on her heel. 'My dream must've been wrong.'

Aylie stepped forward and tried to stop her. 'Your dream? What did you dream?'

The woman laughed. 'Oh, you want to know, do you? It'll cost you, lady . . .' Her voice took on the wheedling note that gypsy women used when they came round the doors selling clothes pegs to the cottagers. Aylie knew that she was being mocked but she had to find out why the woman had come.

'How much do you want? I'll pay you.'

'You can't give me what I want,' was the reply. 'What I want is for you and my Hugh never to have met. You can't give me that. If my dream comes true you'll find out soon enough – and maybe you'll wish you hadn't.'

She marched off down the lane but before she disappeared, she turned back and shouted to Aylie, 'I came to tell you something else. My man Gilbert Kennedy died last week. We burned his bothy yesterday.'

Hugh, 1849

'Hang on, hang on ...' The words rang in Hugh Kennedy's head as he sat with his back against a sun-warmed wall, a half bottle of rum in his hand. He often listened to the words in his head as if they were a sort of background music to his life, but it was not always easy to understand what they meant. His memory was vague, he could not remember very much of what had happened to him before he arrived in Sydney but he was grateful that his life had been less brutal for a couple of years now. He was a ticket-of-leave man and had found a job on a large stud farm on the outskirts of the sprawling settlement round Sydney Bay. His knowledge of horses and his ability as a rider made him invaluable to the owner, a gentleman from England who had travelled voluntarily to Australia to make a new life in the emergent country. Like many other new settlers he was mad on racing and because he was rich, had been able to establish a magnificent stud like nothing Hugh had ever seen before. There were forty thoroughbred brood mares grazing in fenced paddocks and five proud Arab stallions rearing and kicking in spacious boxes in the stableyard. When he was working with the horses, he was happy and his confusion left him but when he was alone, a terrible feeling of sadness would sometimes sweep over him, a feeling of loss which was only assuaged by drinking rum.

Liquor was used like currency among the convict population and it was easy to come by. It brought oblivion for hours and even the next day, when he awoke, his head hurt too much for him to be able to think of anything else. He knew he should be saving money for a passage home but each time he was on the verge of getting enough, he went on a drinking spree and ended up days later in some harbourside brothel, agonized and repentant. His boss at the stud farm always took him back – drunk or sober, Hugh Kennedy was the best stud groom he had ever employed. The gypsy could turn out a horse in the pink of condition, its coat shining like satin and every nerve in its body ready for peak performance. Horses that were looked after by him swept the boards in local races and silver cups lined up like soldiers on parade on top of the owner's imported mahogany sideboard in the vast dining room of his new house.

So eager was he to keep Hugh that if he had been sober too long – for there was no secret made of his intention to get back to Scotland – the stud owner would deliberately ply him with rum and off the rails he went again.

His head was pulsing with pain and his mouth was rasping dry one morning when the owner brought a party of ladies and gentlemen to look at his mares and foals. The women were of the sort that were not often seen by Hugh, for they were pretty, crinolined visions with frilled parasols held coquettishly over straw bonnets. Ribbons floated from their hats and their sleeves so that they looked like a collection of china dolls. The convicts in the stableyard gaped at them in open admiration but as far as the women were concerned, they did not exist. Convicts were commonplace sights, like stray dogs, and less highly regarded.

Hugh led out the best mare, an elegant chestnut, who came trotting along the path at the end of the halter rope with her foal at her side. He stroked her muzzle gently and told her to stand still while the party crowded round her making cooing sounds of delight. The foal, tempted by the delicious smell of women's perfume, stuck its head forward and its mother shivered in apprehension, turning her head to watch what her precious child was doing. Hugh put up a hand and rubbed her ears confidingly.

'It's all right lass,' he told her. 'Nobody'll hurt your bairnie.'

The mare trusted him and calmed herself again while the foal raised its soft lips and nuzzled a piece of sugar from one girl's hands. Hugh felt the girl's eyes on him as he stood with the mare resting her head confidingly against him.

'She seems to like your groom,' said the pretty girl with a dimpling smile at the proud stud owner.

'Oh, all the horses like Kennedy. He's got a way with him. He's a gypsy, you see,' he explained to the gathering as if Hugh were deaf.

'A gypsy!' The women shivered in apprehension and looked at Hugh with new interest. Now that he had a good job and was being fed regularly, he had regained his stature and his strength. In spite of his drinking, he was an imposing man with his straight back and his silver-streaked hair. The intense animal attraction he had for women as well as horses was still with him.

The pretty girl came forward and asked him, 'Can I stroke the mare, please?'

'Put your parasol down then,' said Hugh gruffly. 'You'll scare her if you don't.'

The girl flushed slightly and lowered the pale pink parasol. When she did so, he could see her more clearly and as he cast his eyes over her, he saw that there was a wreath of white satin roses twined along the brim of her hat. Lovely white satin roses, as full flowered as if they had just been picked from the bush on a hot summer's day. Their petals were tightly curled one over the other and the white leaves gently cradled the flowers like loving hands. He staggered slightly as a terrible pain hit him like a fist thrust into his gut. Aylie, oh, Aylie! He'd given Aylie a sprig of roses just like those on their wedding day in Coldstream. Now he knew why he had to leave Australia, he had to go back to Aylie!

Of all the jobs around a farm Aylie enjoyed rick building best. It was a heavy job for a woman but she was proud of her prowess, standing on top of the rick of sheaves and building them up around her until they reached the

257

proper height. Then she felt as if she were a queen on top of a battlemented tower gazing down at the rest of the world.

From her eyrie on top of the rick she watched the line of carts coming into the stackyard, one after the other, pulled by patient horses and loaded down with the harvest for 1851. It had been a good year, a plentiful year, a year when the sun had blessed them as they worked in the fields and the corn was gathered in without a single day of rain.

Good harvests meant good wages and the workers were as jubilant as the farmers. All over Britain, the yield had been good and the newfangled steam threshing mills would soon be busy beating out the wheat that would go to make flour to feed the workers toiling away in the country's fast-growing industries. Great Britain was reaching a peak of prosperity, fortunes were being made by people of enterprise, and abroad the whole world was there to be conquered by a race with imperial ambitions. The British felt their country was the centre of the universe and no other people on earth could match them.

One of the labourers called up to Aylie, 'Are you tired, Missus? I'll give you a spell if you like.'

She stretched her arms above her head and thought that a cup of cold tea from the bottle she had brought with her might go down well, so she shouted back, 'All right. I'll come down,' and swung her booted feet on to the ladder that leaned against the rick side. When she reached the ground, a man was holding the ladder steady for her so with a smile, she turned to thank him for this unusual courtesy.

'Aylie,' he said. 'Oh, Aylie.'

It took her a few seconds before she realized who he was. As she stared at him she noticed that his face was very brown and deeply wrinkled and his two front teeth were broken. A strong smell of tobacco and rum came from him as he moved towards her. Putting out one hand she fended him off but he was not to be deflected.

258

'Aylie, darling, don't you know me? It's Hugh, back from Botany Bay.'

'Oh, my God,' she gasped, unable to conceal her shock. 'Oh, my God, Hugh. What's happened to you?'

Then, to cover up this mistake, she threw her arms around his neck and clung desperately to him. She was in such a state of shock that she was afraid her heart was about to stop beating.

Both of them had dreamed so long about this reunion. He had lain in convict cells thinking about how he would go back to sweep her up in his arms and they would fall into bed together, as fierce and compatible in sex as they were before. She had dreamed romantically of him coming back and holding out his hands gently to her while speaking words of love. In her dreams the returned Hugh looked the same as he had done when he went away, still as strong, as handsome and as admirable as her gypsy husband had been on the day that Patie Mudie married them.

In the event, they were both disappointed though they felt that their disappointment was something which they should cover up even to themselves.

Hugh Kennedy had been broken and aged by his years of transportation. His hair, once as blue-black as a raven's wing, was streaked with grey, and bad diet had rotted his fine teeth. The sun had baked his skin to the texture of leather, and dust and dirt from years past seemed to be engrained in the folds of the wrinkles along his brow and round his eyes. He looked wary, suspicious, distrustful, a man who trusted no one and who had no loyalties. After he had left you, there would be an impulse to pat your pockets.

When he looked at her, he saw the girl he had married, but in the body of an older woman. Of course, he had not expected anything else.

Aylie was still beautiful, dignified and ladylike, with the grace and reserve that had attracted him to her in the first place, but after so many years apart she had withdrawn from him. Living so long on her own had made her self-reliant and she no longer needed his protection. The impulse to protect her had been a large part of his love for her. He still longed to look after her.

With pride she showed him the little cottage that she owned; she told him about her work and he realized that she had her independence. His return was not going to improve her life.

The worst thing was that they felt so awkward when they talked to each other. She told him about the main events that had taken place since he left, about his father's death and the death of her own mother.

He could see that the memory of Jane still pained her and said in an effort to console her, 'But she was an old woman, wasn't she?'

'She was fifty-five. That's not old,' Aylie replied shortly.

She was eager to hear about Australia but its sun-soaked land seemed mercifully removed from his life and he was reluctant to discuss what had happened there. He knew nothing of the political events of his homeland over the past years and had little interest when she talked about them.

She was surprised to realize that her involvement in the labour reform movement did not please her returned husband, who sternly warned her off it by saying, 'Get out of it now. I remember a convict called old Parr who sailed with me on the *Eden*. He was transported because of politics and he told his wife to keep their bairns out of them. I think the same as he did. Politics only get you into trouble. Leave them alone, Aylie.'

The only time the clock turned back for them was when they were in bed together. It was the place where the differences that had grown up between them over the years of separation were swept away. They were as passionate as when they first married and for many months the exaltation this caused Aylie closed her mind to other, less pleasant aspects of resumption of married life with Hugh. When they made love her heart broke for him because it was then that she saw the hideous scarring of his back.

260

'Oh my God, Hugh, what happened to your back?' she asked the first time she felt the scar tissue under her hands.

'Don't talk about it, Aylie, don't ever ask me about it,' he warned her.

He found it difficult to get work. Not only were farmers wary of taking on a returned convict, but his old reputation as a troublemaker was well remembered by people whose memories were long because so very little ever happened to them.

After his experiences in Botany Bay, Hugh was not anxious to buckle down to the life of a farm hind, to the regular drudgery; the early mornings; and, worst of all, the forelock-touching that was demanded of employees by many farmers. He'd had enough of that, the years of the lash and the shackle had left scars on him that were deeper than even he realized. He was full of unresolved and unfocused hate.

In the beginning Aylie did not press him to get work. She continued her own method of earning, going out in work gangs when money was required, but now that she had two people to feed, she had to work more frequently. Something warned her not to tell Hugh about the nest egg she kept in the bank at Melrose, and when he inquired how she had managed to buy the cottage, she told him it had taken all of the small legacy left to her by her mother. Some small warning voice counselled her to keep her secret from him. She would draw on the money to help him if necessary but that would be her decision – not his. She also knew that under the law he could claim any money she possessed as his own, and that was another reason for keeping quiet.

He lounged about the house and garden with his moods varying from high exaltation to deep depression. When he was exhilarated, he rode off on a borrowed horse to Yetholm and sometimes stayed away for two or three days at a time.

When he returned he explained that he had been caught up by his 'own people'. He asked her to

261

accompany him on these outings but the memory of his witchlike mother who, aged though she was, still ruled the Kennedy family with a rod of iron, kept her away.

When he was depressed he sat around the cottage or slumped in a chair on its doorstep, head hanging low and scarred hands idle in his lap, just thinking – what thoughts she dared not inquire. Coming out of those moods, he embraced her, hugged her to him as if she were his only treasure in the world, and even wept, a thing which she had never seen him do before. Then she loved and pitied him most of all for he seemed like a defenceless child who needed her comfort.

Sometimes, usually after an outing to Yetholm, he would have money in his pocket and then he bought extravagant presents for her or new clothes for himself, flashy clothes that made him look even more like an unreliable gypsy horse trader than he did when dressed in old working rags. His army of vagrant cousins enlisted his help in their horse-trading businesses and other unspecified pursuits, and with them he went off to Appleby in May and to the July fair at St Boswells where he trotted out horses and praised them in honeyed words that enraptured would-be buyers. He was very good at that, his golden tongue had not deserted him.

He had been at home for over a year when Aylie discovered that she was pregnant. This was the answer to her dreams . . . a baby at last! She could hardly wait to tell him.

'I'm pregnant. We're having a baby, isn't it wonderful!' she told him, but he received the news with a good deal less enthusiasm.

'Do you want to have it?' he asked. 'If you want rid of it my mother knows a woman . . .'

She was shattered with disappointment. 'Rid of it? Of course not. I'm longing for a child. Don't you want a baby?'

He was dressing to go out on one of his escapades, and paused a little while before replying, 'It wouldn't make much difference to me. I'm happy here with just

262

you and me. Chavies yell and make a lot of noise. I don't like noise much.'

She thought he was being flippant and so she flounced off, saying, 'I'll keep it quiet, don't you worry. I manage everything else round here.'

When they could not make love any longer because she grew so bulky, the breach between them widened. He often came home reeking of rum and fell fully dressed on to the bed, where he lay snoring till the next day. She resented the fact that, though pregnant, she had to go on working in order to support them both, for if he earned any money it was quickly wasted. Tales came back to her through neighbours about the generosity of her husband to his cronies in the Melrose alehouses . . . 'A man aye eager to stand his hand,' she was told.

She listened to this impassive faced, though inside she burned with anger. The money he was wasting on impressing people who cared nothing for him would have put coal in their hearth and food on their table. Eventually she tackled him about it. 'I'm going to stop working now,' she said in early March. 'You'll have to bring in money for a change. The baby's due soon and I'll need all my strength to deliver it. It's a big bairn, I can see that by my belly, and I'm not so young, so I might have a hard time.'

There was genuine anxiety and love in his face as he looked at her.

'Oh Aylie, take care of yourself, I'll help you. Don't worry about money, my people have a big scheme coming off soon . . . We'll be in the money and you won't need to work any more.'

In a flashback she remembered him promising her a silk gown in the days when he went smuggling, and the memory gave her a spasm of fear.

'Hugh, forget the big schemes, just take work in the labouring gang. It's good money and the farmer'll take you on in my place. I've already spoken to him.'

He banged a fist on the table. 'I'm not labouring in any gangs. I've had enough of gangs for the rest of my life. I'm better than that, I'm cut out for bigger things! You wait and see, I'll show them all, I've a scheme that'll take us out of here and into a mansion.'

This was too much for Aylie.

'You damned fool,' she snapped. 'This little place is good enough for me and it's better than anything your family ever had. You talk about mansions but every time you get a few pence together you go out and drink it. I won't wait for your mansion or I'd be sure to be disappointed.'

After he slammed out of the house, they did not speak a civil word to each other for more than a week. What broke the impasse was Aylie going unexpectedly into labour in the middle of the night. Hugh had to run for the midwife who lived in the same hamlet and throughout the long labour he sat in a rocking chair by the fire, paralysed with fear.

The busy howdie, passing and repassing him, looked with curiosity at his trembling body, the hands twitching as they hung by his sides and the head slumped on his chest. No matter how she tried to chivvy him, she could arouse no response. Even when the child was born, and she presented him with a son tightly wrapped in a white blanket, he seemed little interested.

'Is Aylie all right?' he asked dully.

Urged to go up the rickety little stair to see her, he did so and at the sight of her waxen face among the pillows, he put his hands over his face and began to weep heart-brokenly. She could do nothing but hold her hands out to him and he fell on the bed beside her, utterly broken. When she eventually fell asleep, he threw on his coat and went out to get drunk. He did not come back for two days.

Hannah, 1858

They called their son Adam after Jane's father and he grew into a handsome child. When he was five years old Aylie, to her consternation, found she was once again pregnant in spite of having taken all the precautions she knew against conception. Both she and Hugh were reluctant parents-to-be and she was worried because, at the age of forty-three, she dreaded another delivery. It was a wet and clammy summer and she could hardly drag herself to work.

Her dread proved to be fully justified because it was a slow and painful delivery. She went into labour on a Sunday. Hugh was in the house recovering from a hangover, but when her pains started he pulled himself together and helped her. When her suffering became acute, however, his distress was so evident that the howdie, remembering his reaction to the birth of Adam, sent him downstairs.

The pain was excruciating and it was impossible for Aylie to stifle her cries of agony. Soon her moans became screams and the noise of them was heard not only in the house but throughout the whole hamlet where white-faced women huddled in their kitchens remembering the pains of past labours they had suffered themselves. In Aylie's cottage her husband sat with his hands over his ears trying to shut out the sound, his face contorted as if in pain.

Then suddenly he went berserk, throwing himself around the room, smashing furniture, breaking china and, worst of all, howling like a maddened dog. Leaving Aylie, the midwife leaped down the ladder and tried to restrain him but it was like wrestling with an octopus and she had to ask some of the neighbours for help. It took five men to hold him down and even after he was tied up he did not seem to know who or where he was. It was as if he had been stricken with total amnesia.

In the middle of all the turmoil, their daughter was born.

After having looked the same for many years, Jock Hepburn was an old man. The reddish-coloured bush of hair was grey and his once straight back was so bent that he was supporting himself on a stick when he arrived at Aylie's cottage with Sandy, now a grave-faced, middle-aged man who had the same air of rugged reliability as his father.

Aylie knew that Jock would never make the trip to see her on a working day without good reason so when she had brewed a pot of tea for the visitors, she sat down at her scrubbed kitchen table and waited to be told the reason for the visit. In the absence of a father or a grand-father, Jock had always played the male role in her young life. At times of trouble it was he who had come to help her mother and now he was doing the same for her.

'How's the bairns?' he began by asking, and she indicated her son Adam, playing happily about on the rag hearthrug while the baby slept peacefully in the wooden cradle by the fire.

'They're fine, Adam's getting big. He'll have to go to school soon,' she said with a smile.

Jock sipped his tea and his son gazed out of the cottage window at Aylie's kitchen garden where the beanstalks were tall enough to tap on the window panes.

'What name are you giving the wee girl?' was Jock's next question, and Aylie's face fell.

'I wanted to call her Lark – that's what my real name means in English – but Hugh laughed at the idea. He's calling her Hannah after his mother.'

She saw Sandy shoot a look at her when she said this and she hoped her deep dislike of the old woman would not show in her face.

'Is your man all right these days?' asked Jock, and she

realized that the reason he had come to her cottage was to discuss Hugh.

She looked bright. 'He's fine. He's been away with his cousins at Newmarket. They have some relative who's a jockey down there.'

Jock nodded, putting down his tea cup. 'Aye, so I heard. Aylie, you should try to keep him at home or he'll get into trouble again.'

Her face froze. She hated it when people reminded her of Hugh's time as a convict.

'He's not doing anything wrong. He's learned his lesson,' she said defensively.

'No, it's not that. It's just — it's just that he talks a bit strange at times. People are noticing it and when the bairn was born — well, people said he went fair mad.'

She had grown used to Hugh's outbursts of violent activity; to his swift swings of mood from exhilaration to depression. But she was not afraid of him because he was never violent towards her though she had heard there had been fights in alehouses in which his companions had to hold him back, so terrible were his rage and energy.

'Do you mean you've heard that he's been fighting?' she asked Jock. She was not angry at his attempt to talk about her husband although she would not have allowed anyone else to do so.

The old man shook his head. 'Not just that, it's the wild way he's behaving in general. It's the way he talks sometimes — he's been on about big schemes for making money, about backing horses that cousin of his rides in England — and he talks about selling horses to the Duke of Grafton and things like that, but nothing ever comes of them. They're all in his imagination.'

She nodded sadly. She'd heard Hugh's wild talk herself and had long ago learned to take it with a pinch of salt.

But Jock was not finished. 'I think you should get him to see a doctor, Aylie. It's not normal the way he's going on. It was how he had to be tied up when the bairn was born that made me afraid for you.'

Startled, she stared at his face and saw the concern in his eyes.

'A doctor? What sort of a doctor?'

'There's a man lives near Harestanes who's a retired doctor from Edinburgh. He'd have a look at Hugh if I asked him.'

She shook her head defensively. 'There's nothing wrong with Hugh, I'm sure of that. It's only because he's had such terrible experiences in Australia that he behaves the way he does. Oh, if you only saw the marks on his back, you'd know what I mean. Things like that make a man a bit strange. There's nothing wrong with him!'

Old Jock looked solemn and very sad. 'All right, Aylie, but think about what I said. If you change your mind, just send me a message and I'll get the doctor to have a look at him.'

The visit unsettled her and she began watching her husband more closely. It was true his moods varied violently – sometimes he would be melancholy in the morning and as happy as a drunk man, though no liquor had passed his lips, at night. When he had money he spent it wildly, coming home dressed like a lordling with silver spurs and a tall beaver hat that gleamed when the sun hit its velvety nap.

This outraged her because it happened on the same day as she came home tired from a day's work in the fields and found that her son, who had been entrusted to the care of a neighbour, had burned his hands badly on the hot door of the oven. In a rage she swore at Hugh who put both of his hands up over his head and seemed on the verge of striking her before he pulled himself together.

Later he came to her and said in a low voice, 'Don't shout at me like that again, Aylie, because I'm afraid of what I'd do – without wanting to if you see what I mean.'

Shaken, she nodded and they clung to each other, frightened as children at the thought of what had almost happened.

He could not tolerate noise so she taught the children

to be very quiet. The house was hushed and silent whenever he was in it and she worried in case her children
were being brought up in an unnatural way. Then he
began to lose his memory, forgetting things he had done
and said the day before, wandering in his speech and
sometimes thinking he was back in Sydney. These
episodes terrified her and she decided to take Jock's
advice.

The woman with the infant wrapped in a shawl at her
breast and the other child clinging to her hand looked so
defenceless to the doctor that he tried to break the news
to her gently.

'I've had a look at your husband and I think that – I
think that perhaps he needs treatment, Mrs Kennedy.'

'Treatment? What sort of treatment?' she asked, obviously afraid.

'He ought to go away for a little while.'

'Where to?'

'There's a hospital in Edinburgh that takes people like
him.'

'Like him? What's wrong with him?' she asked.

He looked intently into her face and respected the
intelligence he saw there. 'Have you ever heard of syphilis, Mrs Kennedy?'

She nodded, silent and shocked.

'I think your husband must have been infected by syphilis during his time in Australia. You said he was there
for ten years, didn't you? It's endemic among the – er –
the convict population, I believe. The disease could just
be reaching the madness stage now.'

As soon as he said it he knew it sounded tactless.

'The madness stage . . .' The words seemed unreal to
her but she nodded, too full of emotion to say anything
more.

She did not blame him, really. He'd been away for
such a long time and she knew his strong appetites, his
overwhelming life force and its need for assuagement.

269

She had never asked him about women, not wanting to force him into telling her lies.

She looked back up at the doctor. 'But he's not really mad, he only has these outbursts now and again. I'll look after him and see that he doesn't get into trouble. Please don't send him away again.' She was pleading for him.

'I'm afraid he can only get worse. He might even become dangerous, to others or to himself. You've got to be aware of that.' The doctor was obviously upset at having to break such bad news to her.

Aylie still had hope however. 'Just let him be, doctor. If he has another attack, I'll let you know but he's been so calm since the baby was born. I'm sure it'll pass.'

He shook his head doubtfully. 'I know I shouldn't do this but I'll not report him at the moment – I hope you're right, Mrs Kennedy.'

When Hannah was a year old her father's mental equilibrium snapped completely. He had been prey to delusions for several months, thinking everyone in the hamlet was plotting against him, sure he was being followed by spies each time he left the house.

Eventually, after a long spell of silent depression, he ran amok in the middle of the night and killed all Aylie's hens as well as cutting the throat of the pig she had been fattening for winter. He was about to come into the house with his knife dripping blood when he collapsed on the doorstep.

'There's no alternative. This time he's got to be confined. He's had his chance. If he's not put away he'll kill you all,' the doctor told her very firmly.

'But he won't hurt us, he loves us, I know he loves us,' she protested.

'That's as may be but he's not rational any longer. You know as well as I do that your husband's mind has gone. If you won't commit him, I'll do it over your head to protect you and your children – not to mention the people living round about you.'

270

When the cart with two male attendants came to take Hugh away he did not seem to realize what was happening and walked quite calmly out to it, his arms pinioned at his sides in the tightly bound strait jacket. Aylie and the children watched from the window as he was driven away to board the train that would take him to Edinburgh, to the madhouse where, they had been told, he would be kept until he was better. In fact the doctors knew quite well there was no question of recovery for Hugh Kennedy. His madness could only become worse and in a short time he would recognize no one, remember nothing of his past life. He would even forget his wife, the person to whom he had clung in fact and in memory all those years. He was irrecoverably insane.

Dark-haired Hannah sat hunched up on the cottage door-step and listened to her mother and her brother talking inside the cottage.

With a tremor in her voice, Aylie was saying, 'Of course I won't stand in your way, Adam. I'll miss you — very much — but I realize there's nothing here for you . . . you're right to get away.'

'Come with me, Mother,' pleaded Adam. 'You and Hannah come too and I'll look after you.'

Hannah peered in through the half open door and saw her brother standing in the middle of the kitchen floor. Although he was only fifteen years old, he was tall and manly, far older-looking than his age.

Aylie told him, 'I can't come. You know why. Your father's still in that place in Edinburgh — and, besides, I can't imagine living anywhere but here.'

Adam sounded angry. 'Forget about Father, he doesn't even know who you are. Every time you go there he's just the same, a mindless animal. That's wrong, I take it back, animals have more intelligence than he has.' There was always scorn in Adam's voice when he talked about his father.

And, as she also always did, Aylie was quick to Hugh's

271

defence. 'You shouldn't say things like that about him. He couldn't help it. They sent him away to Australia and it turned his brain.'

Adam was exasperated. 'Mother, you're telling lies and I know it. His trouble comes from venereal disease, from syphilis! I've known what was wrong with him for years.'

There was a long silence and then Aylie said, very slowly, 'But he couldn't help it, Adam. Can you imagine what it must have been like to be sent away for *ten years*? There was no certainty that he'd ever get back home again. I've never held it against him . . .'

'But you should,' said her son loudly, 'you should hold it against him. Don't you realize that both Hannah and I could have been infected, we could be syphilitic idiots now because of him.'

Hannah put her hands over her ears but she could not cut out the sound of their voices.

Her mother sounded infinitely sad. 'I know. The doctor told me. He said that if you'd been infected it would show when you were still young. I've watched you both and thank God you're safe. The doctor said that Hugh's infection had probably burned out by the time he got home – he'd no sores, you see.' Her voice was shamed, for she was timid about discussing such personal things with her son. Then after another silence, she continued, 'But it had infected his brain and there was nothing they could do about that.'

'Come to Canada with me, Mother,' said Adam roughly. 'Come with me. He wouldn't even know you'd gone.'

Hannah heard her mother sob, 'I can't, I can't. I hate to lose you, but I've got to stay here. Perhaps if you make your fortune you'll come back to see me one day.'

There was a scrape of chair legs on the floor and she heard her brother saying in a choked voice, 'I'll do well, I'm determined on that. Don't worry, Mother.' Then Hannah slipped off into the garden, not wanting to be found eavesdropping.

He left next day and his mother and sister accompanied

him to Melrose station where, with his brass-bound chest neatly labelled for the ship that was to carry him across the Atlantic, he boarded the train for Liverpool. As she looked at her son, Aylie realized that it had always been inevitable she would lose him. He was too good, too ambitious and too intelligent to settle for the life of a labourer, which was all that was open to him at home. Adam had been a good scholar but he left school at twelve to train as a shepherd with a relative of the Cannon family in the Cheviot Hills. He had the makings of a good shepherd but as he stared out over the empty expanse of hills that surrounded him, he felt his life was being wasted. Eventually he saved enough money to pay for a passage to Canada where there were already many Borderers living. From what he heard, it seemed that Canada was a glorious land of opportunity and Adam Kennedy was determined to make good. He was no stranger to hard work and it did not frighten him. His only regret was leaving his mother and sister, but when he spoke about those doubts, Aylie pressed him to go. She saw that it was his only chance.

As he kissed and clung to them on the station platform, Aylie kept outwardly calm though she felt her heart was breaking once again. Her son had always been her most loved child, the one with whom she felt the closest affinity. Now, as he left her, it seemed that her life was one of continual partings – first from Hugh, then Jane and now from Adam.

She had no certainty that she would ever see her beloved son again and there was none of the hope in her heart that had nourished and sustained her during Hugh's absence. Now, looking back, she realized that it would probably have been better if Hugh had not returned, for the man who came back was not the man she had dreamed of during the years of separation. The day Hugh Kennedy was marched in chains out of Jedburgh's Bridewell was really the last day she had seen her beloved husband. She did not however confide any of those thoughts to her daughter.

Hannah had been a distant and self-possessed baby. She had brushed away embraces, shared no confidences, required little reassurance and, worst of all, she very closely resembled the grandmother for whom she had been named and who was still alive, still as wrinkled, black-visaged and broken-toothed as ever.

From time to time Hannah Fa' turned up unannounced at the cottage, not to see her grandchildren but to berate Aylie for sending Hugh away to the madhouse. 'You sent him away, you got rid of him, you sent away my son, curses on you!' she would chant malevolently.

Aylie was used to her cursing and she stood, blank-faced, staring bravely into the flashing black eyes. As she scrutinized the old woman's face she saw Hannah in her – in the broad high cheekbones and the wide mouth; in the boldness of the dark eyes and the way the hair grew thick and curling on to the forehead. Young Hannah was a gypsy all right although her hair was brown and not raven black. Send her out wrapped up in a tattered grey shawl with a basket on her arm and she would be able to intimidate cottage women into buying anything she had for sale.

Four years after her brother left home, the girl was still attending school, helping to pay for her continued education by teaching the smallest children in the schoolroom.

The gentle old schoolmaster was fond of saying to Hannah's mother, 'You were a clever bairn, Aylie, but your lassie has you beat. I don't think I've ever had a cleverer pupil under my care. It's a pleasure to teach her.'

Hannah sucked in learning with a hunger that frightened Aylie.

'But what good will it do her?' she asked the schoolmaster. 'What can she do with all this learning? It'll only cause her grief because it'll make her want more than she can ever have.'

'She has a mind. It has to be fed. Learning is never wasted,' said the old man, but he added, 'I know what you mean, though. She won't ever be happy working as

274

a bondager when she's thinking about Homer. You'll have to get her a place in a big house, Aylie, where she might go on to be a lady's maid or even a governess, she's bright enough for that.'

Sometimes Aylie would take Hannah along with her when she went out to attend the meetings which were still held round about. The child sat beside her mother, listening intently to the speakers, and would question Aylie about what she'd heard as they walked home. Her mother often told her about the political activities of Hugh when he was a young man and Hannah drank in those stories greedily. Her father was her greatest hero and she liked the idea of him being a political martyr which was how Aylie painted him to her.

Aylie herself had lost none of her convictions but she had become inactive through her years of bringing up the children alone, and Mrs Williamson was now the unchallenged chief spokeswoman against the bondage system. She published broadsheets and pamphlets advocating the need for reform but Aylie was sad to note that these pamphlets never acknowledged that the women on the land had as deep, if not deeper, grievances than the men. Though the tide was turning in favour of change – one by one more enlightened farmers were improving their cottages and not insisting on bondagers being provided by every hind – these changes would not bring equality to female labourers.

Aylie was right. The women lost out because although they were soon to be able to make their own bargains with the farmers, they were forced to accept the status of second-class labourers and were paid even lower rates than before. Added to that they lost the security of being fed and housed by their hind. The worst cottages and the poorest places went to women looking for farm jobs.

When Aylie talked about this to Hannah, the girl's fury at injustice reminded her of the way she herself used to feel before the fight had been driven out of her.

'It's no use,' she told her daughter. 'We can't do

275

anything about it. I tried and your father tried and we both lost.'

'You didn't try hard enough! You gave in,' cried Hannah. 'I won't give in. I won't stand for it, Mother.'

At the time of the Lammas Fair, Aylie's old friend May came down from the hills with her shepherd husband and while he toured the sheep pens at Melrose, she walked over to Charterhall to visit Aylie.

Drinking tea from thin china cups which were brought out specially for the occasion from the tiny 'press' at the side of the hearth, the two women sat and discussed what had happened to them over the past year.

May was careful never to mention Hugh until Aylie brought his name into the conversation, for the news of him was never good. His madness was irrevocable and his wife had accepted that now. She knew that he would never be allowed out of the asylum again. Once a year she made the trip to Edinburgh in the train but he did not know her any longer and she came back sunk in a depression that would take weeks to shift.

'I went up to see Hugh again last month,' she told May. 'I so wanted to tell him that they've made it legal to form a trade union . . . He'd once have enjoyed hearing that. But he didn't understand what I was talking about.' She passed a plate of shortbread over to May, urging her to take a piece, and then she added, 'I took Hannah up to see her father.'

May stared at her friend over the rim of the gilt-edged tea cup and asked slowly, 'Was that a good idea?'

Aylie shrugged. 'She insisted. She'd not seen him since they took him away. I think she half believed what his mother says – you know, that I had him shut up to suit myself.'

May shook her head. 'Oh, it must have been a shock to her when she saw him then,' she said.

Aylie was pouring tea with hands that shook slightly but otherwise she was in control of her emotions.

'Yes, she was very upset. He didn't know who she was.

He's forgotten he ever had children. He shouted and swore at her. He seemed to think she was some woman he'd known in Australia . . .'

The women looked at each other wordlessly, their thoughts unspoken.

Aylie continued, 'Poor Hannah, she's been a lot quieter and easier to get on with since we came home.' She had never made any secret to her friend about how difficult her daughter was to bring up.

May asked, 'She's sixteen this year, isn't she? What's she going to do? She can't go on at school any longer.'

'I wish she could, poor Hannah. The schoolmaster says she's the cleverest girl he's ever had to teach. I don't know where she's got it from.' Aylie sounded confused. Her maverick daughter was a mystery to her.

May shook her head in shared sympathy for Hannah as well as for Aylie. 'Oh, it's not good if a lassie's clever. If she'd been a boy she could have gone to college and been a minister or something like that – but not if she's a lassie.'

'It's unfair, isn't it?' asked Aylie. 'It's just another of the things that are unfair for women in this world.'

'But what's she going to do? Will she go on the land like you did?'

Aylie shook her head. 'I suggested that but she was furious, she says women who work on the land are nothing better than animals . . . She's very proud, like her father was.'

May clicked her tongue. 'Pride's all right but you've got to live, haven't you? If you hadn't worked on the land all those years, where would she be now?'

Aylie nodded. 'I know, but you can't tell a headstrong girl that. I sympathize with her in a way. I know what it's like to look at rich women and compare the way they lead their lives and how you lead yours . . . Don't you ever wonder about that, May?'

But May was not strong on imagination and she shook her head before saying proudly, 'My youngest lassie's going into service in the big house near us. She's starting as a kitchenmaid but the family go to London every year and they might take her with them. They're aye looking for girls because the housekeeper's such a tyrant. Would Hannah like me to speak for her there?'

'I don't want her to go too far away at first. Perhaps she'll take a job round about here for a while,' said Aylie. 'But if she doesn't like it, I'll ask for your help, May. It's kind of you to offer.'

Before the shepherd's wife left the cottage, Hannah came sweeping in. There was a great change in the girl since the last time May had seen her and she was surprised at the feeling of energy that came off Hannah, the sense of movement, of drive – and she had to admit it, of defiance and rebellion. Hannah was very tall and erect in her bearing, she walked like a duchess although her clothes were shabby. She was also as haughty as a duchess and scarcely spoke to her mother or the visitor, flashing her dark eyes and furrowing her brows as she passed them. May instinctively drew back from her as she always did from the predatory gypsy women who accosted her in the lane near her home, begging for money or food.

When she met her husband that evening, she was looking solemn.

'Poor Aylie's got her hands full with that lassie, she's a right Romany,' she told him.

The winter of 1874–75 was bitter. Snow and cold winds came sweeping down from the north; farm workers and animals huddled together in the sheds; birds fluffed out their feathers and crouched down in the lowest branches of the hedges; the earth took on the look of cold steel and the unrelenting frost stiffened tufts of moss on the tops of walls and froze the water of the animals' drinking troughs so hard that even steel-tipped crooks could not break through the ice.

During the hardest grip of the frost, old Jock Hepburn died and his grandson walked across the fields to take the news to Aylie. 'He was eighty-two and he just fell asleep,' said the boy.

'I can't stand it . . .' Every time Hannah came back from yet another job, Aylie knew what she would say: 'I can't stand the people, I can't stand the noise, I can't stand the way they treated me.'

When she came back for the third time, Hannah's mother was grim-faced as she listened to the reasons for unemployment again.

'I can't stand being ordered about. And what was worse, I can't stand the way the master and mistress treated me. They looked right through me as if I wasn't there.'

'People don't usually pass the time of day with their kitchenmaids,' said Aylie wearily.

'But they're such *fools*,' spat Hannah, her eyes flashing. 'All they ever think about is hunting and horses!'

Aylie's face softened as she recalled her own youth when horses totally filled her mind. 'That doesn't mean they're fools,' she ventured, but Hannah would have none of it.

'I couldn't stand them, Mother. I couldn't stand having to step back against the passage wall and look down at my boots every time one of the household passed me.'

Aylie was cleaning her own working boots as she listened and she reflected that labouring women had done far more demeaning things than drop their eyes for an employer. 'The trouble with you, Hannah, is that there's not a job in the world that's going to suit you. When you went to the weaving mill in Galashiels, you couldn't stand the noise and the other girls.

'When I got you a job on the farm, you didn't last a month. Now you've left the job that May got you – and it had prospects. If the housekeeper liked you she'd have taken you to London like she did with May's girl.'

Hannah flushed angrily at her mother's criticism.

'You agreed with me about the mill. You said yourself it would be like Hell to be shut up all day. You understood why I left the farm, there just wasn't anybody there to talk to. They're like animals, those people.'

Aylie nodded, her face bitter. 'I know, you said we were "red-faced rustics", if I remember rightly.'

'Not you, Ma, of course not you, but those others. Even your precious Hepburns are nothing more than rustics. None of them has ever even been to Edinburgh far less over the Border into England.'

Aylie, who thought the Hepburns were the finest family in the world, rose to their defence. 'If only you could settle down with somebody like one of the Hepburns, I'd be a happy woman. But not you . . .'

'No, not me.' Hannah was really angry now. 'Not me. I'll not settle down as you call it with anybody. Look what happened to you when you "settled down". Is that the life you want for me? It's not the life I want for myself. I've made up my mind, Mother. I want to go to London, and if I do it won't be because some housekeeper takes me to scrub away in a basement kitchen. No, I'll go on my own and make my own way.'

Memories of Rosie came back to Aylie. What had happened to her friend, she wondered? No one had heard from Rosie since she left, not even her mother.

'What do you think you'll do in London?' she asked her daughter.

'What does it matter? I'll survive. There's plenty of things I could do. I'm going, Mother, you can be sure of that.'

A week later she went out early in the morning and when she returned at midnight, she was looking happier than she had done for some time.

Aylie asked, 'Where have you been till so late?'

Hannah said airily, 'I went over to Yetholm to see the Kennedys. My father's mother's still alive and she likes me. She says I look like she did when she was a young woman.'

'That's true, she did look like you, I always thought you took after her,' agreed Aylie carefully.

'She's given me the money for the fare to London, she

thinks it's a good idea for me to go there,' said Hannah triumphantly, unable to keep this bit of news to herself any longer.

'So that's her last bit of revenge against me,' said Aylie bitterly.

The parting on Melrose station was not as affecting as the parting from Adam had been. As she waved from the train window Hannah looked raffish, in much the same way as Hugh used to do when he dressed as a gentleman. What would her girl do in London, Aylie wondered. How would a young woman of twenty, who had never lived anywhere else except in the backwater of the Borders, cope with the wicked city? Then she remembered Hannah's gift of invective and her powerful rages – Hannah, she decided, would cope very well.

As Hannah waved her hand at the dwindling figure of her mother, tears of pity pricked her eyes.

Her mother did not understand her, Hannah was sure of that. She had never understood her. How could Aylie be content to live the life she did, trudging out into the fields early in the morning wearing those heavy working boots and that servile costume? When she had tackled her mother about it, Aylie would run her work-chapped hands down over the heavy apron and say, 'But we've always dressed like this, we bondager women.'

'Bondagers! What a name! You don't have to sign a bond with a hind any more, so why do you keep the name and why do you keep that stupid hat?'

Aylie bristled. The bondager costume was the thing she liked best about her working life. She was proud to go out in the morning, smart as paint. Before nightfall she might end up grimed and dirty, but in the morning she must look smart. It was a matter of pride with her.

She tried to explain this to Hannah but her daughter spat back at her like a cat. 'You've told me how you used to stand up and speak against the bondage and now you're just a lackey like the rest. You make me laugh, Mother, you really do.'

281

Standing on the station platform, watching her daughter disappear into the distance in the winding train, Aylie remembered their quarrels . . . 'A lackey like the rest!' She supposed she was, but there had been little alternative for her. At least she had her own house and her little nest egg in the bank so she need not be afraid of ending her days in the poor's house like so many of her friends and associates. Far away in Canada Adam had not forgotten her and sent small sums of money in his letters. She saved carefully so that she'd be able to die in her own house, among her own things, not depending on grudging handouts from charity or the parish.

Hannah was cut in half by her triumph at getting away at last and regret for what had never been said between her and her mother. She loved Aylie but her mother represented a way of life and expectations which her daughter had been educated to challenge. Hannah knew she was as good as anyone else; she knew she was cleverer than most; her gift of comprehension and analysis, however, had proved to be a barb in her side for it made it impossible for her to accept the way of life led by her forebears.

She would never martyr herself for a man or for a place as Aylie and Jane Cannon had done. She, Hannah Kennedy, longed to change her circumstances, to mix with people who could give her the excitement that was impossible to find at Charterhall. She wanted to be accepted for what she had to offer and not as a representative of a class or a family as she would always be if she stayed at home. Even though part of her was weeping at leaving her mother and the place where she had been born, she had to get away.

She sat with her face pressed against the window, taking in every detail of the soft hills, the clustering woods and the silver rivers. She looked out at neat farmsteads with grey stone buildings and the flocks of sheep and herds of brown and white cows grazing in lush meadows. Her eyes were dazzled by the pale wash of the sky with its drifting trails of cotton clouds.

'There's always so much sky in the Borderland,' she said to herself as her lids drooped in sleep. When she woke she was in another world – a flat, grey world that looked as if it had been dusted over with dirt. Factories and workshops clustered up against the railway line and outside the factory gates she saw lines of sordid little brick-built dwellings, not unlike the pig sty in her mother's cottage garden.

Women with their arms crossed over their bosoms stood staring at the passing train while small children played in the dirt at their feet. Everybody she saw looked white-faced, thin and hungry, a bitter contrast with the healthy people who worked the land she had left.

She would never have admitted it but London terrified her when she stepped off the train. The bustling people, all of them intent on their own business, all of them looking perfectly at home and able to cope with the din and the jostling, swept past the girl tightly grasping her carpet bag. Her gypsy grandmother had given her the address of some relatives who lived in Stepney in the East End, but she had no idea how to get there and after wandering around the station for some time, she stopped a man in porter's uniform to ask for directions.

'I don't know! The best thing you can do is take a hansom,' was his reply, and Hannah was forced to draw on her meagre finances for the fare. Turning up in the narrow, smelly East End street in a hansom however gave her a status among her family and their neighbours which she was to retain for ever. They thought she was a very grand lady indeed in her big hat with the flower in it, her tightly fitting dress and her hansom . . . If they wanted to go anywhere in London, they walked.

Hannah's Kennedy relatives lived in a couple of filthy rooms that they shared with an army of rats. When she arrived, they crowded round her, exclaiming at her clothes and fingering her possessions with evident avarice. The ragged children, whose faces showed an artfulness that more than equalled their parents', rummaged into her carpet bag and before she fully realized what was happening anything she had of value simply disappeared. It was obvious that links of blood did not prevent the gypsies regarding any newcomer among them as fair pickings. The women earned their money by begging, thieving or prostitution; the men by occasional work in the docks, pimping or robbery.

'You're a real lady, you are,' said one of the younger women in the curiously wheedling tone that so many Kennedys could turn on at will. 'Why don't you get yourself up West and make a copper or two?'

Hannah was so innocent that she felt complimented, smiled and said, 'Perhaps I will. I'll have to earn money somehow. Is there good work to be had up West?'

The hags screeched in laughter. 'Plenty of good money for them that can take it!'

When Hannah realized that the work they had in mind for her was either prostitution or picking pockets, she almost wished that she had stayed at home in her safe Borderland.

Now that she was in London, the object of her dreams for so long, she saw that her travels had taken her from one world to another that she could never have imagined, and the contrast was so marked that for several days she felt lost and disoriented.

She had been used all her life to being wakened in Aylie's cottage by the sound of birds singing in the pear tree beneath her window. In London she woke to the eternal rattle of traffic mingled with the sounds of fighting women and wailing babies inside the cramped room.

The nights at home had been vast velvet black bowls of silence. Now and again an owl would screech or a badger rustle in the grass of the lane but that was all she ever heard. The nights in London however were even noisier than the days. If people were not fighting or making love in the Kennedys' rooms, others were doing these things next door or in the slime-streaked alley outside the broken window beneath which she slept on a bed made by her own cloak and empty carpet bag.

Standing in a London street, Hannah realized fully for the first time the immense and mysterious power that her mother's beloved Eildons had cast on her young life.

They were always there, brooding on the landscape like guardian angels, gathering the people into their skirts and watching over them. Now she had no blessed view to contemplate and wherever she looked there were hostile people, intent on their own business, and squalid houses, leaning higgledy-piggledy against each other, broken walled and broken windowed. The alley beneath her feet was not a daisy-fringed lane but a chaos of broken cobbles running with green slime, and the air did not smell of new-cut hay but revoltingly of sewage.

In spite of her dislike of having to admit to a mistake, she knew she hated the people among whom she now found herself. They had no sense of kinship or loyalty, no finer feelings at all as far as she could see. They smiled at you while they robbed you; they would stab you in your sleep if there was any advantage to it. The children persecuted unwanted kittens and puppies that crawled around scavenging for dropped food and the adults persecuted each other. They were idle, untruthful, scheming and untrustworthy and she quickly learned two things – one was to sleep with a half brick at her hand in case one of the drunken men tried to molest her and the other was never to believe one word any of her relations said.

Their original affability soon wore thin when Hannah refused to turn out at night with her cousins, the street-walkers who hung around Covent Garden enticing drunken clients and more often picking their pockets than giving them the favours that they expected.

'You think you're too grand to make a copper, do you?' asked one toothless crone whose exact relationship to everyone else – and to Hannah – was unclear.

The girl shook her head. 'It's not that, it's just . . . I don't want to be a prostitute.'

The crone mocked her. 'A prostitute, that's a fancy police court word. We don't call them that – we call them slags. But they make enough money to pay for their food and keep. That's more than you do.'

Hannah had learned to keep what money had escaped the itchy fingers of her family by stitching it into her underclothing and now she reached into her bodice and took out a coin, flinging it angrily at the old woman and saying: 'There's my keep for this week! You've all had plenty off me. You've taken nearly everything I had.'

Yet, in spite of her disillusion, she did not want to go home. It was not just pride that kept her in London. It was the energy, the variety, the eternal fascination of the pulsing, thriving, jostling city.

She walked through the East End marvelling at the squalor of the houses and the engraved-glass, polished-brass grandeur of the pubs where people went to lose themselves in a world of make believe. Even in the morning drunken women sat on the walls around gin palaces, breastfeeding their babies and begging from passers-by with one hand outstretched. Somehow, even in the most squalid streets there always seemed to be music playing – perhaps an organ grinder with his sad-faced monkey, a pub piano or a street singer belting out some music-hall favourite. It was impossible for young Hannah Kennedy's blood not to run faster at the feeling of excitement and danger the city gave her.

She walked all day, every day, ending up in the West End and gazing in amazement at the fashionable crowd riding along in their carriages, thronging the pavements and clustering around the well-stocked windows of luxury shops. She felt as if she had wandered into fairy land. Melrose was the biggest town she had ever been in apart from the sad visits with her mother to Edinburgh's madhouse to see her father, and then they never went into the centre of the city because Aylie said she hated it.

Hannah had never seen so many well-dressed people – men in tall hats and beautifully cut suits, swinging silver-topped canes as they strolled along; women in a multitude of colours, silks, laces, feathers, ruchings, ribbons and artificial flowers. They looked like glorious dolls, good enough to eat. The well-to-do people in the Borders had been sober dressers and any woman who turned out in daytime wearing the sort of outfit that went almost unremarked in London would have scandalized the entire neighbourhood.

The huge London emporia, selling everything anyone could possibly want from all over the world, entranced the girl. She walked from street to street gazing at the goods displayed, imagining the lives of people who would eat off the gilded silver and the painted plates or wear the corseted ball gowns and beautifully trimmed straw hats that she saw displayed.

When Aylie and Hannah went shopping in Melrose it was a once-a-year expedition for a new bondager's hat, a pair of sturdy boots or a length of printed cotton.

They rarely went into the town grocery shop because they grew most of their food. In London Hannah wandered round food shops selling huge pink hams, rounds of cheese as big as cart wheels, bottles of preserves and pickles, crystallized fruits in a myriad of colours, tea and coffee from open crates that scented the air outside on the pavement.

It was the largesse of London that she found so astonishing – nothing was done in small measures.

It took a week before she was definitely sure that she wanted to stay in London. The memories of her home faded gradually away till they caused her less anguish. If she was to survive at all, however, she knew that she had to get away from the Kennedys and she had to find some work . . . but what could a girl with no training and no references do? She looked around on her walks and saw that the busiest places in London seemed to be the public houses. They must always be in need of staff. She'd be a barmaid.

She was lucky. Her first job came her way because the owner of a large and busy bar in Cheapside was impressed by her majestic appearance. He put her behind the china-handled beer pumps with the instructions, 'Take no cheek, gal, just look at them with those eyes of yours and you'll have no trouble.'

Clerks from nearby offices came into the hostelry and stared in amazement at the new barmaid, a disdainful Fury with her thick, dark curling hair and striking face, for although Hannah did not have the refined beauty of her mother and Jane, she exuded an energy that drew men to her like flies to honey. She did nothing to encourage this, in fact quite the opposite, because she treated her admirers with a scorn that only made them keener.

One of the other barmaids was a buxom girl called Bella Marshall whose slanting, knowing brown eyes made her look as if she was always three jumps ahead of everybody else. She took a fancy to Hannah and invited her to share her room in an alleyway off Fleet Street. The offer was eagerly accepted because Hannah was glad to get away from the gypsy family. She was tired of having her possessions systematically fingered over and stolen every time she left their overcrowded hovel.

In the 1870s and 1880s London was a refuge for political agitators from all over the world who fled to its anonymity and crowded into its bars and eating houses, talking agitatedly among themselves, holding surreptitious meetings and making abortive schemes for world revolution under the indulgent eyes of authorities who did not take them very seriously. Bella knew a good many of them and listened to their talk with cheeky dimples marking her cheeks and a sceptical look in her eyes.

One morning when Hannah got up to make their morning tea, Bella was standing staring out of their window and stretching like a surfeited cat.

She smiled at Hannah and, gesturing with her thumb over her shoulder, said casually, 'Meet Gunther.'

A blond-haired young man was still reclining, naked

as far as Hannah could see, between the crumpled sheets of Bella's bed.

Hannah was used to her friend's casual pick-ups and she nodded briefly in Gunther's direction while she went on making their tea. That first day she hardly noticed him but he came back so frequently that in time she accepted him as a semi-permanent fixture in their lives.

'Where do you come from, Gunther?' she asked him one day.

'I'm from Potsdam,' was his reply.

'What are you doing here? What do you work at?'

'I'm an artist.' He had a guttural accent but his English was very good.

'An artist, are you? But you never seem to do any work. Have you a studio?'

He grinned, his face lighting up like the face of a naughty small boy. 'You're right, Hannah, I don't do much work. You're very observant.'

She felt that he was making fun of her and she reverted to being stiff and disapproving with him, an attitude that seemed to make him even more eager to tease her. He annoyed her most when he criticized her political beliefs.

'You're so bourgeois, Hannah. You say you want to change the world but you're stuck in the old ways. You believe people should work and earn money, don't you? Have you ever considered alternative ways of living?'

'Of course I have but I also know that everyone has to eat . . .' She resented the charge that she was conventional in her attitudes. It reminded her too strongly of the accusations she used to throw at her mother.

Gunther liked a discussion. 'But that could be arranged if property was redistributed, couldn't it? There are far too few people owning far too much – the rest of us have to scrape along as best as we can. I'd like to see things arranged differently, wouldn't you?'

She nodded vehemently. 'Yes, of course, but I'm beginning to think it's impossible. I've been in London for five months now and I'm still amazed at the lives people lead in the richest city in the world. In one district they're

289

living in luxury but only a mile away, others are dying of starvation.'

'You have such fervour!' teased Gunther. 'You should come to our meetings. On your next night off, I'll take you.'

Her free night was Sunday. He took her to an attic room in Clerkenwell above a tailoring workshop where women were still working though it was after ten o'clock. A group of Gunther's friends, men and a few women, were gathered together, all arguing loudly in a variety of foreign accents and drinking bottles of ale brought in from the public house next door. There were two Russians; a Frenchwoman; three vehement, noisy Scots from Glasgow; an intense-looking Englishman and another woman; Gunther and Hannah. No one took any notice of her at first but when she heard the Englishman, who had a very upper-class accent, expounding the theory that everyone should leave the city and go to live in the country in order to create the perfect Utopian society, she spoke up loudly, though none too tactfully, in protest.

'Oh, you're talking rubbish, you don't know anything about what it's like to be one of the labouring poor. I come from a family of agricultural labourers and I can tell you there's nothing Utopian about it. People like you only see the country in good weather – if it's too cold or too wet, you rush back into your big houses and sit round the fire – a fire that's made up for you by a housemaid. You don't even carry your own coal! Have you any idea of what it's like to work in mud that reaches your thighs, to carry bags of corn on your back that weigh more than you do, to chop up turnips with frozen fingers to feed cows that are better housed than you are? I bet you haven't!'

Her scorn was magnificently withering and the crowd in the room looked at her with awe. Before she left, a bearded man came over and said to her with approval, 'You spoke well, young woman, but have you any suggestion that would be better than his?'

Hannah flushed scarlet. All eyes were on her and she had to justify herself so she thought rapidly and said, 'There must be some way of removing inequalities, there must be a better way than sending everybody back to the land. You can't turn back the pages of history, can you? Manufacturing is necessary. It's just that all the profits should not go into so few pockets.'

The bearded man nodded sympathetically and said in a friendly way, 'My name's Kropotkin, Peter Kropotkin. I'm an exile from Russia because of my political beliefs. You and I seem to think the same way . . . Tell me your name, tell me about yourself.'

Peter Kropotkin was an aristocrat who had become converted to the theories of Anarchistic Communism and his advocacy of it meant that the Tsarist authorities threw him into prison. He had escaped in 1876 and arrived in London, by way of Switzerland. Around him the London Anarchist movement was rapidly growing. Hannah, dazzled by his conviction and charisma, became one of his most enthusiastic followers. Gunther was one already, but much more lukewarm than she rapidly became.

The dashing-looking girl with her intense, slanting cheekboned face made a charismatic representative for Kropotkin's movement because she could talk with authority about the life of the poor − not only because of what she saw in the East End but because of the way she had lived as a child and, most especially, because of her bitter memories of her father's fate. She built Hugh into a sort of folk hero, ignoring the fact that his transportation sentence had been for smuggling, and painting him as a political martyr. Talking about her father, whom she hardly knew and had only really seen when he was a raving lunatic − made her incandescent with rage.

She became the perfect mouthpiece against the wrongs society inflicted on its people. As she talked and lectured, as she persuaded people to follow Kropotkin, she became more and more convinced that anarchy was the answer to society's problems. Only when the people were prepared to take the law into their own hands, to kill and steal if necessary for the cause, would things ever change, she said.

'It's no use waiting for legislation, it always comes too late and in a watered-down form. What is needed is a root and branch attack – a cut at the heart of the world we know.' Her argument, combined with her exotic appearance and burning conviction, brought many followers to her in dazzled admiration.

Hugh Kennedy had not been expected to live more than ten years when he was admitted to Craighouse Asylum but the strong body that had kept him going through the privations of Australia sustained him again and he stayed alive for more than twenty years. He was blind, he was raving, he knew no one, but he kept on living. Each year when his wife made her pilgrimage to the hospital and stared at him through the bars of his cell door where he was kept chained to his bed like an animal, she silently prayed that he would die soon. It would be a merciful release.

In the autumn of 1885 the news of his death finally arrived at Charterhall in an official letter from Edinburgh. She felt no great grief as she read the words, for the man she had married on that winter day in Coldstream had died long ago as far as she was concerned. His death would be a blow for Hannah, however, for she had always cherished an unreal idea of her father. Aylie sat down and wrote her daughter a tender letter. When she finished, she stretched back in her chair and her eye wandered out into the garden where the leaves were drifting down from her apple trees and the last of the flowers were slowly fading.

I'm in my autumn too, she thought, I'm fading just like my flowers and I'm so lonely . . . so terribly lonely.

The world of 'it might have been' was too painful to contemplate so as usual she closed her mind to such thoughts and went bustling about preparing to take Hannah's letter to the post. She was grateful that her health was good and she was still able to turn out to work in the fields at harvest time or hay making. She thought nothing of walking miles to visit friends, among whom the most highly regarded were the Hepburns. Sandy was a middle-aged man now and his son John was almost grown up. There had been much sorrow when Sandy's wife died but eventually he had married again, to a much younger, pleasant girl who had given birth to a daughter and was once again pregnant.

Aylie took a great interest and pride in all of the Hepburns and they regarded her as an honorary aunt, including her in all their family celebrations, weddings or christenings. They filled the yawning void left by her own children – Hannah far away in London and Adam even more distant in Canada. Adam wrote to tell her that he was thriving, the proprietor now of his own wood yard in Nova Scotia, and twice a year a remittance from him was paid into her bank although she always wrote back to protest that she did not need the money . . . 'I've nothing to spend it on, dear Adam. Keep it for yourself. It's time you were getting married and raising a family,' she wrote.

When Aylie's letter reached Hannah, she was plunged into depression but it did not last, she had far too much energy to languish for long. Now the telling of Hugh's story was even more passionate – he had died for the people's cause, she told her listeners.

Along with the principles of Anarchism, she had embraced the theory of free love and took lovers from among Kropotkin's followers whenever she wanted. They were not hard to find because as the years passed she grew even more impressive, and her slim figure and sensual face attracted many men. She had also adopted the medieval style of dress favoured by Pre-Raphaelite women, most successfully by William Morris' wife Jane, and the loosely flowing, brightly coloured clothes suited Hannah. They made her look like a character from a fairy tale – a wicked witch, said some catty women.

Among her casual lovers were a young Scot called John

293

Mackay and a Prussian ex-army officer called Von Egidy, but they came and went. The man to whom she was most faithful, perhaps because it had to be kept a secret, was the blond and indolent Gunther. Ostensibly he was Bella's man but when she was absent, he slipped into bed with Hannah. It was difficult for her to rationalize Gunther's attractions, for he was lazy and unreliable and his political convictions were never as strongly held as hers but, when he chose, he was charming, attentive and amusing.

One day Gunther said, as casually as if he were announcing his intention to stroll down the street to take the air, 'I'm going back to Germany, Hannah. I'm leaving tomorrow.'

'Are you going for a visit?' she asked, but he shook his head.

'No, darling, I think I'll stay. I'm tired of politics. My father's died and I've come into my estate.'

'What estate? You never said anything about an estate.' It struck her as ironic and typical of Gunther that the Anarchist follower should be the heir to an estate.

He waved an airy hand. 'Oh, we've a palace near Potsdam. I'll go back there and paint. My mother says I ought to get married and I suppose she's right. There's someone she's got lined up for me.'

Hannah felt the cold hand of jealousy grip her heart. She had never expected to feel that way about Gunther.

'Take me with you,' she pleaded and he was genuinely surprised at the request.

'You, dear Hannah? But you'd hate Germany – it's so property conscious. No, you'll be far better here with your friends, trying to change the world.'

She knew he was teasing her again and hated his flippancy. She regretted allowing her guard to slip and feeling even the smallest affection for him.

'You're no revolutionary, I never thought you were. You're like all the rest, as soon as you get your hands on money, you're off to take care of it. I'm glad to have seen through you at last. Get out, get out and never come back,' she shouted.

He had been gone for a month when she began to suspect that all was not well with her . . . By the time another month passed, she knew for certain that she was having his child.

Lark, 1891

One look was enough for Aylie to realize what had brought her daughter home.

She hugged Hannah tight in her arms and then led her inside the cosy little cottage, crooning over her as if she were a child again. When her cloak was off and she was seated in the chair beside the fire, Aylie simply asked, 'When's it due, Hannah?'

The girl lifted her head and said wearily, 'In about two months, I think . . . I'm not quite sure of when I conceived.'

Aylie thought for a moment and then said, 'That'll be the middle of April then. It's a good time to have a baby, in the spring when the blossom's on the apple trees.'

'Oh Mother, you never change do you? You always think of dates in terms of what's growing,' said Hannah with a fond laugh.

They were friends now, their old differences forgotten as they sat side by side in front of the glowing hearth at night, talking about the past or Hannah's vision of the future. What she said appalled her mother – 'But you can't think it's right to kill people if they represent things you disapprove of,' she protested.

'Why not?' Hannah's face had a hard look as the flames flickered on it. 'Political assassination is a potent weapon, it's been used with effect in the past and will be used again in the future. Nothing else works, does it?'

She told her mother that during her time in London she had been briefly involved in the movement for women's suffrage but she was disillusioned with the Suffragettes. 'They're far too soft and middle-class in their way of getting things done. They'll never achieve anything.

They're just waiting for something to happen. If they get the vote in the end it'll be because it suits the men – not because women have forced it through. Besides, I'm not so sure that it matters whether women have the vote anyway. If you vote you're subscribing to a system that's corrupt, you're maintaining it. I wouldn't vote, even if I could.'

Aylie stared longingly into the fire and said with a sigh, 'I'd love a vote. I'd love to be able to express my opinion like a man. I don't think it's right for women to be treated like children or lunatics.'

'Of course not, but we could construct a world in which we all had an equal share, men and women. Voting won't bring it to us,' said Hannah vehemently.

Aylie was frightened by the passion in her daughter. 'Don't go around here talking like that,' she warned. 'If they hear you, you know what they'll say . . .'

'They? Who's they?' asked Hannah scornfully. 'You mean the authorities, the upper classes, the masters, don't you? And what would they say, Mother? They'd say that Hugh Kennedy's daughter is going the same way as her father. First a rebel and then a lunatic. That's what they'd say, isn't it?'

Aylie put an arm round her daughter and hugged her tight. 'Oh, don't be so angry, Hannah. What are you so angry about?'

Aylie was never to know who fathered her granddaughter, for she never asked Hannah any questions. It did not matter, for when the baby girl arrived she was beautiful, very blonde, ivory-skinned and perfect. Aylie had never seen such a lovely child and she held the tiny body in her arms with love and adoration showing in her face while the howdie finished settling Hannah. It had been a straightforward birth and Hannah, true to character, was stoical throughout. Now she lay back against the pillows and, with a smile, watched her mother cuddle her daughter.

'She looks like you, Mother. It's a good present I brought back to you from London, isn't it?'

Aylie looked up from her scrutiny of the tiny face with tears shining in her eyes. 'Oh Hannah, will you please call her Lark? I wanted to call you Lark but your father wouldn't let me.'

Hannah frowned. 'He was right, Lark wouldn't have suited me one bit – but, to please you, I'll call her Lark. It's a pretty name really.'

Morning and evening, rain or shine, Aylie walked around her garden, checking on her plants and staring out at the countryside that spread around her home. From the upstairs window Hannah watched her mother gazing about as if she were seeing the world for the first time, and every day the routine was the same.

When Aylie came in, she might say, 'It'll be sunny by dinner time' or 'It's going to rain all day . . .' and sometimes she would rush in, gasping, 'Come and look at this sunset. I've never seen such a wonderful sky!'

'You're so pagan, Mother, I've never known anyone so rooted in the soil as you,' said Hannah shortly one day. Her mother's unchangeable programme was beginning to annoy her.

'I suppose it's because I come from a long line of people who've always lived close to nature,' said Aylie.

'But what about your aristocratic French father – he couldn't have been so bucolic?'

'The rest of my ancestors overcame his influence, I expect,' Aylie replied. 'Anyway I don't feel half French, I feel – sometimes I feel as if I was like that tree growing out there, I'm so rooted in this earth.'

'I'm not,' said Hannah fiercely, 'I can't stay too long in any one place. I need excitement . . .'

'That's the gypsy in you, I expect,' said her mother. 'Your father's people were always on the move – they spent the whole summer wandering about. They settled down in Yetholm in the winter time, but when spring came their feet itched.'

'I know the feeling,' was the wistful reply. 'When I

298

look out at your precious hills all I want to know is what's happening on the other side of them.'

Aylie's face looked sad as she leant down and lifted the baby out of its nest of blankets in the cradle. As she held it in her arms it opened its brilliant blue eyes and stared silently back at her. Hannah, watching them, turned her head away as if to shut out the sight. That night, when they had eaten supper, she suddenly laid the baby in her mother's lap.

'Here, Mother, you take her. You really love her, I can see that, and I don't feel I can stay here any longer. Will you keep her for me?'

Aylie cuddled the baby, smelling the sweet milkiness of it.

'But I'm nearly seventy-seven years old,' she protested. 'It wouldn't be right for an old woman to bring up a little child, she'd be old before her time.'

Hannah snorted. 'Nonsense, you're the youngest seventy-seven-year-old I've ever known. You're well in yourself, aren't you? You're not sick? You can still walk ten miles a day and never feel tired.'

'Oh I'm well enough, it's her I'm worried about. What if something happens to me?' Aylie wanted the baby but she saw the dangers more clearly than her daughter did.

Hannah swept her objections aside. 'I'll keep in touch all the time, I promise. If you get sick or too tired, I'll take her back, I promise you, Mother. She'll be better off with you. My life in London isn't a good life for a child.'

Aylie had realized that long ago, and it had worried her, so she nodded.

Seeing her weaken, Hannah pressed on, 'I haven't much money but I'll send what I can.'

Her mother shook her head, she had made up her mind . . . 'Don't worry about money. Adam sends me money regularly. I'll use it for Lark, he'd like that.'

Once the agreement was made between them, Hannah could not wait to leave the country. Within a week she was back in London, back to her old haunts, among her revolutionary friends. Kropotkin encouraged her to write pamphlets setting out the Anarchist beliefs and she proved so effective at this that her name soon became known in revolutionary circles throughout Europe.

Having Lark to love transformed Aylie's life. No longer was she lonely, no longer did she feel like a useless old woman. People who saw them together wondered at her energy and, because her hair was still only lightly streaked with grey, a few short-sighted individuals thought that she was Lark's mother, who had produced a baby late in life.

Lark was an easy child to rear, perhaps because she was instinctively aware of her grandmother's limitations. She was never unruly, never tried to run away from home like Hannah used to do. She caused Aylie no anxiety at all. Having her in the house was like having a friend, a confidante, a companion.

They talked together in adult terms from the time the child was very young and Aylie loved to tell her stories of the past. She talked more freely to Lark than she had ever done to her own children.

The life the little girl led was exactly like the childhood of Aylie herself, a gentle childhood among the fields and woods, a childhood closely linked to the rounds of the seasons and the weather.

Their favourite excursions, always by foot, were to the Hepburns' farmhouse, to some local fairs and, most of all, to the ruined abbey at Charterhall where they inspected the family grave and stood in awe in the cave where Jane had lived for so many years.

'It must have been very cold here, Grandmama,' said six-year-old Lark with a shiver one winter afternoon.

'Oh, not when my mother was here. She had a fire in that corner and everything was so snug and cosy. She was so happy here. I think if she'd ever had to leave this place she'd have died of a broken heart.'

The child gazed at the ruins with round eyes. 'It's lovely, and it's so old. But it's awfully sad somehow. It makes me want to cry, Grandmama.'

The Hepburns were growing richer with every year that passed. In spite of the severe downturn that hit agriculture in the 1880s the family thrived through hard work and enterprise, so when other farmers were being driven out of business it was often to Sandy Hepburn that their land was sold. Yet in spite of success, the family stayed simple in their tastes and as considerate towards their workers as old Jock had been. To the farm labourers round about, a place on a Hepburn farm was the most highly desired of all. Hepburn workers were not crowded with their families into ramshackle sheds and bothies, for even before Jock's death, building had started on lines of neat stone cottages for the workforce.

Aylie was as full of pride at Sandy's achievements as if he had been her own son. When she took Lark to visit the Hepburns, the child sat stiffly on the edge of a high-backed chair that prickled her legs through her dress and gazed in awe at the massive furniture. She liked it best when Mrs Hepburn played the piano and sometimes Lark would be asked to sing for it had already become obvious that she had inherited Jane's beautiful singing voice.

With tears of pride and happiness in her eyes Aylie sat and listened to the young treble voice singing the old ballad songs. 'You sound exactly like my mother,' she told the child.

Kirsty, Sandy's daughter by his second marriage, was some six years older than Lark, and she had a brother, two years her junior, called Simeon, but always referred to by his family as Sim. He was a lanky lad with his grandfather's bush of reddish hair and from his eminence he stared down at little Lark who, as soon as she could walk, began following him around like an adoring puppy. She watched everything he did, listened while he talked to the men in the farmyard and trailed after him when he took his gun into the woods in search of pheasants. Her devotion sometimes irked him but he was nearly always tolerant and only when she got in his way or was in danger of being peppered with shot did he shout at her to go home.

*
301

Hannah kept her promise and did not abandon her child entirely. From her travels around the Continent during the ten years after Lark's birth, she sent regular letters and postcards. One from Madrid announced in breathless style her survival from the riots that had broken out during an Anarchist assembly there.

These missives were received with wonder by the old woman and the child at Charterhall village, and Lark carried the Madrid card to school to show to her teacher and the other children. It gave her a feeling of great importance to have a mother who had seen such wonderful things as riots.

On the two occasions when that wonderful mother actually came to visit, however, she proved to be a disappointment. The first time was when Lark was three years old, and later she could remember little about it except that her mother brought her a white lawn dress with ribbons at the neck and deep broderie anglaise ruffles round its hem. She wore the dress for ages after it no longer fitted her, even until it was in danger of splitting down the back every time she moved her arms. Then she used it to dress her doll.

The second time Hannah came, Lark was seven and growing into a leggy tomboy whose only ambition in life was to have a pony. On that visit Hannah arrived in a great state of agitation, bursting into the cottage crying, 'I've come to say goodbye. I'm going to a meeting in Vienna and they might assassinate me there!'

With a warning look towards the child, Aylie rose from her chair and said, 'Oh, Hannah, don't be so dramatic. Of course nobody will assassinate you.'

'They've assassinated others. I've been warned,' said Hannah with utmost satisfaction at this proof of her standing in the movement. 'But I'm not afraid. I just wanted to say goodbye to you both before I went.'

'It's a long way to come just for that,' said Aylie in a dampening way, and bustled about preparing an extra place at the table.

Lark and Hannah had little to say to each other and

302

she was acutely embarrassed by her mother's bizarre dress, which was so very different to anything worn by the other women in the district. Hannah still favoured loose-flowing medieval robes in brilliant jewel-like colours, which suited her well but made her stand out in the crowd of more conventionally dressed people.

When the children at Lark's school teased her about her funnily dressed mother, she ran home in tears but would not tell Aylie what she was crying about. However, her grandmother had a good idea of the reason.

Hannah stayed for two days, sleeping most of the time, and when she departed she left a greatly relieved daughter behind her.

In the summer of 1901, Aylie was eighty-six. It was a hot June and the sultry weather slowed her down, making her move slowly. She was showing her age at last and Lark hated having to leave her grandmother on the fine sunny mornings to sit in a stuffy schoolroom chanting tables and reading laboriously from the tattered primers. It would soon be holiday time, she thought, as she fidgeted in her seat on the bench beneath the high window. Then she would be free to run wild from morning till night and Sim would be home too. If he let her, she'd wander around with him. His pony was out at grass so there would be no riding, but they could go fishing, or exploring the ruins of the abbey perhaps . . . Her mind wandered off at pleasant tangents and she did not hear the schoolmistress, who had replaced Hannah's old dominie, sharply calling her name. . . .

'Yes, Miss.' She sprang sharply to attention when her neighbour dug an elbow in her ribs. The teacher had someone else beside her – it was Mrs Gillespie, their next-door neighbour from the village.

'Come up here a moment, Lark dear, will you?' the teacher's voice was unusually kind.

She stood up, carefully adjusting her white bibbed apron, and walked through the lines of the little ones' chairs to the front where the two women stood whispering.

Mrs Gillespie's eyes were red-rimmed as if she had been crying, and she tried to put her arms round Lark when the girl stepped on to the dais on which the teacher's desk stood.

'Take her outside, don't tell her here,' said the teacher.

Mrs Gillespie led a scared Lark into the passage outside the schoolroom door where she stopped and whispered, 'Oh, Lark, it's your granny, she's – she's not very well.'

Lark felt her chest close on her heart and it was difficult to breathe properly.

'What's wrong with Granny? Can I go home to see her?'

Mrs Gillespie gave a sob. 'Oh Lark, she's dead, your granny's dead. I saw her lying in the garden beside her raspberry canes and when I went over to her she was dead . . . She couldn't have felt anything, bairn.'

'Granny dead!' Lark could not believe it. Her mind simply could not take it in and it was a long time before she wondered what would happen to her now that her grandmother had gone.

Hannah was still in Vienna. Sandy Hepburn wrote to her via London and also to Adam in Canada to tell them about their mother's death. Adam wrote back quickly and offered to take Lark to stay with his family, for he had married a Canadian girl and they had a young son.

The Hepburns held a family conference to discuss what should be done.

'She'd be better off with Adam in Canada, I'm sure of that,' said Sandy's eldest son John, who had not been impressed by what he'd seen of Hannah.

'But we can't send her there till we hear from her mother. We'll have to wait a little while longer,' protested his stepmother.

In the meantime Lark stayed with them, but every day she walked back to the cottage and wandered through its rooms, examining everything minutely, dusting her grandmother's ornaments and plucking the weeds in her beloved garden. Aylie's savings, the cottage and everything in it had been left to Lark and when she was told this, she said to Sandy, 'I want to keep it just like it is now.'

To her friend Sim, who was very gentle towards her that summer, she said, 'If I've got to go away I want you to look after the cottage for me, Sim. Promise you will. One day I'll come back and live here.'

They linked little fingers as they had done since they were very small and he gave her his solemn promise to look after Aylie's home.

A month after her mother had been buried in the Cannon grave in the abbey grounds, Hannah arrived in a smart gig driven by the livery man from Melrose. She looked exotic and Continental as she swept into the Hepburn farmhouse, perfunctorily kissing the women and charming the men.

'I came as soon as I got your letter,' she told Sandy. 'I was broken-hearted to hear about my mother. You say it was very sudden – I hope she wasn't ill for long.'

'She was never ill at all. If she did feel unwell she never mentioned it. She just dropped dead,' said Sandy.

Hannah wiped her eyes with a handkerchief trimmed with lace and said, 'That's the way she would have wanted it. But what about poor little Lark, she must have taken it hard?'

Mrs Hepburn, a tender-hearted woman, nodded. 'Poor little thing, she did take it very, very hard. And she's been so quiet since it happened, not her usual self at all, that we're all quite worried about her. Your brother Adam wrote and said he wanted her to go to Canada but we thought you should make the decision yourself.'

'But of course she must come with me,' said Hannah. 'I couldn't bear to send her away to Canada. I'd never see her again. No, I'll take her with me, she's big enough to cope with London now.'

Her misery was totally engulfing. It made her grow thin

and dimmed her golden hair. When her skin took on a glossy waxen pallor even Hannah began to notice that her daughter was ill and heart-breakingly unhappy.

'What does she do with herself all day?' she asked her friend Bella, who was married now to Bill, the landlord of a busy tavern called the Queen's Head in a Spitalfields alley. Hannah and the child had been lodging with Bella, whose dimpled, motherly arms often engulfed the white faced Lark in a sympathetic hug.

'She helps me in the kitchen sometimes but then she just wanders off. I've seen her beneath the tree in that little churchyard up the lane. She sits there staring into space . . .' Bella said in a doleful voice, for she was sorry for the child. Lark was so obviously out of place in the city that she made Bella, a country-born girl herself, remember what it was like to yearn for green fields when you are shut up in London slums.

Hannah had no such memories and she shrugged. 'She misses her grandmother. That's what's wrong, she's just getting used to the idea that she's dead. They were too close. I suppose I shouldn't have left her there so long. She'll get over it though.'

Bella nodded. 'You must be a bit of a stranger to the kid right enough. She doesn't know you, really. It's very lonely for her here.'

Hannah was busy, gathering up her coat and a bundle of papers in preparation for yet another meeting with her revolutionary friends. In a cheerful voice she repeated, 'Yes, she'll get used to it, just keep an eye on her for me, Bella, will you?'

With a sardonic expression Bella watched her tall, dark friend sweep out into the road. Hannah was and always had been the toughest woman she'd ever met. There was no sentiment about her at all. Even when she'd had the child, she'd never mentioned who the father was – though as soon as she saw ten-year-old Lark, Bella knew at once that her father had been Gunther. There was his smooth blond hair, his aquamarine eyes. Crafty old Gunther, he'd had them both! She laughed without rancour at the idea and then, still dimpling at the memory, bustled into the bar where her husband was pulling pints for a group of draymen.

A big, upright man with a waxed moustache, Bill had taken over the bar after serving in the army and he still had his stiff military bearing. He was fifteen years older than Bella and as indulgent towards her as a love-stricken youth. She could do anything with old Bill.

When he saw her smiling he smiled proudly back at her and asked, 'What's the joke, Bella? You're grinning away like a cat that's caught a canary.'

She patted him fondly on the bottom and said, 'Just old memories, Billy. Have you seen the kid anywhere?'

One of the draymen answered. 'Hannah's kid? I saw her sitting under the tree in the churchyard, that poor kid looks as if she's fading away.'

'We'll have to do something to cheer her up,' decided Bella, 'I'll have to get to work on her.'

Lark had grown in the past few months, shot up like a sickly sapling, and her energy seemed to have left her entirely. When the rain started she came out of her hiding place among the old gravestones and walked slowly down the lane, stepping carefully so as to avoid the puddles of dirty water that filled the gaps in the cobble-stones. From the corner of her eye she could see that she was being watched by a group of tousle-haired women and ragged children who clustered in the door of one of the houses. The fall of rain was heavy so her cotton dress clung to her back and the weight of her soaked hair bowed her head. Her attitude as she walked along summed up the overpowering misery that filled her heart.

For the first ten years of her life she had never travelled more than five or six miles from her home. She knew everyone in the district where she had grown up and everyone knew her. There was a wonderful security in that unquestioned identity . . . she was Aylie Kennedy's granddaughter and everyone knew and respected her grandmother.

Until she came to London she had no idea of what it felt like to be among strangers, and hostile strangers at that. When she said 'Good morning' as she had been taught to do, to the women or children in Bella's lane, they stared blankly at her and then laughed for they could not understand what she said, her Scottish accent was so alien to them. They called her Scotty, and little boys ran jeering after her when she ventured into the street. She was terrified of them but her terror made her stiff and disapproving, so they thought that she felt herself to be superior to them, and their dislike increased.

'Oh here she comes, the little lady!' The woman who called out as she passed had a high-pitched whining voice that rendered the word 'lady' as 'lydy'. Lark lifted her head and stared at the woman, wondering for a few seconds what the strange word meant. As she looked at the woman, with her hair loose and tumbling from its pins, her clothes filthy and ragged and equally filthy children clinging to her skirt, she saw naked hatred in her eyes.

Why does she dislike me so much? she wondered with a chill in her heart. She did not realize that her persecutor was drunk. Earlier that day Bella's husband had thrown her out of the Queen's Head bar for fighting and swearing.

'There goes our fine litle lady, back to old Bella's. Where's your ma, then? Off walking the streets in Piccadilly is she?' The harridan came close up to Lark and screamed in her face.

Another of the women laughed, for they all disliked Hannah with her airs and graces. Tied in by their own poverty, their children and their hopelessness, they resented the way she came and went, sometimes affluent and sometimes penniless. It was a constant subject of debate among them what she did to earn her money. Hannah for her part never noticed their animosity because as far as she was concerned they were a different species to herself. She did not associate her political theories with people like that and if she was battling for the betterment of mankind, it was not for that sort of mankind.

The woman who had called after Lark addressed her again. 'What's your name, dearie?'

The girl stopped, surprised at this question which she took to be a gesture of friendship. She thought she had misjudged the woman after all, so she smiled politely and said, 'It's Lark.'

The woman and the children hooted, they screeched and threw themselves around in glee. 'She's called Lark! That's some name. Who gave you that name, your fancy mother? Lark, what a name! You might as well be called turkey or peahen . . . what a name!'

A sea of jeering little children surged round Lark's legs, jumping about like frenzied imps urged on by their mothers. In the middle of them the girl stood bedraggled and stricken, terrified by the dislike she felt flowing towards her. Tears rose in her eyes and she was staring around like a cornered animal, looking for some way of escape, when Bella, alerted by the din, came bursting out of the stained-glass door of the snug bar.

She was red faced with rage as she rushed up and threw a chubby arm round Lark's shoulders, saying soothingly, 'Come on, gal, you're safe with me. Don't let them rile you.' And then, turning to the jeering women, she yelled in an ear-splitting voice, 'You cows, don't you know better than to turn on a kid? You drunken bitches, none of you'd better show your dirty faces in my pub again or I'll get my old man to kick your arses out the door!'

Bella was childless but it had never bothered her much. Bill did not yearn for a family, in fact she suspected that somewhere in his past he had left a wife and children behind him and did not want to repeat the experience. As a couple they were comfortable and cosy together. Babies would only have disrupted their routine. She cuddled up to him in bed at night, and during the day helped him out in the bar, her deep gurgling, sensual laugh enchanting both him and the customers.

She felt safe to flirt when Bill was there to protect her

and he liked to see the other men staring at her with frank admiration, comparing her with the raddled, gin-soaked women who crowded into the pub to drink themselves to oblivion. The Queen's Head was in an insalubrious part of the city, the haunt of pimps and prostitutes, pickpockets and burglars. The people who made up its clientele lived by their wits, teetering always on the brink of disaster, but they were sustained by an optimism and ebullience that Bella and Bill enjoyed and admired. Any snooping policemen who came around asking awkward questions about their regulars were sent away unsatisfied. 'We're not coppers' narks,' Bill and Bella agreed together. What they knew about the lives and affairs of their customers, they kept to themselves.

They also kept tight lips about what they knew of Hannah and her friends. When she swept off to Madrid or Vienna, they asked no questions and told no tales. When she sat in their parlour talking about her foreign friends, the Germans, the Russians or the Frenchwoman who looked like a wrinkled nut and who'd spent years in prison as a dangerous revolutionary before fleeing to London, they took it all with large pinches of salt. Bella's common sense helped her to see the flaws in Hannah's fiercely expounded theories and a little light of amusement sometimes danced in her brown eyes as she listened to her friend . . .

'What is it that you and your friends want really?' Bella asked Hannah one night after they had been disputing Anarchist beliefs over a few bottles of beer. 'You don't want rid of the old Queen?'

Hannah laughed in scorn. 'The Queen! That old widow of Windsor! She's nothing but a symbol of oppression. Of course we want rid of her. She's just lucky. There's been seven attempts to kill her already but she's always got away! We've killed rulers in other countries, you know. All rulers are oppressors.'

Hannah sank her voice to a conspiratorial tone, implying she knew more about political assassination than she cared to admit. Bella dimpled. It amused her to listen to Hannah on this tack.

'But if there were no rulers, no policemen or anything like that, how'd you keep people in order?' she asked.

Hannah's face took on its visionary expression. 'People don't need keeping in order. They should be allowed to do as they like. Then you'd see that people are basically good. Our aim is to overthrow all governments and allow people to get back to a state of innocence.'

Bella made a rude scoffing noise with her ripe red lips. 'That I'd like to see. If there wasn't any law this lot around here would be cutting each other's throat for sixpence, I can tell you that. You'd not get up the street in your fine cloak without somebody having it off you.'

'You're like all the rest,' mourned Hannah. 'All you worry about is property. Don't you realize that all property is theft?'

Bella and Bill were proud of their pub and particularly of the new piano they'd bought for their parlour. They did not want to hear that their piano was theft.

Bill was proud to go out with Bella in her big feathered hats and boa and she was proud of him, especially when he wore his fine gold watch with the chain made up of what looked like gold nuggets. To be told that their pride in their cherished property was wrong made Bella bridle.

'You do talk a lot of rubbish, you really do. If it wasn't for your friends looking after you, you'd have died of starvation years ago. I don't see you turning down money when some of your pals hand it out.'

Hannah knew Bella too well to take offence. 'It's only right that we help each other,' she explained. 'We're all fighting for the same end and so we depend on each other.'

Bella stood up and shook a cloth over the round mahogany table. Bill would be needing his late-night supper soon. 'It seems to me that some of us do more depending than others,' she said sourly. Sometimes she found it difficult to be tolerant about Hannah's idiotic ideas and all the more so recently when she saw how

311

indifferent her friend was to the child who was at that very moment sleeping on a tear-soaked pillow upstairs.

They were sitting in a dark little room near Eastcheap, some sort of committee room where Hannah and her friends met occasionally. Hannah had taken Lark along, but the presence of her daughter was soon forgotten as she plunged into political argument and discussion. She seemed to be asking for money for some planned expedition, but the child was not very clear where her mother intended to go or whether she was to be taken along as well. As she looked at her mother, for a fleeting second a glimmer of scorn showed in her eyes. Hannah had been a rare visitor in Lark's young life and all her ideas and attitudes had been formed by Aylie. Her real mother's infrequent appearances had been occasions for indulgence and excitement, too short for the child to really study the stranger or to question what she said or did. Now, in London, when she was more exposed to Hannah, she listened to conversations which she barely understood but she could tell from the cadences of her mother's voice, by the way she gestured with her head and arms and by the way she looked at the person she spoke to that she was nearly always acting a part. Her mother was not the heroine from a distant country that Lark had once imagined, she was a fake and a poseur.

'But you must go to Scotland and see the bondagers at work,' Hannah was saying to a gangly young woman with earnest eyes and red chilblained hands. 'I'll tell you where to go. The lives they lead are *incredible* – they work like animals and they live in *squalor*.'

Lark cast down her eyes so that neither of the women could see her scorn. She remembered with great clarity the bondagers she saw every day working in the fields round her cottage home. Those proud women with their brightly polished boots and immaculate aprons would be horrified to hear Hannah's description of them. And their immaculately clean houses, though poor and crowded, put the houses of this neighbourhood to shame.

312

'I've never heard of bondagers before . . . would they let me draw them?' asked the woman who was listening to Hannah with deep interest.

'Of course. I can vouch for that. My mother was a political activist, you know – so was my father. That's why he was sent to Australia. I'd be glad to help you put the case of those women in front of anyone who would take an interest. Sylvia, you *must* do it. They can't help themselves. They need someone like you to help them.'

It all sounded very good, thought Lark, but when you knew the facts the attitudes of people like Hannah and her friend Sylvia were patronizing in the extreme. The bondagers who were her grandmother's friends did not need that sort of treatment from them or anyone else. She was suddenly angry on their behalf and wanted to shout at her mother, 'What do you know about it? You only worked on the land for a couple of weeks. Aylie told me about that. You've no idea of what it's like to be a bondager.'

It was dark by the time the meeting broke up and Hannah seemed pleased with the outcome. Taking Lark's hand, she said to Sylvia, 'I'll have to take her back to Bella's. Look, she's exhausted. Come on, darling, don't dawdle.'

When they were out on the street she said to the girl, 'Do you have to look so glum all the time? Weren't you interested? That was Sylvia Pankhurst I was talking to. She's very famous, a Suffragette like her mother. I don't approve of them really, but they can be useful, you know.'

Heavy-eyed and yawning, Lark glanced up at her fierce-looking mother. 'What's she going to do in Scotland?'

Hannah explained, 'She's planning to do a book of drawings showing the lives of working women. It makes me laugh really. None of them know what work is! I told her about the bondagers, though. They'll make good subjects for her book, so picturesque.'

So picturesque! thought Lark, and tears pricked her

313

eyes. She would far rather be working in the fields than trailing through the gaslit streets of noisy East London with her mother. They dodged a line of racing hansom cabs at the foot of Fleet Street in order to cross the road and Hannah stared longingly into the window of a brightly lit public house.

'Come on, hurry up,' she said sharply. 'I'll have to get you back to Bella's.'

Bella's face was stiff with disapproval as she listened to Hannah.

'But you can't send her off to Canada on her own just like that. She's only a child. If she was going to her uncle, she should have gone when he said he'd take her. He might have changed his mind by now.'

Hannah threw out her hands. 'But what can I do? I've got my work. Louise wants me to go to Seville for the political congress. It's a great opportunity for me, I'll meet all the most important people in the movement. She's going to give me the money but she won't pay for me to take a child with me. . . .'

Bella scoffed. 'Louise! That wrinkled old witch. If you don't watch out you'll end up the same as she did – in jail. I don't know how you can bear hanging around her and her smelly female friend. They're not natural, those women, they make me sick.'

Hannah drew up her shoulders and said, 'Don't be so narrow-minded, Bella, you don't understand. Those women are revolutionaries in every way, sexually as well as politically. They've suffered for the cause. Louise was in a penal colony for years but she never lost her convictions; she's one of the most influential woman in the European movement. I'm very lucky to be taken up by her.'

'She fancies you and she knows she's got a parrot in you, that's why,' said Bella rudely, pushing past Hannah on her way into the bar. 'But I'm not bothered about Louise Jumeau. It's that kid that bothers me. You should never have brought her down here if you weren't

314

prepared to look after her properly. She'll end up on the streets because she's a pretty little thing. Some white slaver'll get her, that's what's going to happen to little Larkie.'

Hannah looked cunning. 'It might, that's true. So what can I do, Bella? Will I send her back to Scotland?'

'What would she do there? Who'd take her in?'

'The Hepburns would take her, I'm sure they would. They're my mother's friends and they're well-off farmers . . .'

'I thought you didn't approve of people like that.' Bella had heard Hannah's political opinions expounded often enough.

'I don't, but they're my mother's friends, you know. They'd take her because of that.'

'You've no conscience, Hannah. You never had much, but the older you get the worse you get. I know what you're driving at. I'm not stupid. Bill and I'll take the kid. We haven't any of our own and we're making a bit of money now. But we'll only take her if you promise to leave her alone and not to start filling her head with rubbish every time you land up back here on your uppers and wanting a free meal.'

Bella had never spoken so frankly to Hannah before and the taller woman was visibly taken back. For a moment it seemed as if she would reply in anger but then she remembered what she wanted from her friend so she looked meek and said, 'I promise. I don't think she's politically aware anyway. She's really rather dull, I'm afraid.'

Indulged and loved by Bill and Bella, Lark grew plump and some of her old gaiety returned to her. Her golden hair shone brightly again and Bella bought clusters of pretty ribbons to wind into the thick tresses with careful, loving hands. Encouraged by her, Lark learned to cook and to help serve behind the busy bar, though if there was ever any trouble, any fighting or swearing, Bill hustled her off into their private parlour till the row died down. Like fierce guard dogs, they protected her from the cruelties and crudities of the life that surged and eddied in the streets outside the public-house door.

Neither of them were worried that her education had virtually ceased when she left the Borders. She could read and she could write, which made her almost a scholar in their eyes because, though both of them could sign their names, their reading skills were rudimentary. One of Bill's great pleasures was to listen to Lark reading out excerpts from his favourite newspapers. He was particularly fond of accounts of race meetings and prize fights, so in time the girl became a specialist on those subjects, and amassed a knowledge which she was encouraged to trot out for the benefit of bar customers and caused them a good deal of entertainment.

'What won the Derby the year before last? Who rode it? What was the distance it won by?' They fired questions at her and she could always answer them. As far as proud Bill was concerned, she was a prodigy of learning.

In spite of the care they took of her, however, it was impossible to shield her completely from the realities of life in their corner of the metropolis. She soon learned which women in the bar were prostitutes; which were pickpockets or shoplifters. She knew which of the men were burglars and which were footpads or lived off women.

Many of the young women who crowded into Bill's establishment at night were little older than Lark herself and as she stood behind the mahogany bar in her stiffly starched white apron, looking at their rouged cheeks and tatty finery, she felt amazement not unmixed with envy.

They were so self-possessed, so sure of themselves, and made her feel so young and incapable of looking after herself without Bill and Bella behind her. She tried to imagine what their lives were like and her imagination failed her.

One day Bella took her 'up West' to see the shops and buy her first grown-up dress. This was the sort of expedition that Bella loved, and they wandered slowly along Piccadilly looking in every shop window. To hurry was to spoil the outing. When they reached the entrance to Burlington Arcade, Lark suddenly spied one of the Queen's Head regulars, a pretty young girl called Sadie.

But it was a Sadie she had never seen before, for the girl was all dressed up like a demure lady of fashion in a fine silken crinoline and wearing a straw bonnet with a delicate lace scarf over her shoulders. She looked lovely and very genteel.

Lark grabbed Bella's arm. 'Look, over there, it's Sadie. Isn't she fine? Let's go and speak to her.'

She raised her hand to wave at Sadie but Bella gripped her arm like a vice and whispered urgently, 'Don't look at her, don't say a word. She's working.'

'Working?' Lark looked at Bella in amazement. 'What at?'

'Just watch,' replied Bella with a note of amusement in her voice. 'Stand back here and we'll watch our little Sadie.'

They stood together in front of a large shop window and watched Sadie's reflection in the glass as she sidled up to another fashionably dressed woman and adroitly slipped a hand into the woman's casually carried reticule. It was so deftly done that everything was over in a second and the woman felt nothing.

'Clever little Sadie, she's got her beer money for tonight and a bit over, I'll be bound,' said Bella with an open giggle this time. 'Come on, let's go. She wouldn't want anyone attracting attention to her right now, would she?'

'I saw you in Piccadilly today,' Lark said when Sadie came into Bill's bar.

The Cockney girl, not smartly dressed now but in a plain grey dress and threadbare shawl, looked up at the speaker and grinned cheekily. She had a triangular-shaped face and twinkling hazel eyes that made her look like an imp. 'What did you think of me in my working clothes?' she asked.

'I hardly recognized you. What a pretty dress you had on.'

Sadie giggled. 'I hired it, ducks. It was pretty, wasn't it?'

She moved a little way along the wooden bench and patted the seat beside her in an invitation for Lark to sit down. It was the first gesture of friendship she had received from any of the women who came into the bar.

'Bella and I wondered if you did well,' Lark said.

Sadie swirled the colourless liquid around in her glass. 'Well enough to buy gin. Would you like one?' she asked.

Lark shook her head. She had never tasted anything stronger than Aylie's home-made elderberry wine. 'No thanks,' she said, and then sat silent, not knowing what to say next, overawed by Sadie whose sophistication and way of making a living struck her as very daring.

Sadie took a sip at her gin. 'You're a funny kid, how old are you?'

'I'm nearly fifteen. How old are you?' Lark replied.

Sadie laughed. 'About the same age. I'll be sixteen, I think, in the summer.'

'You think? Why don't you know?'

'Because I don't know when I was born or who my mother was. I was found in a box in the back of an alley up there. An old dame took me in – I was lucky, I guess.'

Lark gazed at the girl with sympathy. She thought only unwanted kittens were found in boxes. It seemed impossible that anyone would casually throw away a baby.

'How long have you been picking pockets?' was her next question.

Sadie stared at her boldly and defiantly for a few seconds to see if there was any hint of disapproval in her face but, satisfied, she said, 'Since I was about seven. The old woman who took me in ran a school for pocket pickers. She was a good teacher, wasn't she? I can take things from right next to people's skins and they don't know what's happening.'

'But what if you get caught?'

'I'll go to jail, I suppose. It won't be so bad. They feed you all right and you get a bit of a rest. But I won't get caught, I'm too quick. Look, just watch me. You see that man over there? He's a pickpocket himself but I bet I'll take that watch off his chest without him knowing a thing about it.'

She got up from her seat and walked over to a group of men leaning on the bar. The tallest of them, a red-faced fellow in a curly brimmed bowler, smiled at her when she slid an arm round his waist and whispered something to him.

They stood together only for a few seconds before she passed on up the bar and even Lark, who was watching intently, did not see her new friend's hands go anywhere near the big gold watch and chain. When Sadie disappeared out of the bar door, however, it was no longer shining on the man's waistcoat.

Sadie came back to her seat, her face alive with cheeky merriment, and whispered, 'There, I did it, look . . .' She held open her skirt pocket to show the gleaming watch nestling in its depths. Then she shouted out, 'Hey, Mally, that's a fine watch you're wearing. Where did you nick it?' The tall man put his hand down to his waistcoat pocket and the expression on his face changed from pride of ownership to consternation when he discovered it was gone.

In a second he realized what had happened and called out, 'You little bitch. You've got it. Give it back.'

He looked threatening as he walked towards them and Sadie rapidly fished the watch out of her pocket to hold it out to him, saying placatingly, 'It was only a joke. I just wanted to show I could do it.'

'You'd better not do it to me again or your fingers won't be so nimble for long,' he warned.

Lark grew up with Bella clucking round her like a mother hen. On her sixteenth birthday Hannah was in Marseilles and forgot to send a greetings card or letter, but Lark did not mind because she felt she was really the child of Bill and Bella, who gave her a privileged life compared to other girls of her own age in their little corner of

London. When she stood in the cosy security of the bar, behind the bastion of the high mahogany counter, she was grateful to her adopted parents for their care and attention. Girls like her friend Sadie had no one to care for them, no one to worry whether they lived or died. If they became prostitutes, as so many did, or took to stealing, it was only in order to survive. She did not condemn them for it. The world of the East End lived by different rules to the fashionable society she saw when she went up to the West End on the horse-drawn tram with Bella.

Sadie was a teasing and amusing companion, worldly-wise in a way that Lark could never be. She felt it was her function to educate Lark.

'You're such a kid,' she told Lark when they were sitting on the doorstep watching Bill's white doves fluttering on the roof of the outhouse in the little yard. 'You don't know anything about real life, do you? You think everybody's decent like Bill and Bella.'

'I don't think any such thing,' replied Lark indignantly. 'I know they're not all decent but I think that inside everybody there must be something good . . .'

Her grandmother had believed that whole-heartedly and her belief had rarely been abused by the people among whom she lived.

'There ain't,' came Sadie's sharp little voice. 'Let me tell you there's a lot of people that's rotten right through like bits of mouldy old cheese.'

Lark stared at her friend's solemn little face, which was set in frowning lines that made her look much older than her seventeen years. Sadie knew things that Lark hoped she would never have to learn.

'I worry about you, you're so green,' Sadie said. 'If anyfing happened to Bill and Bella, what would you do? What if your mother comes back and wants to take you away with her?'

Lark leaned her head on her clenched fist and said, 'I wouldn't go. I think the way she carries on is stupid. All that going on about blowing up people when she's living off the rich . . . It's them that give her money. It's stupid.'

320

Sadie laughed. 'She's a card your mum, right enough. Every time I've see her I think she looks like a highway robber. She shouldn't have had a kid though, she's not interested in things like that. I don't expect my mother should have had me either. I'm going to make sure that doesn't happen to me. I'm not going to have any kids to leave on doorsteps or give away to my friends.'

Lark glanced at Sadie. 'How can you stop it? If you get married you'll have children whether you want them or not.'

'Don't be daft. There's ways. And you don't have to be married to have kids. I could have one now if I wasn't careful. Quinn and me've had plenty of tries at it.'

Lark had often seen Sadie in the company of Quinn, an open-faced young fellow who treated everyone in the bar to drinks when he was flush with money. He was very slim and fit and Bill had told her that Quinn was the most skilful cat burglar in London, who specialized in robbing big houses in prosperous parts of the city.

'You and Quinn?' she gasped. What a lawless pair they made, she thought with admiration.

Sadie giggled and nodded. 'Yes, he's my man. We've been together for four years now.'

'But you were only thirteen then . . .'

Again Sadie giggled. 'That's old enough, kid,' she said.

When Quinn and Sadie were flush with money, they did not work but wandered around London, dressed in their best and enjoying themselves. When the money was spent, they returned to pickpocketing or robbing houses of silver and jewellery.

In the first decade of the twentieth century the metropolis was bursting with prosperity and pickings were rich. Quinn was in fine form with money in his pocket and a happy Sadie on his arm when they paused one evening at the Queen's Head and invited Lark to accompany them to pleasure gardens on the banks of the Thames at Southwark.

She was eager to go but Bella was doubtful. She eyed Sadie balefully. 'Are you working tonight?'

Sadie shook her head. 'No, honestly Bella, I won't put a finger on anybody's purse even if they throw it down at me feet. Quinn's had a good week. We're just out for fun. Let her come.'

'You watch her then, she's not used to places like that,' warned Bella, and Sadie knew that implacable wrath would come down on her if she failed in her responsibility.

The flower-filled gardens were crowded with people who wandered around paths shaded by neatly trimmed trees. In the distance they could hear a band playing catchy melodies and Lark's heart danced as she walked along with her friends, admiring the fashionable throng in their glorious clothes.

From time to time she was aware that Sadie's eyes were fastened on a likely prospect, but when she saw Lark watching she grimaced and gave her irrepressible grin . . . Sadie was *not* working tonight.

With a girl on each arm and his hat cocked on the side of his head, Quinn strode along the path. As she clung to him, Lark felt the whipcord muscles ripple under her fingers and she could well understand why Sadie found him so fascinating. He exuded a sense of danger. Would she ever find a man like that, she wondered? Then her mind roamed off into one of the daydreams that had occupied so much of her waking hours lately.

She was startled back into full awareness when they reached the white-painted bandstand. It was surrounded by a dense throng listening to an orchestra that played away above the heads of the crowd. The music was popular songs and some people began to sing the words till the singing spread like a tide through the crowd. For the first time in years Lark felt an irresistible impulse to sing so she raised her head and really opened her throat, quite unaware that Quinn and Sadie were staring at her in amazement. People closest to them in the crowd had also fallen silent, stopping singing themselves so they could listen to the voice of the blonde-haired girl.

When the song finished some of the couples in the crowd turned towards her and clapped, which made her so overcome with embarrassment that the colour flooded into her cheeks.

Putting both hands to her face in shyness, she said, 'Oh, let's go. Everyone's looking at me.'

'My God,' said an awestruck Sadie, 'I didn't know you could sing like that, Larkie.'

Tugging at Quinn's arm, Lark said again, 'Please let's go. People are looking at us, what's wrong?'

'They enjoyed your singing, that's why they're looking. You've got a wonderful voice. I've never heard anything like it, not even on the halls,' said Quinn.

'Oh, don't be silly, my singing's nothing special. I've always been able to sing.' She had never recognized her gift as anything extraordinary. Now she felt that she had drawn attention to herself in some unpleasant way.

'I'm going to ask the band if she can go up and sing with them,' said Sadie suddenly, and before Lark could stop her she rushed towards the bandstand and reached up to grab the coat tails of the bandleader. He did not seem too keen on her request at first but Sadie had a way with her and before long, she was back, red-faced with excitement. 'He says you've to go up and he'll play something you can sing. Come on!'

Lark nearly dropped dead with fright. 'I can't. I can't go up there. All those people looking at me . . . I can't.'

But Sadie was determined and she literally pulled her to the bandstand, saying, 'You can. I've told that man you will. Come on. You can do it. Don't be so silly.'

Lark looked at her face. It was obvious that the idea of appearing on a bandstand in front of a crowd held no fears for her and she expected her friend to feel the same way. 'But what if I make a fool of myself? What if I sing wrong notes? I don't know the words of many songs. . .'

'Just make them up as you go along,' said Sadie urgently. 'Come on, he's waiting.'

'What do you want me to play?' asked the bandleader, and Lark's mind went blank. The only songs she could remember were the old ballads she'd sung as a child and some rollicking songs the customers of Bill's bar belted out on Saturday nights. A music-hall song made popular by Vesta Tilley flashed into her head and she whispered to the bandleader that she'd sing it. In surprise he raised his eyebrows slightly but he started the orchestra playing and Lark was off . . .

'For when a fellah has turned sixteen,
You bet your life he knows a bit,
It's no good to take him to the pantomime,
When he winks at the principal lady all the time.
When he talks, you know, of Maud and Flo,
And in the West End clubs he's seen,
He's no kid, for a fellah is a fellah
When a fellah has turned sixteen.'

Strangely enough, as soon as she began to sing, her nerves vanished and she felt music flowing from her. She discovered that she loved performing, she loved the feeling of people listening to her, she wanted to make them laugh and cry with her voice. She felt the power of the born performer stir inside her. As she sang, she so much forgot her shyness that she strutted across the front of the bandstand in imitation of a fashionable dandy, and the crowd loved it. When she finished they stamped their feet, whistled and cheered in approval. In the front she could see the delighted faces of Sadie and Quinn, who were basking in the glory of their protégée.

'They want you to sing again,' said the bandleader who, like the others, was astonished at the girl's performance. 'Do you know anything else?'

'Only some Scottish songs. Do you know the one that goes "It's oh but I'm longing for my ain folk . . ."?'

There was a Scotsman, a violinist, among the players who knew the tune and he said he would play it for her.

With her hands folded in front of her skirt she faced

her audience again and poured into the words of the old song all her poignant longing for the Borders, all her sense of loss and painful love for the countryside she thought she would never see again. The depth of her feeling reached out to the crowd and some of them, exiles too from various lands, felt tears rising in their eyes. Lark had inherited Jane's power to stir the deepest emotions with music. When the last notes died away, there was a strange, stricken silence before the cheering began. And how they cheered! Hands reached up to help her down from the bandstand, people crowded round and asked her name. A few even asked where she was performing, so sure were they that she was a professional. Quinn and Sadie bore her home to Spitalfields in triumph, her head ringing with the compliments she had received.

The bar was crowded every Saturday night when Lark did her turn, and the sight of the entranced faces of her listeners filled her with a strange exultation, a wild and thrilling feeling of power. The whistling and stamping were sounds that she loved to hear. She did not realize how much she changed as soon as she began to perform.

It was dark outside and the gas lamp on the pavement cast a pool of light at the saloon bar door where a knot of men in dark suits were standing listening. Among them was a tall man with a smouldering cigar in his hand and as she sang she was conscious of him watching her with an intent and unsentimental gaze. His calculating gaze disturbed her.

Later, when she was helping Bill behind the bar, the cigar smoker thrust his way through the throng and addressed her in an unceremonious way.

'You did well. I've heard about you. You've got a good voice but you need training.'

She stared at him. 'Thank you. But I don't want training. I'm quite happy the way I am.'

He gave a short laugh. 'Don't be silly. You could be on the halls. You'd be a celebrity. I could make you a fortune.'

Bill, who had been listening, came over protectively and told the stranger, 'Our girl doesn't want to go on the halls. That's not the life for her. She's quite happy here, doing a turn on Saturday nights.'

'Yes, sure, it draws in the customers, doesn't it? But, believe me, this girl could be singing for the world instead of for a few gin drinkers in the East End.'

Bill stared aggressively at the arrogant face of the stranger but this was no ordinary Queen's Head customer. His suit was of good cut and fine material and his cigar smelt rich and aromatic, not pungent like the small black cheroots smoked by people like Quinn.

'What is it you want?' asked Bill. 'What's your business? Say it or get out of my pub.'

The stranger reached into the breast pocket of his grey waistcoat and drew out a square of pasteboard which he handed over the bar.

She glanced over her adopted father's shoulder and read:

Henry Beauchamp Chapman
Proprietor
Alhambra Theatre
The Strand

Bill's face changed. He had obviously heard of Henry Beauchamp Chapman, who then said, 'I want to give your girl a chance on the boards. Send her along next week and I'll listen to her. If I like her act, I'll put her on the bill.'

'Oh Bella, I can't do it. I'll make a mess of it. I'll forget the words of all my songs . . .' She was near to tears as they walked towards the ornate entrance of the Alhambra Theatre.

Bella laid a comforting hand on her arm. 'Don't worry, ducky, it doesn't matter a farthing if you do forget — but I know you won't. Just don't let Henry Thingummy What's-His-Name upset you. They say he's a real tyrant.

326

But I won't let him push you around, you can be sure of that.'

Lark managed a smile. She almost relished the thought of Henry Beauchamp Chapman and Bella locked in combat. They would be worthy adversaries.

At the theatre a grumpy man who was swabbing the marble floor of the entrance hall turned on them with rage as they tried to walk over his wet steps. 'You can't come in here. It's not open.'

'We've come to see Mr Chapman,' said Bella haughtily. 'Kindly tell him Miss Kennedy and Mrs Richardson have arrived.'

'Gawd, you tell him, Missus. But go round the back like all the rest of them. Only paying customers comes in this way.'

The stage door was dark and shabby compared to the glamorous entrance and Bella and Lark were shown in by another old man in a collarless shirt and an open waistcoat.

'Come for an audition, have you?' he asked. 'Well, you're in luck, he's in a good mood today for once.'

The stage was almost in darkness and Lark stood awkwardly at the side, almost hidden by a heavy red velvet curtain that smelled strongly of dust. A few gas lights flickered behind metal hoods at her feet and she shaded her eyes with her hand as she tried to stare into the auditorium. She had been to theatres many times with Bill or Bella but now, on the stage herself, she was filled with dread. A hostile world was out there waiting to devour her. She shivered with weakness and her stomach churned so violently that she feared she was going to vomit.

'Come into the middle of the stage,' called out a disembodied voice and she stepped forward into a pool of dim light that made her feel even more exposed.

'Turn round,' commanded the voice.

'Why?' she asked.

'Just turn round,' was the abrupt reply, so she did what she was told.

'Take off that hat,' was the next command and she did not question the order but drew out the long hat pins with which Bella had secured the vast hat to her head that morning. As she held it in her hand she could feel her hair slowly uncurling from the series of combs that held it high up on her head and she awkwardly put up a hand to tidy it.

'No, leave it. Let it alone,' came the man's voice. 'Now tell the pianist what you're going to sing.'

She stared into the orchestra pit at her feet and saw a man leaning idly over the keyboard of a piano. 'I'd like to sing "A Bicycle Made for Two" and "Following in Father's Footsteps",' she told him. Then she added, 'And perhaps you could also play these for me.' She handed down a couple of sheets of music, her favourite Scottish songs that Bill had asked a musical friend to transcribe for her.

The pianist put the sheets on the piano and rippled through the notes.

'Is that what you want?' he called up.

Gulping down the lump in her throat, she nodded. 'Yes, that's fine. I'll set the time, just you follow me.'

There was an explosion of laughter from the darkened stalls at this but she ignored it and launched into her repertoire. By the time she was on her second song, all her nerves had disappeared, she forgot she was alone in the middle of a darkened stage in front of critical strangers and sang and sang, entertaining herself. Finally she sang the Scottish songs and once again, her longing and her yearning were poured out in music. She even made herself cry with the evoked memories that song aroused. She could see the soft green slopes of the hills behind Aylie's little cottage; she could smell the old-fashioned apple-ringie herb in the garden and feel the gentle rain on her face as soft clouds drifted over the vast sky . . . Oh, the beloved Borderland, how she missed it.

As the last notes died away into the darkness, she dropped her hands and stood silent, her head drooping like the head of a fading flower. What brought her back to immediacy was the voice of Bella.

'Lovely, lovely! Oh, my God, you sang like a bird, Larkie.'

She smiled at that and lifted her head to see Henry B. Chapman climbing on to the stage with another man, older and more distinguished-looking than he.

'You'll do,' he said to her. 'This is Signor Arnotti, he's going to teach you some tricks of the business, breathing and voice projection, things like that. You'll study with him for a couple of months and then I'll put you on here.'

Bella materialized beside them, red-faced, maternal and anxious. 'And who's going to pay for the lessons?' she demanded.

'I will,' said Mr Chapman. 'You can call it an investment. But I never make investments that don't pay dividends so you'd better be prepared to work hard, Miss.'

Working with Arnotti was hard. Her ribs and diaphragm ached from the singing exercises and her waist hurt because the stage dressmakers tied her stays so tight that she felt they were trying to cut her through the middle like the woman a magician sawed in half each night on stage.

Chapman and his cronies criticized her to her face . . . 'She's too skinny up top,' said Chapman to the dressmaker. 'Do something to plump out her tits, will you?' So a high corset that cruelly shoved up her breasts was laced round her until a satisfactory cleavage was produced.

'Her hair's all right but make it hang free, she needs to look a bit more wanton . . .' was another Chapman comment, and two women with sizzling curling tongs heated in the gas ring descended on her, frizzing and singeing the fine hair till her nose was full of the smell of burning and a curtain of coy ringlets hung round her temples. They slapped paint and powder on her face so that when she stared in the mirror before going on stage

329

she felt like a clown. They taught her to step across the boards in a coquettish way when she was singing the provocative songs that the music-hall audiences loved, but they did not have to teach her how to change from a flirt into a wistful, nostalgic stirrer of hearts when she sang the old Scots songs for which she was to become famous.

Her name appeared on theatre bills, though in small letters and well down at the bottom. But it was not her own name that was used because Chapman had decided that Kennedy was too ordinary a name and when Lark told him that her great-grandfather was a Frenchman called Blaize Chardenel, he manufactured a stage name for her. 'Lark Chardelle, that's what we'll call you . . . it's a perfect name for a singer!'

On the day that Lark was to appear in public for the first time, Hannah arrived unannounced at the Queen's Head. She was irked because no one had time to be very surprised or impressed at her arrival from foreign parts. She was in London to attend a meeting of the Russian Social Democratic Party in exile and longed to boast about her importance.

Bella however only nodded in her direction and said, 'You've gone quite grey,' as she bustled past. She was carrying a long tinsel dress in her arms and looked flustered.

'You're acting as if I've only been away a couple of days,' said Hannah in an aggrieved tone.

'You've been away nearly three years,' replied Bella, 'and would you mind getting out of the way? I've got to take this dress out to Larkie's hansom cab.'

'Larkie? I hate it when you call her that. Her name's Lark, it's a beautiful name. Where's she going in a hansom cab?'

'She's not going anywhere, she's there. The cab's taking her dress to the Alhambra Theatre. I've just been putting the finishing touches to it.' And Bella raised her voice in an unladylike yell: 'Sadie, where the hell are you? Sadie, come and get this dress.'

Sadie, in her street clothes, came out of the parlour and took the dress from Bella, who delivered it up with a stern warning.

'You make sure you take good care of it and that she looks her best. It's your responsibility – and don't let those old cows lace her up too tight. She's got to sing and we don't want her fainting from tight lacing. All they worry about is making her waist look as small as possible.'

Sadie nodded and bustled off into the waiting cab.

'Would you mind telling me what's going on?' asked Hannah. 'What's Lark doing at the Alhambra Theatre?'

'She's singing there tonight. It's her first night. We're all going to hear her. You've just arrived in time.'

'She's on the stage!' Hannah was astonished. Her memories of her daughter were of a small, pale-faced child who was too timid to talk far less sing in a theatre. For a moment she wondered if Bella had taken leave of her senses.

'She's going to be a famous artiste,' said Bella proudly. 'She's going to make a lot of money.'

Hannah sniffed. Her principles did not permit her to enthuse about that.

'Well, I'll come along with you and hear her singing,' she said, but Bella looked none too pleased.

'You can only come if you sit in the theatre and keep quiet. I'm not having you rushing in and upsetting her before she goes on the stage. She's got enough to worry about without you!'

Bella, Bill, Sadie, Quinn and Hannah sat in a row in the Grand Circle, their elbows on the gilded rail, impatiently awaiting Lark's debut. When she stepped on to the stage, shining in the tinsel dress and with her golden hair tumbling round her face, each one of them drew in their breath with a gasp. No one gasped more loudly than Hannah.

Signor Arnotti's teaching had not been wasted. Lark controlled her voice superbly; she knew every trick for holding an audience and drew them to her like an enchan-

331

tress. In every seat people sat with their eyes abstracted and their fidgeting stopped as she weaved her spells around them. The shy girl, who blushed when people spoke to her and who moved awkwardly when she was embarrassed, had totally disappeared and a singing siren had taken her place.

Hannah sat silent, her mind in turmoil but her predominant feeling one of regret. She should have got to know this child better; she should have taken trouble with her. Anyone who could sing with such conviction, who had such power over other people, must have depths that she had never suspected. But she was not going to show her regret to Bill and Bella, who were behaving like the managers of a successful prize fighter. They wept and clung to each other; they wiped their eyes and sighed in sheer bliss. The audience were cheering and their darling was a success. That was all they wanted.

Afterwards, in the cramped communal dressing rooms which all the lesser female artistes on the bill shared, they crowded round Lark who once again became shy and blushed if a stranger spoke to her. The unexpected appearance of Hannah did not have the devastating effect that Bella had feared, for the girl had long ago stopped thinking about her mother. Now this tall, gaunt woman was back, thrusting herself forward and talking, talking, talking as she had always done . . .

'I'm in London for a conference, darling. Lenin's here – what a man, Lark, a real genius! And he's very impressed with me. I backed him up today when he pressed for the party being given the name Bolshevik. Don't you think that's a good name?'

Bolshevik? What's a Bolshevik? Lark wondered, but agreed, 'It's a very good name, Mother,' while Sadie gently rubbed cream into her face to take off the heavy make-up.

As Hannah watched this process, she saw the daughter she remembered emerge from under the stage paint.

'You look so very like my mother, Lark,' she said suddenly, 'it's quite amazing.'

She could not have said anything that gave her daughter more pleasure. A smile of beautiful brilliance swept across the girl's face and, rising to her feet, she threw her arms around Hannah and hugged her.

Lark, 1914

'You really need somebody to look after you, you do,' said Sadie disapprovingly, twitching away at Lark's skirt in the dressing room filled with flowers which she now occupied alone as befitted her star status.

'But I couldn't refuse her, I've plenty of money,' Lark excused herself, but Sadie was unimpressed.

'Money doesn't last long unless you look after it. Don't do it again, even if she gets down on her bended knees. What did she say she wanted it for?'

As she spoke she was bustling around, arranging the pots of stage make-up on the dressing table and reading the cards on the bouquets of flowers that had been handed in at the stage door by admirers of Lark Chardelle, 'The Sweetest Songbird'.

'She said she needed it to go to Russia. Apparently there's something going on there.'

Sadie looked relieved. Russia was a long way away and she was always very irritable when Hannah descended on their little household and unashamedly preyed on Lark, who at twenty-three was the toast of London. Invitations to grand houses flowed in; photographers pleaded to be allowed to take her picture; postcards of her posing against a background of flowers in a tight-waisted stage costume were bought in their thousands by her admirers; sheet music of her Scottish songs sold in every music shop. When she appeared on stage, queues formed to buy tickets and the applause was rapturous.

Chapman was still her manager and he insisted that she confine her appearances to his theatres. There was to be no chance of the public growing tired of his Songbird through hearing too much of her, he said.

In spite of her success and the money that was flowing

in, Bella and Sadie still felt that their little Lark was too innocent and naïve to face the world alone. They clucked round her as much as ever and though she now lived in an elegant apartment in Mount Street, Mayfair, Bella made regular visits with steak and kidney puddings wrapped in white cloths, for it was her conviction that Lark did not eat enough. While the tiny span of her waist delighted her admirers, it terrified Bill and Bella, who thought women should have a generous layer of fat on them.

Sadie had taken on the role of Lark's dresser and protector, her guard dog in fact, snarling angrily at any young man who tried to penetrate the barrier of the stage door to speak to his idol. Everyone in the theatre was terrified of Sadie and her sharp Cockney tongue. Lark had bought her and Quinn a little house in Pimlico where they lived in semi-sparring bliss but neither of them were much there because Sadie could not bear to leave Lark unprotected and Quinn was at the moment languishing in prison. As he grew older, he was less nimble and it was easier for the officers of the law to catch him.

Lark was anxious to divert her friend from the subject of Hannah, for she was apprehensive of what Sadie would say if she knew that Lark had given her mother one hundred pounds.

'When does Quinn get out?' she asked.

Sadie's face brightened. 'The day after tomorrow. I'll go up to Pentonville with a cab and collect him, if it's all right with you.'

'Of course, bring him back here. We'll have a bottle of champagne to celebrate. Chapman's coming round because there's some contract he wants to discuss with me.'

'Don't you agree to anything till I'm back here,' warned Sadie anxiously. 'You don't want him trying to put one over on you. I don't trust that man.'

'Oh Sadie, he's done well by us. I'm rich. Look at what we've got.'

'You're rich because you're the best singer in London,'

said Sadie. 'You'd be rich no matter who was managing you. Chapman's got rich out of you and he doesn't want to let you go. He needs to be watched and if he wants you to stay with him, he's going to have to make it worth your while.'

Lark smiled. She knew that between them Bella and Sadie would see that her interests were protected. She felt as safe as a cherished child with the people who cared most for her, and not even when Hannah was at her most flattering did she ever feel like that about her mother.

Chapman's offer was for an American tour with appearances in theatres in New York, Boston and San Francisco. The magnitude of the idea made both Quinn and Sadie suck in their breath in astonishment. The money he was talking about was immense, two hundred pounds a week, more than middle-class family men in London earned in a year. Lark remembered how her grandmother laboured in the fields for tenpence a day, and she gave a little shiver at the memory. To be offered so much money for singing seemed immoral.

But the expressions on the faces of Sadie and Quinn brought her back to reality.

'I'll go,' she said.

The American trip was planned for the winter and she was to spend the summer resting and rehearsing a new programme. She took a house near Bognor Regis and every day lay on the terrace in a long chair, staring out at the sea.

Now that she was rich she could well afford to go back to Charterhall, but something kept her away. It was better, she thought, only to remember it. Perhaps to see it again would spoil those memories. She wrote to the Hepburn family to ensure that the cottage was kept watertight, and Sim answered her letter with a polite note. She could tell from the tone of his reply that he thought he was writing to the child who had left them years ago. When she herself tried to imagine what he would be like, she could only summon up the tousle-haired, lean and daring boy she had hero-worshipped.

She was tired, very tired. Chapman was right, she needed a rest. When invitations came in asking her to join parties for the Derby, she turned them down. She had been there last year when the Suffragette Emily Davidson threw herself in front of the King's horse, and the memory stayed in her mind in horrifying detail. Fanaticism seemed to be all around her, blaring out from every newspaper she opened. Other Suffragettes tried to blow up Lloyd George's house; at the end of June the Austrian Archduke Ferdinand and his wife were assassinated at Sarajevo by a student called Gabriel Princip. She read those reports and thought of her mother. It seemed that Hannah's type of militant action was at last taking over the world. Frightened, she stopped reading the news and it was a surprise when Sadie came running onto the terrace brandishing a copy of *The Times* . . .

'Look at this, Larkie, Germany's declared war on Russia. Your mum's still there, isn't she?'

She sat up and took the newspaper. Its black headlines made her stomach lurch with apprehension, not just for Hannah but for something much deeper.

'Yes, the last I heard she was in St Petersburg but that was in the spring. There's no knowing where she is now,' she said.

Sadie, who was reading the news over her shoulder, tried to console her. 'Your mum'll be all right. But it's not nice, is it, all this talk of war? We'll be next.'

Suddenly the sunshine that was blazing down on to the pretty garden was dimmed. Three days later, on 4 August, Britain declared war on Germany and the world went mad.

The American trip was called off but Chapman was not too dejected because he had other plans for Lark. He launched a series of patriotic shows because he realized that masses of men would soon be on the move and London theatres would be packed out with them. His

Songbird, Lark Chardelle, would entertain the soldiers. She would spearhead the theatrical war effort.

Her restful summer ended abruptly. The hopeful suitors who made appointments to take her on the river, or escort her to picnics in lovely private parks, were disappointed, for she was back in the theatre every day, rehearsing a series of songs calculated to stir the blood of the British. Wrapped in a Union Jack, with a gilded helmet on her head, she sat on a huge throne and belted out lyrics extolling home and country, urging every young man to enlist in the forces and help to defeat the wicked Hun.

They stamped and cheered when she appeared on stage as Britannia but it was still her nostalgic yearning ballads that really brought them to their feet. Her songs of loss and homesickness touched a raw nerve now and people wept openly in the theatre. The nation was girding up its loins for a terrible war.

A kind of desperation seized everyone. Young men flung themselves at her feet in the street and pleaded with her to marry them. Then Quinn and Sadie surprised her one morning with the news that they were going along to St Bride's Church in Fleet Street to be married. She watched them standing in front of the clergyman, their tough faces solemn, and tears slipped down her cheeks.

She had been courted by many men. She'd liked some of them and been entertained by others but she had never felt love and certainly not passion for anyone. Her apparent immunity to this obsession that took over other people worried her. Was there something wrong with her? Was she incapable of love? Even Bill and Bella, growing old now, had that strange bond between them that she recognized between Quinn and Sadie, that knowingness, that acknowledgement of a mutual secret, that sensual enjoyment in each other's presence that she longed to experience.

When they came out of the church, Quinn paused on the pavement and kissed Sadie on the cheek.

'Well, that's that,' he said, 'you're really my old woman

now, gel. Just go back to the theatre with Lark and I'll meet you there in half an hour. I'm off to join up.'

Stunned, the two women walked slowly back up the Strand to the theatre which was plastered with huge posters bearing Lark's name. Already a queue of men in khaki was forming on the pavement so, with heads down to avoid Lark being recognized, they scuttled round a corner to reach the back door.

'They're from that Sir Harry Lewis again. They must have cost him a pretty penny,' said Sadie approvingly as she brought in a huge cane basket filled with orchids. Lark was making up her face in the mirror and the magnitude of the basket made her eyes widen in surprise.

'I wonder which one he is,' she said as she rouged the line of her mouth. 'He's never spoken to me, he just keeps sending those flowers every day.'

'Quite romantic that, really,' said Sadie, who since her own marriage had begun to want a similar status for her friend. The trouble was, in her view, that none of the men who worshipped at Lark's feet was half good enough for her. They were all young men about town who made a habit of courting actresses and whose intentions were rarely honourable.

The arrival of the soldiers however had changed things. As far as Sadie could see, a nicer class of man was coming to town. This Sir Harry was evidently rich and generous, for his flowers had arrived every day for a fortnight – and he was not pushy, either, because he had not followed them up as the others did. Besides, Sadie loved a title and the idea of her Larkie as *Lady* Lewis delighted her. What a slap in the eye for Hannah with her 'all titles are corrupt' cobblers!

The war lurched on inexorably but Lark did not have time to brood on the killing toll that mounted daily. Her task was to entertain those who were about to die.

She stepped forward to the front of the stage for the last part of her act and looked down at the faces of the men lifted towards her in the stalls. Some were dark, others fair; some old, but most of them were very young, little more than schoolboys. She sang with extra feeling tonight because just before she had gone on stage, Sadie had told her that Quinn was going to France. She had hoped that his age – he was over thirty – would have excused him but as the death toll in the trenches rose, more and more men were needed.

As she turned to leave the stage, she saw a thin young man standing up clapping in a box on the right-hand side of the theatre.

That's him, she thought, that's my mysterious Sir Harry.

He spoke to her when she was getting into her cab at the stage door. 'I hope you like my flowers,' he said, and she paused on the step to stare at him. He was dressed in officer's khaki with a gleaming Sam Browne belt that made him look like a schoolboy dressing up, for he was in his early twenties at the most and very thin, with the sort of yellow hair that looked as if it were dyed, so pale was it. His voice was soft and he sounded nervous, like a lovesick boy.

She smiled and said, 'Thank you, they're beautiful, but you shouldn't spend your money like that on me.'

He shrugged and smiled sweetly back at her before drifting off into the crowd.

He asked for nothing but his constant presence in the box and the daily arrival of his flowers made her very conscious of him. She wanted to know why this young boy was so taken with her and what he wanted from her, but though she often saw him outside the stage door after the show, he never again spoke to her. One night however his flowers failed to appear and his seat in the box was occupied by a group of older men in the scarlet uniforms of a mounted regiment. Her heart sank. Had that child been sent to France and killed? He looked so like a sacrificial victim.

Three months later however he was back, announcing his arrival with a bouquet of roses so big that the florist's man could not get them through the narrow stage door and had to bring them in by the front. That night she smiled brilliantly at his box and as he saluted her, she saw that he looked stronger, browner, more manly than before. Whatever he had seen, it had made him grow up.

As she left the theatre he was in the crowd, so she told Sadie, 'I've got to talk to him, ask him to come over.'

Sadie pushed her way through the crowd and grabbed his sleeve, tugging him after her into the cab. This was the first time she had seen him really close and she noticed that his eyes were very pale blue and that he was indeed young, not long from school. Her heart filled with pity for him, such a child having to face this terrible war!

The two women questioned him as they drove along — where had he been for the past weeks?

His eyes darkened and his face stiffened. 'I've been at the Front . . . I'm on leave now for seven days so I thought I'd come across and see your show. I think you're wonderful, Miss Chardelle.'

'The London flower shops must think you're pretty wonderful too,' said Sadie with a giggle. 'They must be glad to see you back. Do you send flowers to all the stars?'

He grinned slightly. 'No, this is the first time I've done it. You make me think of flowers every time I see you, flowers and the countryside, like the place I come from.'

'Where's that?'

'A place in Herefordshire near the Welsh border. My family have a house there.'

Sadie was a good interrogator. 'Do you come from a big family?'

'Not really, there's just my grandmother . . . and my mother, but she's not at home. My father was killed in the Boer War and my grandmother didn't want me to join up, but when I left school I enlisted. It seemed so cowardly not to.'

Men, mused Sadie, thinking of her Quinn, are such hopeless romantics. She then asked him a very direct question: 'How old are you?'

341

He straightened his shoulders and looked her in the eye. 'I'm twenty-five,' he said.

They knew he was lying but he awakened their maternal instincts and so they invited him into the Mount Street house for supper.

When he left he gravely kissed Lark's hand and said in a low voice, 'I'm madly in love with you, you know that, don't you? I want you to marry me, that's why I came back from France.'

'Of course I can't marry you,' she told him, but he ignored her protests and kept coming back to invite her to spend the day with him driving in the London parks or wandering along the crowded streets where he paused in front of jewellers' shop windows, trying to persuade her to allow him to buy her a ring. She steadfastly refused to accept his offer.

He pleaded, 'Why can't you marry me? You're not promised to anyone else, are you?'

She shook her head. 'No, I'm not, but you're too young for me. I'm twenty-four this year. You're probably five or six years younger, if you told the truth.'

He grinned and said, 'Actually, I'm five years younger. But that's not important. I feel about twenty years older than you.'

As he spoke his face hardened again into the grim lines she had seen when she saw him in his box on the first night of his return from France.

'Oh, marry me, Lark, I've never felt like this about anyone before. I've got to go back to France the day after tomorrow. You don't know what it's like over there. If you marry me or even just promise to marry me, I'll have something to live for.'

A cold shiver made the hairs on the back of her neck stiffen. She had heard stories of the war in the trenches but preferred not to think about them. Yet here was this boy ageing visibly as he remembered the war that was being waged only a few miles away in a world so very different from busy, fashionable London. She felt a great sympathy for him and took his hand softly between her gloved ones.

'Harry, my dear boy, if I married you, your family would say I'd only done it because I wanted your money or your title.'

He laughed uproariously at that. 'You've more money than I have, Lark. I only get an allowance from my grandmother and I spend most of it on flowers! As for the title, it's nothing special. The real gentry that live near us think we're very vulgar because my grandfather got his title for lending money to Edward VII and he'd made that money when he was a mill owner in Yorkshire. No, if you marry me, you won't be marrying into the real aristocracy. I know you could do much better for yourself than me.'

She sent him back to France without any promises but her heart was sore for him and she lay awake at night wondering what would have been so wrong in making him happy with a promise to marry . . . His voice saying 'It would give me something to live for' kept ringing in her head.

Next day Quinn came home on leave, transformed into a smart sergeant in well-pressed khaki who came striding into the theatre and surprised Sadie, who had not expected him. He held his weeping woman clasped to his chest and once again Lark realized what it must mean to love someone wholeheartedly.

Sadie took seven days off work to be with him – she had never left Lark before – and when she returned she had just seen Quinn off at the station.

'My God, it was terrible! Victoria was full of men and women all saying goodbye to each other and, Larkie, I couldn't help wondering which couples would never see each other again.'

Lark tried to comfort her friend. 'Quinn'll be all right, Sadie, you know how resourceful he is. He's a survivor is Quinn.'

'I used to think that too, but this is a terrible war. My Quinn cries out at night and grinds his teeth something terrible. One night he woke up screaming . . . My God, it was awful listening to him! He told me some horrible things too, about rats that grow fat as cats on dead bodies and how the lice infest his clothes. You know how fussy Quinn is? He rubs candle grease along the seams of his clothes and washes himself in paraffin to try to get rid of them but nothing works . . . They feed on him, he says.'

She gave a shudder and went on anguishedly, 'Oh, what'll I do if he gets killed, Lark? He says all his mates have gone already – picked off one by one by snipers. One young lad only lasted five minutes – the first time he stuck his head up, he was shot right between the eyes.'

'Stop it, Sadie, stop it. You know how quick Quinn is and he's so careful, he won't get shot. Stop thinking about it.'

But in the summer of 1917 the dreaded telegram came regretfully informing Mrs Quinn that her husband, Sergeant Alfred Albert Quinn, had died a hero's death at Messines Ridge in the third battle of Ypres. He was awarded a posthumous Military Medal for gallantry in trying to rescue a wounded man on the battlefield.

Sadie collapsed and lay like a shrunken doll in the middle of Lark's vast bed.

Bella came to comfort her and, as she was leaving, she whispered to Lark, 'This is awful. There'll be no men left by the time this war's over.'

After a long gap, a letter came from Harry saying he had been wounded and was in an officers' recovery centre in Derbyshire. 'But I'm better now and will be in London next week. Please marry me,' he wrote.

As she held the thin sheet covered with schoolboyish writing she asked herself, 'What would be so wrong about making him happy?' For herself she felt like an empty shell, and the only time she became animated was when she stepped on to the stage.

'Harry Lewis is coming back, he still wants me to marry him,' she told Sadie.

'Poor kid, he's really gone on you. He's a strange one . . . poor kid.'

Lark knew from her tone that, like her, Sadie thought Harry would not survive the war.

'I think I'll do it, just to please him,' she ventured.

Sadie nodded. 'You might as well, it would make him happy.'

He looked strained and much older but there were no visible signs of a wound – no limp, no folded sleeve. Yet obviously something terrible had happened to him, she could see that from the anguish in his eyes.

'Have you been home to see your family?' she asked as they sat together in her drawing room and she watched him drinking tea with such an uncontrollable tremor that he had to hold the cup with both hands.

He nodded. 'Yes, I went home on my way down from Derbyshire. My grandmother's getting old. She seems to think we're still fighting the Boers.'

'What about your mother?'

'She's still alive but she lives in South America. After my father was killed, she married a jockey and they sent her away. Even for my family a little jockey with a drink problem was too much. I've not seen her since I was five.'

The key to Harry was coming clearer. He longed for love, he needed a substitute for the mother he had never had.

'My mother's a runaway too,' she told him. 'She's in Russia organizing a revolution or something.'

The newspapers had been full of the revolution in Russia and though there had been no news of Hannah, Lark was sure that she would be involved in it somehow. She'd waited so long for revolution, how could she miss it?

She said this to Harry and when he laughed she was relieved to see how it changed his face. It made her feel she had the power to transform him to what he had been when he first sent her the beautiful bouquets of flowers, so long ago it seemed.

'Have you thought any more about marrying me?' he

asked suddenly. 'Please say yes, Lark. I don't think I could go back to France without that. I've thought of nothing else since I went into hospital. It's kept me going through everything.'

'What happened to you?' she asked.

He stood up and walked across to the tall window overlooking the street and his voice was harsh as he said, 'I went mad. I started to scream and scream and one of the other officers was going to shoot me, but fortunately I had a friend in the trench and he stopped him. Shell shock, they said! They brought me home and got me better so that they can send me back again.'

With a sharp movement he turned back to stare at her. 'And believe me, I don't want to go. I have nightmares about it. I'm terrified but I've got to go . . . All the men who've been killed will come out of their graves and haunt me if I don't go back.'

She ran across the floor and grasped him in her arms. 'Oh Harry, it's so awful. Of course I'll marry you, of course I will.'

It was a quiet wedding held on the day before he was due to return to France, but the newspapers got hold of the story and announced that the famous music-hall artiste had married a young peer and war hero. She was back on stage on the night of the ceremony and the audience stood up and cheered when she began to sing.

They spent their wedding night in the Savoy Hotel but when they were in bed together he clasped her in his arms and said through clenched teeth, 'I don't think I'll be able to do anything, Lark. I've never done it with anyone but a prostitute when I was at school . . . hope you won't be disappointed.'

She felt relieved but soothed him, feeling old and wise though she was even more virginal and inexperienced than he. Years of listening to the uninhibited conversation of Sadie and Bella however had left her with some knowledge.

'It's all right, it doesn't matter, it happens like that

sometimes. You'll be all right tomorrow,' she whispered to him.

'But I want you so much, I want you so badly.'

She held him close and stroked his hair. 'Ssh, don't worry,' she crooned, 'just talk to me. Tell me about what it was like when you were a little boy.'

He talked for hours, telling her about his home, his pony and his boyhood friends. But as dawn began to streak the sky outside their window, he started to talk about the war though she tried to stop him . . .

'Let me tell you about it,' he whispered, 'I want to talk about it. I want to clear it out of my mind. I want to tell you about the time we fought for three days to capture a foxhole with three Germans in it. We could see them, crouched over their guns, firing out at us and we had to keep trying to get in to their foxhole and kill them. My best friend died, my captain was killed, our sergeant was shot down, the men were slaughtered one after another but we were ordered to go on till we took that foxhole. On the third day we made it, we got in and – you'll not believe this – the Germans were all dead. What we had been seeing were three corpses. They were crouched up in there in shooting positions with their eyes staring at me and – the smell! My God, I can't describe the smell!'

Without speaking she drew him to her and he fell asleep, his head on her breast.

1918

At last it was beginning to look as if the war was coming to an end. Both sides were exhausted and the women whose men were still alive were hanging on to the hope that, in the end, they would survive.

The spring was chilly and Lark's energy was low. She was still in bed when Bella arrived at Mount Street looking grim. She sat down on the bed and nodded to Sadie to bring in tea before breaking the news which she so obviously carried with her. Alarmed by her grimness, Lark sat up anxiously and stared at her.

'What's wrong, Bella? It's not Bill is it, he's all right is he?'

Bella never believed in beating about the bush and she blurted out her story.

'Bill's fine, so am I. Don't worry about us. It's your mother, Larkie. An odd little man came in to the Queen's last night and gave me a package. He said it'd been sent over from Russia. It's your mother's papers and photographs – apparently she was shot some time during the winter in St Petersburg. He didn't know who did it – or if he did, he didn't say.'

She reached into her carpet bag and fished out a bundle of papers wrapped up in dirty, stained canvas. Lark slowly untied the frayed string that held them together.

All that was left of her mother's life was some closely written pages that looked as if they had been torn out of a child's exercise book; four printed sheets in Cyrillic letters which she could not read; and a small sheaf of photographs on card mountings, most of them showing Hannah with various male comrades in high-necked Russian shirts. At the bottom of the pile there was a publicity postcard of Lark herself in stage costume.

Wordlessly she held this out to Sadie and Bella, who looked on silently, not knowing how she was going to react to Hannah's death.

'She was very proud of you,' ventured Bella.

'Was she? I suppose she was. I didn't know much about her, really. Aylie used to say that she was very clever as a child, really brilliant. She could have done so many things . . .'

Lark carefully wrapped the papers up again and laid them on the bed at her side. She needed time to think about Hannah. As she drew on her wrapper and looked up at the concerned faces watching her so closely, she knew that if she had just been told about the death of either of them, her grief would have been real and true. How sad she could not feel like that about her mother.

The telegram about Harry arrived three days later – killed on the Somme where he had cheated death for so long. She crumpled up the thin sheet of official words in her fist and wondered if Harry's ghost would wander that desolate shell-pitted landscape for ever.

It did not occur to her not to go to the theatre. Accompanied by a silent Sadie, she rode there in a cab, staring blindly out of the window. She had not loved him but had felt great pity and affection for him. She had married him from compassion and now he was dead, a sacrificial victim to the Gods of War. Her sorrow was mixed with a terrible anger at the waste of human life. She stared out of the cab window and realized that an all-pervading feeling of grief filled the streets of London. It was no longer a bustling, happy city but a place where grey-faced women in black walked with bowed shoulders along the streets. It was a city full of mourners.

Chapman was waiting in her dressing room. Publicity conscious as always, he had alerted the newspapers and a few reporters were clustered in the passage outside the door as she came in, but one look at Sadie's face was enough to quell their questions.

'You don't have to go on,' said Chapman, 'I'll put on

your understudy – or I'll close the show for the night if you want.'

She shook her head. 'I'll go on. I'll finish it. Just go away and let me get dressed.'

He rushed out and told the press that in spite of her grief, Lady Lewis had decided not to disappoint her public. She would sing for the soldiers as a tribute to her dead husband.

The theatre was packed when she stepped on to the stage. People were even standing in the aisles. A hush swept over them when the curtain rose and they saw her standing very still in the middle of the stage, wearing a cream silk dress with a long train and large pink silk cabbage roses tucked into her corsage. Deliberately she had made herself look as splendid as possible, with diamond bracelets on her wrists and a necklace of brilliant stones glittering round her neck. Her yellow hair was piled high in a thick crown and into it Sadie had tucked an elegantly curved white aigrette.

The cheering died away when she spread out white-gloved hands to silence the crowd and gestured to the orchestra to strike up. Tonight there would be no cheeky, sexy songs, tonight she would only sing of emotions, of love and longing. Her voice was magnificent and it soared out into the dark theatre like a benison, soothing the listeners, taking them away from their everyday concerns into a land of enchantment.

She knew that she had never sung better. Like a swan in its death throes, her magic was more intense than it had ever been. She had reached her peak.

Then she began to sing a series of popular war songs but she sang them with such poignancy that the words achieved a new meaning. The roses that bloomed in Picardy were roses of blood; the road that was winding ahead of the singer was the road to eternity; 'Cheerio, Toodle-oo, Goodbyee . . .' was a brave gesture against certain death. Finally she sang the most moving song she remembered from her childhood. It was an old song of mourning still sung in the Borders for the men who fell in the sixteenth-century Battle of Flodden, 'The Flo'ers o' the Forest'.

Her voice rang out with words that moved every heart:

'I've seen the smiling of fortune beguiling,
I've tasted her pleasure and felt her decay,
Sweet was her blessing and kind her caressing,
But now they are fled, they are fled far away.
I've seen the Forest adorned the foremost
Wi' flo'ers o' the fairest baith pleasant and gay,
Sae bonny was their blooming, their scent the air
     perfuming
But noo they are withered and a' wede away.'

Halfway through, her voice cracked and wavered. The tears began to flow down her carefully rouged cheeks, and she put her white gloves up to her face for a second but pulled herself together and re-started the song. The audience gasped and rustled in sympathy as her voice rang out stronger than ever, and when she finished, everyone in the theatre was in tears as well. Chapman gave orders to the stage hands to drop the curtain on Lark who was standing, head drooping, sobbing openly. But as the red velvet wall slid along before her, she swept it aside and stepped in front of it.

Holding out her arms to the audience, she cried, 'This is a terrible war. We have all lost so much, we are all mourning. Be brave, be brave!'

Then Chapman and a stage hand rushed on stage and led her away.

Everyone was worried about her, she would not eat and she could not stop weeping. A series of doctors were called and they prescribed rest, port wine, and a change of air. Chapman sent her back to Bognor where Bella and Sadie fussed round her. She was still there on the day that the Armistice was announced.

'But I don't understand, he said he wasn't rich. I wouldn't have married him if I'd known he was so rich . . .'

The lawyer, a prim little man called Octavius Pike, looked at her in a sceptical way. He had never before heard a widow complaining about her husband being richer than she thought.

'Lady Lewis,' he said patiently, 'Sir Harry was sole heir to a considerable fortune, a very considerable fortune.' His voice had a plummy sort of satisfaction for he enjoyed dealing with estates of consequence.

'But his grandmother . . .'

'His grandmother died last winter and she also left her grandson a sizeable inheritance. As his wife, it all comes to you. He was an only child, as you no doubt know.'

The lawyer did not really believe this actress person when she protested that she had not realized Sir Harry Lewis was one of the richest young men in England. He had no doubt that the wealth had been a major factor in her decision to marry him – after all, he was considerably younger than she was. But Lark had not been so calculating as to check up on Harry and the news that she had been left hundreds of thousands of pounds and several properties by him was quite literally a shock.

'Perhaps you could put me in touch with your financial advisers and your own lawyer,' suggested the little man who was perched on the edge of her sofa like a tetchy toy.

She shook her head. 'I haven't any. I've never needed any. Chapman pays me my money and Sadie looks after everything else.'

'Chapman? Is he a lawyer?'

'No, he owns the Alhambra Theatre,' she said and the lawyer reeled. There was no way he was going to allow the Lewis fortune to pass into the hands of a theatre proprietor.

'Perhaps it would be best if I continue to handle legal matters for you,' he suggested, and she was grateful for the offer.

'But are you sure it's all mine? He said his mother was still alive in South America.'

'Sir Harry's mother is now Mrs Lafferty and she has

352

been taken care of by the estate. She has no claim on Sir Harry's will,' was the reply. Mrs Lafferty was obviously the skeleton in the Lewis cupboard.

'You're rich, you're really rich. You're as rich as the finest duchess in the land,' cried Sadie exultantly. 'You can go out and buy anything you want. For God's sake, Larkie, do something! Let's go out and buy you some new dresses at least.'

Lark was still unable to stir herself from her lethargy. She sat in her bedroom window, watching the back gardens of the neighbouring houses.

'I don't need any new dresses, I've a cupboard full of dresses.'

'Let's buy you a lapdog then, or a parrot or a motor car . . .' Sadie's mind ranged over all the things she could think of that might interest Lark.

'What a selection,' was the reply. But it was said with a laugh, which was a good sign. 'All right, I'll come out with you but not to buy a lapdog or a parrot and certainly not a motor car. I'm not used to being so rich, I want to let it creep up on me gently.'

Mr Pike organized a trip for her to visit Harry's Herefordshire properties. There were several large farms and a massive house with turrets and sweeping lawns, set in a walled park. She stared at it in disbelief as her hired car swept up to the front door where a line of curtseying maidservants under the command of a stern butler were waiting. Inside it was gloomy and depressing, a house of mourning for two dead heirs.

'I hate it, I'm not staying here. Let's go, Sadie,' she said abruptly only half an hour after being shown into the drawing room. Leaving behind an outraged butler, she returned to London and gifted the Herefordshire house with two of its supporting farms to an organization that looked after severely wounded soldiers. Mr Pike was disapproving of this largesse but she mollified him by saying it was a gift in memory of Sir Harry and a charity should be set up to run it under his name.

*

353

Winter was ending, spring was coming and with it came Chapman, bearing a new contract.

'How would you like to go to America now?' he wheedled. 'I've got it all down here in black and white – they'll pay you anything you want.'

She did not even open his contract.

'I'm finished with singing. I'll never appear on a stage again. That night when I broke down was my very last appearance and don't try to coax me round because I mean it.'

He knew better than to argue. The timid little Larkie had disappeared and been replaced by this firm, determined woman. Money and a title had really brought a change in her, thought Chapman bitterly as he left the house.

'So what *do* I do?' she asked Sadie after he had gone.

'You're not one for good works,' was the reply, 'I don't see you chairing committees or running charity balls. You'll have to do something, though, or you'll fade away.'

Sadie was concerned because Lark was as thin as a walking stick. Her carefully corseted cleavage had completely disappeared.

'You remember that I once said I wanted to go back to the Borderland? Well, this is the time to do it. I want to see if my memories are right, is it as wonderful as I remember? We're going north, Sadie – and don't object, you'll love it. It's a beautiful place – I think.'

Spring came late to Scotland in 1919 and there was still a dusting of crisp white snow on the ground when she turned the key in the lock of Aylie's cottage. It turned easily – the lock was well oiled in spite of the years the cottage had been empty.

The main room was empty but in a corner there was a pile of trunks and boxes, covered by a faded patchwork quilt. The light coming in through the warped, greenish glass of the window had a strange radiance from the reflected snow outside. A dusting of ashes and soot lay around the blackened hearth and on the mantelpiece still stood a few little bits of pottery that her grandmother had loved, the fairings from long ago.

She left the door open and walked slowly across to the boxes. The old quilt felt soft to her fingers and when she held it to her nose, it smelt of apples and lavender, Aylie's smell.

The first box was full of books, pots and cooking bowls. She heaved it off the pile and laid it down in the middle of the floor. The second box contained old bedding, lace-trimmed pillowcases and the padded quilts. They were faded and splitting now but she could make out the minute stitching and the scraps of coloured materials that had gone into them.

At the bottom of the pile she came on Aylie's treasure chest, the dome-topped, brass-bound chest that had come from Jane's cell in Charterhall. The key was in the lock but it was rusted and she had to prise the box open with an old kitchen knife. When she looked inside she found a layer of thin paper covering a bundle of old manuscripts on vellum and beautifully illustrated. With reverent fingers she turned the pages, but was unable to make anything of the Latin words.

Then she found the silver and Alice's books of medical cures, written in what looked like rust-red ink by a slanting hand. Some of the writing had faded away to nothing with age but occasionally a little drawing had been added, an outline of a snowdrop with its bulb or a sketch of a foxglove head.

At the bottom of the box she found the greatest treasures. Wrapped in a scrap of silk was a little spray of white satin roses, yellow with age and sadly crumpled. Lark remembered Aylie telling her about her wedding at Coldstream and how, even as a child, she had recognized the genuine love that filled her grandmother as she told the story. The romance of Hugh and Aylie had been very real and very true – but so tragic. Tears filled her eyes as she held the satin roses in her hands, then she re-wrapped them reverently for her grandmother's sake and put them back in the trunk. The last thing in the box was the French Hussar's jacket. Its colours were still strong and although the sleeves were frayed and the loops of gilded braid tarnished, it looked magnificent and proud. She took off her fur-trimmed tippet and tried on the jacket.

The sleeves hung down over her hands but it sat firmly on her shoulders and made her feel very grand and brave indeed. She knew how Blaize Chardenel must have felt when he put it on.

Wearing it she climbed the rickety ladder to the upper floor. Her bed was still there, the straw mattress in its striped cover split and spilling out from the depredations of generations of mice. There was a basket chair in the corner of the room and a wool rug, unfurling now, in the middle of the floor. She looked around and was in the act of climbing back down when she heard a noise in the open doorway.

A tall man was standing there, his lean figure only a black silhouette against the brilliant whiteness of the snow. He stood perfectly still and watched her as she climbed slowly down.

Then she heard the anger in his voice as he asked, 'What do you think you're doing here? This is private property. What right have you got to go opening those boxes?'

She was flustered by his anger. 'I've bought Charterhall, the big house down there,' she told him.

There was scorn in his voice. 'I know where Charterhall is. So you're Lady Lewis. Buying a big house doesn't give you the right to go poking around other people's property. We heard some lady from the south had bought Charterhall. It's been empty for a while and we wondered who'd get it. But, like I said, that doesn't give you the right to go snooping round here. This cottage isn't yours. It's on the borders of your estate, your ladyship, but it's privately owned.'

His sarcasm and arrogant manner angered her and she snapped back, 'How do *you* know that I don't own it?'

As he stepped into the cottage, she could see that he limped badly. His left leg was hurting him. He sounded short. 'Because I know who does, that's why.'

'And who's that?'

'It's not really your business but it's a girl called Lark Kennedy. This was her grandmother's cottage and my family are looking after it till she comes back from London.'

She stepped nearer to him and looked at his face. The skin was brown and weatherbeaten and the eyes a clear, golden colour like syrup. His hair was reddish brown and though it was closely cropped, it showed signs of wanting to stick out like a bush.

'Are you a Hepburn?' she asked.

'Yes, how do you know?'

'Which one are you?' It had to be Sim, she prayed.

'My name is Simeon Hepburn and I farm the land next to Charterhall. I'm your neighbour, Lady Lewis.' He pronounced her name in an exaggerated, sarcastic way.

She rushed towards him. 'Oh Sim, don't you know me! Look at me. Have I changed all that much?'

He was startled and stared at her incredulously. Before him stood a slim, tall woman in a dark coat and skirt with Aylie's Hussar's jacket slung over her shoulders. Her hair was fair and – heavens, yes, she looked like old Aylie Kennedy!

'You're not Lark?' He obviously could not believe it.

'Yes, of course I am. I'm Lark Kennedy. The Lady Lewis bit always makes me feel awkward. I'm not used to it. I saw Charterhall estate advertised for sale in the newspaper and my lawyer bought it for me . . . I had to buy it back for all those Cannons who lived there and loved the place so much but never owned it. I bought it for the abbey really but I'll probably live in the house – at least for a while.'

Sim was obviously dumbstruck with surprise. 'But I can't believe it. No one said anything about it being you who'd bought the place. I can't believe it. I thought you'd still be a young girl . . .'

'And I thought you'd be a leggy lad. Our memories play us false, don't they? A lot has happened since we last met, Sim.'

He sat down on the window ledge and said, 'Yes, that's true. Let me look at you, Lark. Now I see it's you after all. But round here they're saying that Lady Lewis was a famous music-hall star who married some young chap for his money, is that true?'

She nodded. 'Well, part of it's true. I was on the stage but I didn't marry Harry for his money. I didn't even know he had any. I was Lark Chardelle. Perhaps you've heard of me?'

He grinned. 'I've heard of you all right, but I never knew you were our little Lark. Though the first name should have given me a clue, shouldn't it?'

She gestured towards the leg that obviously hurt him so much. 'Were you wounded?'

He nodded. 'Yes, at Gallipoli. But I reckon I'm lucky. At least I'm alive.'

'I'm sorry,' she said. 'What about your brother?'

'He's dead, so's my nephew, his only son. But Kirsty's all right and mother's still alive.'

'Have you any family?' she asked. It was an important question to her and her heart leapt when Sim shook his head.

'I'm not married. I was too busy working before the war and fighting has kept me occupied for the past four years.'

Suddenly she felt young and joyous again, younger and happier than she'd been for years. She'd found Sim again and this time she was going to keep him. Walking towards him, she held out her hand. 'Come on, Sim, walk back to Charterhall House with me. I want you to meet my friend Sadie. She's a real Londoner and all this open space and wild countryside terrifies her. She won't come out. I want you to let her see that there are some nice normal people around.'

He laughed at that and her happiness transferred itself to him as arm in arm they left Aylie's cottage. In the little

358

garden they paused and stared around them just as Aylie used to do. The sky was a brilliant egg-shell blue and the surrounding circle of hills, all covered in white, looked as if they had been iced by a giant confectioner. The branches of the trees in the lane were heavy with frozen snow and they stretched overhead like a network of lace.

Lark took a deep breath and let the ice cold air fill her lungs.

'It's so beautiful. It's as beautiful as I remembered. No wonder none of my family ever wanted to leave here. Oh Sim, I'm so happy to be back.'

He looked at her and laugh lines crinkled up the sides of his eyes as he said, 'You look rather strange in that jacket. But don't take it off, it suits you. I'm glad you're back, Lark. I've got a feeling that you're going to stay.'